Steam Highwayman

Volume II

Highways and Holloways

by

Martin Barnabus Noutch

Illustrated by

Ben May

Introduction

Who is the Steam Highwayman?

You are the Steam Highwayman. Whatever brought you here, you now stand on the verge of an exciting adventure. Within this book you can explore a world of different choices and consequences, puzzles, mysteries and quests, discovering your own story as you turn from passage to passage. You will need a pencil and eraser to mark your adventure sheet to track your progress and two dice to help calculate the effects of chance in your tale. Your decisions will be matters of life and death, not just for yourself, but for many others too.

Options

From the very first passage in this book you are presented with choices: where to travel; how to answer a challenge; to kill or to spare a villain. Choices presented beneath a passage's main text are optional; instructions within a passage must be followed to maintain the narrative: this allows you the freedom to make choices but also means you are subject to their consequences. To make a choice, simply turn to the passage indicated and continue to read from there...

Tickboxes

Some passages include tickboxes which track your progress. You will be instructed to tick them with a pencil when you encounter them and either read on or proceed to a different passage. When the time comes to restart your adventure, you will need to erase any ticks before beginning afresh.

Codewords

As you travel throughout the realm you will learn many secrets, hear many rumours and experience strange and wonderful adventures: codewords allow the book to track this. When you gain a codeword, tick that codeword in the back of the book. When you are asked if you have a particular codeword, check to see if it is ticked in your codeword list. Some options are only available if you have a certain codeword, indicated by a codeword in brackets after that option (*Belligerent*). When travelling to another book in the series, retain your codewords, but if you restart your adventure you will need to erase all the codewords you have collected.

Your Adventure Sheet

Abilities

Your adventure will require you to use a diverse set of skills, which the following list represents:

RUTHLESSNESS	How threatening you seem, both in appearance and reputation
ENGINEERING	Your skill with pneumo-mechanics and steam machinery
MOTORING	The knowledge of road lore and the art of handling an engine
INGENUITY	Your ability to solve problems
NIMBLENESS	Your physical quickness and agility
GALLANTRY	The appeal of your manners, words and deeds

To make an ability roll you must **roll two dice and add the total to the appropriate ability score**, plus any modifiers. If the total score is **greater than** the difficulty, you have succeeded.

Bonus Skills

During your adventure you may gain additional specialist skills such as **animal friendship**, **legal knowledge**, **explosives expert** or **medical training**. When you learn one of these, you will gain a **level** in this skill and should note it on your **Adventure Sheet**. Possessing a level of **animal friendship** or three or more levels of **legal knowledge** may help you with specific ability rolls or may allow you to access unique quests and adventures.

Possessions

You will collect, find and buy many items as you travel the land. You may carry up to 12 possessions in your inventory (representing your saddlebags) at any time. In addition, you may carry 12 small items in your **jewellery pouch**. These may only be small objects that would fit within the hand, such as **keys**, **rings**, coiled **necklaces** or similar. Flat objects, such as **punchcards**, **tickets**, **notebooks** or **posters** may be carried in your **satchel**, which can hold 12 paper or card items. If in doubt, act like a Steam Highwayman. Remember - this is intended to be a fun adventure, not a lesson in inventory management!

Many items modify your Ability scores. These modifiers are cumulative as long as the items are unique. For example, your ENGINEERING score of 4 could be improved by possession of a **pneumatic manual (ENG+3)** and an **adjustable wrench (ENG+1)** to total 8, but could not be improved by two adjustable wrenches. Some options are only available to you if you possess a certain item, indicated by a bracketed item (**grappling iron**). If these do not indicate that you should discard or use up the item, you may retain that item for later. You may come across limited use objects. These have a number of tickboxes beside them which you should tick on each use. Bonuses to ability scores are temporary and will revert after a single fight or skill check. After the final tick, erase the object from your Adventure Sheet.

Money

The realm uses the Imperial monetary system - pounds (£), shillings (s) and pence (d). You will normally deal only in shillings, but when making deposits at the bank or expensive purchases you will need to do a little maths: there are 20 shillings to the pound or sovereign, and 21 shillings to the guinea. Paper money is normally only used by the wealthiest and is not always easy to exchange. A bundle of notes such as **thirty guineas in notes** may not be spent as normal - you will need to find someone to accept it as a deposit or exchange it for hard money (sometimes at a discount). Paper money does not take up a possession slot in your inventory.

Bank Deposits

Should you wish to deposit your money in a bank account, you will need to subtract amounts in multiples of ten guineas (**£10 10s**) from your purse and write this amount into the account space on your **Adventure Sheet**. If you travel to another book, write this number onto the new **Adventure Sheet** as your account will be available at other branches of the bank, where you may withdraw it with the same restriction.

Noted Passages

Within the text you may be asked to note a certain **passage number** on your **Adventure Sheet**. Shortly after this you are likely to encounter an instruction that indicates that you should turn to your **noted passage**. This should be your most recently **noted passage number**, as you will never be required to note more than one passage number at a time.

Hidden Links

Not every choice in *Highways and Holloways* is marked with an option: keeping your eyes peeled and learning from the adventures you encounter may lead you to making leaps of faith from one passage to another. In general, these will involve making calculations based upon the **passage numbers**, so you are advised to calculate carefully and to keep note of the passage you are leaving in case you need to return there.

Weapons

Shooting Guns

Each gun has an ACCURACY rating (eg **blunderpistol (ACC 6)**). To shoot, roll two dice and add the score to your gun's ACCURACY together with any other modifiers. A score **greater than** the difficulty is a success. Of course, should you lose your firearm, you should not choose any option that would require you to take a shot.

Fighting enemies

Combat proceeds in rounds, and in each you have an opportunity to wound your opponent before they have a chance to hurt you. When the number of **wounds** you have inflicted is equal to your opponent's TOUGHNESS, or when you have **five wounds**, the fight is over. To calculate whether you wound your enemy, roll two dice and add the score to your NIMBLENESS, together with any modifiers. If the total is **greater than** your opponent's PARRY, you will succeed in wounding them.

Your opponent then has the same chance: the roll of two dice is added to their NIMBLENESS and if the total is **greater than** your PARRY then you gain a **wound**. Your PARRY score is the total of your NIMBLENESS plus the PAR value of your weapon. Note that if your opponent has a weapon with modifiers, these have already been added to the NIMBLENESS, PARRY and TOUGHNESS scores printed. You make take your opponent's weapon if you win.

Wounds

A highwayman's life is a dangerous one: you may be wounded in single combat, shot at by angry Constables or hurt in a road accident. Keep track of each **wound** on your Adventure Sheet, as normally your fifth **wound** will incapacitate you and may hasten the end of your adventure. You are able to treat your **wounds** in a safe location either through rest or paying for medical treatment, which will normally result in your **wounds** converting to **scars**.

Scars

The normal process when a wound is healed is to erase the **wound** from your Adventure Sheet and add a **scar** to your scar tally. Sometimes you will be prompted to roll two dice and a score of 11 or 12 will result in an **intimidating scar (RUTH+1)**, which should be noted in your **Other Modifiers**.

Velosteam

Your velosteam is your most prized possession: a finely-tuned and carefully engineered two-wheeled road engine of unsurpassed mechanical beauty, it runs on readily available coal-gas and can achieve considerable speed. However, it can be damaged by accidents or risk-taking. Keep track of any **damage points** on your Adventure Sheet, along with any customisations that you manage to fit. You must take care! Your velosteam can sustain three **damage points**, but should you suffer the fourth your machine will be **beyond repair**. At this point you will be forced to abandon your adventure on the road - so ensure you know a trustworthy mechanic who can help you repair your velosteam before that stage.

Reputation

As you proceed about your lawless way you are bound to make enemies as well as friends. Record your notoriety (for example, **Wanted by the Coal Board**) and your friendships (for example, **Friend of Lord Dashwood**) on your Adventure Sheet. These will decide your fate at many a turn.

Great Deeds

Some adventures may result in you becoming known for your **great deeds**. Note these on your Adventure Sheet: they will influence your eventual fate when you come to retire from this life. They may also influence those around you, as your legend precedes you in the land.

Solidarity Points

The common people of Britain are oppressed and disenfranchised: their poverty enables the wealth of the landed, the gentry, the industrialists and the political classes. Some of your choices may result in you gaining **solidarity points**, which indicate whether the poor of the land know you as a saviour or as an oppressor. Should you gain 50 or more **solidarity points** you will be known as the **People's Champion**. However, you may lose **solidarity points** for participating in the oppression of the common people. It is not possible to have a negative number of **solidarity points.**

Retirement and the End of your Adventure

Once you have fully explored the world of *Highways and Holloways*, you may adventure on into the other books in this series, riding airships, infiltrating government, fighting for Cornish independence or riding the Great North Road. However, your good fortune cannot last forever and when you decide to settle down and retire from the road you will be invited to turn to the **Epilogue**. Several important factors will decide the happiness and security of your later years: the number of **friendships** that you have made, the amount of money you have banked with Coulter's Bank, the number of **solidarity points** and **great deeds** that you have collected and your health, represented by the number of **scars** you bear. All of these will also help you calculate a score to share with other riders of the midnight road, or to better in another adventure.

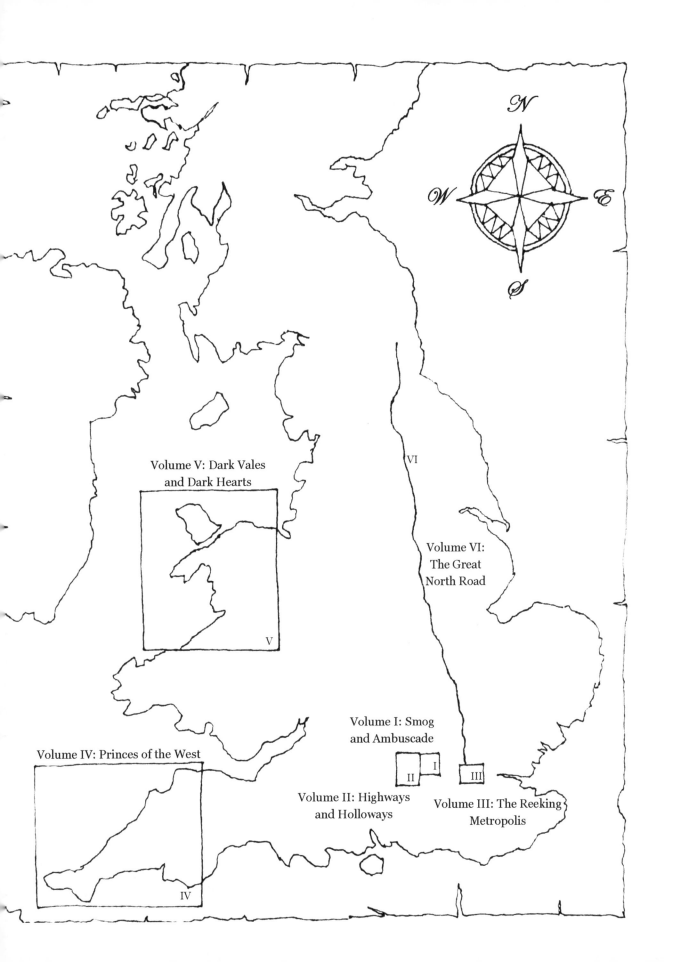

Volume V: Dark Vales
and Dark Hearts

V

VI

Volume VI:
The Great
North Road

Volume IV: Princes of the West

Volume I: Smog
and Ambuscade

II I III

Volume II: Highways
and Holloways

Volume III: The Reeking
Metropolis

IV

1

That rumble betrays the approach of a heavily-laden steam carriage through the night. Any moment now, the glow of the fore lantern will split the darkness. Then, as the mighty wheels roll past, your moment will come: sudden surprise, ruthless violence and escape.

Here you have waited in the shadows of the woods, patiently maintaining pressure in your velosteam's boiler, ready to speed alongside a passing engine at a moment's notice. No trace will be left other than the terrifying reputation of the Steam Highwayman.

The steamer comes into view bearing a regimental crest on its doors, just as your informant told you. Why are you robbing this carriage?

"I hope to make my fortune."	**84**
"I seek vengeance for my fallen comrades."	**170**
"It is time for the revolution to begin."	**526**
"Poverty has left me with no other choice."	**837**
"The steam age is an age of opportunity."	**931**
"We of the nobility must change our ways."	**1085**

2

In the parlour of the Angel at Henley a fine bow window looks out over the bridge and the water. Day and night the road-trains crawl across, their heavy wagons clanking and grinding against the stonework, setting the old inn a-shudder. Customers come and go, occasionally peering at the tattered wanted poster hanging by the door. If you choose to take your ease with a pot of ale here, you can keep an eye on everything entering and leaving town.

Investigate the wanted poster...	**545**
Stay and watch the traffic... (**2s**)	**44**
Return to the marketplace...	**702**
Head out of town...	**586**
Return to your boat... (**moored at Henley**)	**818**

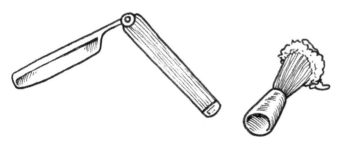

3

The village of Bix profits from the traffic on the road here: the road between Henley and Wallingford is maintained by a company owned largely by the nobility roundabouts. A broad gate closes the road, opened at a steam-powered lever-pull by a tollman - but of course it is no obstacle to a vehicle like your own.

Beside the tollhouse stands a tarpaulin-shrouded sand bunker, a massive rivetted water tank and a scattering of newer cottages. An engine-shed for repairs has also been erected and the sound of hammers on hot metal rings through the woods and down the hill.

All this prosperity has had effects on the parish: the village has out-grown its ancient church and a new, iron-framed sanctuary is being erected.

Visit the workshop...	**283**
Talk to the tollman...	**335**
Investigate the new church...	**387**
Ride on up to Nettlebed...	**394**
Head down the Hill to Henley...	**144**

4

You steam on up the road from Northend to Christmas Common. The Ferguson churns happily away and you are treated to a warm blast of sunshine. The air is clean here, far from workshop chimneys or dusty highways. Here trees dominate, and between their roots grow woodland flowers. If you have a **steam fist (RUTH+3)**, turn to **59**.

Continue on uphill...	**617**

5

The tournament will be played to house rules, as befits a frequent country gathering. "Oh, Miles insists we should play association," complains the Viscountess, "But then I would really have little to do as umpire. All you need to know is that I award a bonus whenever I can. Now do you have a partner, or would you like me to find you one?"

The guests include several local notables - do you recognise any of them?

Partner with Major Redford...	**917**
Partner with the tall lady... (**burnt rose**)	**1241**
Partner with Earl Brigg...	
(**Friend of Earl Brigg**)	**1175**
Partner with Susan Tenney..	
(**Friend of Susan Tenney**)	**1353**

❧ 6 ❧

You leave Henley behind and steam up the road westwards. Dogs bark and run into the street as you pass the terraces and the tin shacks thrown up for workers along the roadside. A lumber yard, a furniture warehouse, an industrial laundry and a tile-yard each take their place beside the dusty way. Then the hedgerows take over and you are in the country again. Still, the road bears signs of countless heavy wagons coming this way. A regular locobus carries passengers from the wharf, the station and the market square up to the airship depot at Rotherfield Greys. Then there are all the Atmospheric Union wagons, hauling supplies up to their compound.

Plan an ambush here among the hedges... **72**
Ride on to the airfield... **454**

❧ 7 ❧

If you have the codeword *Bernadette*, turn to **151** immediately.

An officer of the Union tells you what they know about Captain Coke. "He's a dreadful fellow. He certainly has people inside our guild: he robbed a transatlantic last month and killed eighteen people. We reckon that he must have a base of his own near here, but no-none has ever found it and the people won't tell. He flies a slim Marcozzi with a blue envelope - but normally flies the black jack. We can't send anyone up at the moment without a heavy guard and it's eating into our profits dreadfully. If you can capture or kill him, there's a five hundred guinea reward. Keep that poster by you so you can recognise him - but be careful of his tricks."

Leave the office... **454**

❧ 8 ❧

The Oxford road stretches uphill through the trees towards Stokenchurch here and off, through the tiny village of Piddington, towards Wycombe. It is a well-used, expensively maintained route. At the steepest points there are iron grips set into the tarmacadam for steamer wheels, chained bollards at the roadside and a water tank at both top and bottom, secured with Haulage Guild padlocks. At the side of the road, early blackberries ripen in the sun. A patch of thick mud shows the marks of heavy Wheels.

Prepare an ambush here... **957**
Ride up the hill to Stokenchurch... **308**
Head into the woods to the north... **872**
Take the road east... *Smog and Ambuscade 546*

❧ 9 ❧

If you are **Wanted by the Constables**, turn to **146** immediately. Otherwise, read on.

A patrol vehicle is making its way towards your ambush. Even if you are unknown to the Constables, this is no place to be caught and questioned about your business. You had better head on your way directly.

Towards Woodcote... **488**
Towards Wallingford.... **860**

❧ 10 ❧

The obelisk stands on a plinth carved with dozens of names: men of the village and region fallen in colonial wars over the decades. Freshly-cut names list those killed in the Iberian conflict:

Pte. K.E. Massey	Ox
LCpl. G. Gerrard	Herts. Fus.
Pte H. Junforth	Ox
CSgt. L.S. Bamford	Ox
Lt. A. Brittey	Ox

These men are not long dead. Their mothers and sisters still live down the lanes. Their brothers are in the workshops, the fields, or the trenches of Valencia.

Return to Whitchurch... **749**

❧ 11 ❧

With your help, the steam wagon is soon freed from the mud. "So the Steam Highwayman is more than just a road thief," says a passenger. "When you rode up I thought we was going to be robbed!" Gain a **solidarity point**.

Go on your way... **488**

❧ 12 ❧

The short lane from Skirmett to Fingest winds around several cottages and a short terrace that enterprising villagers have built into the roadway. As you ride past, several women with laundry-baskets on their heads are trudging down to the river, children in tow. If you have the codeword *Beneficent*, turn to **835** immediately.

Continue on to Fingest... **867**

❧ 13 ❧

The Constables have you in their gauntleted grip. A bored Sergeant leafs through a sheaf of vulcanized printofits in a wallet, searching for your likeness. How they treat you will depend upon the crimes associated with your Citizen Number. Check the options below and total the number of points indicated by relevant conditions.

If you are...

Wanted by the Constables...	**5 points**
Wanted by the Haulage Guild...	**4 points**
Wanted by the Telegraph Guild...	**4 points**
Wanted by the Wallingford	
Town Guard...	**3 points**
Wanted by the River Guild...	**2 points**
Wanted by the Coal Board...	**2 points**
the **People's Champion** or a	
Famed Lawbreaker...	**5 points**
a **Member of the Compact for**	
Workers' Equality...	**4 points**
If you have the codeword *Bursting*	
or *Bolster*...	**1 point each**

If your charges total **20 points or more**...	**24**
If your charges total **10-19 points**...	**140**
If your charges total **5-9 points**...	**219**
If your charges total **0-4 points**...	**407**

❧ 14 ❧

Three steam vehicles are parked outside the Flowerpot: a local haulier's trade wagon, much-repaired, mud-splashed and dinted, a Telegraph Guild carriage for transporting personnel between sites, and a long-distance private steam carriage. The last is plainly the transport of someone important enough to afford their own staff and guard, judging from the exterior seats.

Search the Telegraph Guild carriage...	**1496**
Bribe the driver and guard of the private	
steam carriage...	**1153**
Enter the pub...	**348**
Leave the pub...	**280**

❧ 15 ❧

You have been taken prisoner by the Telegraph Guild. They will treat you completely without mercy, maintaining their own reputation for terror and ensuring that you do not trouble them again. First they strip you of all your **possessions** and **money**. Then they chain you and take you to their compound at Caversham Hill and put you to work hauling on a windlass.

In the process of the months of forced labour you receive many beatings, poor rations and little rest. Lose a point of NIMBLENESS and a point of ENGINEERING but you can turn one **wound** into a **scar**. Convinced that they have taught you a thing or two, they turn you out onto the road and you will no longer be **Wanted by the Telegraph Guild** - if you ever were!

You have enough spirit left in you to find where they have stored your velosteam and you steal it back at night, but it has **serious damage** after being joyridden by unappreciative young officers. Finally you head back out into the woods.

Turn to...   807

❧ 16 ❧

□

If the box above is empty, put a tick in it and turn to **46** immediately. If the box is already ticked, read on.

The glum passengers empty their pockets, muttering together as your back is turned. None dare resist you directly, but this will harm your reputation with the common people. Lose a **solidarity point** and roll two dice to see what you collect.

Score 2-3	**18s**
Score 4-5	**£1 6s**
Score 7	**£2 4s**
Score 8-9	**£3 5s** and a **wheel of cheese**
Score 10-11	**£4 15s** and a **silver bracelet**
Score 12	**ten guineas in banknotes** and **£3 1s**

Ride away...   **noted passage**

❧ 17 ❧

The package is a set of miniature industrial components that needs to be conveyed to a Manchester mill as soon as possible. Once delivered, the mill-owner will scale them up and fit them to his steel-rolling machinery to increase efficiency. The **leather satchel** is small but heavy and the porter making the handover has a steely look in his eye.

"These are worth a lot in the wrong hands," he says.

It is not long before you are in the saddle of your velosteam once more. The despatch riders see that your water tank is full, your coal-gas reservoir pressurised and your pistons oiled. "It'll be a famous run, I'm sure," calls Desdemona Wren, as you set off. "Only one thing! Watch out near Stoke! The Compact..." The rest of her words are lost in a squall of wind and rain.

The journey will be long and tiring. Riding non-stop, you might make it within the two days. Make a MOTORING roll and add 1 for each **customisation** (such as **off-road tyres** or **reinforced boiler**) that you have fitted to your Velosteam.

Score <11	A slow ride	**167**
Score 11-15	Hard steaming	**187**
Score 16+	A record-breaking time	**206**

❧ 18 ❧

If you have the codeword *Bressingham* and a **mechanical arm**, turn to **98** immediately. If not but you have the codeword *Bother*, turn to **456**. If you have neither of these, you leave your velosteam by the Chequers and take a short turn around the pretty village of Fingest. Roll a dice to see what you encounter:

Score 1-2	A misty evening...	**92**
Score 3-4	Gambling priests...	**125**
Score 5-6	A country engagement...	**153**

❧ 19 ❧

You dismount and take a seat on the step of Barsali's colourful steam caravan.

"How are your family?" you ask.

"Well - and the boy is still at large, by grace. My daughter's birthday approaches again. I believe I met you around that time, is it not so?"

You chat together of the wandering life. Barsali envies your freedom, untrammelled by possessions, unburdened by the responsibilities of caring for a family. Do you envy his comforts and the presence of his family?

He tells you about local happenings too. "There are many angry people in Stokenchurch. It's all about water - whose it is, what to use it for. I won't be surprised if I hear of violence." He sighs. "And their football team is in need of a new coach too."

"A new steam coach?"

"No. A new trainer - a sports coach."

He brings out a bottle of hedgerow wine. The stars rise into the sky beyond his campfire. "Do you have anything to sell?" he asks with a sideways grin. "I always made a good profit with your help."

Food and Drink	To buy	To sell
bird's eggs	-	3s
rabbit	2s	1s
pheasant	-	2s
deer carcass	-	£1 5s
bottle of whisky	£2 2s	£2
Clothing	To buy	To sell
mask	4s	-
lace shawl	£1	£1
silk scarf	6s	-
cloak	15s	-
dark cloak (RUTH+1)	-	£4 10s
fur coat	£4	-
hair matches (R+2) ☐ ☐ ☐	£2	-
Jewellery	To buy	To sell
locket	-	10s
pocket watch	-	£2
silver ring	-	10s
silver bracelet	-	18s
silver necklace	-	£1 15s
gold ring	-	£2 8s
gold bracelet	-	£2 10s
gold necklace	-	£3
sapphire pendant	-	£25
pectoral cross	-	£12
Jousting Cup	-	£4 6s
Medical	To buy	To sell
bandages	3s	-
poison	15s	10s

Leave Barsali...	**308**

❧ 20 ❧

The clerks are four nervous-looking men travelling for business, but emboldened by their numbers, they believe they are a match for you. You must fight them!

Clerks	Weapons: **rapiers (PAR 4)**
Parry:	8
Nimbleness:	4
Toughness:	8

Victory!	**311**
Defeat!	**999**

✎ 21 ✎

Has something about the ghost's plea moved you? Or is the prospect of making trouble simply irresistible? Either way, you turn up at the doorway of Fingest Manor and hammer on the door until it opens. Something about your attire or your attitude convinces the footman to bring you to Lord Burgess, who listens as you explain your encounter with his ancestor's ghost. He looks around, motions to his staff and wordlessly dismisses you. They bundle you up and literally toss you out into a heap of dung in the yard.

Will you accept this treatment? You have several options open to you: bloodthirsty revenge, which could increase your reputation as a ruthless and desperate persecutor of the nobility, a trickier route of terrifying Lord Burgess into submission which might have its own satisfactions, or to swallow this insult and do your best to forget about it. Whatever you decide, gain the codeword *Bother*.

Decide to haunt Lord Burgess...
    (**lantern**, **cassock** and **nephritic**
    solution or **fluorspar powder**)   **448**
Blow up the manor house... (**explosives**)   **81**
Return to the village...   **867**

✎ 22 ✎

When you make your offer, Parson Twinge laughs nervously. "You may have greater luck than me. I suppose if I tell Reverend Prattle that you are my new curate he may find the switch fair. But you will need ready money to put down - I have none."

"I will make the stake." (**£10 10s**)   **1503**
"You must be responsible for your bells."   **867**

✎ 23 ✎

You talk a little longer with Miss Evans before taking your leave. She shows you the books of work she must mark, nightly, although the girls rarely respond and nobody seems to value her hours. "At least it means I know where they each are," she says optimistically.

Head down towards Henley...   **702**
Ride to Lower Assendon...   **163**
Steam east along the valley...   **62**

✎ 24 ✎

The officer leaps from his seat when he recognises who you are. He rings a bell at his belt, summoning his superior immediately. They have a hushed, rushed conversation while the men holding you tighten their grip.

"There is a reward out for you," sneers the commander. "A substantial reward for your capture leading to your execution. No plea will help you now."

You are held until a prison wagon arrives to take you away to Gallowstree Common.

Turn to...   **493**

✎ 25 ✎

A group of rag-tag deserters are sat around their bivouac, staring into the campfire and talking amongst themselves. If you have the codeword *Betrayed*, turn to **1174** immediately. If not, but you have the codeword *Bought*, turn to **1135**. If you have neither, you can settle down and hear their stories of the battles fought, the injustices done to and by them.

"Worst of all was Valencia. Corp was there, weren't you? Just ordered out onto the bleedin' plain."

"Half of Spain's red with the blood of Bucks boys," says the corporal gruffly.

Leave them...   **102**

✎ 26 ✎

The baker puts out a floury hand to shake on the agreement and then goes over to her account book to write a contract for Miller Fursham. Perhaps you could have got him a better price elsewhere, but at least this should allow him to return to making a profit once more. The baker hands you the **baker's contract** and you leave her chewing through the fine golden-crusted loaf.

Return to Stokenchurch...   **308**
Leave town...   **660**

✎ 27 ✎
☐

If the box is empty, tick it and read on. If it is already ticked, turn to **193** immediately. A familiar horse-drawn wagon is making its way towards you. Bells chime in time to the horse's feet and you can see the shape of a steam-organ beneath the canvas. A halloo rings out.

"Well met, you fine dancer! How goes the toll business?" Goodman Butt halts the wagon and leaps down to shake your hand. Several of his morris-men smile and call their own greetings. One lies dead drunk on the wooden boards, reeking of cider. "Sammy's gone on a bender again. His brother found out what he does for a living and he drank himself silly of the shame. We're heading to Reading for a little kickup!" A cheer from the morris-men - those that are awake. "When we left Mapledurham, there was a fancy carriage getting up steam. Some business chappie who'd come up to the country. What say we pull a little trick on 'im? We'll make a distraction, you rob 'im blind and then we'll split the proceeds and go drink cider?"

Agree to the ambush...	**234**
Wave them on...	**803**

❧ 28 ❧

The tiny hamlet of Cadmore End is simply a cluster of cottages and huts housing several families scratching their living off the land. Some are indentured labourers for nearby landlords, others depend on remittances from sons and daughters working in service in London or in the military. Small, over-worked gardens provide most of the people's food.

A tiled church building with a bell stands behind a stand of trees.

Enter St Mary's Church...	**536**
Distribute money to the poor... (**£5**)	**466**
Take the lane to Stokenchurch...	**142**
Ride east up to Bolter End...	**546**

❧ 29 ❧

A bold young woman with a basket on her arm stands from her seat on the top deck and challenges you. "What makes you think you can thieve from us? Just 'cause you're armed and have some flash machine to ride on, you think you can do what you like? We're just trying to get by!" The passengers begin to throw anything they can at you - fruit from their shopping baskets, their clogs, whatever they can lay their hands on. You cannot simply massacre unarmed townspeople, so you ride out of range and head elsewhere.

Ride away...	**noted passage**

❧ 30 ❧

You steam carefully between the lighters, rowboats, steamers and barges to Spiller's Quay. The boat-builder and dealer here will repair, upgrade or buy your boat. He will not pay any more for your boat if it is customised: his customers are more likely to want a plain craft. He says.

Customisation	To buy
cargo crane	**£18 5s**
enlarged cabin	**£20**
Perkins engine (Allows you to carry refrigerated cargoes like **Ice** and **Frozen Meat**)	**£28**
strengthened screw	**£12**
butty boat (allows you to carry three more units of cargo)	**£30**

Boat	To sell
Small skiff	**£12**
Medium launch	**£18**
Large barge	**£30**

If you sell your boat, turn to **297** immediately.

Return to the river...	**495**
Head downstream... (**4s**)	**319**
Head upstream towards Wallingford... (**8s** or a **Bargee's Badge**)	**305**

❧ 31 ❧

From the river, the gables of Mongewell Park are visible between a row of alders lining the bank. It is a substantial house, built at the end of the previous century for a wealthy churchman. Now it is the home of the Tenney family, made rich by their part in the Atmospheric Guild designing, manufacturing and testing airships.

Beyond the house runs Grim's Ditch - the unnaturally straight dyke leading from the riverside up into the Chilterns. It forms a choke point through which road traffic must travel to reach Wallingford from this side of the river. However old it truly is - Saxon, Roman or prehistoric - its origins are lost in time. The devil, they say, threw it up in a night.

Moor here... (**Friend of Susan Tenney**)	**94**
Sail on towards South Stoke...	**271**
Sail upstream towards Wallingford...	**943**
Moor at North Stoke...	**383**

You swiftly turn about and head towards Stonor, where you know the villagers are desperate to get their hands on a working traction engine. When you tell them of the abandoned Guild road-train they are overjoyed and set out immediately to claim the machine for their own. Gain **two solidarity points** and remove the codeword *Bonnington*.

Turn to...   **430**

To treat your **wounds**, you will need a **bandage** or a **cloak** of any kind to staunch the bleeding. Remove this from your possessions and make an INGENUITY roll, adding 2 for each level of **medical training** you possess and 1 if you have a bottle of **soothing ointment**.

Score <10	A problematic injury: the **wounds** remain...
Score 10-14	Healed: replace one **wound** with a **scar**
Score 15	A dramatic result: replace one **wound** with an **intimidating scar (RUTH+1)**
Score 16-18	Healed: replace two **wounds** with two **scars**
Score 19-20	Healed: replace three **wounds** with three **scars**
Score 21+	Healed: replace two **wounds** with a single **scar**

You may also treat the following ailments:

If you have a **fever** take a hot bath, drink a bottle of **whisky** or **cough medicine** and take three **white pills (ING+2)** ☐ ☐ ☐
If you have a **burn** you may heal it with a bottle of **soothing ointment** and any piece of **clothing** (both to be discarded)

If you are struggling to tend your own hurts, perhaps you had better seek help at a house of charity such as Elvendon Priory or St Katharine's Convent. The trained medics of the Telegraph Guild and the Coal Board might also be able to help - provided you have not previously made an enemy of them.

Turn to...   **noted passage**

It was less than wise to climb up into the narrow branches of the ash trees here. A branch snaps beneath your feet and throws you to the ground amongst the smashed nests. Gain a **wound** and if you have **five wounds**, turn to **999** immediately.

If you survive the fall, you should go and seek treatment immediately.

Ride to Gallowstree Common...	**600**
Head towards Woodcote...	**488**

Your bullets achieve nothing. The guards, on the other hand, send their shots whistling about your head. To continue now would be folly: all you have done is to make the Guild aware of your presence in the region, and you will now be **Wanted by the Haulage Guild** unless you possess a **mask**.

Ride away...   **noted passage**

The owner of the Chequers has invested in a Westwood Automated Fryer and offers fried potato slices with the beer. The aroma of hot fat and vaporised vinegar hangs over a crowd of hauliers sat at the benches, sharing road news and pots of ale.

Take a seat with the hauliers... **(2s)**	**121**
Buy a drink and settle by the fire... **(2s)**	**745**
Leave the parlour...	**867**

Leaving behind all your **possessions**, your **weapons** and your purse, you drag yourself onto your velosteam one last time and kick the friction-starter. Weaving along the lanes and making many turns by instinct alone, dodging the oncoming traffic of the falling night, you somehow reach Valentine Wood and collapse on the driveway to Mr Sands' cottage.

You awake under a quilt that smells of dogs and cordite, unable to tell how long has passed since your collapse. Your **wounds** are in the process of healing - remove them and replace them with **scars** - but each has left you with an ache in the bone. For each **wound**, roll a dice and on a score of 5 or 6 you must lower one of your attributes by 1 skill point.

Sands reappears in the evening and grunts appreciatively to find you awake. "Didn't know if you'd wake," he says, "You were so cut up."

It takes several weeks to recover yourself enough to try riding again. You hobble around the gamekeeper's smallholding with a stick, but he is only able to spare you a little time and seems nervous about having you staying with him. It is clear that you should leave as soon as you can.

"It's better if you don't come back here," he says, part insistent and part dismayed. "I shouldn't be mixing with the like of you." You are no longer the **Friend of Mr Sands** - although you will surely still remember everything he taught you.

Leave the cottage...   **600**

❧ 38 ❧

As you skirt the edge of Great Wood, the distinctive smell of aircraft dope reaches you: the solvent-heavy mixture applied to canvas and linen airship coverings. Could you have stumbled across Captain Coke's hideout at last?

Leaving your velosteam at the wood's edge, you creep along animal paths, following your nose, and emerge at the edge of a ramshackle encampment. There you see all manner of ruffians tending to a large blue airship - and patiently watching, you even catch sight of the distinctive Captain Coke himself.

Wait until nightfall to capture Coke...   **65**
Head on to Turville...   **947**
Return to Stonor...   **430**

❧ 39 ❧

If the total of your **wounds** and **scars** is 15 or more, you are overcome and never awake again: turn to the **Epilogue** immediately. However, if you still have the sufficient strength, you can drag yourself back to your trusty velosteam and make for safety.

Head for Culham Court...
        (**Friend of Earl Brigg**)   **328**
Look for the gypsy encampment...
        (**Friend of Barsali**)   **507**

If you cannot choose any of the options above, you are left entirely without hope and recourse. Think on your need for allies and friends in this life of difficulty as you bleed your life's strength out on the roadside.

Turn to the **Epilogue**.

❧ 40 ❧

The dogs are easily avoided: spaniels make poor guard dogs at the best of times and these seem more interested in each other than in anyone approaching the house. You quietly roll up to the house out of their view and take a light from your velosteam's burner.

A bundle of sacking, half a bale of straw and some scraps of wood jammed beneath the scaffolding and soon you have a fire roaring up the wall. It is time to make a getaway. As you ride off, the dogs at last realise that something is wrong and begin barking.

It is some days later when you hear that Lady Pomiane perished in the fire. Of course the hearing decides in the Earl of Macclesfield's favour and when you return to Shirburn Castle a bag of coin is waiting for you: gain **£50**. The Earl is far from keen to be seen talking to you, so you are quickly sent on your way.

If you are a **Member of the Compact for Workers' Equality**, gain the codeword *Bolster* if you do not already have it.

Ride on...   **710**

❧ 41 ❧

Your escape route takes you flying up the lanes past Crazies Hill. The steep roads, the sharp corners and the confusing changes of direction will give you a chance to get away - if you can stay upright on your heavy Ferguson and if it can cope with the strain you are putting it under. Make a MOTORING roll of difficulty 11, adding 1 if you have **off-road tyres**.

Successful MOTORING roll!   **313**
Failed MOTORING roll!   **1042**

❧ 42 ❧

The baker shakes her head. "And I can't profit from it at that price." You have been unsuccessful here - but if you were to take a sample to another bakery in the region, perhaps you would get a better offer.

Return to Stokenchurch...   **308**
Leave town...   **660**

❧ 43 ❧

You do not scruple to use every trick and wile at your disposal to bring Reverend Prattle to grief. By midnight you have won back the bells, your own stake (regain your **£10 10s**) and a fine **dark cloak**

(RUTH+1) that the vicar of Hambleden was unwise enough to wager. He shakes his head. "Your curate enjoys divine favour with cards, brother Twinge. I shall send the bells back directly."

As you leave, you hear the cocky and perhaps rather foolish Parson Twinge suggest playing for the Hambleden bells next. Gain the codeword *Bellingham*.

Leave the gambling vicars...	**343**

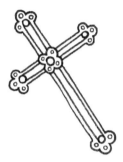

❧ 44 ❧

If you have the codewords *Breadbasket*, *Beyond* or *Bodacious*, erase them now.

Before settling down to watch the road you dismiss a townsman from your preferred seat with a scowl and a grunt. He gets up sharply, leaving his meal partly-finished on the table. With a tankard of reliable Brakspear Best in your grip, you peer out at the bridge, noting anything out-of-the-ordinary or strange about the comings and goings of local traffic. Roll a dice to see what you notice.

Score 1-2   A long-distance Haulage Guild convoy. Gain the codeword *Breadbasket*.

Score 3-4   Observe a private steam carriage setting out. Gain the codeword *Beyond*.

Score 5-6   See a Constables' prison wagon crossing the bridge. Gain the codeword *Bodacious*.

The beer has a very light nose, like a summer ale or a homebrew, but it follows up with a gradually strengthening savour of nuts, malt and baked fruit. There is something buttery about it - perhaps the contribution of an unfamiliar hop?

Return to the parlour...	**2**
Head into Henley...	**702**
Leave town...	**586**
Pursue the vehicle directly...	**830**

❧ 45 ❧

You have been given a comfortable room in the inn with a window overlooking the mill and the moorings on the river below. A sturdy door fitted with heavy bolts should prevent you from being surprised.

If you wish to take one of the following actions, note the current passage (**45**) before turning to the indicated passage.

Tend to your **wounds**...	**33**
Repair your velosteam in the yard...	**180**
Open a **strongbox**...	**138**

You may leave items here in safety, together with money hidden behind a brick in the fireplace. If you wish to do so, write them into the box below.

Leave your room...	**118**

❧ 46 ❧

You terrify the people into handing over everything of value and gain **£2 1s**, a **pocket watch** and a **silver necklace**. Your reputation will be directly affected - gain a point of RUTHLESSNESS but lose a **solidarity point**. You will also be **Wanted by the Constables** now, unless you have a **mask**.

Ride away...	**noted passage**

❧ 47 ❧

An open-topped steam carriage approaches where you stand beneath the tree. You can hear an argument rising from the passengers as they approach.

"You said it would only be a shower!"

"That was a shower."

"I am absolutely dripping wet. My hat is ruined!"

"Oh, bother your hat!"

A **wide-brimmed hat** comes sailing out of the carriage and lands on the roadway. You may take it if you like as the carriage continues on, the argument becoming only more unreasonable.

Ride on...   **807**

❧ 48 ❧

You manage to make it back to Shiplake. Your butler meets you at the door and helps you across the threshold into your sanctuary. Your body begins to heal - remove a **wound** and replace it with a **scar** - but to fully recover, you will have to spend some time getting yourself back to strength.

Turn to...   **1073**

❧ 49 ❧

Your accelerating machine terrifies the Constables who dive aside as you crash through the old gates. The damage to your machine is considerable: you must either remove a **customisation** or gain **two damage points**. If your machine is now **beyond repair**, turn to **874** immediately.

Unfortunately in your haste to get away, you have left several of your belongings behind. For each item in your **possessions**, roll a dice and discard it on a score of 5 or 6. Now where will you go? The Constables are sure to pursue you!

Ride towards Valentine Wood...   **364**
Head for Aston Ferry...   **137**
Make for Culham Court...
　　(Friend of Earl Brigg)   **41**

❧ 50 ❧

Remove the codeword *Baggage*. A set of heavy wheel-ruts turn off the road near the farm sheds. Following them, you bump through a disused yard to find the abandoned missing Haulage Guild roadtrain that the Tollman at Bix spoke to you about. No-one is around and the wagons seem intact and unlooted.

Tell the Haulage Guild representative
　　at Nettlebed...   **105**
Loot the wagons yourself...   **93**
Light a flare... **(purple flare)**   **71**
Inform the Stonor villagers... *(Bonnington)*   **32**
Ride away...   **939**

❧ 51 ❧

The talk at the bar is of Goodman Butt's morris-dancing troupe who have recently passed through, the arms fair down in Reading and Captain Coke's most recent escapades in the skies above. "I 'appen to know," winks one drinker, "That he lands his airship over near Christmas Common. That's where he has his depot and refuels and suchlike."

Your Silkflower Ale is pale, fresh and sweet, only lightly hopped and reminiscent of hay meadows and spring woods.

Leave the pub...   **977**
Return to the parlour...   **585**

❧ 52 ❧

You pull over briefly in the tiny village of Britwell Salome. The muddy road shows tracks of pneumatic tyres leading on towards Watlington, but a sidelane leads up towards the high ground at Eatonsfield Shaw.

Take the lane...   **110**
Head on to Watlington...   **303**

❧ 53 ❧

Remembering the directions to the secluded village of Maidensgrove, you turn off the main road beside the sand bunker and follow a narrow lane between cottages and squatters' huts. A field-edge track takes you past stubble and hawthorn hedges springing with life, through a dairy-farm and up onto the hill. Somewhere a blackbird is singing.

On the hill you bump over flints and chalk, over rich ochre mud and out to where the view breaks out. It is a glorious place t ride.

Continue to Maidensgrove...   **344**

❧ 54 ❧

At Culham engineers of previous generations cut a narrow channel across the meadow, avoiding the treacherous ground of the Sutton pools. The resulting man-made stream runs swift, dark and cold.

A pleasure cruiser is drifting without helmsman or crew. No steam rises from its funnel and the side lamps are unlit.

Investigate the cruiser...   **825**
Sail on...   **210**

55

If you have the codeword *Bellyache*, turn to **793** immediately.

Heavy rain has churned up the road surface and strewn gravel unevenly across the slope: make a MOTORING roll of difficulty 10, adding 2 if you have **off-road tyres**. If you are unsuccessful, you unfortunately lose control of the velosteam and tumble to the ground, causing one **damage point**.

If your velosteam is **beyond repair**...	874
Otherwise...	793

56

The offices of the Atmospheric Union have a ticket office and an enquiries desk. There is also a recruiter for the Union at her stall, keenly crying the benefits of a career with the Union. Crisp, machine-printed posters paint the delights of far-flung destinations, all reachable by Union airships, however strange and exotic their names are to the locals.

Talk to the recruiter...	160
Look for Judge Hector's son... (*Abapical*)	154
Ask about the bounty on Captain Coke...	
(**wanted poster**)	7
Leave the offices...	454
Leave the airfield...	68

57

You leave the tiny village of Skirmett and cut through a field towards Turville, avoiding the junction at Fingest and remaining unseen by anyone. The high hedges hem you in on either side, absorbing the sound of your heavily-breathing velosteam. A kite screeches and swoops down past your head, diving at some rodent in the grass.

Continue on to Turville...	947

58

It was unwise to come this way while the Constables are searching for you. As soon as they recognise you, they mount their velosteams and give chase. Which way will you turn?

Towards Sonning Bridge...	692
Into the woods east of Woodcote...	364
North towards Stonor and Ibstone...	459

59

A small boy has his head trapped in railings beside the road. He wails desperately while his friends look on. With your steam-powered fist, however, you are quickly able to wrench the bars apart and free him. He runs off happily.

A man approaches. "What have you done to my fence?" he asks. Roll two dice: if you score more than your current number of **solidarity points**, gain **one**.

Ride on...	617

60

□

If the box above is empty, tick it now and read on. If it is already ticked, turn to **268**. You have come across the Constables' prison wagon that you saw from the window of the Angel in Henley. It is halted on the uneven verge while driver and guards stand around. The furnace shutters are open and you can hear someone chopping wood. It seems that they are low on fuel. Remove the codeword *Bodacious*.

Creep up and release the prisoners...	78
Fire on the Constables...	434
Leave them be...	313

61

Of course there is a branch of Coulter's Bank here in the heart of Reading. You will be able to enter as long as you are not **Wanted by the Constables**, in which case you should return to **297** immediately.

Inside the bank you will be able to place money in an account, saving it for a rainy day or for your eventual retirement. To do this, you must deposit multiples of ten guineas (**£10 10s**) in coin or **banknotes** and write this amount into the bank account space on your **Adventure Sheet**. Note that you can also withdraw money with the same restrictions, but that if you have made deposits elsewhere with Coulters (for example, in High Wycombe) then you will be able to add to or access the same amount here.

You can also exchange **banknotes** for coin here. Simply remove them from your **possessions** and add the correct number of pounds and shillings to your wallet. Remember that **one guinea** is equal to **one pound** and **one shilling**, or **twenty-one shillings**. I f you have **Sackler's cheque**, turn to **231** immediately.

Leave the bank...	297

❧ 62 ❧

The road between Henley and Marlow may be as direct as it can be, its curves and twists echoing the river's way, but it is by no means a fast road. To the east is Mill End, a clustered village clinging to the riverside, and the high hedgerows hiding the road from the meadows make this lane seem even narrower than it truly is. An even camber to the branches overhead betrays the frequency of freight wagons and roofed omnibuses: if you choose to rob the traffic here you will have to work fast. You are no distance at all from Henley.

A side-road through an iron gate heads into the riverside meadows just south of the bend in the road, leading to Fawley Court. The house is a noble family's dwelling and characteristically private. What business can someone like yourself have there? Another turning takes a smaller lane up the hill past a sign marked *Henley Park School - Girls' Boarding*.

Ride south to Henley...	702
Ride east to Mill End...	112
Prepare an ambush here...	508
Enter Fawley Court...	
(letter of introduction)	104
Visit Henley Park School... (*Awful*)	224

❧ 63 ❧

Your attempts to keep time with the morris-men first make them laugh and then anger them. In the first few bars you manage to turn the wrong way and barrel into a large weaver. Then you catch Goodman Butt a crack over the head with your badly-wielded stick. "What are you trying to do?" asks Butt. "You're making us look stupid! I wish I'd never given you this stick."

Turn to...   947

❧ 64 ❧

Through an incredible show of swordplay and many lucky escapes, you defeat the posse of Constables and leave them lying on the floor of your room. You have time to collect all your belongings and to climb out of the window to your velosteam without further opposition. Where will you turn?

North...	682
Towards the Bath Road...	589

❧ 65 ❧

When night falls you creep towards Coke's tent. Drawing the flaps aside, you are dismayed to see him still awake, writing by candlelight. He turns, draws his weapon and leaps up to defend himself. Coke is a skilled and determined fighter: you will be hard pressed to defeat him. He fights with a short-handled hooked blade, which hums with some sort of charge. Every time he bypasses your parry and strikes you, the blade will temporarily reduce your NIMBLENESS by 1: after the fight, return your score to its normal value.

Captain Coke	Weapon: **charged skyhook** (PAR 6)
Parry:	12
Nimbleness:	6
Toughness:	5

Victory!	685
Defeat!	741

❧ 66 ❧

As you ride onto the field and bump over the gravel, guards in the grey livery of the Atmospheric Union surround you. They are heavily armed with rifles and clockwork-powered repeating carbines. It was unwise to come to their headquarters while you are being hunted. You have no choice other than to give yourself up.

Turn to...   77

❧ 67 ❧

To hit both guards while firing from a moving velosteam will be a feat of gunmanship indeed. Make an ACCURACY roll of difficulty 15, adding 1 if you have a **double headlamp**.

Successful ACCURACY roll!	813
Failed ACCURACY roll!	35

❧ 68 ❧

You are on the high road between the airfield at Rotherfield Greys and Henley-upon-Thames. The noise of nearby cranes and cargo-shifting wafts on the breeze over the hedges.

Plan an ambush here...	72
Ride to the airfield...	454
Take the road east...	158
Head downhill to Henley...	702

❧ 69 ❧

"You teach the girls? What an idea! But perhaps it would work - after all, you have already proven that you can charm them. You would need considerable patience, I warn you. But if you are serious, I will talk to the headteacher and he will write you a short-term contract. We really are desperate."

How has the road led you here? Is this the life you imagined would accompany your ruthless brigandage on the midnight road?

In the morning you are given a class in the school workshop: you will need both wit and charm to engage and interest the teenage girls. Fortunately you have been given students who are keen to learn. Add your INGENUITY score to your GALLANTRY.

Score <11	**169**
Score 11+	**183**

❧ 70 ❧

A cool young man with a floppy bow tie seems quite unworried by your sudden arrival. "So, some sort of highway robber, eh? I'll teach you a thing or two." He draws a sabre and attacks you with the vigour of youth.

Baronet Fuller	Weapon: **sabre (PAR 3)**
Parry:	11
Nimbleness:	8
Toughness:	4

Victory!	**351**
Defeat!	**999**

❧ 71 ❧

You light up a flare and within a few minutes, Captain Coke and his crew arrive from the air to salvage the wagon. "This is a good haul, matey," he says. "Come back to our hideout and I'll make sure you get your share." Gain the codeword *Bragging*.

Turn to...   **939**

❧ 72 ❧

A farm track into a field provides you a place to wait to see what approaches and a gooseberry bush heavy with sharp green globes refreshes you. Note **passage number 433** and roll a dice to decide what next.

Score 1	A supply wagon...	**194**
Score 2	Passengers for the airfield...	**1244**
Score 3	The Telegraph Guild...	**198**
Score 4	A private steam carriage...	**103**
Score 5-6	The Constables!	**757**

❧ 73 ❧

If you have the codeword *Brazen*, turn to **350** immediately. Mapledurham Manor is a fine Elizabethan house with fine chimney stacks and a pleasing symmetry. The whole place is a little overgrown, perhaps indicating that the owners' priorities are elsewhere.

If you have the **Whitchurch ballot list**, turn to **215** immediately. Otherwise your options are limited: if you know the lady of the house, you might manage to speak to her. And then there is always burglary.

Talk to Leticia Forebury... (*Beaurigarde*)	**260**
Consider robbing the house...	**381**
Leave the house...	**864**

❧ 74 ❧

You have the innkeeper roll out a barrel of beer for the voters and announce that they will each have another waiting for them at the ballot, together with a side of bacon and a new pair of boots fitted at your expense. Well, that is enough to sway the most worried voter. They line up to make their mark alongside their name on your paper: remove the **Whitchurch ballot list** and replace it with the **Whitchurch affidavit**. Also gain the codeword *Blameless*.

Return to the parlour...	**529**
Leave the Ferryman...	**749**

❧ 75 ❧

It is almost as though you return to your woodland camp by instinct alone, like a homing pigeon or a snail. Like a snail, you leave a trail of your life's fluid behind and almost pass out at your camp. There you are able to bandage and rest: remove a **wound** and replace it with a **scar**, but to recover fully you had better hope in your supplies stashed here.

Turn to...   **962**

❧ 76 ❧

Anita is in her tent, peering at the insides of a crow she is dissecting. Obsessed by the intricacies of anatomy, she only has the briefest of time for you and your requests.

Medical items	To buy	To sell
bandages	3s	-
poison	15s	5s
bottle of chloroform	£2	15s
pink pills (NIM+2) ☐ ☐ ☐	£2 5s	-
false teeth	£1 2s	6s
gold tooth	15s	8s
stethoscope	£1 8s	15s

Medical treatment	To buy
Treat a **burn**...	12s
Heal a **wound**...	£1 1s

If you take her treatment for a **wound** or **burn**, convert it into a **scar** on your **Adventure Sheet**.

Return to the encampment...   **819**

❧ 77 ❧

The Union guards confiscate all your **possessions**, your **money** and your velosteam. Granted the right to police their own affairs by parliament, the Union have a system of punitive labour intended to extract payment through work for all the misdeeds of those who have acted against them, whether sky-pirates, brigands or thieves.

Your sentence is harsh, intended to terrify other would-be robbers. First you are mechanically flogged and thrown into a cell for several months. Your back heals, but you are badly and permanently scarred: gain **five scars**. When you are well enough to work, you are assigned to a chain gang breaking stone for the airship runways, hauling iron frameworks for a new launch ramp and shifting cargo.

It is a long year and more before your sentence is considered complete. You are re-united with your velosteam, which has been repainted in Union grey, and let loose on the road once more, penniless and without any possessions. At least you are no longer **Wanted by the Atmospheric Union**.

Turn to...   **68**

❧ 78 ❧

You leave your velosteam between two thickly-leaved hazel coppices and slowly proceed along the woodbank towards the parked machine, keeping the iron-barred cage between yourself and the dismounted Constables. Make a NIMBLENESS roll of difficulty 11.

Successful NIMBLENESS roll	**759**
Failed NIMBLENESS roll!	**486**

❧ 79 ❧

The labourer appreciatively climbs aboard your Ferguson and clings on as you power up the hill towards Woodcote. In no time, you drop him off at a crossroads where a foreman stands with a clipboard.

"That were proper of you," says the workman. "I'm sure you're that Steam Highwayman I've heard of. Well you might be the one to sort out all the hoo-ha down in Whitchurch. Election's due and there's been no end of fuss. Brawling, bribing. It's all down to the families there, you see. The Forbury candidate should take it, if you ask me."

If you are a **Member of the Compact for Worker's Equality**, turn to **182**. If not, but you are **Wanted by the Constables**, turn to **146**.

Enter Woodcote...	**488**
Choose an onward route...	**659**

❧ 80 ❧

At the departure lounge you may wait in style while waiting for a flight - or even hobnob with the off-duty officers about their travels. Wealthy passengers sit in their furs and flying suits, ready to depart with a change in the wind.

If you have the codeword *Believer*, turn to **1391** immediately.

Board the flight to Belize...
(*Balance* and **emerald jewellery**)	**1365**
Chat with the airship officers... (**10s**)	**1410**
Return to the airfield...	**454**

∽ 81 ∾

Lord Burgess will regret the way he has treated you and the disregard he showed to his ancestor's unhappy spectre: you are the vengeful spirit of vengeance itself! Late by night you carefully distribute the **explosives** around the manor (remove them from your possessions) and join them with a carefully-linked fuse. Make an ENGINEERING roll of difficulty 12, adding 2 for each level of **explosives expert** that you possess.

Successful ENGINEERING roll!	**289**
Failed ENGINEERING roll!	**1512**

∽ 82 ∾

The decorations and luggage on the steam wagon warn you to expect a sportsperson: the carcass of a mighty stag lolls on the roof of the compartment. As you move to open the door, a woman in tweeds leaps out, slashing at you with a hunting knife, and you gain an immediate **wound.** "So you'd try to hunt the hunter, would you?" she snarls. "You'll get what you deserve, roadside scum!"

Huntress	Weapon: **hunting knife (PAR 1)**
Parry:	10
Nimbleness:	9
Toughness:	3

Victory!	**1461**
Defeat!	**999**

∽ 83 ∾

You pull your velosteam into view and draw your weapons. The driver may well stop without a fight if you are terrifying enough. Make a RUTHLESSNESS roll of difficulty 10 adding 1 if you are **Wanted by the Coal Board** and 1 if you have a **double headlamp.**

Successful RUTHLESSNESS roll!	**497**
Failed RUTHLESSNESS roll!	**1342**

∽ 84 ∾

The open road is your only home and your velosteam your only companion. Whoever approaches, by robbing them you will continue to maintain your proud independence and your liberty. The region's lanes, highways and hidden paths offer you places to hide and ambush, secretive villages and friendly landlords to host you. Perhaps in the vulnerable houses of the great you will find the wealth you so covet.

You have in your possession a **blunderpistol (ACC 6)**, a **sabre (PAR 3)**, a **mask** and a **tarpaulin.** Your ability scores are:

RUTHLESSNESS	4
ENGINEERING	4
MOTORING	6
INGENUITY	4
NIMBLENESS	3
GALLANTRY	3

Turn to... **1440**

∽ 85 ∾

Your shot goes completely astray, passing well overhead. The driver laughs scornfully and accelerates past, entirely unimpressed by your attempt. If you wish to hit what you are aiming at, you had better invest in some practice - or a more accurate firearm!

Turn to... **171**

∽ 86 ∾

The cards simply deceive you: every time you gather a flush, Reverend Prattle lays out a run. Whenever you gather a full house, he manages to conjure a house of aces. At the end of the game he takes your stake and nods to Parson Twinge. "I'll send some men for your final bell," he says. "You'll have to call your parishioners with a bird-scarer. And I do hope this new curate of yours takes better care of your flock than of these cards." Gain the codeword *Bellbottom.*

Leave the gambling vicars... **343**

∽ 87 ∾

To intimidate the voters you will need to convince them of your ability and willingness to pursue and punish them, should they vote for anyone other than his Lordship. Make a RUTHLESSNESS roll of difficulty 13.

Successful RUTHLESSNESS roll...	**97**
Failed RUTHLESSNESS roll...	**149**

❧ 88 ❧

You are a short distance from Frieth village on the road towards Marlow. A lane between trimmed black-thorn hedges leads south, without any sign or indication where it might lead.

South along the lane...	**226**
Into Frieth village...	**896**
East towards Marlow...	*Smog and Ambuscade 288*

❧ 89 ❧

"Be off with you," shouts the woman. "You'll have nothing from me! You don't dare kill!"

Before you can reach for your weapon, Goodman Butt taps your elbow. "No need to spill any blood," he says. "We've had the luggage off the back anyways."

The morris-men reattach the drive-chain and cheer the carriage off. They offer you first choice from the luggage - you may take any two of the following: a **clockwork bird**, a **picnic hamper**, a **cloak**, or a **silver bracelet**. The woman's description means that you will be **Wanted by the Constables**, if you are not already.

"We'll see you again," says Butt. "Off to make trouble across the river now."

Ride away...	**433**

❧ 90 ❧

As you steam down the Thames, the sound of throbbing propellors approaches over the wooded hills. An airship hung about with bloodthirsty sky-pirates is flying low, keen to snap up any ill-defended cargoes. As you watch, it begins hovering over a craft around the next bend like a kite poised to strike.

Wait until the airship has gone...	**495**
Rush to the aid of the other rivercraft...	**1029**

❧ 91 ❧

A row of wooden grain warehouses stand along the dusty Sonning street between the Methodist chapel and the wharf. Beside a bridge over the Thames is the French Horn, a coaching inn that was once a regular stop on the long-distance turnpike. Recently the improvement of the Bath Road has taken traffic around the village and the fortunes of the Horn have fallen in response.

The village is mostly timber-framed cottages built with flint. There are few shops and they only sell the most meagre of local produce.

Enter the French Horn...	**358**
Cross the river...	**682**
Head out onto the Bath Road...	**589**
Go aboard your boat...	
(if **moored at Sonning**)	**750**

❧ 92 ❧

☐

If the box is empty, tick it and read on. If it is already ticked, turn to **473** immediately.

The sun is low as you stroll between the cottages, the occasional brick-built house where a son of the town has made good, the barns and the gardens. A mist sinks down from Hanger Hill and soaks across the village street. You are returning to the warmth of your velosteam when a figure stumbles out of the mist towards you. An old man in a cassock, bare-headed and wild-eyed immediately fixes you in a strangely magnetic gaze. "A helper," he says. "A helper for the people. As I should have been. Their common land taken from them, in my selfishness, how long ago? And my heirs so hard and obdurate. I brought such suffering on them in my pride. My heirs must return the land to the people and you must bring this to pass!"

As he finishes his words, the man drifts strangely out of vision and into the mist. You have encountered the ghost of Henry Burghersh, the fourteenth-century Bishop of Lincoln, who enclosed much of the common land hereabouts. Interestingly, the current Lord of the Manor is indeed descended from the ancient churchman.

Visit the Lord of the Manor and tell him the ghost's wishes...	**21**
Ignore the ghost...	**867**

❧ 93 ❧

Amongst the wagons you find a variety of tools and machinery parts: an **axe**, a **shovel**, a **net**, a **high-pressure valve**, some **copper pipe**, some **welding tools** and a pair of **goggles (MOT+1)**. If you have an ENGINEERING skill of 8 or higher you can also take a **pump and filter** from the engine and fit it to your velosteam.

Turn to...   **939**

✎ 94 ✎

Note that you are now **moored at Mongewell Park**. You and your mate hammer in mooring stakes on the grassy bank beneath the willows. "We are guests here," you remind him. "Best behaviour."

Turn to...   **1028**

✎ 95 ✎

The ladies and gentlemen can see that you are not joking and a respectful hush falls. After all, a sportsperson devoted to their discipline garners a great deal of esteem from these classes. Your next shot passes cleanly over the lawn and you shoot **two hoops** in turn.

Turn to....   **1476**

✎ 96 ✎

The branches of hawthorn, hornbeam and beech whip at your face as you take the bends towards Deadman's Lane. The heavy tyres of the velosteam grip into the verges, propelling you over the hollows of rabbit burrows and wheel-ruts as you cut every corner, leaning out boldly to balance your machine's powerful weight. Your pursuers are close on your tail: make a MOTORING roll of difficulty 11, adding 1 if you have a **reinforced boiler**.

Successful MOTORING roll!   **396**
Failed MOTORING roll!   **1042**

✎ 97 ✎

You lower your voice and begin to tell the voters how you know their names, business and dwelling-places; how you have treated those unwise enough to cross you previously; how his Lordship's wrath will fall on them. They silently line up to make their mark on the ballot list, terrified of what will happen if they do not: remove the **Whitchurch ballot list** and replace it with the **Whitchurch affidavit**. Also gain the codeword *Blameless*.

Return to the parlour...   **529**
Leave the Ferryman...   **749**

✎ 98 ✎

You seek out Elias Croney and find him at work weeding a garden for pennies. He recognises you and shakes his head. "I ain't been able to lift that sack," he says. "Still a bachelor."

"I have something that might help you," you reply. Remove the codeword *Bressingham* and the **mechanical arm**, which you help him strap to his stump. He is amazed - with linkages that help it move in tandem with his whole, right arm or in a series of complementary motions, he discovers a strength he never had before and expresses his gratitude tearfully.

"I'm off to get the vicar! We'll be married this afternoon! Oh, Delia!"

And indeed the wedding goes ahead. You are one of the guests of honour, amongst the villagers who flock to the long-awaited celebration. A feast follows in which you are toasted and give toasts in turn. The bride is no slip of a girl but a hearty, sensible country woman with a big heart - whom Elias happily carries over the church gate to the sound of hearty cheers and sliding hydraulic pistons. You eventually leave them, still celebrating into the warm night, warmed yourself by what you have been able to do. Gain a **solidarity point** and the codeword *Bumpkin*.

Return to Fingest...   **867**

✎ 99 ✎
☐

If the box above is empty, put a tick in it and read on. If it is already ticked, turn to **233** immediately.

The door to the director's office is marked with a brass plate and opens to the touch. Inside, a short-haired woman is poring through a catalogue. She looks up suspiciously, but when you explain why you have come, she begins to smile. You hand her the **treasure trove** - remove it from your possessions - and she begins to peer at it through a magnifying glass.

"Incredible! Look at these markings! What a find! It shall have pride of place in the East Gallery! Yes, this will put them in their place. Close the museum? I should think not! Tell me how you came by this fabulous, fabulous discovery. We have a lot to learn from it."

You tell her how and where it came into your possession and she quizzes you for almost an hour, keen to wring as much understanding about the object's provenance and context as possible. In the end she sits back, shaking her head in wonder.

"Incredible. This may lead to us re-thinking the entire field. I shall certainly have to visit the site. How wonderful." She looks you in the eye. "Now, my friend, what can I do for you? No, let me tell you. The museum is not rich but what influence I have is at your disposal." She pulls out a fine fountain pen and writes you a **letter of introduction**. "Show this to any person of nobility and you will receive a glad welcome." As well as this reward, you can now count yourself the **Friend of Professor Challing**.

Leave the museum...   **702**

❧ 100 ❧
The John Barleycorn at Goring takes its name from the ancient folk song. Outside a smiling straw head swings from a bracket, greeting the traveller. On a plain door to the back room hangs a poster advertising a drink called Vlaada Original.

Buy a pint...	(2s)	**218**
Enter the back room...		**721**
Leave the pub...		**487**
Mount up and leave the town...		**911**

❧ 101 ❧
You climb onto a tall stool and watch a game of darts as you drink your ale. A local farm labourer has been challenged by a nun - and she seems to be beating him hollow. Watching and sipping your cloudy, sweet and mild Forshaw's Summer Ale, you study her.

The nun is not old but clearly of middle age. She moves with a happy confidence amongst the men and drinks from her own pot of beer. She is Sister Celandine of the Order of St Katharine, from the convent south of Frieth near Heath Wood. She is an interesting woman, trusted by her mother superior to check on the welfare of serving girls in the great houses nearby.

"Where do you go, mostly?" you ask.

"Stonor House, Hambleden Manor, Fingest House. Some of the maids are novices, you see, and some of the others are just needy of a friendly ear and someone on their side. The gentry will take advantage of them otherwise, you see," she smiles. "They need confronting at times. Like when that girl was so badly beaten for cleaning the computing engine wrongly..."

"Where was that?" you ask, but she refuses to talk any more.

Return to the parlour...   **405**

❧ 102 ❧
The road here follows the very top of the hill crest, so that as breaks in the trees appear you are treated to glimpses of the wide Oxford plain, surmounted by the smoky smudge of the city on the skyline. Thick, ancient woods stand all around: beeches of incredible age grow here, some fallen, some rotten through, one even with a young holly tree sprouting from inside its hollow trunk. The woods are quiet now, but in the distance you can hear sawmills whirring and the clanking of iron couplings.

Take the road to Aston Hill...	**710**
Ride on to Stokenchurch...	**308**
Head to Christmas Common...	**617**

❧ 103 ❧
Your best chance of success is to threaten the driver and intimidate them into halting the engine and then deal with the passengers. Make a RUTHLESSNESS roll, adding 1 for each **Wanted** status you possess:

Score 10 or less...	**782**
Score 11-14...	**164**
Score 15-18...	**212**
Score 19+...	**242**

❧ 104 ❧
Your **letter of introduction** opens the gate for you and soon has the lady of the house out on the terrace greeting you politely, if with bemusement. Remove the **letter of introduction** from your possessions.

"My," says Viscountess Bell-Happing, "What an interesting machine! Don't tell me that you oil it yourself. These machines and vehicles are all very well but, oh, so messy. Come and join us in the garden."

The Viscountess is hosting a croquet tournament. Having handed you a drink herself, she drags you around into the rear garden where you are met by a crowd of the most interesting people. Among them is Major Redford, the commander of the Henley Constables. He does not recognise you - he is famously short-sighted and enjoying his punch rather too much to worry about arresting people.

"You've turned up just in time!" he says cheerily. "I can't find a partner. But you look like you've got a good arm. Join me on the court!"

Turn to...   **5**

❦ 105 ❧

You ride back up to Nettlebed and steam into the Freight Yard. The Haulage Guild representative is busy in her office, but you insist on seeing her and tell her about your discovery. She sniffs. "That driver wasn't one of ours," she says. "We'll send a crew to go and pick it up."

Turn to...   677

❦ 106 ❧

The market at Watlington spreads out across the road where the junctions meet. Great untidy piles of freight stand alongside local produce - who is buying, who is selling and what exactly is for sale is anyone's guess.

Food and Drink	To buy	To sell
bird's eggs	4s	2s
rabbit	2s	1s
pheasant	4s	3s
deer carcass	£2	£2
wheel of cheese	£2	£1 1s
bottle of wine	10s	8s
Clothing	To buy	To sell
mask	4s	-
lace shawl	£1 5s	15s
bow tie (GAL+1)	£1 10s	£1 5s
silk scarf	-	15s
cloak	£1	-
goggles (MOT+1)	£2 15s	£1 15s
Jewellery	To buy	To sell
locket	-	6s
pocket watch	£3	£1 18s
silver ring	10s	8s
silver bracelet	£1	16s
silver necklace	£2	£1 10s
gold ring	£3	£2 5s
gold bracelet	£3 5s	£2 8s
Tools	To buy	To sell
snare	2s	1s
net	6s	4s
Weapons	To buy	To sell
billhook (PAR 2)	-	10s
catling knife (PAR 1 NIM+2)	-	£3 1s
razor (PAR-1 NIM+3)	£1 15s	18s

Leave the market...   360
Leave the town...   637

❦ 107 ❧

You climb up into the branches and throw down the nests. Perhaps it is cruel to prey on a predator like this - or perhaps it is all part of the responsibility of caring for the land. You may take a handful of **bird's eggs** if you wish. It takes you some time to deal with each of the kite's tree-borne nurseries and when you are done, dusk is falling. Mr Sands appears, tramping between the trees. "Very nice," he says approvingly. "Come this way to my cottage for a spot of tea."

Follow Mr Sands...   646

❦ 108 ❧

"An escape? Perhaps that is what I need. I have longed to travel the world. But I am not paid until the year's end, and then the headteacher docks all my expenses. It is dreadfully hard to save what I need. I have no travelling clothes or money for a ticket."

"Perhaps this will help." (**fur coat, £15 15s**)   447
"I will return when I can help you."   415
"I can only advise self-discipline."   23

❦ 109 ❧

"So many of you are considering voting for the Duke's candidate," you say.

"Well, it's his daughter what convinced us," one replies. "She says that we need to get someone into Parliament what'll help with all the slums in the cities. But that's a long way away, ain't it? Things are fine here for now."

"You should vote for the Duke's man and think
          of others, not just yourselves."   240
"Vote however you believe you should."   181
Bribe them to vote for Sir M'Dow... (**£20**)   74
Intimidate them into supporting Sir M'Dow...   87

❦ 110 ❧

You have come to a cross-roads at the high ground above Watlington, right at the edge of the escarpment. Roads leave here in five directions, unmarked, but the heaviest wheel-tracks run north and south.

Head north to Watlington...   360
Ride north-east along the high road...   746
Steam south-east towards Pishill...   370
Turn due south towards Nettlebed...   920
Take the smaller road north-west...   307
Investigate Swyncombe House... (*Burnett*)   590

❧ 111 ❧

A haulier's engine trundles towards you, splashing through the ruts and rocking from side to side. Several wagons swing round the bend behind it. How will you proceed?

Attempt to unlink the last wagon...	**184**
Threaten the driver...	**202**
Jump aboard and fight it out...	**239**

❧ 112 ❧

The lock here across the Thames is named for Hambleden Manor to the north but the scattering of houses astride the road is known as Mill End. A run of massive watermills use the river's power to grind corn, mash cloth into paper and cut wood from the nearby hills. Like many riverside settlements, it was built around natural islands in the stream, cut and reinforced by the iron-powered hand of man. A long catwalk stretches out over the weir. As you approach, one of the giant undershot wheels begins to turn, slapping the water again and again with its baffles in slow celebration of profit.

Atop the mills you can see the livery of the Imperial Northern Milling and Manufacturing Company and a small telegraph tower winking away.

Go aboard your boat... (if **moored** here)	**855**
Steam east towards Marlow...	**801**
Ride west towards Henley...	**62**
Take the road up the valley to Hambleden...	**343**
Board the ferry to Aston... (**2s**)	**280**

❧ 113 ❧

The Thames bends back and forth, almost as if with the weight of the freight barges that clog the stream. You wind your way between side-paddle, stern-paddle and screw-driven steamers, doing your best to keep to the upstream lane but continually harangued by unreasonable and time-pressured bargees. Reading will no doubt be just as busy and unwelcoming.

Turn to...	**540**

❧ 114 ❧

If you are the **Friend of Professor Challing**, turn to **1407** immediately.

The archaeologist is a dour old man travelling to the museum in Henley. You may take his **shovel** and **£4 3s**. "It's a shame," he says glumly. "How can a humble archaeologist get by nowadays? They may well have to close the museum in Henley. Not enough visitors. But I'll tell you why - they need a new exhibit. And now you've come to steal my shovel."

You will now be **Wanted by the Constables** unless you have a **mask**.

Turn to...	**noted passage**

❧ 115 ❧

As soon as the ferry sets off across the river, you move your boat into position and come alongside. A steam vehicle and several local people are aboard: whether this will prove profitable you are unable to say. Standing on the gunwale with your weapons on show, you must make a RUTHLESSNESS roll of difficulty 10 to see whether you can terrify the passengers into surrender.

Successful RUTHLESSNESS roll!	**1447**
Failed RUTHLESSNESS roll!	**463**

❧ 116 ❧

"Here you are at last, matey," cries Coke. "I was struggling to keep a-hold of your share of the booty from that last raid. The lads was wanting to drink it!" Roll a dice to see how much you have been apportioned.

Score 1-2	**£8 10s** and a **gold ring**
Score 3-4	**ten guineas in banknotes** and **£1 8s**
Score 5-6	**£14 3s**

"Got any more flares? Just shoot one off and I'll be there," says Coke. Remove the codeword *Bragging*.

Return to the hideout...	**819**

❧ 117 ❧

The Theatre has an entrance for the rich and an entrance for the poor, seats for the nobleman and for the urchin, but one performance for them all. Dancing girls are promised - a drama - a performing ape - jugglers - a skilled soprano. In a private box above the show, Lord Barrymore and his friends play at cards throughout, barely noticing the performers and talking, laughing and shouting regardless. You must have paper money for your stake if you wish to join them.

Watch a show... (**4s**)	**290**
Join the gamblers...	
(**ten guineas in banknotes**)	**213**
Leave the Theatre...	**702**

❧ 118 ❧
□ □ □ □

If you are **Wanted by the Constables**, tick one of the boxes above. If they are all ticked already turn to **214** immediately.

Board your boat... (**moored at Sonning**)	750
Head into Sonning village...	91

❧ 119 ❧

After crossing the ditch beside the holly-topped beech, you find the path the children told you about. It is only just wide enough for your velosteam to thread between the tree-trunks. You wind downwards into the valley as quietly as you can, past clucking pheasants and drifts of leaves, until you reach the rear of Wormsley Park itself. There, as the children said, you find **peacock feathers** lying about - take one if you wish.

Continue on towards Ibstone...	977
Retrace your route to the high road...	102

❧ 120 ❧

You plunge into the narrow valley, then descend even lower as the lane becomes a deep, steep-sided holloway. Sunlight glances inbetween the beeches, but this is a precarious place for heavy engines and their loads.

Prepare an ambush here...	968
Take the lane to Turville...	947
Ride across the field to Ibstone...	977
Head west to Northend...	595

❧ 121 ❧

You take a seat and put down your florin. A dish of 'chips' is placed before you and a tall beaker of the house ale drawn smoothly from the barrel. Your neighbours on either side lean in to take their share of the hot fresh potatoes. If you have a **Guildsman's medallion**, turn to **729** immediately. Otherwise, read on.

The hauliers are mostly talking about the road conditions, watering places and fuel stores on their various routes. One has just returned from a long journey to Wales. She shakes her head remembering the difficulty she had keeping her water tank full. "There's plenty of watering stations," she complains, "But all owned by the blamed Haulage Guild. It ain't easy keeping the tank healthy full."

"I done got the blacksmith at Turville to build me a pump and filter," says another. "Long journeys no object, you see. I can even steam on ditch water."

"Ditch water? Ain't you got no self-respect? Your boiler won't last the year!"

The draught in front of you has no such risks. It is crystal clear - limestone clear. You raise the beaker to admire it and a haulier opposite raises his in reply. "Good health," he calls. "Good health, pressure to your boiler and grip to your treads!" The beer is light on foretaste and sweet - perfectly refreshing - but it runs through a steady drinker quickly. In fact with the salted potatoes it seems a good earner for the innkeeper. You ask what they call it.

"Ain't got no name," says the maid. "Just our Light Chequers Ale, I guess. We make the dark one wintertime."

Leave the pub...	867
Return to the parlour...	36

❧ 122 ❧

If you are the **Friend of Goodman Butt**, turn to **129** immediately.

The morris-dancers are preparing for a session at a nearby celebration. They have gas for their handcart steam-organ, flowers for their hats and fresh starch in their handkerchiefs, but are unable to dance. The leader of the group points to one snoring dancer. "Sammy be dead drunk! How can we dance a fourteener with only thirteen? Our reputation as the foremost morris troupe in the region be at stake, here!"

"You'd better wake him somehow."	405
"Pass me a stick. I can dance your fourteenth man."	196

❧ 123 ❧
□

If the box is empty, tick it and turn to **696** immediately. If it is already ticked, read on.

You wait beside the road as afternoon turns to evening, preparing your weapons and keeping your eyes ready. Note **passage number 839** on your **Adventure Sheet** and roll a dice to see what you encounter:

Score 1-2	A private steam carriage...	103
Score 3-4	The Constables...	1396
Score 5	A farmer...	1163
Score 6	A locobus...	440

The doorguards put down their lemonade and give you a look, but a word or two convinces them that you are a member of the Compact and they allow you through. In the lounge are several members peering over maps and ledgers. They are planning for the coming revolution. "Comrade!" A thin man with a walrus moustache grips your shoulder. His name is Plunkett. "The time approaches. But we need to convince more to join the cause. We need men and women of determination. Go and spread the word for us in the navvies' camps, the workshops, the factories. Win who you can! There is, after all, a bounty paid on their membership. But only to reflect your expenses."

The members of the Compact will sell you a little equipment from their stores and will also buy valuables with interesting histories.

Clothing	To buy	To sell
cloak	£1	15s
dark cloak (RUTH+1)	-	£2
engineer's gloves (ENG +1)	£3	£2 5s
hair matches (RUTH+2) ☐☐☐	£4	-
Tools	To buy	To sell
rope ladder	9s	7s
wirecutters	12s	9s
grappling iron	12s	8s
jeweller's loupe (ING+1)	£2 2s	£1 5s
telescope	£4 10s	£2 5s

Weapons	To buy	To sell
club	3s	1s
razor (PAR-1 NIM+3)	£1 15s	18s
sabre (PAR 3)	£3	£1 10s
blunderpistol (ACC 6)	£4	£1 10s
gamekeeper's shotgun (ACC 7)	£10	£6
Constable's Carbine (ACC 8)	-	£10
Jewellery	To buy	To sell
locket	-	4s
pocket watch	-	£1 15s
silver ring	-	7s
silver bracelet	-	10s
silver necklace	-	£1 5s
gold ring	-	£1 1s
gold bracelet	-	£2 2s
gold necklace	-	£5
diamond brooch	-	£23
sapphire pendant	-	£24
emerald jewellery	-	£50
Other items	To buy	To sell
revolutionary poster	1s	-
gold cup	-	£15
gold bar	-	£25
ten guineas in banknotes	-	£6
twenty guineas in banknotes	-	£14
thirty guineas in banknotes	-	£22

Return to the parlour... 1515

Head out into Reading... 297

If you have the codeword *Bellingham*, turn to **512** immediately. If you have the codeword *Bellbottom*, turn to **537**. Otherwise, read on.

The church of St Bartholemew is an interesting place. It stands at the lowest point of the village and lush grass and puddles in the churchyard witness the seasonal pond that floods the graveyard, but the church building itself is also far from ordinary. The yellow walls and lichen-covered tiled roof give the place a homely feel, but the square roughstone tower is plainly very old: two tiny windows mark a stairway's progress up to the belfry where eight Norman arches pierce heavy walls, topped by a twin tiled gables presumably added sometime in the eight-hundred years the tower has stood.

A single bell begins to toll. In the valley it is the loudest sound by far. For folk who have never ventured to Reading or Wycombe and who rarely see a steam engine, the homely ringing defines volume, but you can see that there are gaps where other bells have hung.

Venturing into the cool, you meet the vicar, who is tearfully wringing his hands. "Reverend Prattle has won them all in play," he complains. "We have played cards together for many a year, but when I wagered the bells I was sure of my hand. Now we only have the one left. I am to play him again tonight at his vicarage in Hambleden and how I wish I might regain my peal!"

"I have never heard anything so foolish." **867**
"Shall I help you to win them back?" **22**

Henley recedes behind you and the Marlow road lies flat and firm beneath your wheels. What is there like the pleasure of being astride a machine built for speed, racing over good tarmacadam in the summer sunshine?

You manouevre around a long road-train negotiating the town toll-gate and accelerate northwards. Smoke rises ahead of you: roll a dice to see what you encounter.

Score 1-2	Hedge-layers	**831**
Score 3-4	A football team	**852**
Score 5-6	A Telegraph Guild survey team	**942**

The markets at Oxford are some of the largest in the region, but many stalls and shops sell things entirely useless to you, such as second-hand textbooks, small porcelain models of the university and singlets printed with strange slogans like 'I have been to Oxford City of Knowledge'.

Food and Drink	To buy	To sell
bird's eggs	4s	2s
rabbit	2s	1s
pheasant	4s	3s
bottle of wine	10s	8s
bottle of champagne	£1 5s	18s
bottle of whisky	£1 10s	£1
pork pie	3s	2s
picnic hamper	£3 3s	£2 10s
Clothing	To buy	To sell
bow tie (GAL+1)	£1 10s	£1 5s
silk scarf	-	15s
cloak	£1	10s
cassock	£4 8s	£2 10s
golden monocle (GAL+2)	£10	-
top hat	£4	£1 5s
wide-brimmed hat	-	£1 10
Jewellery	To buy	To sell
locket	-	6s
pocket watch	£3	£1 18s
Medical	To buy	To sell
bandages	3s	-
cough medicine	5s	3s
soothing lotion	2s	-
bottle of chloroform	£2	£1 10s
stethoscope	£1	10s
Weapons	To buy	To sell
billhook (PAR 2)	-	10s
catling knife (PAR 1 NIM+2)	-	£3 1s
razor (PAR-1 NIM+3)	£1 15s	18s
sabre (PAR 3)	£1 5s	8s
rapier (PAR 4)	-	£4
blunderpistol (ACC 6)	£4	£2
duelling pistols (ACC 7)	-	£10
Other items	To buy	To sell
deck of marked cards	£1 5s	5s
punchcards (Selladore V)	-	£14 5s
punchcards (Livingstone M)	-	£15 6s
sketchpad ☐ ☐ ☐	3s	1s

Leave the market... **688**
Leave the town... **970**

❧ 128 ❧

☐

If the box above is empty, tick it now. If it is already ticked, turn to **807** immediately.

A working man is walking up the hill ahead of you, a shovel and an axe on his back and a parcel of food strung from his belt. You slow to speak with him.

"I've heard there's a chance of work up in Woodcote," he pants. "And I'll get there soon enough if I can."

Offer him a lift...		**79**
Pay him to fill in potholes...	(10s)	**365**
Ride on by...		**807**

❧ 129 ❧

Goodman Butt and his troupe are in their accustomed places once more, enjoying an afternoon's refreshment. "We won't be dancing this evening," says Goodman. "Come and have a drink with us."

You spend a pleasant evening drinking and talking with the troupe, hearing of Butt's growing family, his son's reluctance to learn the steps of the family dances, his new grandchild and all the everyday cares of the men who come together to drink, and dance.

Bid them farewell...	**405**

❧ 130 ❧

You have now travelled into the very heart of Heath Wood. The trees beside the track are no longer coppiced and tended: they have become wild. If you stop your velosteam, you will hear no human noise at all. A blackbird will warble or a pheasant cough and cry. Rustles betray the presence of deer abroad even at this hour. That is all.

Head north to St Katharine's Convent...	**226**
Ride towards Skirmett...	**969**
Steam to Hambleden village...	**343**
Head east into the wood..	*Smog and Ambuscade 118*

❧ 131 ❧

As you steam into Wargrave the silhouette of a D-Class Telegraph Tower can easily be seen on the crest above the village. A Freight Yard behind the wharf handles all the cargo that is transhipped onto wagons for the Bath Road, and consequently there are always gangs of labourers ready to give a hand with cargo.

	To buy	To sell
Charcoal	**£13**	**£12**
Furniture	**£30**	**£26**
Machinery	-	**£25**
Pottery	**£18**	**£17**
Cotton	-	**£4**
Woollen cloth	-	-
Coal	-	**£12**
Beer	-	**£15**
Wheat	-	**£4**
Malt	**£5**	**£4**
Frozen meat	-	-
Ice	-	-

If you want to moor here, mark **moored at Wargrave** on your **Adventure Sheet** and turn to **418**.

Moor at the quarry... (*Breaker*)	**1485**
Head upriver through Shiplake Lock...	
(2s or a **Bargee's badge**)	**471**
Head downstream towards Henley...	
(2s or a **Bargee's badge**)	**982**

❧ 132 ❧

Spiller's boatyard occupies a thin strip of land between an iron foundry and the dirty river. Boats in various stages of repair and construction stand on the hard and are moored up, three deep, on the water. The foreman looks at you skeptically when you mention that you are looking for a boat. He shows you three sizes that would allow you to travel the waters, carry some cargo and ship your velosteam safely. He can even find you a crewman to mate your vessel.

Boat	Cargo	To buy
Small skiff...	1 unit	**£15**
Medium launch...	2 units	**£25**
Large barge...	3 units	**£35**

If you purchase a craft, note it on your **Adventure Sheet** and turn to **495** immediately.

Return to the city...	**297**

❧ 133 ❧

You settle into a winged chair and raise the glass of Ferry to your lips. What a taste you are rewarded with! A careful balance of fruitiness and bitterness, bright and zesty yet smooth on the palate. Sinking further into the chair, you slowly release all the stresses and anxiety of nights on the road, putting aside the threats and punishments you have been forced to make. For a few minutes you have nothing else to concern you other than the delicious, cool contents of the glass.

If you have any levels of **medical training**, turn to **380** immediately.

Return to the parlour...	**529**
Leave the Ferryman...	**749**

❧ 134 ❧

Wormsley Park stands within a fine, manicured parkland and a gorgeous garden. Peacocks strut proudly around, shrieking in their angry way. If you have the codeword *Blouse*, turn to **1357**. Otherwise, read on.

Ambush Lord Ponsonby...	**1385**
Leave the park...	**977**

❧ 135 ❧

After choosing a likely-looking depression between the stones, you begin to dig. The ground is stony and you make slow progress, but you do open up several rabbit burrows. In one you find a garnet ring. A promising beginning!

You are knee-deep in your hole when you realise that you are being watched. A man in a long waistcoat is pointing a shotgun at you. "What do you think you're doing?" he asks.

"Digging for a treasure trove," you begin to explain.

"What nonsense!" he scoffs. "This isn't even a real grave site! All the stones come from Jersey - my great uncle shipped them here for some ridiculous reason of his. There isn't anything historic here!"

"But what about this ring?" you ask.

He snatches it. "I wondered where this went. Confounded magpies! Now get off my land! You'll have better luck digging around Wyfold Castle!"

"Where's that?"

"The old fort in the wood behind Gallowstree Common. Archaeologists! If you had asked, I could have saved you the bother digging. Go on, get out of that ridiculous hole!"

You loosely shovel some of the man's dirt back into the hole and return to your velosteam, taking your **shovel** with you. Erase the codeword *Bonehunter* but gain the codeword *Benign*.

Travel down the road to Wargrave...	**418**
Ride along the river towards Henley...	**1251**

❧ 136 ❧

A private steam carriage approaches. If you have the codeword *Blarney*, turn to **1499** immediately. Otherwise, read on.

You quickly notice the armed guard sat atop the carriage: plainly whoever is inside is rich enough to be able to afford some protection. Whether they are bold enough - or well-armed enough - to resist you is another question.

Demand the driver stop...	**1400**
Shoot at the guard...	**1416**

❧ 137 ❧

You set off in the direction of Aston, first taking a farm-track heading north, then cutting through an open farm gate and across a wheatfield. As you reach the crest of the hill and glance back, two Constable velosteams are plainly visible behind you, following your trail through the crushed stalks. This momentary hesitation against the skyline costs you: a shot rings out. Roll a dice to see the effect:

Score 1-3	It whistles overhead...
Score 4-5	A **wound**...
Score 6	A **damage point**...

If you now have **five wounds**, turn to **39**. If your velosteam is **beyond repair**, turn to **874**. Otherwise, you press on, racing down the hillside and bursting through a hedge onto Aston Lane.

The ferry is only a short distance ahead and you can see it moored against the near bank. You race on down, judging your speed carefully. Will you be able to stop on the rickety wooden platform without overshooting and ending in the river? Make a MOTORING roll of difficulty 12, adding 1 if you possess **improved brakes** or **off-road tyres**.

Successful MOTORING roll!	**1008**
Failed MOTORING roll!	**781**

❧ 138 ❧

To open the strongbox yourself, you can either attempt to dismantle it or to pick the lock. To do the former, make an ENGINEERING roll of difficulty 14. To do the latter, you will need a set of **lockpicks** or a **skeleton key** and will need to make an INGENUITY roll of difficulty 12. If you would rather wait until you are better prepared, you may turn to your noted passage.

Successful ENGINEERING or INGENUITY roll! **964**
Failed ENGINEERING or INGENUITY roll!   **998**
Leave the **strongbox** for now...   **noted passage**

❧ 139 ❧

The men are effusive, nay, grandiloquent in their thanks and appreciation for your goodness in transporting them across the fluvial barrier to their onward travels. "If I could have written us a ticket across that stream," effuses the grey-beard, "Then I would have written us a pretty ticket indeed. If you need anything writing prettily, come and find us at the sign of the Dolphin."

As they make their way though the deep grass of the riverside pasture, you realise that as well as chicken-thieves and forgers, one of the men must be a skilled pickpocket. Remove **£4 10s** from your wallet (or whatever you possess, if it is less than that.)

Sail on...   **495**

❧ 140 ❧

The charges against you impress your captors. They are sure they have got their hands on an important and well-connected criminal. You are bound and taken to Wallingford, the centre of the Constables' power in the region. Your **money** and any **weapons** are confiscated before you are taken for interrogation.

"Who do you answer to? Nobody flouts the Constables' law alone!"

"The Compact for Workers' Equality!"   **622**
"You fool! I work for you!"   **661**
"Nobody gives me orders. My choices
    are my own."   **705**

❧ 141 ❧

You begin to describe how you could imprison the wretch in a dripping-wet shelter in the woods, fed on nothing but raw game, while the slow message reached his family demanding guineas for his release. He shivers and babbles and quickly opens up a compartment in the carriage wall. "Here, you really don't need to kidnap me. You wouldn't enjoy my company anyway." He thrusts **£5 2s** into your hands.

Leave him...   **noted passage**

❧ 142 ❧

The air is full of soft drizzle, beading on your velosteam's iron-work as you gently steam up the road. What need is there for speed here? Sometimes it is enough to be astride a self-powered machine, open to the wind and the air and the birdsong, and to breeze past the woods and fields like a bird a-wing.

Smoke rises from a steam caravan parked beside the lane here. If you are the **Friend of Barsali**, turn to **477** immediately.

Steam on towards Stokenchurch...   **308**

❧ 143 ❧

"Welcome back!" says the organ-inventor. "Sales are going well. We've built several mechanical organs on the model we came up with together. The church in Marlow bought one recently!"

He nods towards the computational engine's punchcard hopper. "Are you thinking of running something? Be my guest - you can use the engine all you like. It's fully steamed and ready to calculate. Very exciting, eh?"

Leave the workshop...   **771**

❧ 144 ❧

The road down to Henley flattens out into a long, straight stretch, bounded by broad grass lawns, fine trees and middle-class villas. It would be pretty if it weren't so unadventurous.

Ride on down to Henley...   **1251**

❧ 145 ❧

You step into the Cherry Tree and look around. Dogs lie at the fireside. Two farm labourers feast on bread, cheese and pickles before returning to the harvest.

Buy a beer... (**2s**)   **815**
Leave the inn...   **457**

❧ 146 ❧

The Constables have caught up with you at last! You see one of their Imperial velosteams gaining on you: you have barely a moment to decide your route.

Head down Deadman's Lane...	**96**
Try to lose them in Valentine Wood...	**364**
Race for Sonning...	**692**
Lose your pursuers down Straw Hill cowpath... (*Butterchurn*)	**161**

❧ 147 ❧

Remembering the account you have heard of the earthworks around here, you resolve to take a look around the wood. After some time tramping beneath the trees, it certainly seems that these banks and ditches were once a hill-fort - perhaps from pre-Roman times.

There are no signs of anyone excavating anywhere, and your instincts tell you that there may be something valuable hidden where few have considered looking.

Dig for antiquities...	**(shovel)**	**635**
Return to the wood...		**401**

❧ 148 ❧

The accuracy of your fire shocks and terrifies the guards. They look about, quite convinced that a posse of brigands is firing on them, turn and leap the ditch into the woods beyond. The driver and engineer quickly follow them, meaning you can approach the wagon at your leisure. Roll a dice to see who is in the wagon.

Score 1-3	A murderer	**576**
Score 4-6	Protestors	**779**

❧ 149 ❧

Your attempt to threaten the voters leaves them unimpressed: they return your threats of violence with a heavy beating and throw you out. "We'll vote however it pleases us," they say, as you hit the road. Gain **two wounds**: if you now have **five wounds**, turn to **999** immediately. Otherwise you must pick yourself up. At least you still have the list - perhaps another tack would be more productive.

Turn to...	**749**

❧ 150 ❧

Your shots bring down the nests one after another and fill the woods with the sound of gunfire. The noise attracts Mr Sands, who appears some time later and surveys your handiwork. "Well done," he says. "Those birds won't trouble us now. Come down to the house for a spot of tea."

Follow Mr Sands...	**646**

❧ 151 ❧

"Haven't you heard?" asks the officer. "Captain Coke's been taken. Due to be hanged - or was he hanged already? I don't recall. Anyway, it's a long time since he's bothered us."

Leave the office...	**454**

❧ 152 ❧

The occupant of the carriage is an explorer, home from his travels across the vast continent of Asia. He bristles as you tell him to step down and surrender his valuables. "Why, you blackguard scoundrel! I've fought off Kazakhs, Afghans, Gregs and Han! I've scaled Mount Kumbalumba and crossed the Great Dry Vur! You think I'll be scared of you?"

Explorer   Weapon: **sabre (PAR 3)**

Parry:	8
Nimbleness:	5
Toughness:	5

Victory!	**1152**
Defeat!	**999**

❧ 153 ❧

If you have the codeword *Bumpkin*, turn to **211** immediately.

Strolling past the church, you come across a strange sight. A one-armed man is standing by the wych-gate, attempting to haul a massive sack of grain onto his shoulder. He tries to climb the gate, then falls, sprawling on the ground.

It is only polite to help him up and regardless of your further intentions, curiosity prompts a conversation. His name is Elias Croney, a labourer and some-time engine-man, who lost his arm in a Wycombe mill. He has returned to the village and found someone who loves him despite his disability. "But this is the thing! We're to be wed here in St Bart's. I wouldn't have it anywhere else - my old dad married his first wife and my mother here, as did my Delia's parents. And the village saying goes that a groom who lifts his bride over the church gate is guaranteed a happy marriage."

The sack of grain weighs exactly the same as the betrothed Delia - although how this gallant unibrach discovered that is a mystery. He is a strong man but with only one arm he cannot balance the weight.

"I just about get by. I was saving for one of them mechanical arms," he sighs, "But they cost a pretty pound I tell you. And I won't wed until I can carry me bride."

If you have a **mechanical arm** and wish to give it to him, turn to **98** immediately. Otherwise, gain the codeword *Bressingham*. If you should come across someone who can make such a thing, bringing it to him would be an act of real charity.

Return to the village...   **867**

❧ 154 ❧

You ask around and soon discover that the Judge's son has indeed been here: he managed to get a position as a navigator on an airship on the routes north. "Airship A711. But that ship went down months past. Last signal was received as they flew over Stokenchurch. Never found."

Turn to...   **56**

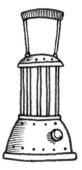

❧ 155 ❧

The Richards brothers specialise in fine pneumomechanics - engine parts, components for calculating engines and fine machine work. Their workshop resembles a hive of bees with dozens of focused workers each hunched over his or her bench, peering through magnifying lenses and working with fine tools to produce brass and steelwork. Jewellery is also turned out here and gold is always in demand as a raw material.

Clothing	To buy	To sell
jewelled eyepatch (RUTH+1 GAL+1)	-	£4 8s
golden monocle (GAL+2)	£10	-
Jewellery	To buy	To sell
locket	-	6s
pocket watch	£5	£2 10s
silver ring	15s	10
silver bracelet	£1 5s	£1
silver necklace	£2 10s	£1 18s
gold ring	£3	£2
gold bracelet	£3 5s	£2
gold necklace	£5	£4
sapphire pendant	-	£25
emerald jewellery	-	£100
pectoral cross	-	£22
Jousting Cup	-	£7
Medical	To buy	To sell
gold tooth	-	£1
Other items	To buy	To sell
ivory fan	-	£1 10s
jewelled bible	-	£12 5s
fine clock	-	£6 3s
pair of golden candlesticks	-	£2 14s
gold cup	-	£15
gold bar	-	£32

As well as more usual machinery for sale, the engineers will manufacture complex machines for you but will require some components as well as payment.

	To buy
mechanical arm	£5 2s and **steam fist** (RUTH+3)
mobile telegraph	£8 10s, **pocket watch** and **ivory fan**

If you have **lost a hand**, you may replace it here with a **mechanical arm**, regaining 2 points of NIMBLENESS and MOTORING. Your mechanical arm should then be noted in the **Other Notes** section on your **Adventure Sheet** and, unlike a **possession**, cannot be lost.

Leave the workshop...   **771**
Return to the town centre...   **297**

156

The regional locobus has a comically short wheelbase and an underslung boiler: the passengers must climb a set of steps to take a seat inside or up a steep stair to the upper deck, for a cheaper ride. The smoke-stack protrudes from the rear, for the sake of the upper-deck passengers, who merely have wind and rain to contend with.

As the locobus approaches, you may consider how to respond. With no guard and only simple folk aboard, intimidating them should be relatively simple, although you will probably be rewarded with slim pickings.

Rob the passengers...	**621**
Redistribute some wealth...	**1193**
Let the locobus pass...	**noted passage**

❧ 157 ❧

This workshop rings with a different collection of sounds: hoots, ringing resonant bells and whistling tones. The proprietor is an inventor who works on many projects but is most keen on his automatic organ. If you have the codeword *Burnish*, turn to **143** immediately.

"It's almost ready," he says, "But I'm struggling to get the timings perfectly right. The synchronisation belt is giving me many problems - but when this is done, my goodness, it will be popular the world over!"

"What do you need?" you ask.

"Someone to look it over with me - to give me their insight into my method. Someone who really understands computational pneumatics." He shows you his steam difference engine. "I've been using this but I need a better program to calculate the complexities of tone. If I had the right punchcards I know I could complete my project."

Give him **punchcards (Aramanth A)**...	**375**
Give him **punchcards (Habbukuk K)**...	**391**
Give him **punchcards (Selladore V)**...	**451**
Leave the workshop...	**771**

❧ 158 ❧
A large country house stands a little way off the road here and the airfield at Rotherfield Greys is not far either. Which way will you turn?

Ride towards Henley...	**68**
West towards High Moor Cross...	**939**
Take the road to Cane End...	**421**
East to the airfield...	**454**
Into Greys Court...	**500**

❧ 159 ❧
The tent you have been reserved is little more than a sheet of surplus airship envelope draped over a convenient tree-branch and guyed down. Nonetheless, it is dry. You can rest here, but if you seek to treat your wounds you had better speak to Anita. Likewise, the quartermaster will be able to help you open a **strongbox**. You should **note this passage**.

There is an old crate left here and the normally magpie-like sky pirates will leave any possessions you store here alone: they fear the Captain's reprisals, as you are known to be his particular friend.

Repair your velosteam...	**180**
Return to the camp...	**819**

❧ 160 ❧
"You're looking for work?" The recruiter looks you up and down skeptically. "Well, take a look at these posts. See if they suit." If you choose to take a position, tick the box and turn to the passage indicated. You may not take a position if the box is already ticked.

☐ Sous-chef on Union Flight 6371 to Cairo
You must have at least one level of **haute cuisine** skill to take this position... **175**

☐ Bodyguard on Union Flight 880 to Budapest
To take this position, turn to... **188**

☐ Engineer on Union Flight 7162 to Reykjavik
You will need an ENGINEERING score of 8 or higher to convince the recruiter of your ability. To take this position, turn to... **197**

Leave the office... **454**

❧ 161 ❧
You dash through the market at Goring, scattering housewives and stallholders. Your pursuers crash after you, adding to the chaos. You surge on through the yard at Hardwick House and swing onto the cow-path. The mud seems to have got even thicker since you last rode this way: make a MOTORING roll of difficulty 10, adding 2 if you have **off-road tyres**, to leave the Constables behind.

Successful MOTORING roll!	**864**
Failed MOTORING roll!	**13**

162

The Whistlers bears a sign of a jaunty harvestman, but inside you are told that the name commemorates a local legend of whistling wanderers on Cobblers Hill, who appear on summer nights and unpredicatably help or hinder the harvest, dependent on their whim. "Been a good year so far," says the garrulous local. "But I haven't heard whether they've been out a-whistling yet."

Buy a drink...	(2s)	709
Leave the inn...		515

163

You close the regulator and coast to a stop at a sign-post. The few houses here are known as Lower Assendon - Middle and Upper Assendon are hamlets on the road to Stonor, on the right. The other way is the toll road leading uphill to Bix and Nettlebed.

Another iron sign points the way to Henley Park School for Young Ladies - but you could scarcely ride into there unannounced. Perhaps if you knew somebody there?

Visit the Henley Park School... (*Awful*)	224
Take the left road...	330
Take the right road...	208

164

The quivering driver pulls on the brakes and halts the steamer at a bend in the road. He was not expecting to be stopped and was looking forward to his refreshment at the next inn. Now he must do his best to stay alive. Roll a dice to find out who is travelling inside.

Score 1	A man and wife	186
Score 2	A madam	237
Score 3	A well-known chef	274
Score 4	A foreign noblewoman	468
Score 5	An artist	489
Score 6	A travelling preacher	554

165

You explain how the Telegraph Guild are intending to turn Cobstone Mill into a telegraph station. As soon as you mention them, the baker changes his tune. "The Guild crushing another craftsman? I tell you, they still owe me pounds for supplies sent on to their towers. What price does he need?"

You agree a price of sixteen shillings a hundred-weight for Fursham's best flour and the baker sets you out a **baker's contract**.

Leave the bakery...	418

166

The steep hill here provides a perfect opportunity to stop the traffic. A driver would have to be confident indeed to steam up the slope here under fire - or under the threat of fire. Note **passage number 550** on your **Adventure Sheet** and roll a dice to see what you encounter.

Score 1	A private steam carriage...	136
Score 2-3	The Haulage Guild...	408
Score 4-5	The Coal Board...	223
Score 6	The Telegraph Guild...	198

167

The bad weather sets in and you soon find yourself riding through rain and mud, dodging unwary engines on narrow roads. A wrong turning in the murk has you lost north of Bicester on the first day and you have to push to make up time. Then, as if the journey could get no worse, you are surprised when a posse of Constables appear as you are re-filling your water tank. If you are **Wanted by the Constables**, read on. Otherwise they will let you go and you should turn to **442** immediately.

The Constables check your details and quickly decide they should take you in for questioning. Naturally you take advantage of the first opportunity to make a break for it and speed off back the way you came.

The roads are lathered in mud and your velosteam chokes and shudders as you splash through the puddles: clearly one of the intakes has become blocked. Dare you stop to clear it?

Stop and clear the intake...	555
Ride on...	580

168

The Livingstone punchcards clatter as they flip through the machine. It pauses, almost as if taking breath. What will you instruct it to do?

Analyse other punchcard patterns...	1389
Leave the machine...	noted passage

∾ 169 ∾

Teaching the girls is difficult. You begin by using your velosteam as a demonstration but you are forced to continually re-word and re-explain yourself. At the end of the lesson it is hard to tell who is more exhausted - yourself or the girls.

"I am not cut out for this," you tell Miss Evans. "I have more respect for you than ever."

"Not everyone can do this job, although everyone seems to think they can," smiles Miss Evans. "I'm still grateful for your desire to help. Do come and visit again."

Turn to...   23

∾ 170 ∾

Many have tales of the Spanish War: many have tales of woe, heartbreak and sorrow. The grounds of your demobilisation were nominally a 'lack of character sufficient for duty' - but even in the lengthy formal interviews you were unable to plumb the depths of all the reasons for your disillusionment in the cause. Then, how cruel, to return from your tour of duty to your home village and find it swallowed by the nearby city sprawl, cottages replaced with rows of terraces and tenements, giant steam-mills occupying the village green, roads and lanes completely overlaid with an impersonal grid of ordered progress.

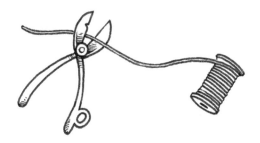

And those you knew in the cottages, dispersed. A few remained working in the new mills, eking out their existence, choking on cotton waste and oily smoke. Your family - vanished. What little you could gather implied ruthless destruction on the developers' part: cottages were demolished on top of their stubborn occupants, buried with the rubble.

So with your roots cut through, as with a billhook, you have become a wanderer. You exchanged your remaining service pay and the shameful medals for the machine beneath you and sped far away from that cursed town.

Your comrades suffered for nothing. The officers who commanded them must be found and punished. Perhaps at the regimental headquarters in Wallingford you can find information to lead you to those responsible, or perhaps the surviving veterans in the pubs and bars of the region can tell you more.

You have in your possession a **blunderpistol (ACC 6)**, a **sabre (PAR 3)**, a **mask** and a **locket**. Your ability scores are:

RUTHLESSNESS	6
ENGINEERING	4
MOTORING	3
INGENUITY	4
NIMBLENESS	4
GALLANTRY	3

Turn to...   1440

∾ 171 ∾
☐ ☐ ☐ ☐ ☐

If any of the boxes above are empty, tick one and read on. If all are ticked, erase the ticks and turn immediately to **310**.

You cannot stay around here after making so ruthless an attempt. Choose a route to follow, to put some distance between yourself and your crimes:

Head to Stokenchurch...	**308**
Find shelter at Christmas Common...	**617**
Ride towards Pishill...	**370**
Take off in the direction of Nettlebed...	**791**

∾ 172 ∾

The rain continues to sheet down. Water gurgles across the roadway, swelling to a stream. In the distance you hear the chugging of an approaching engine. Note **passage number 171** on your **Adventure Sheet** and roll a dice to see what you encounter.

Score 1	A farmer...	1163
Score 2	The Constables...	1434
Score 3	A private steam carriage...	136
Score 4	The Atmospheric Union...	1244
Score 5	The Church's emmissaries...	666
Score 6	An independent haulier...	1285

∾ 173 ∾

Dewsbury and Knight are the local vehicle engineers. They are reputed to be the best at repairing and building reliable steam engines and their yard is full with a range of steamers in various states of repair. They will happily take a look at your velosteam as there is much for their apprentices and their more experienced engineers to learn from its fine mechanical workings.

Velosteam Customisations	To buy
muffled exhaust	**£4 2s**
off-road tyres	**£7s 3s**
gas pressuriser	**£12 12s**

Repairs	To buy
Per **damage point**	**£3**

Leave the workshop....   771

771

❧ 174 ❧

You are recognised from your description and the Constables are summoned. You will have to leave the station and Henley behind you. Which way will you turn?

Towards Sonning...   **692**
Head north towards Stonor...   **459**
Try and reach Pishill...   **1368**

❧ 175 ❧

Flight 6371 is a fine touring craft, fitted out with luxurious cabins, saloons and promenades for those rich enough to afford a long and pleasant flight to Cairo. When you report to the staff boarding ramp you are given a white jacket, a grey apron and a paper cap, then sent up to meet the chef, Monsieur Ramboutarde. He has little time for you.

"A new sous-chef? The last one threw 'imself off over Gibraltar. Here, check this list for me. Ensure that the delivery has been made correctly."

The paper list details the greengrocer's order: you will have to check the delivery boxes for new potatoes, zucchini, tomatoes, satin carrots, chayote, eggplant, tenderstem broccoli, and lettuce.

The potatoes are easy enough to spot. A large crate of tomatoes contains some beautifully striped fruit of different sizes. Then there is a box of glossy, purple things, some leggy green sticks topped with tiny florets, some small, orange carrots, some cylindrical, striped squash, a box of what seem like very hard, long green apples - but uglier - and lettuces of various colours in paper bags.

"I think everything is here."   **994**
"You've not been given the right carrots." **974**
"I think you've been given a replacement
for the chayote."   **953**

❧ 176 ❧

The Aramanth punchcards set the machine whirring. It settles into a steady rhythm of calculation. What will you ask it to do?

Analyse Telegraph Guild Codes...
    (**telegraph observations** ☑ ☑)   **252**
Decode the Valencia Orders...
    (**punchcards (Valencia Orders)**)   **1498**

Leave the machine...   **noted passage**

❧ 177 ❧

If you have the codeword *Bergen*, turn to **254** immediately. Otherwise, read on.

The Telegraph Guild maintain a small post here - merely a few guildsmen relaying freight messages from the wharves and taking up lower priority messages from the nearby A-class towers at Caversham and Waltham. There is no compound and no guard.

Burn the tower down...   **706**
Return to Wargrave...   **418**

❧ 178 ❧

Valentine Woods are owned by the estate of Hardwick House, down at the riverside and patrolled by gamekeepers. You see no-one, however, as you coast between the trees and make your way over the uneven ground.

Lay a snare... (**snare**)   **532**
Put out poisoned meat... (*Bestial*, **poison**
    and **rabbit** or **pheasant** or
    deer carcass)   **842**
Ride towards Gallowstree Common...   **600**
Head deeper into the wood...   **401**

ꙮ 179 ꙮ

The chef at the French Horn is a talented and passionate man. He delights in producing good food and in teaching others his craft. If you are patient and willing, he will show you the secrets of **haute cuisine**.

☐ "Teach me to cook like you."
    (**deer carcass**, **bottle of wine**)   **275**
☐ "Show me how to prepare this." (**large pike**) **309**
Return to the parlour...   **358**

ꙮ 180 ꙮ

To bring your velosteam back to full working condition you will need to spend some considerable time repairing it. If you have the required items indicated below, make an ENGINEERING roll. If you do not have what you need, you may return to your **noted passage.**

Minor damage	**copper pipe** or **brass flange joint**
Serious damage	Above item and **high pressure valve** or **pocket watch**
Critical damage	Above items and **titanium alloy** or **ultra-tensed wire** or **welding tools**

Score <10	Failed and gashed your hand! Gain a **wound**.
Score 10	Failed and broke a part: remove one of the **items** you were attempting to repair with
Score 11	A fair start: remove the parts and remove **one damage point**
Score 12+	Success: remove the parts and remove all **damage points**

Turn to...   **noted passage**

ꙮ 181 ꙮ

The voters are quite bemused by the concept of having free choice. They continue to argue, some preferring the persuasive words they have heard from Letitia Forebury, but most preferring the status quo under his Lordship. You will find out how the election turns out eventually. Gain the codeword *Blameless*.

Return to the parlour...   **529**
Leave the Ferryman...   **749**

ꙮ 182 ꙮ

You tell the labourer about the Compact, painting a convincing picture of their ability and intention to overthrow the powerful and instate a government of the people. He listens carefully. "Seems like they 'as the right idea," he says. "You may've found yourself a recruit. I'll ask around in Reading - I'm sure there's a cell there." Gain the codeword *Bargain* if you don't already have it.

Enter Woodcote...   **488**
Choose an onward route...   **659**

ꙮ 183 ꙮ

You seem to be a natural teacher. The girls enjoy their practical lesson and you are also energised by their genuine enthusiasm for mechanics. You decide to stay at the school for a week and proceed with the project, much to Miss Evans' delight. Make an ENGINEERING roll to see the outcome.

Score <10	Repair any **damage points** and receive **£4 4s**
Score 11-14	Build an **enlarged fuel tank** for your velosteam and receive **£4 4s**
Score 15-18	Build a **reinforced boiler** for your velosteam and receive **£4 4s**
Score 19+	Create an **autogauge (MOT+3)** and receive **£4 4s** pay

At the end of the week you are tired out, but Miss Evans is delighted. "Do come back and teach some more," she says. "The girls get so much out of your lessons."

Turn to...   **23**

ꙮ 184 ꙮ

As the wagons rumble past, you steam out from behind the hedge and match speed. You must lean inbetween the wagons and uncouple the heavy chains that hold the wagons in line. Make a NIMBLENESS roll of difficulty 13, adding 1 if you have a **grappling iron** or a **wrench** of any kind.

Successful NIMBLENESS roll!   **320**
Failed NIMBLENESS roll!   **1376**

❦ 185 ❧

☐

If the box above is empty, tick it and read on. If it is already ticked, you have already made observations here and can gain little more: you must head to another Telegraph Guild tower and turn to **617** immediately.

Night falls as you take up position in a tree a short distance from the tower. You watch carefully as the shutters open and close, as the apprentices oil the mechanisms and switch the long control rods by lamplight. The soft glow of the oil lamps blurs in the rising mist and soon the tower suspends its messaging. Nonetheless, you believe that you have identified several patterns in the codes that may help you understand them. If you possess a set of **telegraph observations** ☐ ☐, tick one of the boxes. If you do not own such an item, add **telegraph observations** ☐ ☐ to your possessions. You will need to observe the codes on three unique towers and then to run a set of appropriate **punchcards** in a computing engine to analyse your results.

Leave the tree...   **617**

❦ 186 ❧

A man in a well-worn suit and his wife in a travelling dress emerge worriedly from the carriage. "I knew hiring a carriage would only attract trouble," says the man. "Now look!"

"I told you I'm not travelling in a public carriage to visit my mother," replies the woman sharply. "She thinks you're an important city man."

You may take **£1 8s**, a **silver necklace** and a **parasol** from them. If you have a **mask**, they will be unable to give a description: otherwise, you will now be **Wanted by the Constables**.

Turn to...   **noted passage**

❦ 187 ❧

You make good time over the first part of your journey despite the heavy rain and the drifting fog. At one point you are nearly struck by an engine hauling a trailer loaded with lumber, but the nimble Ferguson responds to your touch like a well-trained steed.

The roads are being re-laid near Lichfield, so you are forced to find your way through the lanes and villages and you reach Stoke-on-Trent behind schedule. Pressing on into the dusk, you are suddenly set upon as the road enters a wood. A cable stretched across the road catches your front tyre - you are thrown clear and land in a bush - but the moment you are up, you are grabbed by armed figures. Their red sashes clearly indicate that you have fallen into the hands of the Compact. If you are a **Member of the Compact for Workers' Equality**, turn to **222** immediately. Otherwise, you must fight them off. Outnumbered as you are, it will be a nasty brawl.

Revolutionaries	Weapon: **clubs (PAR 2)**
Parry:	8
Nimbleness:	6
Toughness:	8

Victory!	**314**
Defeat!	**336**

❦ 188 ❧

A rich businessman has requested that the Union provide him with a bodyguard on his flight to Budapest. "He has business there that may prove controversial," explains the Union Officer. "Take this slip up to the lounge and report there."

Another officer briefs you more fully and you are led aboard the European-styled Gringbach airship tethered in the centre of the airfield. The passenger cabins line the outside of the broad gondola while the centre and the two waist cars are reserved for fuel and baggage. You are given a tiny private cabin connected to your employers.

When he arrives he proves to be a white-haired gentleman with a bushy moustache and a rather shy manner. He is almost apologetic. "Ah, well, you'll be the, er, bodyguard? Excellent. Pleased to meet you. Death threats. Death threats, you see, they can do a lot to a man's confidence."

You proceed to shadow Mr Knapp during the flight. He has no valet and looks after himself mostly, but he is extraordinarily jumpy and you do your best to keep him feeling his best.

In the meantime, you travel in a strange limbo, not quite a servant nor a fee-paying passenger, you are ignored by most of the others aboard and have no time 'off-duty'. Nonetheless, you manage to spend a little time with the engineers and stokers aft, who are straightforward men and women, unimpressed by the wealth of their passengers or the attitudes of the officers. Amongst them you even find members of the Compact, as well as people who have heard of your own exploits.

In Budapest things turn sour quickly. Mr Knapp becomes jumpier than ever. On the first evening you accompany him to a meeting in the industrial district where all the talk is in Hungarian. You do your best to anticipate trouble, but on the way back to the hotel you are jumped by three attackers in the dark. There is no warning and you have to be quick to draw your weapon.

Attackers	Weapons: **knives (PAR 1)**
Parry:	7
Nimbleness:	6
Toughness:	6

Victory!	1213
Defeat!	1257

❧ 189 ❧

You are ushered through to see Comrade Plunkett. He turns from his business and greets you warmly. "Ah, our recruiting friend! More and more flock to the cause - no small thanks to you." Your work of arguing the Compact's purpose has won you some popularity here: you are paid a Comrade's Bounty of **£2** and given **brass disc 7821**. "This marks you out as an individual we can trust. " Remove any of the code-words *Bargain*, *Chosen* or *Driven* you possess.

There is little small talk amongst the desperate men and women of the Compact. They are disciplined to wait for you to leave before continuing with their plans.

Return to the parlour...	1515
Head out into Reading...	297

❧ 190 ❧

A trio of long-distance Haulage Guild engines have just entered the yard ahead of you: it is not easy to find space to manoeuvre or anyone to listen to you. Nonetheless, there are some supplies available if you are determined and ready to pay the high prices. If you are **Wanted by the Haulage Guild**, turn to **966** immediately.

Tools	To buy	To sell
rope	4s	2s
snare	2s	1s
net	6s	4s
rope ladder	9s	5s
lantern	6s	4s
shovel	8s	6s
axe	8s	6s
wirecutters	12s	8s
adjustable wrench (ENG+1)	£1 8s	18s
welding tools	£2 2s	£1
brass flange joint	8s	4s
copper pipe	6s	3s
high pressure valve	18s	10s
telescope	£4 10s	£3 5s
Repairs	To buy	
Per **damage point**	£2 4s	

Find a haulier for Miller Fursham...

(baker's contract)	919
Leave the Freight Yard...	360

❧ 191 ❧

The Selladore punchcards travel slowly through the computational engine: it is almost as though the great brass mechanism requires time to chew each mouthful. What will you instruct it to do?

Reconstruct missing information...

(torn manifest)	228
Write a piece of music...	1511
Leave the machine...	**noted passage**

❧ 192 ❧

If you are **Wanted by the Coal Board** then you will be recognised immediately and handed over to the Constables: turn to **13**. Otherwise, read on.

The offices of the Coal Board are largely concerned with their contracts to supply the municipal councils, the factory consortiums and the transport companies of the region. However, a poster indicates that the Regional Director is looking for 'Resourceful

Types' to carry out 'Delicate Work."

A trained doctor is on hand to treat members of the guild - but her services can be obtained for a price.

	To buy
Heal a **wound**...	£1 10s - replace with a **scar**
Treat a **burn**...	15s - replace with a **scar**

Talk to the Coal Board Regional Director...	1040
Leave the compound...	308

✎ 193 ✎

You recognise the wagon of Goodman Butt's morris troupe approaching. They stop briefly to share a swig of cider and laugh about their recent exploits. "Sammy fell in the river again!" says one.

They move off and you are left on the empty road. Note **passage number 306** on your **Adventure Sheet** and roll a dice to see what you encounter.

Score 1	An independent haulier...	1027
Score 2	The Atmospheric Union...	194
Score 3	A farmer...	294
Score 4	The Haulage Guild...	408
Score 5	The Telegraph Guild...	198
Score 6	A private steam carriage...	103

✎ 194 ✎

The approaching steam engine is recognisably an Atmospheric Union vehicle towing three wagons of goods. Not only is the livery of grey and blue easy to spot, but the unique fairings and design of even their supply wagons are designed to catch the eye and to reinforce the glamour of air travel. You can trust in your ruthless reputation and demand the driver halt, shoot at the driver immediately or ride alongside and unpin the rear-most wagon.

Demand the driver halt immediately...	1125
Fire at the driver...	1133
Ride alongside...	1164

✎ 195 ✎

If you are the **Friend of Professor Challing**, turn to **1501**. Otherwise, read on.

Henley Museum has plainly seen better days. The dirty windows allow only a little light into the galleries and the display cases are half-filled with broken tools, unidentified artefacts and disappointing reconstructions. Anyone can see why the museum is threatened with closure - but should this concern you?

You see a model of a strange circle of stones claiming to be a passage tomb - apparently situated between here and Wargrave on the eastern side of the Thames. The label reads 'The Druid's Tomb, Park Place, Remenham' but nothing more. It might have been too much to expect an interactive hands-on display with a mock excavation or an animatronic reconstruction.

Make a donation to the museum...	
(**treasure trove**)	99
Return to Henley...	702

✎ 196 ✎

The dancers lead you on to the wedding where they will be dancing and entertaining the guests. You are fitted out with a natty waistcoat, ribbons, bells, hat and stick and charged to follow the pattern closely. The accordion, mechanical organ and fiddle strike up a tune: make a NIMBLENESS roll to decide the outcome.

Score <9	Two left feet...	63
Score 9-12	An imperfect step...	217
Score 13+	Born to dance...	258

✎ 197 ✎

"So, you can work with an aerial engine, can you?" asks the thin, harassed-looking woman. She is the Chief Engineer for this chartered flight to Iceland. "The mate has got himself arrested on some ridiculous Constable business and we need to fly. Bring your tools."

You are first put to work with the stoker, shovelling coal and pumping the bellows to get the furnaces up to temperature. When the steam pressure is raised, Mrs Betting telegraphs through to the Captain. A reply comes clanging back and she releases the steam into the massive pistons. A swishing, churning dance like the sound of giant horses' hooves starts up - a sound that will dominate your waking and sleeping hours - and the giant propellors aft begin to swing .

Once moving, she shows you the gauges and dials that are your responsibility. A great deal of your job is simply to regularly lubricate the moving parts. "Eight gallons of good, sweet oil, on a flight this long," says Mrs Betting. "I don't want to hear a single squeak or a dry joint the entire flight."

If you have the codeword *Believer*, turn to **1230** immediately. Otherwise, you will continue with your duties in the engine room.

Turn to...   **1304**

❧ 198 ❧

A slow engine tows three green-painted wagons up the road. You can see three armed Telegraph Guild guards seated on top of the supplies in various states of boredom or readiness. To block the road and demand they stop would require a very ruthless reputation indeed - so you consider other options.

Threaten the driver...	**446**
Shoot at the guards...	**510**
Let the wagons pass...	**noted passage**

❧ 199 ❧

"I say! What a scoop! The Steam Highwayman in person!" The journalists whip out their notebooks and stenomatics. "Can we ask you a few questions about your escape? Is that your getaway vehicle? Where is your hideout?"

"My abode changes always."	**357**
"I escaped with help from one of my many allies and friends."	**371**
Ignore their questions....	**noted passage**

❧ 200 ❧

Up the retaining wall, up the rear of the terrace, climbing up a drainpipe, over an outshut roof licked by flames, and then to the window. You find a girl clutching her baby sister and put them both over your shoulder. Then back to the window, over the roof and to the edge. The mate puts out his arms and catches first the baby, then the terrified girl. You dive into the river, your clothes alight. Gain a serious **burn**, meaning you must lower your NIMBLENESS and your MOTORING by 1 until it heals. If you have a **hat** or **mask** of any kind, their burnt shreds are torn off.

The townspeople are amazed and impressed by your bravery: gain **two solidarity points**. They take the girl to her family and set about making the ruins safe. Several have died today, but your quick action lessened the count.

Turn to...   **719**

❧ 201 ❧

You are shaken hard. "You should know better than to come blundering in where you ain't got no business," you are told, and then thrust out into the street.

Turn to...   **487**

❧ 202 ❧

You step out into the road and raise your weapons. "Stand and deliver! I'll have your coin and your paper money, or you'll give me your blood!"

Make a RUTHLESSNESS roll of difficulty 8, adding 1 if you are **Wanted by the Constables**.

Successful RUTHLESSNESS roll!	**277**
Failed RUTHLESSNESS roll!	**243**

❧ 203 ❧

In the Red Lion, dogs lie underfoot like rushes in an old house. You have to pick your way through them to reach the bar where the landlord is deep in argument.

Buy a beer... (**2s**)	**930**
Leave the inn...	**488**
Leave Woodcote...	**659**

❧ 204 ❧

You are pulled a characteristically single-hop blonde beer, with an interestingly fruity aroma. It has a freshness suited to a hot afternoon at the waterside, so you carry your pint of Fresco Gold over to a table on the terrace and watch the barges chug past. A large number are carrying food supplies into Reading, including several sporting modern-looking steam-powered refrigeration devices. "Perkins Engines," says a waterman at the next table. "Quite a smart move. Good for keeping things cold. Freebody's Yard at Hurley fit 'em - but so does Micklewhite up in Oxford, and for a better price."

If you have the codeword *Barbaric*, turn to **850** immediately.

Return to Wargrave...   **418**

❧ 205 ❧

You speed along the road, kicking up a fine cloud of dust behind you. The summer sun dries out the road quickly, even after this morning's rain. Ahead is the village of Shirburn, clustered around the farm serving Shirburn Castle - once a famous place indeed, when the Earls of Macclesfield held sway in this land.

Prepare to ambush the passing vehicles...   **123**
Continue on to the foot of Aston Hill...   **710**

❧ 206 ❧

Soon after leaving Oxford the rain sets in. You are treated to a day and night of some of the worst weather you have ever ridden through - rain, unseasonal sleet, fog and thunder. The roads run white with chalk or become thick quagmires. Nonetheless your Ferguson is more than a match for the task and you steam into Manchester as the sun rises, just within your deadline. The clerks at the mill are waiting for your delivery in response to the telegraph from their Oxford agent, and the moment you hand the **leather satchel** over it is whisked away to the workshop.

A cigar-chewing woman claps you on the back. "An impressive ride," she says. "We should have our machinery refitted before the next cotton shipment makes it in. We'll be in position to buy twice as much stock." She hands you **ten pounds in notes** and **£2** in coin and directs you to the factory canteen where you are fed well before your return journey.

Return to Oxford...   **688**

❧ 207 ❧

As you ride up to the gates of the Telegraph Station, an officer hails you from an observation post up one of the towers. "Business here?" he asks. "No loitering!"

If you have the codeword *Befriend*, turn to **1334**. Otherwise you may try to find work with the guild, or see their emergency medic, who will grudgingly bandage up your wounds - as long as you can afford his fee..

	To buy	
Heal a **wound**...	**£2** - replace with a **scar**
Treat a **burn**...	**8s** - replace with a **scar**

Seek work with the Telegraph Guild...   **1377**
Leave the tower...   **617**

❧ 208 ❧

The long lane leads along the valley floor, slowly rising towards Stonor. The cottages of Middle Assendon squat behind their coppices and the beeches stand guard on the steep slopes either side. This is not a busy road - but that may lend you some safety if you manage to stop one of the rare steam vehicles that come this way.

Prepare an ambush here...   **220**
Head north...   **286**
Ride towards Henley...   **144**

❧ 209 ❧

The transporter is a multi-wheeled Haulage Guild low-loader, carrying a dismantled crane towards Henley. It is unlikely to be carrying much worth stealing, but the size of the machine itself is awe-inspiring. Machinery grows as calculating engines help engineers to create stronger and more efficient designs, just as the heights of buildings are increasing with iron frames in the city.

Watch it pass...   **3**

❧ 210 ❧

The passage up the Thames is mostly quiet. True, steam-barges and pleasure-craft chug past, but for most of the way you can hear birdsong. Eventually you come to Osney Lock at Oxford.

Turn to...   **868**

❧ 211 ❧

Wandering through the village, you come across a cheerful and immediately-recognised face: the one-armed groom you helped to wed. He gives you a warm and semi-mechanical embrace, chattering gladly about the reliability and the strength - the surprising strength - of his arms.

"Why, I'm the strongest chap in the village now! Mrs Croney is ever so appreciative. And I can also whisper you that we are expecting!" He insists you step into their cottage, a short walk along the lane, where you find the ample housewife preparing a simple meal. Their fare, though common enough, fills your belly and sets all things right for a brief evening. You leave them enjoying their marriage, their home and their security - a far cry from the life you are destined to lead, perhaps, but maybe you have done something for Mr and Mrs Croney that is entirely without regret. You regain some strength: if you are wounded, you may remove one **wound** and convert it immediately into a **scar**.

Return to the village... **867**

Your shouted threat obviously terrifies the crew of the vehicle, who draw to a halt just beneath your position on the roadside. Roll a dice to decide your encounter.

Score 1	A young nobleman	**70**
Score 2	A huntress	**82**
Score 3	A famous archaeologist	**114**
Score 4	An explorer	**152**
Score 5	A mysterious woman	**322**
Score 6	A woman of means	**399**

9 213 &
If you have the codeword *Bloodied* turn to **1215** immediately. Otherwise, read on.

Your stake lies on the table with the banknotes of the other risk-lovers. Lord Barrymore laughs. "A mysterious stranger. Perfect. If you are cheat I'll run you through and hang your craven corpse from Henley bridge."

The game is a played with a spiral of cards laid on the table. As each is drawn, responses, bids and threats must be made. Card-counting would help if it weren't so fast - each hand whizzes by and the cards are laid out again. Make an INGENUITY roll, adding 3 if you possess a **deck of marked cards**.

Score <9	Bad luck...	**1104**
Score 9-14	Fair play...	**1116**
Score 15+	Aces high...	**1123**

9 214 &
As you are gathering your belongings and preparing yourself to leave in the early mists of the morning, you become aware of whispering voices outside your door. You freeze like an animal hearing the hunters and faintly make out the clink of scabbards and swords.

The Constables have found you: surely an informer has claimed a reward for giving away your hiding-place. You must make a quick decision.

Draw your weapons...	**267**
Climb out of the window to your velosteam...	**395**
Climb down to your barge...	
(moored at Sonning)	**403**

9 215 &
You knock on the door, explain why you have come and are shown into a high hall with a roaring fire. A woman approaches you. "Are you one of M'Dow's lackeys?" she asks.

You show her the list and she nods. "My father is Duke Forebury. He has lent his support to M'Dow for a long time - and M'Dow is not a bad man by any stretch. But he is slow to change. He is only interested in preserving what is, not in defining what will be. Parliament needs more men who will grasp the future and ensure that it is fairer for the poorest and least fortunate. I have convinced my father to sponsor a candidate for the election - Mr Elfinstone - who is ready to see some change for the better. It is not enough to sit on our wealth and security when the workers are being abused. Revolt and disunity mar our nation. The interests of the Guilds must be challenged."

You explain that Sir M'Dow has promised to have your record cleaned and that if you convince the voters to support him, he will pay you as well. She shakes her head. "My father doesn't have that influence. He is an old and frail man now and keeps to his books and his dogs and his chair. But I know someone who can help you gain a new identity. Have the voters in Whitchurch support my father's candidate." Gain the codeword *Betterment*.

Leave the house... **864**

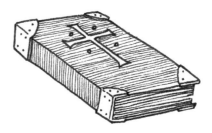

9 216 &
From the escarpment you can see the traction engines setting out from Watlington below. Most head to Wallingford or Oxford, but a few set out up the road into the hills, carrying supplies for the industries in Nettlebed or Stokenchurch.

Prepare an ambush here on the hill...	**166**
Steam on down to Watlington...	**360**
Ride uphill to Christmas Common...	**617**

The steady whine of the accordion and the clack of the sticks begin to get into your pulse. After a few simpler dances you feel ready to dance anything.

Off you go - stripping the willow, dosey-doing and wheeling, spinning, even making an attempt at a clumsy basket. The troupe are pleased with your help and you are now the **Friend of Goodman Butt**. However, as a result of your participation in the troupe you must lower your RUTHLESSNESS score by 1 - can anyone take a morris-dancer seriously?

Return to Turville...   **947**

☐

If the box above is empty, tick it and read on. If it is already ticked, turn to **1431** immediately.

You take your pot over to a corner table and take a few sips. It is a pleasant, somewhat spicy brew with a reddish tinge. The barman was proud that a cousin of his brewed it nearby, and called it Carrington's Red Ale. There's a

A one-armed man begins singing a long ballad about the Iberian war. After he finishes his song, nodding in thanks to his patrons for the line of beers mounting at the table, you ask him about his regiment.

"The Ox and Bucks boys? They're all gone. Almost. Ordered onto the plain at Valencia, right into the fire of the Spanish guns. Ground up like mincemeat. It was a catastrophe - a massacre. Some fool gave the order and some fools had to carry it out - that was us. They're trying to rebuild the regiment at Wallingford garrison, but whether anyone'll volunteer to join the cursed ranks, I don't know. But the commanding officers are holed up there, and let me tell you, they're the ones to answer for it. The records will show!"

He tells you how the modern Imperial Army logs all orders with punch-card code so that every initiative can be tracked. The punch-card stacks are holy and can never be destroyed, however compromising their contents. "I know some as would pay dearly to get their hands on those orders," he says, "And find out who murdered us." Gain the codeword *Benediction*.

Return to the parlour...   **100**
Leave the John Barleycorn...   **487**

The Constables chain you up with several other vagabonds and thieves. Your velosteam, all your **money** and your **weapons** are confiscated and you are marched, slowly and painfully, to Wallingford Gaol.

Turn to...   **841**

You roll off the road and take up position just inside a gate, your low machine hidden behind the stone wall. You can then climb a nearby ash for a lookout position. Note the **passage number 433** and roll a dice to see what you encounter.

Score 1-2	The Haulage Guild...	**408**
Score 3-4	A private steam carriage...	**103**
Score 5	A farmer...	**294**
Score 6	A locobus...	**156**

☐

If the box above is empty, tick it and read on. If it is already ticked, turn to **1002** immediately.

You take your pint of Horner's Pale Pride to a table where a weaselly looking man is supping his own drink. He cheerfully raises his glass and watches as you savour the cool, lemony, oaty, lightly-carbonated brew. Then he speaks.

"You look like an investor, my friend. Do you know that there is silver not far from here?"

"I had no idea," you reply cheerfully.

"Well, there is," he replies. "The old lead workings at Culham Court are riddled with silver. My name is Sackler and I am under secret contract to extract this silver by a new method, devised by myself, for the Earl Brigg. I am prepared, for a small investment, to allow you in on the ground floor. My company are still raising capital, you see, and have much equipment to pay. But rest assured, once the process is begun, we will be paying up to seven shillings on the pound!"

"How much do you need?"

He looks you over carefully. "The greater the sum the far greater the return, my friend. Seven hundred guineas would buy you a good share."

"How much has the Earl invested?"

"Far more," he replies, unable to help himself from smiling. "Far more." Gain the codeword *Botanical*.

Return to the parlour...   **348**

❧ 222 ❧

"Wait! Reform and revolution! I am one of you!"

The revolutionaries are sceptical to begin with, but you convince them of your commitment to the cause and they back off.

"Listen," says their leader. "We were told to take a satchel from a despatch rider coming this way. We weren't told you would be one of us."

Give them the **leather satchel**...	**414**
Insist you must deliver it...	**453**

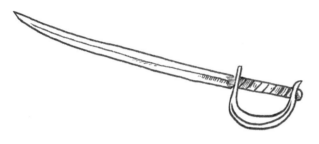

❧ 223 ❧

A dusty black Coal Board engine chugs along the road. It tows several wagons loaded high with coal. Other than a few coins for tolls, the crew are unlikely to have much worth stealing. Nonetheless, if you want to make an impression, there is nothing like a good coal fire.

Threaten the driver...	**83**
Let it pass...	**noted passage**

❧ 224 ❧

You pass through the gates and onto a long drive towards Henley Park School. This is the school whose teacher you entertained when her students mutinied and took their charabanc to the seaside - do you remember?

Asking at the front desk for Miss Evans, you are told to wait while a girl is sent to fetch her. When she does arrive Miss Evans greets you warmly and takes you to her sitting room for buttered toast. "How pleasant to remember that day in the woods," she reminisces. "I have thought of it many times. It was quite an escape for me - an escape from all this responsibility and care here. All these essays. All these longwinded reports. All this assessment."

She tells you about her life as a teacher, longing to share her passion for literature and her interest in cultures with the girls under her care, but the difficulty of doing that within the structure of the school. "It isn't a bad life, though," she says. "I have a roof over my head and food in the canteen. The school is always struggling to find new staff: what they really need is a new Practical Engineering teacher. The girls have little opportunity to apply their abstract understanding of pneumatics, clockwork and mechanical systems, and those really are skills they will need in their lifetimes. The world is changing, is it not?"

"It's been good to see you again."	**23**
"Perhaps I could help teach the girls."	**69**
"Do you need an escape from here?"	**108**

❧ 225 ❧

"What are you doing?" shouts Mr Sands. "You were meant to kill the kites, not the pheasants!" He fires his shotgun, sending a cloud of stinging shot into your leg. You dash to your velosteam and jump aboard before he can fire again. The wounds are not serious, but you will limp for a long time: lose 1 from your NIMBLENESS score. Also remove the codeword *Bestial*.

Head towards Woodcote...	**488**
Head towards Gallowstree Common...	**600**

❧ 226 ❧

You have come to the Convent of St Katharine. It is a place of seclusion and retreat from the world, where women devote themselves to serving one another and the worship of God. Many of the nuns do work in the communities around as well, cleaning, serving or working the land. Some even help with the laundry at the prison on the road to Marlow. One will help treat any injuries you may have - as long as you can make a donation to their work.

	To buy
Heal a **wound**...	£1 - replace with a **scar**
Treat a **fever**...	15s
Treat a **burn**...	4s - replace with a **scar**
Treat a **toothache**...	2s
Treat a **bite on the neck**...	1s

Ask to see the Mother Superior...	
(**15** or more **solidarity points**)	**1180**
Leave the convent...	**88**

❧ 227 ❧

If your boat is a **skiff** (a single-unit boat) then it will pass through St Patrick's stream, leading you out onto the reach of the river near Wargrave: turn to **131** immediately. However, if you have a **launch** or **barge**, you will quickly come to a halt, grounding on the gravel, and must throw all your **cargo** overboard to refloat. Remove your **cargo** from your **Adventure Sheet**.

Turn   to...   **882**

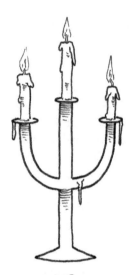

❧ 228 ❧

You feed the torn manifest and the punchcards in together. The calculating engine slowly analyses the data, then begins to print out its predicted completion. Will it be accurate? Who can tell?

Replace the **torn manifest** with a **repaired manifest**.

Leave the machine...   **noted passage**

❧ 229 ❧

You overtake a slow locobus headed out of Wallingford and fly between wheatfields and beetrows towards the village of Ewelme. Clouds are gathering over the plain: rain may be coming. The passengers on the upper deck of the slow-moving locobus will not be pleased. You, on the other hand, can find shelter easily - or dodge the raindrops!

As the clouds break and the rain begins to fall visibility drops. This could be an opportunity for you here on the open road.

Prepare an ambush here...   **172**
Ride on towards Watlington...   **52**

❧ 230 ❧

The cow-lane between Hardwick and Mapledurham is soft beneath your tyes, but in no time you pass the short distance between the two estates, cutting off a great deal of travel time.

Ride to Hardwick House yard...   **460**
Ride to Mapledurham village...   **864**

❧ 231 ❧

When you present the cashier with **Sackler's cheque** he wrinkles his nose. "Another of these? Absolutely worthless, I'm afraid. The gentleman in question has no standing with us - or with any bank, as far as I know." You may remove the **cheque** from your possessions or keep it as a souvenir of your involvement with the unscrupulous Sackler - if that is his real name.

Leave the bank...   **297**

❧ 232 ❧
☐

If the box above is empty, tick it now and turn to **504** immediately. Otherwise, read on.

Returning to Heath Wood, you can see the traces of the scuffle you had here with the brigands - broken branches and a smashed fencepost. The tyre-tracks of your own Ferguson are still just visible in the mud. No-one seems to have visited since then. For a wood like this to be neglected is a considerable waste of resources for the villages - but then maybe they are prevented from taking firewood and timber to repair their houses. Poachers, surely, must find something to lure them beneath the boughs.

Ride further into the wood...   **130**
Return to Hambleden...   **343**
Head to the Marlow Road...   **801**

❧ 233 ❧

Remove the **treasure trove** from your possessions.

"What, another fabulous discovery? Why, you are quite the benefactor!" Professor Challing takes the artefact gingerly, noting the marks and scratches and carefully turning it over. "Fascinating! This will be a compelling centrepiece... Yes, since your previous gift, the fortunes of the museum have improved dramatically. Donors, visitors, events, all manner of people come to see your donation. At this rate we will be the best-known museum in the land!" The Professor will not allow you to leave until she has written you another **letter of introduction** - and then led you around the renewed galleries.

Leave the museum...   702

Leave the museum...   702

❧ 234 ❧

The morris-men love the prospect of excitement. They slew their wagon round, blocking the road, and remove a wheel while you take up position. Sure enough, within a short while a steam carriage with a cog-and-crow crest comes charging up the lane. The driver hits the brakes.

"Can't you bumpkins clear the way? What's your need to block the whole road?"

The driver edges forward to the gap at the side of the wagon. He doesn't see as a morris-man swings under the chassis and disengages the engine's drive chain with a sharp tug on a morris stick. The vehicle stops where it is: this is your moment.

With exaggerated coolness, you swing down from an overhanging branch and peer into the passenger compartment. "Good afternoon. I'm fundraising for the Morris-Men's Benevolent Fund for widows and orphans of morris-men lost in the cause of duty. Very good of you to stop. What sort of donation can I put you down for?"

A business-like lady in a striped dress looks up from a box of papers. "Donation? I only just gave a guinea to a troupe of wretched morris-men in Wallingford - and one of them was drunk!"

You may attempt to charm the woman by making a GALLANTRY roll of difficulty 12 or scare her with a RUTHLESSNESS roll of difficulty 11.

Successful GALLANTRY roll!   248
Successful RUTHLESSNESS roll!   349
Failed either roll!   89

❧ 235 ❧

The track between the trees is barely noticeable: Coke's crew use it as little as possible and camouflage it when they can. It leads you up and down ridges, deeper and deeper beneath the green shade into the heart of his hideout.

You know that you are getting near when the smell of dope for treating the airship linen wafts between the trees.

Turn to...   819

❧ 236 ❧

You ask the smith about the **mechanical arms** that you have occasionally come across in your travels. She smiles and shakes her head. "Now they take fine work, fine work indeed. Beyond me, I'll confess. All can say is that they're based on a **steam fist** and then take some more work from there. Down in Reading you might find an artificer able to piece one together, but they're mortal tricky to balance, I can tell you."

Return to the forge...   340
Leave the forge...   947

❧ 237 ❧

The door to the passenger compartment opens with a gust of scent. A hard-faced woman sits with her account book open. She judges you for a moment, then gives a smile. "And what can I do for you?"

A glance at the book reveals the names of dozens of women, their prices and the profit she has made from them. "What sort of a way is that to make a living?" you ask.

"I am no robber," she replies. "Every one of these has a warm place to sleep and food in her stomach. Who do you think you are, to pass judgment on me?"

"I should set them free from your grasp..."

"Free?" she laughs. "Better with me than in the workhouse. Kill me and another pimp will come and prey on them. Wake up, dearie. This is the real world."

"Hand over your money!"

The madam has **£8 3s** in cash and **ten guineas in banknotes** on her, as well as a **silver ring** and a **locket**. You will now be **Wanted by the Constables**, unless you have a **mask**.

Turn to...   **noted passage**

❧ 238 ❧

The road takes turn to the right as you leave Stoke Row and continues beneath the branches towards High Moor Cross. Muddy and rutted passing-places have been hacked into the hedgerow to allow steam engines and their wagons to pull in, but even on your velosteam it is as if you could reach out and touch the leaves either side.

On to High Moor Cross...   939
Prepare an ambush here...   366
Straight on to Nettlebed...   791

As the haulier turns the bend beneath the high bank where you wait, you spring aboard and clatter onto the footplate, knocking the driver down. He quickly regains his feet and hauls on the whistle. You must fight him!

Driver	Weapon: **shovel (PAR 2)**	
Parry:	7	
Nimbleness:	5	
Toughness:	4	

Victory!	**277**
Defeat!	**999**

You have to work hard to convince the voters that they should exercise their right decisively and selflessly, but you also promise to protect them against any repercussions from his Lordship. Gain a **solidarity point**. In the end they agree: they will vote for the Duke of Forebury's candidate. Gain the codeword *Beaurigarde*.

Return to the parlour...	**529**
Leave the Ferryman...	**749**

The forge has stood cold and empty ever since the blacksmith's arrest. One bold villager tells you that it was on account of assisting you - the famed and dreaded Steam Highwayman - that the Constables came and took her away. "Although it may have been she angered some other person of power."

Return to the village...	**947**

Your reputation precedes you: even before you open your mouth, the driver recognises your fearsome silhouette and releases the steam pressure from the engine. It shudders to a halt. Roll a dice to see what you encounter.

Score 1	A military officer	**1375**
Score 2	A widow	**1380**
Score 3	A high-ranking Constable	**1363**
Score 4	A Member of Parliament	**1387**
Score 5	A businessman	**1402**
Score 6	A doctor	**1415**

Your attempt to scare the driver has failed! You are forced to dive aside into the ditch to avoid the massive wheels of the steam vehicle.

Remount your velosteam...	**171**

Your cuisine has made a great impression upon the passengers: the Captain arranges for a bonus payment of twenty guineas (**£21**) and one of the guests graciously bestows a **gold ring** to remember her by. You whistle as you saunter down the boarding ramp, return to the shed where you left your velosteam and head off, on solid ground once more.

Turn to...	**454**

You open up your sketchpad and show the Count. "Hmmm, very nice," he says. "I do like how you create that sense of space in the interior here. And very good detailing on the stonework on the tower. Tell me, is it still plastered inside or have they taken it down? They were always going to and it really was not in good condition."

The Count points out several ways in which you could improve your skills and then makes good on his bargain. "Now, I'm not much of a string-puller myself, but in the city I do know a fair few fellows. If you need a favour, just mention my name." Gain the codeword *Blotchy*. He also arranges for his butler to advise you on your manners while you stay with him: the resulting changes give you quite an air of sophistication. Roll two dice and if you score higher than your current GALLANTRY score, increase it by 1.

Leave the house...	**158**

It is a long way to Cobstone Mill. Eventually you pass through Fingest and Turville and head up the slope - such a slope - to the windmill. Your velosteam slips in the mud and you tumble off with a thump, landing on your painfully-cut arm.

In some unlikely and fortunate circumstance, Miller Fursham is just returning from the village. He comes across you lying on the roadside and takes you in.

It is several weeks before you are recovered enough to remount your velosteam - which is now

critically damaged as a result of your accident. Your **wounds** have all become **scars** but it will be a long time before your confidence and bravado are what they once were. Lower your RUTHLESSNESS by 2.

Head down into Fingest...   **867**

❧ 247 ❧

The steep little lane brings you between heavy hazel coppices towards Fingest. Children run alongside on the banks, waving and laughing as you pass. If you have more than **10 solidarity points**, turn to **1232** immediately.

Otherwise you are left alone and whizz past the children, past the orange and red wallflowers, the tall purple towers of the foxgloves and the hollyhocks and into the village.

Coast down into Fingest...   **867**

❧ 248 ❧

"What you have to understand," you continue, "Is the life of hardship and the constant sense of rejection these men have to live with. Their wives won't accept them under their own roofs, their families disown them and their very children are told that their fathers are at sea. Why, milady, would you have your son a morris-man?"

She laughs at last. "They seem to have a friend in you - for unless my eyes deceive me, you are the Steam Highwayman, are you not? Well, I have heard how you care for the needy - although I did not know of your soft spot for folk dancers - so take these." She strips off her two **silver bracelets** and also hands over a purse. Once she is on her way, you split the money with the morris-men and are left with **£7 5s**.

Sammy wakes up briefly. "Is it pub o'clock?"

Ride away...   **433**

❧ 249 ❧

Several men are working with a tip-wagon of steaming tarmacadam and a work-stained, heavy-duty steam-roller. Looking up, one recognises you. "'Tis that Steam Highwayman," he calls to his mates. "Off to rob the rich..."

"And give to the poor I'm sure," says another with a cynical laugh. "We've work to do."

Turn to...   **793**

❧ 250 ❧

The Telegraph Guild depot is bounded by a high wall topped with a new type of wire invented in the Confederacy. Hooked barbs are strung along a sturdy wire, preventing anyone from easily vaulting or surpassing the barrier. If you are **Wanted by the Telegraph Guild** you will have no chance to get inside and should return to **487** immediately. An emergency medic also offers treatments for a fee.

	To buy
Heal a **wound**...	**£2** - replace with a **scar**
Treat a **burn**...	**8s** - replace with a **scar**

Buy drinks for the codesmen... (6s)	**1044**
Steal from the supplies...	**1049**
Buy 'surplus' equipment...	**1064**
Leave the compound...	**487**

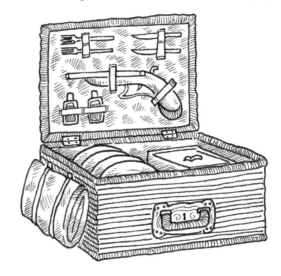

❧ 251 ❧

You are travelling on the Thames past some of its prettiest meadows and hillsides. On the south side stands a fine square house with a long garden running down to the riverbank: that must be Culham Court. A private telegraph tower rises from an outbuilding a decent distance away. A short way upstream is the village of Aston and beyond that is Hambleden Weir, but here the river splits and a narrow channel runs behind a thickly wooded island, known hereabouts as Magpie Island.

Head upstream to Hambleden Lock...	**630**
Tie up at Aston Wharf...	**950**
Steer down the narrow channel...	**482**
Travel downstream...	*Smog and Ambuscade 877*

❧ 252 ❧

Remove the **punchcards (Aramanth A)** and the **telegraph observations** from your **possessions**.

As you input the observations the great machine begins to tick and whine. Steam hisses and condenses somewhere within its workings. Then, with a turn of the dial, the armatures begin to flicker, the great spine of brass levers spins and curls and the printer-reel begins to chatter.

It does not take long to see that you have been successful: the machine has identified the patterns within the observations and deduced the various codes. You now have long reels of paper equivalent to a **Telegraph Guild codebook**. Such a feat of espionage would amaze the world - if you could tell it.

Turn to...   **noted passage**

❧ 253 ❧

He grabs the money hungrily, then begins to whine. "The plans are worth much more than that! They could make a lot of money for the right investor." He looks you up and down. "But I'm sure that isn't you."

Leave him...   **noted passage**

❧ 254 ❧

The telegraph tower stands a blackened ruin, its iron framework smoke-stained and the operator's cabin no more than ash and cold ember. The Guild have not yet rebuilt their station here: the Compact's intention to disrupt communication here has been at least partly successful. It would not be wise to be seen hanging around here.

Return to Wargrave...   **418**

❧ 255 ❧

The man is completely pitiful and helpless: there would be neither glory nor dignity in robbing or harming him. That said, you barely seem dignified hauling him over the saddle of your velosteam and wobbling back the way you came.

The morning mist shrouds the bridge and you are not stopped by any town guards. The Constable has begun to sober up with the cold breeze rushing past his hanging head and he manages to stagger off once you have helped him dismount outside the Constable's post, muttering gruffly. "Can't be late, oh no, Captain'll skin me. Got to make my report... it's the Fleur de Lis he wants, the Fleur de Lis. We'll burn

them to the ground."

Once he has disappeared into the mist you notice he has dropped his **Constable's whistle**, which you can take if you wish. Then you turn back the way you were headed and take the road to Wargrave.

Turn to...   **418**

❧ 256 ❧

Someone has recognised you and the River Guild have laid out booms across the river to halt your boat and board you. If you have a **strengthened screw**, you may churn straight through, laughing, and turn to **495** immediately. Otherwise, the Constables will come running out along the floating booms and try to leap aboard. You must fight them!

Constables	Weapons: **truncheons (PAR 2)**
Parry:	8
Nimbleness:	6
Toughness:	5

If you are defeated, you must remove your boat and its cargo from your **Adventure Sheet**.

Victory!	**495**
Defeat!	**13**

❧ 257 ❧

You return to where you moored your barge, remembering how worried your mate was to be tied up close to the navvies' camp. Roll two dice to see whether anything has happened, adding 1 to your roll for each **5 solidarity points** you have and **2** if you are a **Member of the Compact for Workers' Equality**.

Score 2-6	Wrecked by destructive drunks! Remove your boat and cargo from your **Adventure Sheet** and return to **584**.
Score 7-8	Cargo pilfered and ruined! Remove your cargo from your **Adventure Sheet**.
Score 9+	Everything safe.

Take on cargo at the wharf...	**263**
Head onto the river...	**271**

❧ 258 ❧

At the start of the music you give a leap, a spin, and throw yourself into the dance. The steps do not challenge you and you begin embellishing them with flicks and turns and tricks. The fiddler, keen to inject some energy, responds to your nods with a rising pace and soon you are running the other dancers out of breath. "What are you doing?" asks Goodman Butt, snatching the stick and hat back after a reel. "You want to show us all up? Why don't you go enter one of them ballroom competitions in Reading instead?"

Return to the village...   947

❧ 259 ❧

The long road to Oxford stretches out ahead of you, passing through villages and small, overlooked towns like Chislehampton. The sun sinks into the west and you are soon steaming along in the dusk, your lime lantern cutting a beam into the night. Roll a dice to see what you encounter:

Score 1-2	Deer by night...	517
Score 3-4	An empty road...	990
Score 5-6	A rivalry!	292

❧ 260 ❧
☐

If the box is empty, tick it and read on. If it is already ticked, turn to **1510** immediately.

Leticia Forebury is not at home to greet you, but the old Duke does appear to warmly shake your hand. "Ah," he says, "The Kingmaker! You're the one who did so much with the voters. Well, we'll see if it comes out right at the election. Now, she did leave some things for you."

He hands you a **letter of introduction** that his daughter has written, together with a fine **rapier (PAR 4)**, a purse containing **£28** and a note that reads: "Jermyn Bigod at Exeter College in Oxford can help you to disappear from the Constables' lists. Take him a clockwork bird for payment."

Leave the manor house...   864

❧ 261 ❧

"Come over here to the vestry where we can talk," invites Father Patrick. "Now what do you have to tell me? There is no compulsion in our communion to confess aloud, but I know, oh yes I know, how very necessary it can be to the individual."

He makes no sign of amazement as you describe those things that bring you guilt. But when you finish, he looks into your eyes. "Now I know you better," he says. "Do not make the mistake of believing that you are beyond forgiveness - or without the need for change either. Each is a path to a hard heart."

Remove the codewords *Barbaric* and *Bronte* if you have them.

"How can I help the people?"   279
"The Constables pursue me. How can
   I be free?"   385
Leave the church...   3

❧ 262 ❧

As you open the poorbox, a sharp snap accompanies the closing of a metal-jawed trap that has been fitted inside. Gain a **wound**! If you now have **five wounds**, turn to **999**.

Leave the church...   308

❧ 263 ❧

South Stoke has swollen as the railway navvies have built a camp nearby. It has greatly increased trade, as they demand machinery and beer to carry out their earthworks for the Imperial Western Railway. Wheat produced on the plains north and west of here is being transported down to a new quay, where River Guild barges are lined up to carry it to a mill downstream.

	To buy	To sell
Charcoal	£13	£12
Furniture	-	£27
Machinery	-	£25
Pottery	-	£20
Cotton	-	£4
Woollen cloth	£5	£4
Coal	£14	£13
Beer	-	£18
Wheat	£2	-
Malt	-	-
Frozen meat	-	-
Ice	-	£10

To ship **Ice** or **Frozen Meat** you will need a **Perkins engine** to refrigerate your cargo hold. The navies are unable to fit such machinery themselves, but you are told that you can find these customizations in both Oxford and Reading.

Moor here...	**823**
Head upstream...	**305**
Steam downriver towards Reading... (8s)	**658**

❧ 264 ❧

The farmer tells you about a strange man his children found sleeping in the barn. "They said he could talk to animals," he says, "And was whistling to the rats when they found him. They said he was Jesus and were stealing food from the kitchen for him, the little blighters. I turned him off the farm, of course. He went off south-ways."

Turn to...   **595**

❧ 265 ❧

The firm road surface carries you south-east across the Oxford plain. Maintaining your speed you are easily able to overtake the lumbering road trains, weaving elegantly past and around them. At Aston Hill you climb up into the Chilterns, forced to slow somewhat, but still too fast to be bothered by the glimpses of an ambush laid at the roadside. On, on, on, past Stokenchurch, Piddington and West Wycombe until you approach High Wyombe itself.

A queue of vehicles ahead indicates a roadblock or some accident. You lower the pressure and coast forward: a posse of Constables are checking vehicle details and looking for trouble-makers.

If you are **Wanted by the Constables**, turn to **359** immediately. If not, you have nothing to fear from the law and can proceed straight on up the long road to London.

Ride on...   **417**

❧ 266 ❧

At last Union Flight 6371 returns to Rotherfield Greys and moors to its post. The passengers depart and you are dismissed. If you have **three or more levels of haute cuisine**, turn to **244** immediately. Otherwise, you are given your payment: **£5 6s** for all your hard work.

You return to the shed where you left your velosteam carefully parked and head off, on solid ground once more.

Turn to...   **454**

❧ 267 ❧

With your weapons ready, you fell the first Constable through the door with a heavy blow to the face. His mates push through the narrow space and surround you. This will be a fight worth remembering!

Constables	Weapon: **sabres (PAR 3)**
Parry:	13
Nimbleness:	10
Toughness:	10

Victory!	**64**
Defeat!	**13**

❧ 268 ❧

You have again come across the Constables' prison wagon. However, since you last tried to release the prisoners, the guard has been doubled. It would be foolish indeed to try to spring them!

Ride past...   **313**

❧ 269 ❧

You recognise Mr Sands beneath his deer-stalker. He lowers his shotgun sadly. "I never thought you would sink so low," he says. "Take the bird." You may take the **pheasant**, but you are no longer the **Friend of Mr Sands**.

Leave the wood...   **600**

Wallingford is a prosperous town controlling both river trade and the toll-roads overland. No wonder that for centuries the castle here has been a royal palace too: it is currently the headquarters of the Wallingford Town Guard.

The Telegraph Guild have a small outpost here, although their larger towers are out on the high ground. They maintain a depot here for resupplying - and for political reasons. The whole town is ringed with an ancient wall and the streets inside are narrow and packed. Houses are jettied outwards to make the most of the space and despite the town ordinances, workshops and lodging houses are sprawling outside the walls too.

Board your boat...
(if **moored at Wallingford**)	**895**
Steam into the Freight Yard...	**653**
Head to the market...	**598**
Visit the Dolphin Inn...	**281**
Steam up to the castle...	**1210**
Leave the town...	**742**

You are on the reach above Cleeve Lock, running past the Stokes and opposite the cluster of dirty hovels known as Moulesford. A recently completed railway bridge crosses the Thames obliquely, its embankments still raw and unseeded. Signals flicker along the track on railway telegraphs - one of the very few licenses that the Telegraph Guild have given for the use of their machinery.

A ferry crosses between Moulesford and South Stoke, carrying foot passengers, farm wagons and the occasional road locomotive. It runs on a chain lying on the river bed, hauled along by a steam winch on the eastern bank.

Cleeve Lock is the first of several between here and Reading, each owned and maintained by the River Guild. Their tolls nibble away at independent freighter's margins, so many rivermen join the guild and purchase a **Bargee's Badge** where they can.

Visit South Stoke Wharf...	**263**
Moor at South Stoke...	**823**
Rob the ferry...	**115**
Head upstream...	**305**
Sail on through the locks...	
(**8s** or **Bargee's Badge**)	**658**

The distant column of smoke rising indicates a heavy road engine, probably towing several wagons. You can make out the green, gold and black of the Telegraph Guild as well as the small optical telegraph mounted above its cab, but to see whether it is defended you will need a **telescope** or a pair of **binoculars**. If you do not want to threaten the driver or ride alongside, a nearby beech branch offers you the chance to swing directly aboard on a rope.

Take another look...
(**telescope** or **binoculars**)	**1390**
Swing into the passing driver's cab... (**rope**)	**1404**
Intimidate the driver...	**1424**
Ride alongside...	**1412**

A Scottish haulier is refreshing himself after a long journey. "You've come a long way," you observe.

"Aye, that I have," he replies. "And still a way to go. I'm hauling chain and shackles down to Salisbury. Take me another few days yet. Still, the journey means I won't be bothering my missus too much - or she me."

Return to the parlour...	**36**

You recognise the occupant of the steam carriage as a well-known chef, renowned for his cookbooks across the empire. "Why, Monsieur du Lac," you begin, but he draws a large kitchen knife in reply.

M. du Lac	Weapon: **knife (PAR 1)**
Parry:	8
Nimbleness:	7
Toughness:	5

Victory!	**302**
Defeat!	**999**

The chef smiles at the quality ingredients you have brought him and proceeds to explain his methods. It is not a short process and you spend several days at the inn, working under the chef and accustoming yourself to kitchen work - a far cry from the rough eating and cooking you have been accustomed to in your bivouacs and roadside dens.

Eventually he claps you on the back. "You will

do. You are beginning to learn what it means to be a chef." Gain a level of **haute cuisine**.

Return to the parlour...   **358**

❧ 276 ❧

Guildsmen surround you as you ride into the compound. "We know who you are!" calls an officer. "Surrender yourself!" If you hope to prove that you mean no harm, you must show that you have sided yourself with the Guild by producing a **Coal Board Accounts book**. If you can do this, they will reluctantly accept that you share an enemy and will allow you to talk to one of their officers: turn to **538**. If not, you will be captured, bound hand and foot and made to pay for your crimes.

Turn to...   **15**

❧ 277 ❧

Robbing the common people of the land will provide you with slim pickings. The haulier has **£1 3s** on him, which you pocket, and you can take as many **bolts of cloth** from his wagon as you can carry. However, lose a **solidarity point** for so ruthlessly taking from someone simply trying to make ends meet.

Leave the haulier...   **noted passage**

❧ 278 ❧

Your journey proceeds without incident until shortly before Oxford, when a skiff appears suddenly from beneath Folly Bridge, right under your bows. With a crashing of wood, your heavier craft tears through the skiff and tosses its occupants into the water.

"I say! How very dare you! I had right of way, you know?" The owner of the skiff is a student at the University. When you pull towards the bank to see if he is alright, his friends mob you.

"Satisfaction!" they cry. "A duel! For honour!"

If you have a **bottle of champagne**, now would be a good time to broach it. These students are easily swayed by bubbly. Otherwise, they will force you to fight their unconventional duel.

Open the champagne...
    (**bottle of champagne**)   **472**
Fight the duel...   **954**

❧ 279 ❧

"You can help the people by ceasing to rob them," says Father Patrick boldly. "Taking what is not yours is no ways to redress the wrongs of the world."

"Other holy men disagree."   **317**
"It is my way of living."   **478**
"And as well as this?"   **513**

❧ 280 ❧

The village of Aston lies in rich meadowland at the foot of Remenham Hill. Most of the inhabitants are tenants of the landowners at Culham House, but the trees hanging with apples, the noisy chickens in every yard and the fresh paint on doors and lintels tell you that life is comfortable here.

The village inn, the Flowerpot, is known as a meeting place for anglers. Outside stand several engines parked in a row. Down the lane past the willows is the wharf where several barges are moored. A boatman also runs a ferry here to the northern side of the river.

Visit the Flowerpot...   **348**
Investigate the parked engines...   **14**
Board your barge... (**moored at Aston**)   **950**
Cross onto Magpie Island...
    (**moored at Magpie Island**)   **870**
Head along the riverbank towards Henley...   **427**
Ride up the hill towards the main road...   **313**
Cross to Mill End on the ferry... (**2s**)   **112**

❧ 281 ❧

The Dolphin is not a fussy or prettified place. The landlord snorts in derision at the trends sweeping inns and pubs. "What do people want coffee for? Or little plates of tiny food? That ain't my business!"

His custom seems to be booming. Members of the Town Guard drink at their own table by the front window. Hauliers and rivermen drink in the garden or at the bar. An urchin selling cut-down shoes from a basket weaves in and out of the customers. A grey-haired man sits at a table in an alcove, watching you intently with beady eyes. He looks hungry and thin.

Order a pint... (2s)	613
Buy a meal for the grey-haired man... (4s)	490
Leave the pub...	270

❧ 282 ❧

You leap aboard the barge and begin cutting down the crew. The water-rats whoop with excitement and press forward. You come face to face with the captain of the barge, who carries a heavy gaff and swings it towards you mercilessly.

Guild Captain	Weapon: club (PAR 2)
Parry:	8
Nimbleness:	6
Toughness:	6

Victory!	784
Defeat!	528

❧ 283 ❧

Here in the workshop, hairy-armed and soot-smeared men are labouring on a variety of road-going machines in various states of readiness. Several boilers are being riveted together and the noise is tremendous. You have to revert to sign language to communicate your wishes to the foreman.

Velosteam Customisations	To buy
muffled exhaust	£4 2s
off-road tyres	£7s 3s
gas pressuriser	£12 12s

Repairs	To buy
Per **damage point**	£2 5s

Leave the workshop...	805

❧ 284 ❧

The Ferguson smashes heavily into the steamer right behind its front axle, knocking the vehicle sideways and into the ditch. Unfortunately you must also gain a **damage point**. The driver is thrown clear and you are able to dismount and throw open the door of the passenger compartment.

The Bishop of Barnsbury tumbles out, smeared in cream from his cakes and still clutching a broken wineglass. He grovels at your feet in the mud. "Spare my life!" If your velosteam is now **beyond repair**, turn to **874** immediately. Otherwise you can turn your attention to the Bishop.

Turn to...	765

❧ 285 ❧

If you have an **urgent parcel**, turn to **1216** immediately. Otherwise, read on.

The Freight Yard here is managing with several road-trains including one pulled by a double-boiler colossus - a long-distance road engine that tows eight self-steering wagons. Several of the hauliers are gazing at it in wonder, resplendent in its Haulage Guild livery. Repairs are offered here and some tools can be purchased as well.

Tools	To buy	To sell
rope	4s	2s
net	6s	4s
rope ladder	9s	5s
lantern	6s	4s
shovel	8s	6s
welding tools	£2 2s	£1
grappling iron	12s	8s
measuring line	10s	6s
copper pipe	6s	3s
high pressure valve	18s	10s
pneumatic manual (ENG+3)	-	£8
autogauge (MOT+3)	-	£18

Repairs	To buy
Per **damage point**	£4

Leave the yard...	688
Leave the city...	970

❧ 286 ❧

The lane rises steadily up Assendon Vale towards Stonor, a huddle of cottages at the head of the valley. The road is not busy but a party of hop-pickers are walking southwards for their harvesting trip.

Talk to the hop-pickers...   **334**
On towards Stonor...   **430**

❧ 287 ❧
☐

If the box above is empty, tick it now and read on. If it is already ticked, turn to **977** immediately, as you have already drawn this building!

St Nicolas' church is a rather odd, idiosyncratic building with the stubbiest of square bell-towers, heavy abutments on the ends of the nave and yellow-rendered chancel. It is neither smart nor imposing, but plainly a building much-adapted for the purpose of housing the worship of God. It does make a very interesting set of sketches. Tick one box in your **sketchpad**.

Leave the church...   **977**

❧ 288 ❧

Tall cow-parsley and meadow weeds flash past as you peer out over the plain. The road to Oxford is dotted with traffic: long road trains managed by independent hauliers, the Haulage Guild, even the black and yellow livery of the Coal Board. At one distant spot the road disappears into a small wood amongst the farmland, but the rest of the way it is open to the elements.

Up here is a different story. The roadway along the crest is poorly-maintained and rutted. It keeps to the high ground, sometimes alongside plantations and sometimes between high pasture. Turning a bend you see a few figures in tattered military uniform resting around a fire beneath the trees.

Stop and talk to the soldiers...   **25**
Ride on by...   **102**

❧ 289 ❧

The charges go off with an almighty crash, tossing stone, wood and tile high into the air. The manor house is completely destroyed and the inhabitants have no chance of survival.

When the terrified villagers emerge to see what you have done, they quickly realise their opportunity to take back their lands and you hear of how several of them have been visited by the ghost themselves. You, however, were the only one determined enough to respond with such destructive violence.

Your reputation will be enhanced: gain **two solidarity points** and remove the codeword *Bother*. The Compact for Workers' Equality will also be very interested in your punishment of the nobility - gain the codeword *Bolster* if you do not already have it.

Steam up to Ibstone...	**400**
Head down the lane to Turville...	**947**
Ride on to Bolter End...	**546**
Take the road south to Skirmett...	**969**

❧ 290 ❧

You take your seat as the small theatre orchestra are warming up and tuning their instruments. As well as a small brass section, there is a multicello and an automatic box-organ in the pit, capable of a wide variety of artificial sounds.

The first act is a comedian who banters about everyday life at the waterside, telling anecdotes at the expense of his employer before going on to juggle puppies. A blind soprano is led onstage and she moves everyone to tears with her sentimental songs. Then a drama follows - a modern piece of writing set in a smoky tenement in which a married couple argue about money. It is received with a quiet disinterest even more damning than ridicule.

Dancers appear in their gauze and net and now the orchestra really come alive and show what they are capable of. Melodies pour out and the dancers perform in all sorts of creative ways, leaping and swirling and launching themselves into the imaginations of their audience.

It is a popular show and much enjoyed by those around you. The wide variety of performers only need to be judged in a competition style to make the thing even more dramatic. Perhaps there is scope for a show with that edge of rivalry, hope and reward?

As you leave, you overhear two theatre-goers talking quietly about the Compact for Workers' Equality: they have a private parlour at the Three Guineas in Reading.

Leave the theatre...	**702**

❧ 291 ❧

You settle into your velosteam's comfortable leather saddle and start the climb up Red Lane. Your coalgas tank still holds plenty of fuel but the water tank shows that you will need to refill soon. Despite all your adventures and the stresses you have put the Ferguson under, its essential mechanics are all in working order. Good honest engineering has produced a machine that is both reliable and fast - as well as being very difficult to stop!

After several miles, the lane runs between two small hills and a full ditch implies a nearby stream. You pull over and find a bright, clear flow of water channelled out from the hillside. The flow is too small to be of use to bigger steam vehicles, but your tank is quickly brimmed up.

Prepare an ambush here by the spring...	**397**
Ride on to Woodcote...	**488**

❧ 292 ❧

Two hauliers are racing one another on the road to Oxford, each trying to out-do one another despite hauling two wagons of cargo. They are taking up the entire road between them and needless to say they are both much slower than you.

Speed around them on the verge...	**1021**
Wait for one to get a good lead...	**990**

❧ 293 ❧

The children cheer again at your approach. They are two brothers and a sister returning home to Shirburn after a day bird-nesting and collecting firewood in the woods. Intriguingly, the girl is carry three peacock feathers along with her faggot of twigs.

"You's the real Steam Highwayman? Wow!" The eldest brother is enthralled. "I's heard of you!" The youngest, barely more than a snotty-nosed toddler, strokes the brass on your velosteam gingerly. He has never been allowed close to a machine like this without being beaten.

Their sister plucks up courage. "We went a-swimming in the big tank above Stokenchurch. It's easy to get in if you know how!

Give them a guinea to take home to their mother... (**£1 1s**)	**918**
Give them a ride on your velosteam...	**902**
Ride on...	**360**

❧ 294 ❧

A rusty Fowler traction engine is dragging a pair of wagons loaded with bales of straw and several milk churns. A farmer stands at the wheel and a youth shovels coal sparingly into the glowing firebox. Their eyes peer at you through bodged, home-made goggles and rising clouds of steam. They have nothing worth stealing and are unwilling to lengthen their already long day by chattering on the roadside.

Turn to...   **noted passage**

❧ 295 ❧

You find Sir Reginald again and hand him the **Whitchurch affidavit** (remove it from your **possessions**). He chuckles. "Excellent. You stay here in the house tonight and dine with me. I'll send a telegraph out to the Colonel and see if we can't do something about your record."

You enjoy an excellent meal and a good night's rest. One of your **scars** heals completely: remove it from your **Adventure Sheet**. In the morning you are given the good news that you are no longer a person of interest: remove any **Wanted** statuses you possess as well. Finally, you are given a bag of forty guineas (**£42**) and sent on your way.

Head towards Mapledurham... (*Butterchurn*) **230**
Return to Whitchurch...   **749**

❧ 296 ❧

The road out of High Moor Cross climbs steeply, winding up the hillside towards Stoke Row. Hedgerows full of summer leaf shade countless tiny cultures of predator, prey and scavenger. Several tall elm trees move in a high breeze that you cannot feel here on the hot road.

Prepare an ambush here...   **366**
On to Stoke Row...   **457**

❧ 297 ❧

Reading sits astride the Thames like a canker on an oak-branch. It swells, daily, as tenements are raised, shacks thrown up on the outskirts and new chimneys climb skywards. It is a vast centre of commerce and industry: Huntley and Palmer's biscuit factory fills the tea tables of the empire's lower and middle classes and the bellies of the Imperial army; the arms manufacturers along the river stamp out thousands of rifle-barrels every month, for government issue and for export; steam-barges are launched here with powerful engines built to haul long trains of barges; boilers are beaten noisily into shape and iron is forge-welded into pre-fabricated constructions that are shipped all over the world. The wharves, the Freight Yard and the airship ground are all rammed with heavy transport.

On every hurriedly-built street, hordes rush to work: children as young as four labour in the factories. The men are called upon in the foundries to shovel and hoist. And over the whole region hangs a pervasive, soot-laden smog, blackening even the brass on your beloved machine.

Head down to the wharf...   **788**
Find somewhere to drink...   **1515**
Visit Coulter's Bank...   **61**
Explore the markets...   **838**
Visit the Abbey grounds...   **1069**
Wander the industrial district...   **771**
Leave the city...   **410**

❧ 298 ❧

Remove the **Cobstone flour** from your possessions.

You do your best to sell the quality of miller Fursham's flour to the baker in Wargrave, but he shows little interest. "We have all the flour we need," he says, "And pay a fair price for it."

Tell him about Fursham's troubles...   **165**
Threaten him...   **438**

❧ 299 ❧

Using what familiarity with airship design as you have, you instruct the machine to calculate the maximum possible buoyancy of an airship using the materials currently available. The machine whirrs and whirrs, frequently asking you to set new parameters. Some you estimate, others you are forced to guess. In the end the machine prints out an **airship buoyancy calculation**. To your eye it may well improve the average carrying ability of airships. Whether it will ever be adopted, you cannot tell. The **punchcards (Habbukuk K)** have been consumed by the machine and you must remove them from your **possessions**. However, you have learnt a great deal. If you have an ENGINEERING score of 10 or less, gain a point of ENGINEERING.

Leave the machine...   **noted passage**

✎ 300 ✐

You dive beneath a dense holly bush. Perhaps you were unrealistic in your attempt to scare the guards?

However, you hear the engine's brake-blocks screeching and the sound of men running. They begin beating the bushes and hunting for you. A cry rings out as they find your velosteam parked a short distance away. You raise your head to see if there is any way out of your predicament and suddenly find yourself looking down the muzzle of a gun.

Turn to...   15

✎ 301 ✐

This man deserves neither your mercy nor your time. A quick blow to the back of his head incapacitates him. He has a **pocket watch**, a **Constable's whistle**, and a **sabre (PAR 6)** on him, but only **3s** in coins. The rest of his pay is presumably behind the bar of the George and Dragon in Wargrave.

Then it is a simple task to drag his unprotesting body the short distance to the river's edge and lump him in. He floats, facedown, for a short while, and then sinks into the mist. Good riddance. Now you can continue on your way.

Add 1 to your RUTHLESSNESS score and gain the codeword *Barbaric*.

Head on to Wargrave...   418

✎ 302 ✐

"You 'ave bested me," says the chef. "Is the world to 'ave no more of my masterpieces? No more Crème du Lac? No more Poulet au Poires?" He collapses into a heap, bleeding badly. You may take **£4 17s** from his purse and a **bottle of champagne** he had on ice, but unless you were wearing a **mask**, you will now be **Wanted by the Constables**.

Turn to...   **noted passage**

✎ 303 ✐

You approach Watlington. A sharp bend should lead you straight to the Freight Yard, but instead you find yourself face to face with a Constabulary road block. You had better have nothing to hide - or be very good at hiding it.

Turn around and speed off...   307
Stop and present yourself...   476

✎ 304 ✐

The route you choose takes you winding through the old villages, along deep holloways and through ancient woods. You stop several times at old haunts and refresh yourself at comfortable and out-of-the-way inns. Eventually you reach the edges of London, all without passing a single Constable's post or roadblock. However, the length of your journey has depleted your purse: remove **15s** for all the food and drink you have purchased on the way.

Ride on...   417

✎ 305 ✐

This is a quiet stretch of the river. With no locks for several miles, craft power on past the cows and bulrushes, careless of the meadows and the riverside communities. They have no reason to stop or pause here and villages like North Stoke and Mongewell are overlooked and ignored.

Steam towards Mongewell Park...   31
Moor at North Stoke...   383
Head upriver towards Wallingford...   943

✎ 306 ✐
☐ ☐ ☐ ☐

If any of the boxes above are empty, tick one. If all four are already ticked, erase the ticks and turn to **146** immediately.

You had better make yourself scarce and put some distance between yourself and the site of your most recent ambush. Which way will you turn?

On to Nettlebed...   791
Towards Reading...   793
Approach Henley...   68

You are on the road to Wallingford across the low hills. The farmlands are rich and well-tended here, but the mechanisation of the harvesting has wreaked havoc in the local labour market: family after family has been forced to move to the cities to find work.

As for you, the breeze and humidity warn you of a rainstorm approaching. You could use the bad weather to cover an ambush or you can plough on towards Wallingford.

Plan an ambush here...	**172**
Continue towards Wallingford...	**800**

Stokenchurch is a busy place, with its position on the road between Oxford and London giving it some significance as a freight town. However, it has also been a prosperous centre of the furniture trade and a market town for the surrounding farmlands and is becoming an industrial centre too as workshops are thrown up. The one restricting factor up here on the high ground is water and the Coal Board keeps a reservoir a short distance away. Prosperity for some has drawn in labourers and that in turn has led to speculative house-building, more employment for the construction companies and more demand for freight. Coal is of course at the heart of the whole process and streams of Coal Board wagons make their way day and night into the compound on the southern side of the growing town. If you have the codeword *Bootlicker*, turn to **1286** immediately.

Investigate the church of St Peter and St Paul...	**979**
Enter the Coal Board compound...	**192**
Enter the Fleur de Lis...	**640**
Visit the shops and market...	**406**
Leave town...	**660**

"What a fine fish! Did you catch this?" The chef busies himself cleaning and descaling the pike. "Many people find pike bony, but it is undoubtably a fine centrepiece to a meal and has a surprisingly delicate flavour. Let me show you what to do."

The chef teaches you many secrets and tricks over the next week or so that you work with him. Gain a level of **haute cuisine**.

Return to the parlour...	**358**

You have attracted too much attention by your presence here on the Oxford Plain and the Constables have despatched a velosteam squad in your pursuit. You must choose a route to escape them - and quickly.

Up onto the hill above Watlington...	**1287**
Over Grim's Ditch...	**1266**
Towards Stokenchurch...	**1299**

The clerks lie about, bleeding but not badly wounded. They quickly surrender their purses and possessions. You may take **£8 2s** from them, together with a **locket**, a **pocket watch** and a set of **blank punchcards**.

Turn to...	**noted passage**

The letter is taken into the house and you are told to wait for a response: remove it from your **possessions** now. If you have the codeword *Broken*, turn to **1339** immediately. If not, but you have the codeword *Brimming*, turn to **1347**. If you have neither, read on.

You are eventually led inside to meet the Viscount Monsberg. He is a fashionable and haughty man with a keen sense of his place in society - a very exalted place - and yours.

"I need someone ruthless. I have a rival for the affections of a lady in London: Sir Peter Fotherill. He lives in the city, near St James' Park. Kill him and I shall pay you well, as well as seeing you are taken under my protection. The Constables will no longer concern you." Gain the codeword *Browned*.

Leave the house...	**937**

The road here runs east to west over Remenham Hill before making its way down to the Thames and Henley. From your velosteam you can see the water of the Thames glinting to the north beyond Aston. A square gatehouse topped with a narrow chimney and a private telegraph relay stands just to the side of the road, with a discreet sign reading 'Culham Court Lodge. Strictly Private'.

Enter the lodge...
(*Botanical* or **Friend of Earl Brigg**)	**885**
Ride down the lane towards Aston...	**280**
Follow the road west towards Henley...	**863**
Prepare an ambush here...	**506**
Head east...	*Smog and Ambuscade 445*

৯ 314 ৵
The revolutionaries are no match for your swordplay. One after another, they fall or disappear into the woods. You are left to remount your velosteam and make your way on towards Manchester, taking **£1 18s** and a **revolutionary poster** from the bodies if you wish.

Ride on...   **442**

৯ 315 ৵
Your footfall on the church doorstep rings loud in the quiet. The church is squat and ancient: a Norman arch opens into the chancel, where the vicar of Ibstone is kneeling at prayer.

He looks up, smiles a strange, faraway smile, and comes directly over.

"Here you are," he begins. "A strange answer to prayer, perhaps, but you're unmistakably the one the Father has shown me."

"What are you talking about?" you reply.

"I've been praying," says the priest. "You never know what you're going to hear when you get down on your knees and talk to God. We need help. I've just been talking with the Rathbones, poor people. Their daughter works in the city, in London in the house of an important man. They haven't heard from her in several months and need someone to go and look for her."

"Aren't your prayers being answered?"

"Yes they are. Last night I dreamed of a figure on a two-wheeled steam machine, swathed in smoke. Now here you are. God has chosen you to help us."

"Where did she work?"

"In the house of Michael Ennis - a banking man. Here - this is the last letter she sent. It may help you to find her." He hands you **Andrea Rathbone's letter**.

You can believe the priest about his dream if you wish. Either way, someone is in need.

Leave the church...   **977**

৯ 316 ৵
Susan Tenney is very pleased. "What an enjoyable game," she says. "Croquet can be dull stuff but you brought it to life, didn't you?" You have learnt a great deal by coming here and observing everything. If your unimproved GALLANTRY score is 10 or less, gain a point of GALLANTRY. Susan Tenney also gives you a **silver ring** in memory of the match.

Leave the house...   **62**

৯ 317 ৵
"You mean my brother in Stokenchurch amongst others, I am sure. Yes, Christ overthrew the tables in the temple. But he also said, 'Give unto Caesar that which is Caesar's'. I do not believe he was a zealot. Read your Gospels again, my child. Invite him to show himself, rather than simply reading to find what you desire."

Leave the church...   **3**

৯ 318 ৵
Before long you are inside the old house. You prowl through the rooms and collect valuables. You may add any of the following to your **possessions**, provided you have space: a **pair of golden candlesticks**, a **fine clock**, a **fur coat**, a **silver necklace**, some **false teeth**, and a bottle of **pink pills (NIM+2)** ☐ ☐ ☐.

However, as you are moving around, you knock a vase off a mantlepiece and awaken the homeowners. You dash out of the house as shouts ring out behind you!

Ride away...   **803**

৯ 319 ৵
You have reached Sonning at last. The lock in front of you has a narrow entrance and there can be a considerable queue when the freight barges are running. However, the River Guild are constrained from widening the lock by the local landowners - for now. Little can stand in the way of money-makers.

Return upriver...   **113**
Head into the lock... (**2s** or **Bargee's Badge**) **750**

❧ 320 ❧

You uncouple the chains and the wagon breaks away from the train, tearing off its pneumatic hose with a cloud of steam and crashing into the hedgerow. Shouts from the engine tell you that your escapade is not unnoticed, but with your armed silhouette atop the wagon, the driver is loath to stop. Your reputation will certainly suffer as a result: lose a **solidarity point**.

The wagon is laden with everyday goods, food-stuffs and supplies. You can take any of the following: a **rope**, a **wheel of cheese**, a **bolt of cloth**, a bottle of **cough medicine**, some **copper pipe** and a **high-pressure valve**. There is far more to take than you can carry here. If you have a **purple flare**, you may use one now, turning to **354** immediately.

Leave the ruined wagon...   **noted passage**

❧ 321 ❧

After tramping around the house looking for a way in or a servant to announce you, you return to the front door and swing the knocker. The sound echoes around the old house like a hacking cough through a decrepit giant's lungs. After some minutes, the door creaks open and you stand face to face with an old lady wrapped in blankets, a shawl and a nightcap. If you are a **Famed Lawbreaker**, or have **15 or more solidarity points** turn to **462** immediately.

She looks you up and down sceptically. "Who might you be?"

"I am a messenger of your doom! Relinquish your claim to the Earl's farms or you will perish!"	**389**
"An interested legal advisor. I have heard you might need help in your current lawsuit?"	**578**

❧ 322 ❧

As you rap on the door of the carriage, the driver leans round. "I'd be careful with this one. Not quite... all there."

The door opens and you see a lady inside. She takes your hand to climb down the steps and smiles weirdly. She is dressed all in white with a white hat, and long, straggling white hair hanging over her shoulders. A hungry look in her eyes appears when you demand she give over her valuables. "Give me a moment, child," she says, rummaging in her bag.

Suddenly she leans forward and bites you in the neck! You thrust her off and draw your weapon. She laughs, tosses you a purse containing **£12** in coins and climbs back into her carriage.

"What is she - a vampire?" you ask the driver.

"Either she is or she thinks she is," comes the reply. "I ain't got it worked out meself." Note that you now have a **bite on the neck** on your **Adventure Sheet**.

Turn to...   **noted passage**

❧ 323 ❧

Wargrave's shops sell typical, everyday items for the most part, but one shopkeeper supplies the boats and freighters hereabouts and another deals in jewellery.

Tools	To buy	To sell
rope	4s	2s
waterproof paint	6s	-
heavy wrench	18s	12s
net	6s	3s
tarpaulin	4s	4s
brass flange joint	8s	5s
copper pipe	6s	4s
high pressure valve	-	9s
Jewellery	To buy	To sell
locket	6s	4s
silver ring	10s	7s
silver bracelet	£1	10s
silver necklace	£2	£1 5s
gold ring	£3	£1 1s
gold bracelet	£3 5s	£2 2s
gold necklace	-	£5
Other items	To buy	To sell
Bargee's Badge	-	£2
Guildsman's medallion	-	6s
gold bar	-	£25
jewelled bible	-	£8 15s

A waterman desperate to raise money tells you that he can steal you a **Bargee's badge** from his captain, for a fee. "I knows where he keeps it and it'll see you a long way up and down the river."

Pay the waterman...	(**£10**)	**887**
Visit the town bakery...	(**Cobstone flour**)	**298**
Return to Wargrave...		**418**

❧ 324 ❧
The Major is overjoyed with your victory. He claps you on the shoulder. "Very good, very good! I had some money on that - let me slip you a little." He puts five guineas (**£5 5s**) into your pocket and then hands you Major Redford's Card. "If you get into any trouble with the Constables in Henley - or pretty much anywhere - show them this card and it might help you out. I don't need my particular friends getting stopped, do I? When can we play again?"

Leave the house...   **62**

❧ 325 ❧
Inside the cabin you find an **autogauge (MOT+3)** in prime working condition, together with an **officer's cap** and a **strongbox**.

Leave the cabin...   **266**

❧ 326 ❧
The gentleman playing yellow crouches to consider his next shot. He turns with a flourish and prepares to knock his ball in entirely the wrong direction! The sharp crack of his shot is followed by gasps as the yellow speeds towards the balustrade, loops up the slope beside the stair, flicks around a decorative pillar and comes flying back from an ornamental fish's tail. You duck and the yellow knocks hard into your black, returning directly through the next hoop and sending you way off course. The audience clap excitedly.

Try to rebound from the yellow...   **1472**
Aim to bounce off the terrace wall...   **1264**
Cautiously position yourself to proceed...   **1132**

❧ 327 ❧
As you make your way down the channel you are forced to duck beneath the low branches of the willows and poplars. Reeds disguise the edge of the channel and several times the tiller shudders as the keel catches on something.

Before long, the screw stops turning. The mate rushes over to release steam from the boiler before the pressure mounts and you both lean over the stern to see something like a wicker-work basket caught around the screw.

"You clumsy landsman!" cries a voice from the reeds. "You've gone and torn up me bucks!"

An ancient, white-haired eel-catcher rises from the riverbank, shaking his fist as he surveys the ruined eel-traps left in your path. Perhaps you can calm him by offering to pay for his traps? Or will you be able to sooth him with an appeal to his better nature, by making a GALLANTRY roll of difficulty 11?

Offer to pay for his eel bucks... (**£2 2s**)   **386**
Successful GALLANTRY roll...   **432**
Unable to calm him down...   **514**

❧ 328 ❧
It is not a great distance to Culham Court but you only just make it. Twice you slip from your seat and only the rugged stability of your velosteam prevents it from toppling over: in your current state you would be quite unable to right it again.

Once at the house, you collapse against the door, where Earl Brigg's footmen find you and bring you inside. The Earl insists that you are treated with the best medicines, the most up-to-date treatments and fed with the most nourishing food and as a result it is not long before you are back on your feet: fighting fit, although somewhat scarred and maybe rather more cautious as well.

Replace each **wound** on your **Adventure Sheet** with a **scar**, rolling two dice for each one and on a score of 11 or 12, converting that into an **intimidating scar (RUTH+1)**.

The Earl warns you before you set out again. "You risk much, my friend. You must consider how you will eventually need to leave this way of life. No-one lives forever. You should settle down in comfort - find an estate of your own where you can live in comfort and peace."

Leave the Earl's care...   **313**

❧ 329 ❧
"I believe that, unknowingly, the previous owners of this place were fascinated by knowledge - particularly secret knowledge. And secrecy has a great deal of power. We need not fear knowledge, but we cannot worship it. God himself is known to us in Christ and yet beyond our comprehension."

He prays once more. As he does, the light in the lantern flickers and then burns more brightly. "That should be the last," he says. "Let's return to the sunlight."

Turn to...   **416**

❧ 330 ❧

You open the regulator and let a little more steam into the pistons: the Ferguson answers immediately and smoothly accelerates up the slope into the hills. A kite, sailing overhead, scans the roadside for prey. Steep-sided pastures and fields flash by and the road climbs on. Note passage number **550** and roll two dice to see what you encounter:

Score 2-5 A rumbling transporter...   **209**
Score 6-8 An empty road...   **3**
Score 9-12 A coal board wagon...   **223**

❧ 331 ❧

The Constable snores messily, so you prop him against the hedge and rifle through his pockets. You find a **silver ring**, a **Constable's whistle**, and **3s** in coins. You could also take his **sabre (PAR 6)** if you want.

He makes a ridiculous sight, sleeping there with his helmet askew. Perhaps one of his own will find him - or one of the many enemies the Constables have made amongst the common people.

Ride on towards Wargrave...   **418**

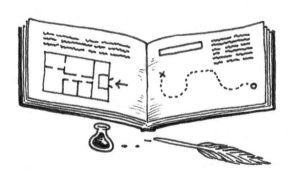

❧ 332 ❧

Pausing for a moment on the bridge, you see the smooth surface of the water broken by a massive pike. Its long jaw splashes above the water for a moment as it snatches at a duckling, then it flips its tail and dives into the murky depths of the water. Gain the codeword *Bitten*.

Ride straight to the French Horn...   **358**
Enter Sonning...   **91**
Head on your way towards the Bath Road...   **589**

❧ 333 ❧

If you have the codeword *Bust*, turn to **986** immediately.

The badger's trail weaves beneath the wire fence and through a thick growth of docks, grasses and teasels before bringing you to the edge of the reservoir itself. Signs marked with the Coal Board insignia stand near the entrance, near the keeper's lodge and the now-quiet steam-pump, but at your end of the compound are merely badger-signs, trimmed grass and a low brick wall.

Lay an explosive charge... (**explosives**)   **1344**
Measure the reservoir's capacity...
          (**measuring line**)   **1366**
Return to the roadside...   **544**

❧ 334 ❧

The hop-pickers tell you about their seasonal work. "Oh, it's long days, but we get good wages currently. Have you heard about the trouble in Marlow? Wethered's couldn't get ingredients. And hops is up all round the country, general-like. On account of all the new breweries."

"A golden age, you could say," says one worker.

"If you fancy new-fangled flavours and all manner of silly over-hopping," growls an old-timer.

Join the hop-pickers for a while...   **382**
Head on to Stonor...   **430**

❧ 335 ❧

If you have a **Guildsman's medallion**, turn to **891** immediately. Otherwise, read on.

The tollman is suspicious. He looks you up and down skeptically and checks his blunderbuss is ready by the door.

"What news on the road, my friend?" you greet him cheerily.

"Little enough news. Same old transport business as ever. Coal Board came down though here to Nettlebed last week - tree fell east of Christmas Common and blocked the way there. But this is a private road and they hates to pay."

"Do all the guilds have to pay to use the road?"

"Not the Atmospheric Union. They loaned a lot of the grading equipment from the airfield, see, so they gets use of it."

Leave the tollman...   **3**

❧ 336 ❧

The revolutionaries beat you to a pulp and toss you into the undergrowth. They take all your **money** and **possessions**, but are particularly interested in the **leather satchel**, which you overhear them discussing as you slip into unconsciousness.

"Here it is, just like she said. Rider on a Ferguson velosteam and a small, heavy leather satchel. I wonder what's in it."

The sound of a blow to the head is heard. "Leave it, you fool. Comrade Feaver will skin you - and the rest of the cadre - if it's tampered with."

Turn to...   **999**

❧ 337 ❧

Here at Goring barrel-staves are being piled onto an open trailer ready to be taken to the cooper in Wallingford. Noisy repairs to under-carriages and linkage-chains make it hard to hear and you see a lot of the haulier's sign language flashing about. The Haulage Guild maintain a presence here but do not entirely dominate the yard yet: in fact, the River Guild are just as powerful in this riverside town. Helpfully, several engineers offer repairs here.

Repairs	To buy
per damage point	£3 4s

Look for honest work...   **1005**
Leave the yard...   **487**

❧ 338 ❧

☐

If the box is empty, put a tick in it and turn to **315** immediately. Otherwise, read on.

St Nicholas' church is cool and quiet. The window glass glows green and gold over the simple, un-adorned interior.

Sketch the church... (**sketchpad**)   **287**
Leave the church...   **977**

❧ 339 ❧

The road between Oxford and Wallingford is empty at this time of the evening. You ride on, passing only a few men and women on foot, returning to their homes after a long day of work.

Turn to...   **800**

❧ 340 ❧

If you have the codeword *Blabber*, turn to **241** immediately.

The smith at Turville is an overalled, middle-aged woman with a muscled and silent apprentice. Conversation about technical matters - the pressure in your boiler, the force of her power-hammer - is tolerated, but most of her responses are grunts. Until you get to talking about inventions, when she begins to open up and show her enthusiasm. She will build you all manner of things - as long as you can get her the parts. And of course she'll do what she can for your velosteam too.

Other items	To buy
winged harness	**roll of oiled silk, brass flange joint** and **£5**
sprung leg braces (NIM +3)	**binoculars, wire-cutters, ultra-tensed wire** and **punchcards (Habbukuk K)**

Velosteam Customisations	To buy
pump and filter	**£8**
double headlamp	**£9 9s**
gas pressuriser	**£10 4s**

Repairs	To buy
Per **damage point**	**£2**

Ask about **mechanical arms**...   **236**
Leave the forge...   **947**

❧ 341 ❧

A strange duo flag you down at the riverside. Two men - a grey-haired, top-hatted figure and a fat younger man - clutching jostling sacks full of stolen chickens want to cross to the other side to flee their pursuers.

Take them across the river...   **139**
Sail on by...   **495**

ᔥ 342 ᔤ

The airship continues its long and leisurely journey back to its port of departure. All the meantime you are kept chained in the hold, fed very little and treated most roughly. The **possessions** and **money** that you brought with you are confiscated, of course, and when you eventually return to Rotherfield Greys, the crew hand you over to the Constables.

Turn to...   **13**

ᔥ 343 ᔤ

You steam into Hambleden along the valley road. It used to be a pretty village, but shows the scars of bad management and emigration. One row of cottages stands gaunt and roofless: the church walls are cracked and rotten with damp.

Ride up to Hambleden Manor...	**372**
Follow the lane towards Heath Wood...	**232**
Ride south to Mill End...	**112**
Ride north towards Skirmett...	**991**

ᔥ 344 ᔤ

Maidensgrove is a tumble of cottages and a few larger houses standing high on the hilltop. The view down towards Stonor shows that progress has encroached as far as smoking chimneys and coal depots, but up here England is unchanged. The routes into the village are narrow and secret and few beyond the immediate area are even aware of the hamlet. There is one semi-public building - the Five Horseshoes - but that is really just a parlour adjoined to the village forge and smithy.

Enter the Five Horseshoes...	**760**
Take the track down to Pishill...	**370**
Take the route towards Bix...	**3**

ᔥ 245 ᔤ

The road passes through a common, largely open but dotted here and there with scrub. You pass a tumble-down farm on your right and a row of freshly-planted willows along the ditch.

If you have the codeword *Baggage*, turn to **50** immediately. Otherwise you continue on through the woods.

Continue on down the road...   **939**

ᔥ 346 ᔤ

You are shown into the conservatory where the eccentric Count Grey is poring over some watercolours. "You're looking for preferment? Or a word with the powerful? I'm happy to sponsor any lover of art. Tell me - do you draw? In my younger days I was working on quite a project, sketching the churches of the region, but I never finished it. It would still be nice to publish one day but I don't get out much at all now. Perhaps you would help me draw the final few?"

"You want me to sketch churches and in return you will help me get into polite society?"

"Yes, exactly. Here, show me what you can do."

Your grasp of perspective and shadow does not exactly excite Count Grey but he helps you with your powers of observation and promises that he will continue to tutor you if you return with a full sketchpad. "Here, take one of my empty ones," he says. Gain a **sketchpad** ☐ ☐ ☐.

Leave the house...   **158**

ᔥ 347 ᔤ

Here in the shadow of Caversham Hill, the road is thronged with a steady traffic. Choosing your target is about waiting for an isolated vehicle, so you must check the road in both directions constantly. Roll a dice to see what you encounter, adding 2 if you possess a pair of **binoculars** or **telescope**.

Score 2-5	Constables!	**9**
Score 6	A locobus...	**156**
Score 7-8	A haulier...	**1285**
Score 9+	A private steam carriage...	**103**

ᔥ 348 ᔤ

The Aston Flowerpot is a destination sportsman's pub. Although the rear parlour serves the men and women of the village and local farms, the servants of the local houses and few hauliers who come down to the ferry, most of the business is built on serving the needs of anglers come to enjoy the fabled fishing spots on this stretch of the Thames. The bar walls are loaded with glass cases of lugubrious-looking fish: pike, perch, carp, tench, all plaster-still and glass-eyed. Paintings of missed catches, retired bamboo rods and torn nets that have witnessed legendary struggles hang above: each is labelled with the name and the date of some real or exaggerated victory over a piscine gladiator.

In the parlour several anglers sit with their pots,

waving hands and discussing exactly how large the last big fish was. If you have a **large pike**, turn to **1003** immediately.

Buy a drink...	**221**
Buy a drink for the anglers... (**8s** and *Bitten*)	**827**
Leave the inn...	**280**

✎ 349 ✎

"I've no time to banter," you say, threateningly. You draw your weapons. "Now - give me everything of value."

She pales and strips off her jewellery. You grab her bag as well and are rewarded with the chinking of coin. "Be sure to tell all your friends," you say, "Of the attack of the Steam Highwayman."

Once the morris-men allow the carriage to go on its way, you split the proceeds. You can take the purse - containing **£6 8s** - or the jewellery - two **silver bracelets**, a fine **pocket watch**, a **silver necklace** and a **locket**. However, the woman's description means that you will be **Wanted by the Constables**, if you are not already.

"We know what to do with our share," laughs Goodman Butt. "It's off to the pub for us!"

Ride away...   **433**

✎ 350 ✎

It is more than brave - foolhardy, in fact - to return to the place you robbed. Your velosteam is recognised by a gateman and he fires his carbine. Roll a dice to see what results!

Score 1-2   Receive a **wound**
Score 3-4   Receive **two wounds**
Score 5-6   Receive a **wound** and a **damage point**

If your velosteam is now **beyond repair**, turn to **572**. If not, but you have **five wounds**, turn to **999** immediately. Otherwise you will need to turn about and make yourself scarce!

Turn to...   **864**

✎ 351 ✎

"Doesn't seem fair," whines the Baronet as he slumps into the mud. "I mean, you're bigger than me. If my footman were here..."

You may take **£7 1s** from his purse, a **top hat** and **silk scarf**. You will now be **Wanted by the Constables** unless you have a **mask**.

Turn to...   **noted passage**

✎ 352 ✎

How you have come to be advising a noble widow on a legal battle over her estate is a question indeed for a road-thief like yourself. Over crumpets and tea by the fire, Lady Pomiane tells you how the Earl of Macclesfield tricked her husband into an agreement that seemed to be a lease of the two most productive farms. She has been unable to get them returned and her estate suffers from the lack of rent. The paperwork is knotty, disorganised and all written in the densest legalese. You will have to make an INGENUITY roll of difficulty 14 to have any chance of unravelling the mess. You can add 1 to your roll for each level of **legal knowledge** you possess.

Successful INGENUITY roll!	**608**
Failed INGENUITY roll!	**638**

✎ 353 ✎

The spaniel becomes aware of your pursuit and puts on a burst of floppy-legged speed, barking indistinctly. It loops round and drops your black in an ornamental fishpond.

"Play on," shouts the Viscountess. "Now we'll see your mettle!"

Your strike does not clear the parapet, but the Viscountess is a stickler and will not permit you to lift or raise the ball by hand. Your opponents have little to stop them from clearing the field and soon the post is struck, the game is over and you have lost. Your partner is unimpressed and heads off to find better company while you squelch to your velosteam, to the laughter of the other guests.

Turn to...   **62**

✎ 354 ✎

You light the fuse of the purple flare (tick one of the boxes or remove it from your possessions) and fire it into the night sky. Fifteen minutes later, the throbbing of engines announces the approach of Captain Coke's airship. Flying low over the escarpment, it descends over the road and grapples come swinging down. Airship pirates clamber down on lines as well and begin to net and gather the wagon's goods.

Coke himself is lowered in a basket, his frock coat flapping in the wash of the mighty propellors. "Nice work," he says, looking at the cargo. This'll be worth a pretty penny. Meet me back at the hideout and I'll give you your share." Gain the codeword *Bragging*.

The pirates are quickly finished, taking even the wheels and linkages of the wagon and leaving just the heavy chassis. The airship ascends again and makes off into the night - as you must.

Ride away...   **noted passage**

✤ 355 ✤

You leave the bustle of Henley behind you, its narrow, freight-clogged streets, its ladies in hats and gentlemen in spats. The road is gloriously clear for the first stretch. Before long a turning to the village of Harpsden on your right appears.

Take the turning to Harpsden...	**494**
Ride on towards Sonning Bridge...	**682**
Ride towards Shiplake House...	
(*Caraway* or *Blended*)	**1091**

✤ 356 ✤

You return to your snare to find a bird with its foot trapped in the wire. As you are untangling it, you hear a heavy tread and turn to see a gamekeeper approaching, his shotgun at the ready. If you are the **Friend of Mr Sands**, turn to **269** immediately. If you have the codeword *Bestial*, turn to **225** immediately. Otherwise read on.

The keeper has you covered. "Leave that **pheasant**," he says. "It belongs to his Lordship. And you are nothing but a common thief. Get out before I pepper your sorry behind with shot."

Leave the wood quickly...   **600**

✤ 357 ✤

You give a short - and largely fabricated - interview, taking care not to give any details that will help your pursuers catch up with you. In the end, the journalists whistle with amazement. "This will please our readers no end! You wouldn't believe how many are

in awe of the Steam Highwayman! I can see the headline now!" Gain a **solidarity point** if you have fewer than twenty already.

Turn to...   **noted passage**

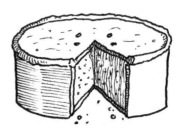

✤ 358 ✤

The French Horn is an upmarket destination eatery as well as an historic inn: the current owner has secured the services of a talented chef and is proud of his menu, served on riverside tables or in the long dining room. Local people eat and drink here in the parlour and they also get to enjoy the delicate flavours of crab cooked in white wine, venison pie and sole bonne femme.

You can take a room here for a payment of **£4**. If you choose to do so, remove the money from your purse and tick the option below. You will then be able to rest, recuperate and take care of your needs - but be careful of giving yourself away to the visitors. Many of them would leap at the chance of a reward for your capture.

Try the house ale...(**2s**)	**450**
☐ Go to your room...	**45**
Visit the kitchen...	**179**
Board your boat... (**moored at Sonning**)	**750**
Leave the French Horn...	**91**

✤ 359 ✤

You decide to wheel about, but the Constables have closed in behind you and are proceeding down the road steadily. They have chosen the position for their roadblock carefully: thick hedges prevent you heading cross-country. As you are deciding what to do next, a Sergeant and his squad appear and quickly immobilise your velosteam with an iron rod through the wheel spokes. With their weapons raised, you have little choice besides surrender.

Turn to...

❧ 360 ❧

Watlington is a small, brick-built town at the edge of the Oxford plain, where the rich farmlands meet the steep hills and woods of the Chilterns. It has a thriving market and the crossroads at its centre is frequently lined with engine-towed stalls selling produce, grain, industrial supplies, worked wood, coal, cloth and every commodity needed for life here. Several tall brick chimneys tell their own story of engines built to pump water out from beneath the hill, to hammer out iron sheets or to cut straw into bales. The Freight Yard is packed with busy men and women ordering and organising their loads, clutching the machine-tickets that organise their cargoes and overseeing several dozen labourers hauling the cargo.

Peruse the market and the shops...	106
Investigate the Freight Yard...	190
Visit the Carriers Inn...	934
Leave the town...	637

❧ 361 ❧

"My story?" Father Patrick smiles. "It is not my story that draws you here. It is His story, you know." He nods to the hanging crucifix. "But He invites us in, so if you wish, I will tell you why I am here."

Father Patrick was born on a tiny Melanesian isle some forty years previously. After a missionary's visit, the islanders abandoned their ancestor-worship for the Christian faith and he desired, of all things, to become a teacher of the Bible. He was chosen to travel back to London and studied theology, but before he could return to his own people, he was required to minister in an English parish under the watchful eye of the area Arch-Deacon. "They wish to see that I behave properly. That my theology is sound. Well, I know that my Lord has called me back to Melanesia. But his time is not yet."

"I want to confess my sins..."	261
"How can I help the people?"	279
"The Constables pursue me. How can I be free?"	385
Leave the church...	3

❧ 362 ❧

You crash to the ground from the first floor window. A sharp pain shoots up your leg - is that a fracture? The commotion attracts interest - a shout and a face at the glass. You haul yourself up and drag yourself away to the cover of the trees. Gain **two wounds** and if you now have **five wounds**, you must turn to **999** immediately.

Head towards Whitchurch...	749
Take the road to Cane End...	807
Steam north towards Cray's Pond...	577

❧ 363 ❧

An overturned carriage lies at the roadside. An anxious gentleman and his driver are trying to help someone out. If you have a GALLANTRY score of 6 or higher, read on. If not, he will have nothing to do with you and you must turn to **55** immediately.

When you offer to help, the gentlemen looks at you carefully before nodding his head. "My daughters are inside. Help us to shift the carriage."

With a few heavy shoves and a rope from your velosteam's tow-ring, you pull the carriage upright. The two young girls inside are shocked but not badly hurt. The gentleman thanks you and gives you £1 15s and a **silver ring** for your trouble.

Ride on...	793

❧ 364 ❧

Branches whip past as you lean into the corners of the twisting lanes. You break out onto the wide road and swerve around a lumbering Haulage Guild engine coming the other way. Speed, speed, speed is of the essence! Make a MOTORING roll of difficulty 12, adding 2 if you have a **reinforced boiler**!

Successful MOTORING roll!	411
Failed MOTORING roll!	1042

❧ 365 ❧

"Two crown for filling in potholes? That's a sight better than I'll make up in Woodcote. Sure I'll take your money." The man pockets the coins and sets about work. "When you come back down this way, you'll find a nice smooth way, I guarantee it." Gain the codeword *Bellyache*.

Ride on up the hill...	807

❧ 366 ❧

The road is quiet for a good while, but if you are patient, something will turn up. Sure enough, you hear something approaching down the hill. Note **passage number 306** and roll a dice to see what you encounter.

Score 1-2	A private steam carriage...	**103**
Score 3	The Haulage Guild...	**408**
Score 4	A farmer...	**1246**
Score 5	The Atmospheric Union...	**194**
Score 6	The Constables...	**1396**

❧ 367 ❧

A farm track leads you up from Stokenchurch to the high road along the hills. First steering around ruts and hollows where cattle have slipped, then over tree-roots and molehills, you turn left out of a farm gate to find the track wider but no firmer. Rain has left wide swathes of mud and you can read the tracks of several farm carts and iron-shod steam wagons too.

Stop in the wood...	**102**
Continue on to Christmas Common...	**617**

❧ 368 ❧

The woman slips out of the cage and you quickly make your way towards your velosteam. She mounts up behind you. "If you take me to the ferry at Aston," she says, "I can repay you. I have money."

You roll slowly between the trees, eventually mounting the woodbank and emerging on Aston lane. You come down towards the ferry, where she dismounts and hands you a **rusty key**. "This is for the box I keep at the Fleur de Lis," she says. "Take what's in it. I'm heading for Argentina." She climbs onto the ferry, smiles at the ferryman, whom she plainly knows, and is gone.

Return to Aston...	**280**

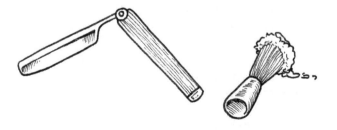

❧ 369 ❧

On the return flight you have a little more time to wander the airship and one night you have the opportunity to break into the Captain's strongroom. To do so is risky - there is nowhere to flee if you are caught - but could be very profitable indeed. If you have a **skeleton key**, turn to **325** immediately. Otherwise, make an INGENUITY roll of difficulty 14, adding 2 if you have any **lockpicks**, unless you wish to bypass this chance.

Successful INGENUITY roll!	**325**
Failed INGENUITY roll!	**533**
Stay on the straight and narrow path...	**266**

❧ 370 ❧

Pishill is little more than a few tiny cottages and their gardens clustered around a rambling old inn at the foot of the hill. There is a miniscule chapel and graveyard but this corner of the valley is really as secluded as possible. A few freight hauliers do come this way on their route from Henley to Watlington and Oxford, but the new, firmer roads through Stokenchurch or Nettlebed are now carrying much of the traffic.

Visit the Crown...	**763**
Ride down to Stonor...	**430**
Take the lane towards Eatonsfield Shaw...	**840**

❧ 371 ❧

The journalists are amazed as you tell them of all the people who have professed friendship with you. Of course, once they publish that information, you may find yourself in a spot of bother. Gain the codeword *Blabber*.

Turn to...	**noted passage**

❧ 372 ❧

The Bishop of Barnsbury owns Hambleden Manor and the surrounding estate, but he shows little care for the people of his domain. A broad iron chimney rises from the yard, indicating a new steam boiler of some size has been fitted - but to what purpose in a rural manor? A wisp of smoke rises from it but those of the house are cold and quiet. A couple of old servants pottering on the steps and in the yard keep the place from appearing entirely deserted.

If you have the codeword *Alacrity*, turn to **503** immediately.

Attempt a break-in...	**1506**
Talk to the servants...	**404**
Leave the house...	**343**

✺ 373 ✺

Eventually you approach Reading. The slopes of Caversham run down to the river, thickly wooded and green, while to the south lies the city itself, shambolic, noisy, ruinous and black. If you are **Wanted by the River Guild**, turn to **256** immediately.

Sail into Reading...	**495**

✺ 374 ✺

Earl Brigg smiles. "You're quite a player," he says. "An impressive show of decision-making." Once again you reflect on how different he is as a sportsman. You can learn a lot from a game like this: if your unimproved INGENUITY score is 10 or less, gain a point of INGENUITY. He also hands you a **bottle of champagne.**

Leave the house...	**62**

✺ 375 ✺

Fox takes the punchcards. "Ah yes, I know this set well," he says. "Excellent for cracking codes or encoding information. Also the best if you need to calculate anything to do with time." He looks through their alignment holes and carefully places them in the machine.

The computational engine begins to work its magic. Brass and steel spin and interlock. A welter of dancing, steam-powered armatures and dials interact in almost unimaginably complex ways. After some minutes, a punch begins chattering away at the other end. Fox grabs the folded output eagerly, then relaxes. "Much as I thought. These are the same conclusions I had reached manually. Aramanth A are not the cards I need." He takes them from the machine and returns them to you.

Turn to...	**157**

✺ 376 ✺

This wanted poster has been printed by the Constables. It describes a dangerous road-thief known to travel on a Ferguson velosteam who is wanted for robbery, murder and reckless driving. The reward is not flattering - but then the Constables are always remarkably stingy.

Return to the bar...	**2**
Leave the pub...	**702**
Mount your velosteam and leave town...	**586**

✺ 377 ✺

Samuel Driver is glad to have struck such a good deal for the quality flour and gives you a hearty handshake and a **baker's contract** to take to miller Fursham at Cobstone mill. "Sooner we get a delivery, the better," he says. "We'll not buy more from the Imperial Northern if we can help it."

Return to Goring...	**487**
Leave town...	**911**

✺ 378 ✺

The river bends westwards here and the road turns to follow it through the flattest part of the valley. A wood tumbles off the hillside and for a short distance the tarmac passes through a tall stand of mixed conifers, dark and over-bearing. Through the trees it is just possible to see the gouges of a quarry on the hillside, where the river, road and steep ground are all close together, but nothing can be heard from here.

Visit the quarry...	**392**
Continue up towards Henley Bridge...	**863**

✺ 379 ✺

The tall lady gives her enigmatic smile. "You are an interesting sort," she says. "Quite a diverse skill-set you have: croquet, dancing, jewel burglary..."

"Where is the Dervish's eye?" you counter. "You took it."

"I did," she replies. "But I don't have it any more. Someone stole it from me."

"Is that so?" you reply skeptically. "Set a thief to catch a thief, then."

"You only want it for its value, don't you?" she asks. "Well I have a much better use for it. Come and visit me in London and help me to regain it. I'll make it worth your while." She gives you **Lady Serene's Calling Card**, which gives the address of her Mayfair house and disappears into the crowd.

It is after she has left from sight that you realise your pockets have been picked. Remove any **money** or **jewellery** you were carrying.

Leave the house...   62

❧ 380 ❧

You are sat at your accustomed table at the Ferryman when a wild figure bursts into the parlour. It is a coachman, or a manservant, plainly of some important household and accustomed to receiving assistance of any kind asked for his Lord. He marches over to the landlord and interrupts a conversation over the bar.

"Medical aid. My master sends me to bring anyone able to tend wounds and treat broken bodies."

The assembled drinkers and regulars watch as the landlord looks around the room before nodding in your direction. "Ask yonder," he says, meeting your eyes, "Though you may get more than you ask for."

The servant comes over and looks down at you sceptically. "You? You are trained to care for the body?"

"Not at all trained. But capable and
  always willing."   1050
"I am not interested in your need."   529

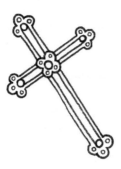

❧ 381 ❧

To rob the house, you will need to break in through a window, either using equipment like a **grappling iron** or **rope ladder**, or an exceptionally high NIMBLENESS score.

Attempt a break-in...   419
Leave it for now...   73

❧ 382 ❧

You join the hop-pickers' party and travel with them to the hop-fields. It takes two weeks' steady work to strip the hop-vines, but the weather is fine and you are happy to sleep out in the open with the other labourers. In doing so you learn much about the countryman's way of life, pick up several songs and dances from the evenings around the fire and even manage to earn some honest payment for your labour. Roll a dice to see what you are paid:

Score 1   **10s** and gain a level of **musicianship**
Score 2-4   **£1 8s** and a **pork pie**
Score 5   **£1 2s** and a **bottle of beehive stout**
Score 6   **£1 15s** but gain a **fever (NIM-1 ING-2)** from working in the hot sun

Return to Stonor...   260

❧ 383 ❧

North Stoke is a tiny, rural village with no wharf or quay. A row of mooring rings have been staked into the riverbank and most of them lie empty and unused. You find one beneath the shelter of two crazily-leaning willows and tie up. Mark **moored at North Stoke** on your **Adventure Sheet**.

Go ashore...   515

❧ 384 ❧

You pass Woodcote church where a group of ladies are washing down the parish locobus in preparation for an outing, and eventually you wind northwards up Red Lane. The road slopes towards the river valley but hides itself in a gully between hornbeam trees for part of its route. In the shade of the iron-grey branches you come to a spring gurgling out into the roadway.

Prepare an ambush here at the spring...   397
Ride on towards Wallingford...   860

❧ 385 ❧

"Be free of the Constables, you mean? Well while your number is known to them, you will always be on the run until your punishment is completed. Either you must find someone to pay for your crimes or you must change your number. That is the sort of thing a punch-card worker will have to do for you, like the man in Maidenhead or a rippler amongst the students in Oxford. I suppose you could always appeal to someone in power amongst the Constables in Wallingford too. But I doubt if any of these will leave you feeling free like you wish."

Leave the church...   3

❧ 386 ❧

At first you offer the old man a few shillings, but his pale face turns cherry-red with indignation and rage. "What? After the many hours a-crafting I put in to them? Not to count all the eels I'll have lost while I plaits me some more."

Eventually he accepts two golden guineas for his loss, and once the money is in his pouch he changes his tune abruptly, humming and whistling with satisfaction. He notices your velosteam under its tarpaulin and quickly puts two and two together.

"I see, I do. You ain't no bargee, with gold like that in your ticket drawer. You'se is the Steam Highwayman. Well, robbin' the rich and redistributin' the wealth seems mighty fair to me. I always heard you was a good 'un, and now I knows it. You could have just steamed on by, but you wanted to see old Henry right. So God bless you, says I." Gain a **solidarity point**.

You put him ashore and steam on upriver.

Turn to...   950

❧ 387 ❧

The new church at Bix is built Paxton-style: elegant prefabricated ribs of iron have been raised over a solid paving and the bays filled in with glass and local brick. It has an airiness unlike any other church building in the region.

The vicar here is a smiling and curly-haired Melanesian man called Father Patrick. How he came to minister in an iron church in the wooded hills of a land on the opposite side of the world from his birthplace must be a story indeed.

Speak to Father Patrick...   839
Give a gift to the poor...   (1s)   814
Leave the chapel...   3

❧ 388 ❧
□
If the box above is empty, tick it now and turn to **783**. If it is already ticked, read on.

Constables and townspeople are here to see the

hanging of another member of Captain Coke's crew. This is not a good place for you to stay! How long until you are recognised and hands are laid upon you?

Ride into the wood...   **401**
Head towards High Moor Cross...   **939**
Steam to Grey's Court...   **158**
Take the road towards Cane End...   **455**

❧ 389 ❧

The lady reaches around her door and reappears with a large and antiquated blunderbuss. "Be off with you, villain!" she replies fearlessly. "Before I set the dogs on you."

You retreat out of sight, but still have an opportunity to try and carry out the Earl's mission.

Set the place ablaze...   **40**
Leave a threatening note...   **409**

❧ 390 ❧

You are now **moored at Mill End**. Note this on your **Adventure Sheet**.

Turn to...   **112**

❧ 391 ❧

"What a lovely set of punchcards," says Fox. "I'm unfamiliar with this programme - wherever did you get it? Well, let's put plenty of tolerance in the system and see what it can do."

A hiss of steam announces the arrival of power into the engine and several large clocksprings are wound into tight snailshell coils. Then with a tug on the initialisation lever, the machine begins to flick through the punchcards and set itself whirring in its unreadable brass dance.

Eventually an output flag is raised and Fox links the machine to a drawing arm. The mechanical pencil details the arrangement of machinery that will help the new organ design read and interpret music. "Ah yes," says Fox. "I can see it now. These cards contain a powerful subroutine for testing alternate options - a machine-driven creativity, if you will. I expect it could be very helpful in a design process or in generating new ideas." He looks at the designs a little more closely. "And very helpful here, but I think still not quite what I need." He returns the punchcards to you.

Turn to...   157

❧ 392 ❧

If you have the **quarry lease**, turn to **1108** immediately. If not but you have the codeword *Breaker*, turn to **1119**. Otherwise, read on.

You unhook a chain and ride into the quarry: it has been worked recently but the tools and machinery stand quiet. At the sound of your approach a foreman appears from a shed and then slumps in disappointment.

"I thought you might be Mister Briggs," he says, "The leaseholder. But he's caused us to stop cutting and all the quarrymen are out of work. I'm only here on a penny a day, waiting for a re-opening."

"What do you mean?" you ask. With their own little quayside across the road, machinery standing about and quarrymen available in the nearby villages, this place should be profitable.

"Ain't in his plan to be working now," says the foreman, "And he don't care if we're simply waiting. I don't know if he'll open it up again - he said he was done with the place, would sell the lease if he could find a buyer. Going to be an auction in Henley."

There is little you can do here.

Ride north...	**863**
Head south to Wargrave...	**418**

❧ 393 ❧

The road to Wargrave stretches across the meadow, tight against the rising ground of Remenham Hill on your left. Your lime-lantern reflects off the early-morning river fog, picking out grotesque shapes of pollarded trees and stray cows. Roll a dice to see what you encounter:

Score 1-2	A puncture...	**543**
Score 3-4	A boy herding cows...	**562**
Score 5-6	A drunken Constable...	**647**

❧ 394 ❧

Leaving Bix behind you and steaming on uphill, the trees flash by. There is a fine straight here leading up towards Nettlebed, an important and prosperous little town, and the road is well-kept and firm beneath your wheels.

Prepare an ambush here...	**470**
Continue on up to Nettlebed...	**791**

❧ 395 ❧

Grabbing your pack, you dive for the window just as the door splinters beneath the boots of the Constables. One grabs at your heels as you are climbing over the sill and tears at your clothing, but you fall down the ivy and into the courtyard. Your Ferguson is warm and ready, but the Constables are closing the gates to the yard. Will you hand yourself in to the authorities, or make a MOTORING roll of difficulty 12 (adding 4 if you have a **ramming beak**) and smash through the gates?

Successful MOTORING roll!	**49**
Failed MOTORING roll or surrendered...	**13**

❧ 396 ❧

How did Deadman's Lane get its name? Perhaps because it leads, indirectly, to the hanging ground at Gallowstree Common. Or perhaps for other, older, less rational reasons. Steaming over the rutted chalk surface, you pass beneath uncounted yew and holly trees, stretching out over the roadway to cover the sky. The distinctive smell of rotting yew needles fills your nostrils, even through the reek of lubricating oil and coalgas. For a moment, the figure of a man appears between the trees, holding out stretched arms, but it is quickly hidden by the gloomy trunks.

Investigate the figure...	**907**
Continue downhill to Whitchurch...	**749**

❧ 397 ❧

You conceal yourself and prepare your weapons. Note **passage number 306** and roll a dice to see what you encounter.

Score 1-2	A private steam carriage...	**136**
Score 3	The parish locobus...	**440**
Score 4	A local haulier...	**1285**
Score 5	The Haulage Guild...	**408**
Score 6	The Constables...	**1396**

❧ 398 ❧

The dog proceeds inside the open summerhouse and drops the ball on the brick floor, losing interest when it sees a dropped parasol. You must play the ball from its unsteady position. It will take a strong blow to send it over the step, across the gravel path, through the shrubbery and return it to the lawn. Make a NIMBLENESS roll, adding 3 if you have a steam fist or a mechanical arm.

Score <11...	**596**
Score 11 to 15...	**553**
Score 16+...	**610**

❧ 399 ❧

A large and bossy woman with a maid, a chaperone and a footman is travelling in style to impose herself upon relatives somewhere in Hampshire. You are able to relieve her of some of her accoutrements, including a purse of **£3 18s**, an **ivory fan** and a **wide-brimmed hat**. The maid has a **silver ring** that you can take if you like. You will now be **Wanted by the Constables** unless you have a **mask**.

Turn to...	**noted passage**

❧ 400 ❧

You coax your velosteam up the hill in the summer sunshine, rising up to where a soft breeze stirs the grasses. The sails of Cobstone mill are still, and the orchard is hung with early fruit. Ibstone is a short distance ahead along the crest.

Investigate the windmill...	**628**
Continue on the road...	**977**

❧ 401 ❧

The track into the wood winds between brambles laden with ripening berries and overgrown hawthorn bushes. The ground shows no sign of other wheels, iron or pneumatic, only a few hoofmarks and horse-shoe prints. Then, as you continue uphill, you come to a bank, a ditch and another bank: it is an ancient earthwork on a long-since wooded hilltop.

Investigate the earthwork... (*Benign*)	**147**
Set up a camp here...	**832**
Visit your camp... (*Before*)	**962**
Steam onto Gallowstree Common...	**600**
Head for Woodcote...	**488**
Steam to Stoke Row...	**457**

❧ 402 ❧

You are not far from Osney Lock when you are flagged down by a University umpire. "Keep to the far bank," he says. "The team are out!"

Several rowing eights are on the water. At the retort of a gun, they lean into their oars and propel themselves downstream. One boat is clearly ahead, its crew wearing red caps and coxed by a thin, straw-headed fellow.

You plough on steadily behind them and soon meet the crews returning to their boathouses. The red-capped crew are singing lustily, plainly satisfied with their victory.

Now roll a dice to see how the remainder of your journey passes.

Score 1-3	Engine trouble...	**983**
Score 4-6	A quiet voyage...	**719**

❧ 403 ❧

You open the window and whistle for your mate. He emerges on the deck of your barge, moored directly beneath you. Over the window sill and a leap into the water! You plunge from your room just as the Constables smash through the door behind you. Your mate has the engine started and hauls you from the river onto the moving deck. In the morning mist you may be able to get away, if you are quick about it.

Unfortunately your dive has ruined any **paper items** in your possession: remove any letters, invitations, calling cards, books or similar.

Head through the open lock...	**113**
Steam downriver...	**882**

❧ 404 ❧

You hide your weapons before approaching the servants and asking about the Bishop.

"Oh the Bishop is a darling man. So generous. Sent a cake to my Maisie last winter. There's wicked folk as curse him but they don't know him like I do."

"When will he return?"

"He's a busy man. Not for some time," replies the old housekeeper, before her husband jags her with an elbow.

"But I see your furnace is lit... I'm a salesman for efficient, smokeless fuels." The quick lie smooths the momentary suspicion rising in their eyes.

"It's a fearful 'ungry boiler," replies the white-haired footman. "And never to go out. Had to buy in wood from Fingest and set the keeper a-coppicing out of season. But the Bishop knows what he's calculating."

Return at night and break in...	1506
Leave the house...	343

֍ 405 ֎

Outside the Bull and Butcher there is indeed a large red Herefordshire bull with a ring in his nose, fenced from the highway but very interested in any passer-by. Of a butcher there is, mercifully for him, no sign.

Inside the cool shade is a haven for the agricultural labourers of the village. Several games of backgammon are in process and the local ale is poured out in heavy clay pots. In the garden sit a group of men dressed in white and bedecked with tiny, tinkling bells. They are morris-dancers, practicing for a local celebration in the way they know best. After all, dancing requires a good deal of energy and the body must be nourished with plenty of beer to dance well.

Order a drink... (2s)	101
Talk to the morris-dancers...	122
Leave the parlour...	947

֍ 406 ֎

The market at Stokenchurch fills the green with noise and movement. As well as the stalls there are several fine shops that specialise in machinery, agents for freight and agricultural produce, a large bakery and the furniture workshops.

Food and Drink	To buy	To sell
bird's eggs	4s	2s
rabbit	2s	1s
pheasant	4s	3s
deer carcass	£2	£2
wheel of cheese	£1 2s	£1
Clothing	To buy	To sell
mask	4s	-
lace shawl	£1 5s	15s
silk scarf	-	15s
cloak	£1	-
Jewellery	To buy	To sell
locket	-	6s
pocket watch	£3	£1 18s
Tools	To buy	To sell
rope	4s	2s
snare	2s	1s
net	6s	4s
shovel	8s	6s
axe	8s	6s
wirecutters	12s	8s
adjustable wrench (ENG+1)	£1 8s	18s
welding tools	£2 2s	£1
grappling iron	12s	8s
measuring line	10s	6s
brass flange joint	8s	4s
high pressure valve	18s	10s
lockpicks	6s	2s
Weapons	To buy	To sell
billhook (PAR 2)	-	10s
club (PAR 2)	4s	-
sabre (PAR 3)	£1 5s	8s
blunderpistol (ACC 6)	£4	£2
Other items	To buy	To sell
sketchpad ☐ ☐ ☐	3s	1s
bolt of cloth	-	15s
fine clock	-	£6 3s
pair of golden candlesticks	-	£2 14s

Visit the baker... (Cobstone flour)	892
Leave the market...	308
Leave Stokenchurch...	660

֍ 407 ֎

You are judged unworthy of any interest from ranking officers and simply thrown into a cell in Wallingford Gaol, where you are kept for several months in appalling conditions. Food is hard to come by and you are forced to spend all your **money** and barter all your **possessions** away to scrape together enough to eat. In the end, you are released back into the world with a stern warning. "Next time you'll be hung! Change your ways!"

Fortunately your velosteam is returned to you. Remove any **Wanted** statuses, since your sentence has been recorded as completed, and you are issued with a **Convict's pass**.

Leave the town...	742
Look around Wallingford...	270

❧ 408 ❧

The hauliers frequenting these roads may well be members of the powerful Haulage Guild - an enemy indeed! The Guild dominate the Imperial roads through their freight tolls and rules. Independent-minded men and women looking to make their own career on the road have a hard time making ends meet, even without the threat of robbery.

The steamer you see approaching does bear the livery of the Guild. It is towing a long train of wagons, probably carrying building materials, goods and deliveries between businesses. Make a RUTHLESSNESS roll to see whether the engine is guarded, adding 2 if you are **Wanted by the Haulage Guild** and 1 for each of your other **Wanted** statuses.

Score <13   **731**
Score 13+   **717**

❧ 409 ❧

You tear a leaf from your notebook and pen a note, warning Lady Pomiane that unless she backs down from her suit, she will suffer punishment. Her house is being watched.

Make a RUTHLESSNESS roll of difficulty 14, adding 3 to your roll if you wish to kill one of her dogs to underline your point.

Successful RUTHLESSNESS roll!   **720**
Failed RUTHLESSNESS roll!   **754**

❧ 410 ❧

You cross Reading Bridge, stubbornly refusing to give way to a haulier and receiving an angry curse in response. The sooner you are on the open road, the better.

Ride west along the riverbank...   **803**
Take the Henley road east...   **726**
Head up into the hills...   **609**
Follow the Bath Road into the West...
Princes of the West 209

❧ 411 ❧

You manage to gain a good lead on your pursuers and then, once over a crest, turn aside into the woods. You dismount and take great care to rearrange the bushes behind you before quietening your steaming machine behind a hazel coppice.

The Constables thunder past, bells ringing. You have avoided them - for now - but they will soon be back. You had better make off and lie low.

Ride off...   **178**

❧ 412 ❧

"Come here boy," you call firmly. Make a GALLANTRY roll of difficulty 12, adding 2 for each level of **animal friendship** you possess.

Successful GALLANTRY roll!   **523**
Failed GALLANTRY roll!   **353**

❧ 413 ❧

Somehow you manage to cobble together something for the passengers to eat during the remainder of the flight, but dish after dish is returned to the kitchen with complaint after complaint. Perhaps you are not cut out for this role after all, and perhaps you have less culinary skill than you thought.

Turn to...   **369**

❧ 414 ❧

Remove the **leather satchel** from your **Adventure Sheet**. You pass it into their keeping and the leader of the group chuckles greedily. "Well, Comrade Feaver will be pleased, won't she? As for you, Comrade, I think you've made the right decision."

There is nothing to be gained from riding to Manchester now. You have made a long and tiring journey to deliver the components into the hands of a group of revolutionaries. Gain the codeword *Bested*.

Return to Oxford...   **688**

❧ 415 ❧

"You do not have to help me. I am an adult woman and I have made my own choices. Savings, my life's direction, these are my responsibilities." The teacher nears tears and gets up to rearrange the few lumps of coal that smoulder in her fireplace.

"No-one can live without help - or friends," you reply.

She turns around. "This is what I dream of. Standing on the promenade deck of a great airship, wrapped in a warm fur coat, a ticket in my hand for a round-the-world-tour. Why, I teach these girls the wonders of Ancient Greece, Babylon, the Holy Land, but I have never seen them myself. I only want a year for myself. Then I would be able to give more than ever."

How small the barriers to adventure are: for this woman, **fifteen guineas** and a **fur coat** are enough to convince her to leave her life and travel around the world. You get her to tell you more of the places she longs to see and then leave, late that night, hers the only lit window in the whole school.

Ride towards Henley...	**1251**
Head to Lower Assendon...	**163**
Steam east along the Thames valley...	**62**

❧ 416 ❧

Something has changed about the Grotto and its grounds, but it is hard to say precisely what. The Shrubhams are grateful and Father Patrick advises them to continue in prayer for their new house. He climbs onto the velosteam and you set off again back towards Bix. It is certainly an experience to think about.

Deliver Father Patrick...	**3**

❧ 417 ❧

The night falls and with it an unseasonable chill. Mounted on your steam-powered steed however, you are warm and ready. You ride on through the night and eventually, late next morning, come down towards the publisher's address. You beat on the door. A man with slick, macassared hair emerges and takes a look at the **tightly tied parcel**. He snorts.

"I don't know why this chap insists on sending us his nonsense. Nobody wants to read his stories about a lot of fairies and goblins. A lot of juvenile fantastic twaddle, that's all. No chance of ever making any money. Still, here it is."

Hand him the **tightly tied parcel**...	**481**
Find another publisher...	**524**
Keep the parcel...	**557**

❧ 418 ❧

If you are **Wanted by the Constables**, turn to **866** immediately.

Wargrave is a large village straggling from the waterside wharves up onto the hillside to the east. Several freight businesses transfer river-freight to road wagons here, which make the run down to the Bath Road and then west across the realm. A brick inn called the George and Dragon has a river-side terrace where all manner of people come to take their ease and a small run of shops provides goods for the local people. A D-class telegraph tower stands on the hillside, built to flicker its messages to Henley and Caversham hill.

Enter the George and Dragon...	**668**
Visit the market...	**323**
Take a look at the Telegraph Tower...	**177**
Take the road north...	**378**
Head south to the Bath Road...	**589**
Board your boat... (if you are **moored** here)	**131**

❧ 419 ❧

Gain the codeword *Brazen*. You make your attempt from the rear of the house, scaling the brickwork with the aid of a tough ivy stem. Make a NIMBLENESS roll of difficulty 15, adding 1 if you have a **grappling iron** and 2 if you have a **rope ladder.**

Successful NIMBLENESS roll!	**318**
Failed NIMBLENESS roll!	**362**

❧ 420 ❧

The track beside the church is narrow and uneven. It has certainly never seen a heavy steam-vehicle. It leads steeply uphill, beside a field verdant with beet-tops and under the outstretched boughs of a wood. Leaf-litter covers much of the way and horse-droppings indicate the preferred mode of transport up here.

Continue to Maidensgrove...	**344**

❧ 421 ❧

You steam down a winding hedged track known as Dog Lane, catching the sound of harp music from a hovel nearby, bump over the tussocks of grass at Peppard Common and find yourself back on the road again. A short distance ahead is the execution ground at Gallowstree Common and the dense Wyfold Wood. Beyond them, to the south-west, lies the village of Cane End and the main road between Reading and Wallingford.

Steam on to Gallowstree Common...	**600**
Head non-stop for Cane End...	**807**

❧ 422 ❧

Before long you are able to gather everybody on his Lordship's list that lives locally. They air their grievances and quickly you realise that they are more than ready to vote for him again. They really have little grasp of the power of their choice. Beer and bacon will sway them - but you will need to make a considerable outlay to impress them. Otherwise there is always the power of fear...

Bribe them to vote for Sir M'Dow... (**£20**)	74
Intimidate them into supporting Sir M'Dow...	87
Talk to them about the other candidate...	
(*Betterment*)	109
Leave them for now...	529

❧ 423 ❧

Remove the **letter of introduction**, which you pass to the footman who answers the impressive clockwork doorbell. After waiting for more than half an hour, he reappears and leads you around the side of the house to a garden, where his Lordship is busy spreading manure onto his cabbage patch. He pauses, wipes his hands on the side of his filthy woollen jacket, and plucks your letter from his pocket.

"Interesting reading, this. You seem like a capable and interesting sort of person. Well, I might be able to use you - as long as you can take instruction. I'm running for re-election to Parliament shortly and I need the local voters to play their part. There are only nineteen of them, for historical reasons. Last time they were perfectly amenable - and they should have been, considering I gave them a side of bacon and a barrel of beer each, but recently somebody has been stirring them up and they seem to want to vote somebody else into my seat."

"Do you want me to intimidate them?"

"Goodness, no. Just make them see sense!" He gives you the **Whitchurch ballot list**. It details exactly who has the right to vote in the tiny borough - largely villagers in Whitchurch, but also the old Duke of Forebury, who lives in Mapledurham Manor. "He's never been a problem - been happy for me to represent the borough. But his daughter has come of age. Of course she doesn't have the vote, but she does seem to have ideas." He looks you in the eye. "I think you could do with a powerful friend. Do this for me and I'll not only pay you, but I'll see that you're pardoned for any crimes you've committed - or are accused of committing. You'll no longer be wanted by anyone."

"I'll make sure they vote the way you want them to, your lordship."	618
"Voters should be able to choose independently."	527

❧ 424 ❧

You take up position in the centre of the road, ensuring your silhouette will advertise your fearsome presence. Make a RUTHLESSNESS roll of difficulty 13 to scare the driver into halting the carriage.

Successful RUTHLESSNESS roll!	715
Failed RUTHLESSNESS roll!	782

❧ 425 ❧

Your shot is close - too close! It strikes the driver in the shoulder, who immediately lurches to the side, slamming on the brakes. The long-nosed engine slews to a halt and the door of the passenger compartment flies open.

"You blackguard scoundrel son of a working dog!" A tall and violently angry man launches himself at you, drawing his sword as he comes. "I'll pay you back for what you've done to Masterson!" You must fight!

Earl Macclesfield Weapon: **rapier (PAR 4)**
Parry:	8
Nimbleness:	4
Toughness:	3

Victory!	516
Defeat!	999

❧ 426 ❧

The road out of Nettlebed is firm and dry: iron posts at its side inform you that you are travelling on the property of the Henley Turnpike Company. Whoever they are, they employ good road-builders. You overtake several heavy wagons setting out from Nettlebed and several more steadily climbing uphill - all making a good speed up the gradient. At a narrowing in the road you find a thicket that might hide you from on-coming traffic, should you wish to surprise anyone here.

Prepare an ambush here...   **470**
Ride on to Bix...   **3**

❧ 427 ❧

The sun beats down on the riverbank, warming the apple trees with their ripening fruit and the plashy cow-mires where the cattle drink. Dismounted, you stroll along for a short distance beneath the willows and spy a path that will lead towards the bridge just a little further along.

Return to Aston...   **280**
Go fishing... (**fishing line**)   **436**
Head to Henley Bridge...   **863**

❧ 428 ❧

The clerk flat on the road surface, you are free to rob the civil servant. You can take **ten guineas in bank-notes**, a **silver ring** and a **bottle of chloroform** from him.

Turn to...   **noted passage**

❧ 429 ❧

It will be difficult to enter Christmas Common without attracting the interest of the Guild: they are looking for you, after all. As you ride up the road, a signal flashes on the massive Telegraph tower ahead of you and you hear shouts and steam rising in the trees around. Which way will you turn?

Observe the tower...
    (**telescope** or **binoculars**)   **185**
Ride south-west along the hill-top...   **110**
Head down Watlington Hill...   **216**
Take the lane to Northend...   **595**
Drive north-east towards Stokenchurch...   **102**

❧ 430 ❧

The village of Stonor is dominated by the vast residence of the Stonor family just to the north. It cannot be seen from the cottages and barns but almost every family works for the 'Big House' directly or indirectly, and the Estate Manager is certainly the most influential person hereabouts. Nobody has the time or capital to start their own business in the village, whether a poor alehouse or a spinning mill, and it seems that things will stay that way.

Talk to the villagers...   **1070**
Ride up Stonor Park drive...   **888**
Head south towards Henley...   **208**
Steam up towards Pishill...   **370**
Steer for Turville and Northend...   **856**

❧ 431 ❧

You leave Ibstone behind you and cross fields to the south, passing a tall barn with freshly-painted doors. A workman with a burgundy cap at a steam machine pauses to watch you pass, then goes back to tossing straw into the hopper. You brake hard as the slope leads you down into a wood, then emerge onto Turville holloway, twenty yards from Turville Valley Farm, where more fresh paint and a Grant model traction engine parked in the yard tell you that someone hereabouts is prospering.

Head west along the holloway...   **120**
Ride into Turville...   **947**

❧ 432 ❧

You manage to calm the old eel-fisher with apologies and flowery expressions of your regret. He smirks. "Well, they was old ones, anyway. Haven't caught a single thinfish down here for months."

You invite him aboard for a brew with something fortifying in it and he tells you all about the mysterious life of the eel: how they appear, almost magically, in any damp place at the full of the moon. Ditches, wet cellars, even low meadows. Then they're drawn towards the water, where they congregate on gravel banks and clean themselves against the stones. "Many's the mystery about the old eel," he says as he sips his hot drink. "Many indeed."

He gives you a **Bargee's Badge** on a faded ribbon. "I've no use for this any more. It can take you a long way, that can."

Next morning you unmoor the boat and steam back out onto the main channel.

Turn to...   **950**

✖ 433 ✖
☐ ☐ ☐ ☐ ☐

If any of the boxes above are empty, tick one. If all five are already ticked, erase the ticks and turn to **757** immediately.

After your ambush it would be prudent to put some distance between yourself and the scene of your crime. Already the alarm may have been raised by a far-sighted Telegraph officer on a tall tower. Where will you head? Do you have a plan for your eventual getaway and a hideout where you know you can safely mend a damaged velosteam and bandage wounds?

Towards Mill End...	**112**
Up to Nettlebed...	**791**
To Cane End...	**807**
To Sonning Bridge...	**690**

✖ 434 ✖
You stop your velosteam at some distance and ready your weapon. Make an ACCURACY roll of difficulty 12.

Successful ACCURACY roll!	**148**
Failed ACCURACY roll!	**1414**

✖ 435 ✖
The houses, workshops and warehouses of Wallingford straggle down to the river's edge, each with its own timber quay or jetty. A pall of smoke hangs over the town, through which at least one church spire can be seen, but never more than one at a time. On the river-front, hard-faced rivermen loop rope and chain around their parcels and tarpaulins. A chute dispenses wheat, unsacked, straight into the belly of a long barge with a rush. Interestingly, nobody is buying beer, malt or hops: supplying the brewery trade is the Haulage Guild's prerogative around here.

	To buy	To sell
Charcoal	£13	£12
Furniture	-	£27
Machinery	-	£25
Pottery	-	£20
Cotton	-	£4
Woollen cloth	£5	£4
Coal	£14	£13
Beer	-	-
Wheat	£2	-
Malt	-	-
Frozen meat	-	-
Ice	-	£10

The Thames continues north: the long journey upriver to Oxford will take you through a series of eight locks before reaching that city of learning and machinery.

Moor here...	**915**
Steam downriver...	**987**
Take the long journey to Oxford...	
(**£1 10s** or **Bargee's Badge**)	**485**

✖ 436 ✖
Now this will call for patience. You cast your line out into the stream and settle down to wait. And wait. A few twitches occasion as weed streams past the hook and you have to check your bait several times. If you are prepared for a long day at the waterside, you will have a much better chance of catching something. Roll two dice, adding 1 if you possess a **pork pie**, 3 if you have a **picnic hamper** and another 3 if you possess **Marvin's Lure**.

Score 1-11   Catch nothing
Score 12+   Catch a **large pike**

Steam to Aston...	**280**
Steam towards Henley...	**863**

✖ 437 ✖
It is nearly dusk when you hear gunshots echoing across the water. The mate looks at you for reassurance, then steers ahead as you nod and ready your weapons.

Around a bend in the river you come across a

skiff of water-rats boarding a heavy River Guild barge. They are struggling with the crew with swords, gaffs and clubs. Pistols are discharged in the chaos and the boat is veering across the river. The fight is right in the balance.

Come to the bargee's aid...	**687**
Help the river-pirates...	**282**

❧ 438 ❧
Make a RUTHLESSNESS roll of difficulty 9 to scare the baker into making an offer for the flour.

Successful RUTHLESSNESS roll...	**552**
Failed RUTHLESSNESS roll...	**418**

❧ 439 ❧
Your snare catches a **pheasant**. After calming it under your coat, a quick wrench of the neck leaves it limp and ready for the pot.

Turn to...	**600**

❧ 440 ❧
☐

If the box above is empty, tick it now and read on. If it is already ticked, erase the tick and turn to **1202** immediately.

"It's the Steam Highwayman!" shouts a child on the top deck, travelling with her mother to market. "Are we all going to be killed in our beds?"

The driver puts on the brakes and the locobus hisses to a stop. He has a long way to drive on his round from Wallingford to Nettlebed and Goring and he is not pleased to be held up. "What's the problem?" he asks. "Nobody's got anything to steal here!"

"I'll tell you what's thievery," says an angry, thin man. "The fares they're charging now! A real hero would make this here driver give us our money back!" There are cries of agreement.

Rob the passengers...	**621**
Chat with the passengers...	**1217**
Force the driver to return everyone's fare...	**1191**

❧ 441 ❧
The rickety bridge at Sonning may be your best chance of escape. If you can cross to the northern bank you will be able to hide in the woods north of the Henley road.

You steam down the Bath road, weaving around a Guild engine and its wagons, cutting the corner onto Sonning Lane and kicking up dust through the village. The Constables are close behind you.

The bridge is raised - but you can see a figure standing by the windlass. If you have **5** or more **solidarity points**, turn to **1311** immediately. Otherwise you will have to make a MOTORING roll of difficulty 12, adding 2 if you have a **gas pressuriser**, to make the jump!

Successful MOTORING roll!	**633**
Failed MOTORING roll!	**13**

❧ 442 ❧
You make it to Manchester but all the delays mean you have spent significantly longer than the two days you claimed to need. You deliver the **leather satchel** (remove it from your **Adventure Sheet**) but the clerk who takes it gives you **£5**, not the promised reward. "This is late," he says. "Production can't wait, you know."

You are forced to return through more heavy weather and eventually you near Oxford, filthy and worn out by your ride.

Turn to...	**688**

❧ 443 ❧
The first evening without Ramboutarde you serve a four-course dinner of grouse, souffle and rack of lamb, followed by an airship trifle. The next night you try something more exotic and create a terrine of goose with capers, a crocodile consomme and songbirds en croute. Several passengers send their compliments after the meal and you go from strength to strength, experimenting and creating dishes that delight and amaze.

After a particularly fine meal, you are invited to the saloon, where you meet a fat broker named Sir

Rodney Battle, who insists that you would find satis-faction in employment at his club in London, the Gu-berstein. He gives you his card: **Sir Rodney Battle's calling card**.

Turn to...   **369**

❧ 444 ☙

To reach Ibstone you first ride along the holloway to Turville Valley Farm, then turn right and cross the fields northwards. You steam on, past the barn, and find Ibstone common right in front of you. The vil-lages are barely a mile apart - yet how distant to these village folk!

Steam into Ibstone...   **977**

❧ 445 ☙

The brickworks is one of the biggest employers in Net-tlebed. It churns out stacks of machine-cut and coal-fired bricks from the excellent local clay, ready to be hauled away to Oxford, down to Goring wharf and wherever the Age of Steam is inspiring new buildings. The furnaces run night and day.

Address the workers... (**Member of the
    Compact for Workers' Equality**)   **1035**
Leave the brickworks...   **791**

❧ 446 ☙

You step to the edge of your cover and summon your most threatening tone: "Stand and deliver!" Make a RUTHLESSNESS roll of 17, adding 2 if you are **Wanted by the Telegraph Guild**.

Successful RUTHLESSNESS roll!   **531**
Failed RUTHLESSNESS roll!   **483**

❧ 447 ☙

Remove the **fur coat** from your possessions and the money from your purse and erase the codeword *Aw-ful*. Gain a **solidarity point**.

Miss Evans is astounded by your generosity. She stutters for a moment, begins to speak and stalls. "No, I shall not ask whence these gifts. What know I of your methods and means? I barely know you at all! But if I wait any longer for an opportunity to change my life, it will pass me by." She goes to her desk in the corner of the room and removes an envelope. "I have had my resignation written and ready for three years," she says. "Now at last I can sign it."

Leaving the letter on her desk for her head-teacher to find, she swiftly packs a travelling bag with her few belongings and accompanies you downstairs and out through a side-door. "My sally-port," she smiles, "Whenever I want to leave unnoticed."

Miss Evans climbs onto the velosteam behind you and you open the regulator: the gravel crunches beneath your tires as you gain speed and head towards Rotherfield Greys.

Late though it is, the passenger lounge remains open and you leave Miss Evans with a ticket in hand awaiting the morning flight to Madeira. Who knows whether you will see her again? Perhaps your paths will cross in the skies once more.

Leave the airfield...   **68**
Stay here for a while...   **454**

❧ 448 ☙

Impersonating the ghost of a fourteenth-century bishop seems a sensible enough way to terrify the no-bility into redressing their wrongs - the real question is how to go about it. You settle for repeated appear-ances by night in the yard of the manor house, clothed in the cassock, carrying a lantern and glowing from head to foot with the flourescent chemical. Remove the **fluorspar powder** or **nephritic solution** from your possessions and erase the codeword *Bother*. Initially you are only noticed by servants, but your nightly return gets Lord Burgess' attention and when you meet him, face to face (although glowing), he is nothing less than terrified. You deliver his ancestor's ultimatum: hand back his lands or face a lifetime's terror and haunting. He gibbers with fear and prom-ises to do as you wish.

Sure enough, in the morning Lord Burgess is gone, permanently, to live in his estate on the south coast. He leaves behind a formal agreement to hand the possession of the estate into the common holding of the people of Fingest. Although they may suspect you had something to do with his actions, you have managed to keep the secret of the haunting from them, and all that follows is a great celebration of your mysterious, though effective, manoeuverings. Gain **two solidarity points**.

Steam up to Ibstone...   **400**
Head down the lane to Turville...   **947**
Ride on to Bolter End...   **546**
Take the road south to Skirmett...   **969**

Since your last visit the house has been emptied entirely. There is nothing of value left here, other than the computing machines in the attic and the few possessions of the servants in the basement.

Return to the attic...	**484**
Leave the house...	**343**

The Riverbed Ale is rich, creamy and flat - clearly influenced by the beer of the Midlands, whence many of the bargee customers hail. It is a nourishing meal in a glass and as you sup at it you fall into conversation with several bargees discussing their trips to Wallingford and back.

"The river's silting up the channel by Eel Pie Eyot," says one. "Won't take a load any more. Main channel gets so busy there - the River Guild should be dredging, or what do we pay our dues for?"

"Them dues is just another income stream for 'em," replies another angrily. "We don't get nothing in return except the right to steam on the river - which is our natural right anyways."

"Coal's down," says another. "Since them big Welsh fields opened up, it's barely a paying cargo. Crocks and fine china's where the money is."

"Fine china? Yours is the dirtiest boat on the river, Gavin! You'll be doing more than sweeping out the coal dust if you want to carry fine china!"

Return to the parlour...	**358**

The inventor is intrigued by the set of punchcards you present him with. They are a slightly different size and have some very unusual punch shapes. "I will have to realign the feed - and replace a reading wheel or two, I think." Fox gets to work and an hour or so later you are able to place the punchcards into the machine.

The movement of the wheels and dials is quite unusual: to your eye, the whirring seems repetitive with tiny variations, much going forwards and back over the same processes. Fox smiles. "I see what this is doing. It is a prediction programme - useful for reconstructing missing data, I'm sure, but vital for the invention of melody. I wonder who programmed this: it really is a masterwork of code."

The engine chatters out its results and Fox im-

mediately calls over his assistants and begins discussing how to complete his mechanical organ. Then he remembers you. "Thank you, a thousand times. This is just what I needed." He returns the punchcards to you and shakes your hand. "You're welcome back to borrow the engine any time you need to calculate something."

Working with Fox has taught you a lot about these punchcards. In future, when you find yourself in a passage in which a computational engine is mentioned, look for the key word 'hopper'. Where you come across this, you will be able to interact with the machine if you possess a set of **punchcards**. As you have no doubt noticed, each set is given a name and an initial. Use the initial (for example, V in **punchcards (Selladore V)**) to identify the next word in the passage beginning with that letter after the mention of the hopper. Count the letters in that word and in the next word to create a two-digit number. Add this number onto the number of the passage in which you find yourself and turn to the resulting passage. This will give you further options or tell you what happened when you fed the **punchcards** into the engine. If the passage you reach is nonsensical, it is either a mistake in your programming or the particular engine does not support that set of **punchcards**. You will also need to note the **passage number** in which you find the computational engine in case you need to return there.

Gain the codeword *Burnish*.

Leave the workshop...	**771**

The road from Oxford takes you past villages and small towns and you see many steam carriages and private steamers of interesting design on the way. Eventually you reach a secluded area more suited to an ambush. Roll a dice to see if you encounter anything.

Score 1-2	The Atmospheric Union...	**1300**
Score 3-4	A quiet journey...	**710**
Score 5-6	A private steamer...	**1325**

You convince them to let you go on your way. They aren't pleased to see you disappearing with the **leather satchel**, but once they believe they risk upsetting their superiors' plans - not that there is a hierarchy amongst comrades - they have little choice.

"On your head be it. If you see Comrade Feaver, tell her we tried!"

Ride on... **442**

Ride on... **442**

✎ 454 ✎

The airship station here is more than simply a grass field. Several massive hangars cover construction yards for Eden's airship builders; a long iron-framed launching ramp strides across the grass; four tall mooring towers stand at corners of the field; a block containing a departure lounge, offices, storehouses and workers' dormitories sprawls over the hilltop. Then there is the vast service arch, wide enough to span the biggest airborne colossus.

If you are **Wanted by the Atmospheric Union**, turn to **66** immediately.

Enter the departure lounge...	**80**
Visit the Atmospheric Union office...	**56**
Head downhill to Henley...	**68**
Ride west...	**158**

✎ 455 ✎

The lane from Gallowstree Common skirts a valuable sweet chestnut plantation and a small fenced coal dump. Birdsong echoes from the trees: the sound of a magpie chattering and a whistling blackbird.

Stop at Cane End...	**807**
Turn left downhill towards Reading...	**560**
Turn right onto the Woodcote road...	**488**

✎ 456 ✎

You return to the walls of Fingest Manor, where Lord Burgess lives in security and wealth. Did you intend to do anything about that?

Haunt Lord Burgess...	
(**lantern**, **cassock** and **nephritic solution** or **fluorspar powder**)	**448**
Blow up the manor house... (**explosives**)	**81**
Return to the village...	**867**

✎ 457 ✎

The village of Stoke Row has a few indications of the advent of industry: a small furnace lets out a pillar of charcoal-smoke and several iron-framed prefabricated houses stand along the roadway. The village inn is traditional enough: it was originally a short row of flint-walled cottages before being transformed into a destination eatery. A short distance behind the houses and workshops stands the village well, which has its own story to tell.

Investigate the Maharajah's Well...	**988**
Pause at the Cherry Tree...	**145**
Head north into Mongewell Woods...	**766**
Steam west towards Woodcote...	**664**
Steam east...	**238**

✎ 458 ✎

If you have the codeword *Artisan*, turn to **859**.

The Freight Yard at Henley runs alongside the wharves, uncircled by any wall or railing. Locomotives and engines are parked about, a mobile steam crane lifts crates, sacks of grain, slings of lumber and barrels of beer from barge to wagon and back again, and on every side men and women, urchins and lads are at work. A bell and an automated ticketing system keep everyone in check, regulating which cargo is in process and which owner needs to pay up next.

The engineers here are interested in your velosteam and ready to offer you repairs, although none has the skill to customise the machine.

Repairs	To buy
Per **damage point**	**£2**

Seek a haulier for Cobstone Mill flour...	
(**baker's contract**)	**958**
Return to the town square...	**702**
Leave Henley...	**586**

✎ 459 ✎

You cut across an open field to save time and send several startled sheep diving out of the way. A sheep-dog barks and comes alongside, but you quickly outpace her and bump through a gateway and onto the lane heading north. The Constables are still on your tail: you open the regulator and feel the air chilling your flanks as you whistle up the slope towards the sheltering valleys. You must attempt to hide in the woods, unseen and unheard by your pursuers. Make an INGENUITY roll of 11, adding 2 if you have a **muffled exhaust** fitted to your velosteam.

Successful INGENUITY roll!	**430**
Failed INGENUITY roll!	**13**

ᔕ 460 ᔕ

A fine brick house with three gabled bays overlooking the river; a tarmacadam drive prepared for his Lordship's steam-carriage; a long series of garages and stables: Hardwick House is a place of wealth and stability. Sir Reginald M'Dow is the owner of the estate, but he is known all around here as simply 'his Lordship'. If you have the **Whitchurch affidavit**, turn to **295** immediately.

Seek out his Lordship...

(letter of introduction)	**423**
Ride past the dairy... (*Butterchurn*)	**230**
Take another road...	**693**

ᔕ 461 ᔕ

If you have the codeword *Bespoke*, turn to **1192** immediately.

"I don't think you're a regular wheat trader," says a narrow-faced woman. "Let me check my list. Nope, no sign of you or your craft. That shipment is forfeit - and the payment must be returned immediately."

Resist and fight your way out...	**1296**
Try to talk your way out of trouble...	**1322**

ᔕ 462 ᔕ

"Oh, I know you," says Lady Pomiane. "You're the Steam Highwayman! Do come in! I am honoured! How nice to meet you. Sorry about the temperature - my steam heating system has been on the blink for a while and there's just no money to mend it. Come and have a crumpet."

Enter the house...	**352**

ᔕ 463 ᔕ

The passengers and ferryman are far from discouraged by your appearance. They laugh - and the ferryman picks up his pole and shoves you, hard. You fall into the water with a splash. Gain a **wound** from the pole and if you now have **five wounds**, turn to **528** immediately.

Eventually you pull yourself up onto your boat again, where the mate shakes his head. "I don't like to see that," he says. "They'll never take us serious at this rate."

Turn to...	**271**

ᔕ 464 ᔕ

You are taken to the headquarters of the Wallingford Town Guard in the centre of the town. They maintain a certain independence from the Constables, but are no less brutal. And they are certainly glad to have their hands on you.

"At last!" crows a Captain as she marches across the yard towards you. "We've been looking for you! We had you down for the paychest job a long time ago."

"Paychest job?" you reply.

"Don't play dumb," she says. "You know exactly what I'm talking about!"

Within their jurisdiction the Town Guard have a terrifying authority: you are charged with a variety of crimes, many of which are quite impossible for you to have committed. No matter: a perpetrator has been found and it will certainly help the Guard to have their unsolved casebook shortened.

There is no jury and no formal sentencing. One morning you are taken out from your cell and chained into a steam-wagon parked in the dirty street.

"Where am I being taken?"

The burly Constable laughs shortly. "Where do you think? Gallowstree Common!"

The wagon moves off...	**493**

ᔕ 465 ᔕ

The Constables must have missed the turning in the rain and dark. You steam across the bridge as quietly as you can and make your way to the shelter of Sonning village, where you may be able to find an inn ready to let you dry off and recover from your ride.

Turn to...	**91**

ᔕ 466 ᔕ

How to be both equitable and helpful? Remembering an old story of Robin Hood, you divide the money into small bags and, soon after dusk, hang one from the door handle of each cottage in the village. Gain the codeword *Beneficent*.

Turn to...	**28**

ᔕ 467 ᔕ

While waiting alongside several other barges at Clifton Lock, you hear a story from London. "The King's Cut has opened all the way to the docks at Limehouse -

but they say King Charlie has his own reasons for wanting a canal. There's tunnels, see, and beneath Islington there are junctions running north and south. Not freight tunnels, no. They're for some other purpose."

"What might that be?" asks a bargee.

"I ain't telling. But there's an awful smell down there. Rotten meat."

Continue downriver...   **435**

❧ 468 ❧

A noblewoman and her chaperone are taking a journey across the country. Needless to say, they are somewhat surprised to experience a robbery as part of their tour! You may take a **fur coat**, a **silver necklace** and **£8 4s** from them. You will now be **Wanted by the Constables** unless you possess a **mask**.

Turn to...   **noted passage**

❧ 469 ❧

The mining engineer is poring over blueprints and measurements and barely acknowledges you. "Money?" he asks. "I'm bankrupt, myself. Trying to sell these designs to the Coal Board." You can take his **mining plans** and his **pocket watch** if you want, but he tells you that he has no money on him. Will the plans ever be of any value to you?

"How about I hold you for ransom?"   **141**
"Take this for the designs." (**£3**)   **253**
Leave him...   **noted passage**

❧ 470 ❧

The vehicles on this road travel quickly and frequently carry armed guards: they can afford to if they can afford the tolls on this privately-owned stretch. You will have to be both clever and quick to rob someone here successfully. Note **passage number 433** on your **Adventure Sheet** and roll a dice to see what you encounter:

Score 1-3	A private steam carriage...	**103**
Score 4	The Telegraph Guild...	**272**
Score 5	The Haulage Guild...	**408**
Score 6	An independent haulier...	**111**

❧ 471 ❧

The stretch here heads close to the hillside on which the road between Henley and Reading runs. A house stands behind a lawn, hidden from the road by mature trees. Further downstream the river winds past two wooded, reedy islands.

Moor at Shiplake House... (*Caraway*)	**1063**
Take a look at Hallsmead Ait...	**894**
Pause by the Lynch...	**935**
Continue upriver to Sonning...	**750**

❧ 472 ❧

Champagne dissolves the students' anger and they let you go. "We were only on the river because our examinations have finished," says one. "Don't really know how to handle a boat."

Leave them...   **868**

❧ 473 ❧

It was on an evening like this that you came across the bishop's ghost. Tonight, however, your walk is undisturbed. Did such a thing ever actually happen, or was it your senses playing tricks on you?

Return to the village...   **867**

❧ 474 ❧

Unable to unlock your bonds, you slump down into the corner of the wagon in frustration. The journey's end approaches... If you are the **Friend of Captain Coke**, turn to **591** immediately.

The wagon stops at the top of the hill, where you are unceremoniously hauled out and dragged to the gallows. A small crowd stand around, waiting to see your demise. Their lives must be miserable indeed if this entertains them.

There is no ceremony and you are given no chance to speak any final words. The guards maintain their vigilance and the noose is slipped over your head before you realise. One short, final jerk and you are suspended by your neck muscles, the rope cutting through most but not all of your windpipe, giving you a long and increasingly delirious hour to cast your mind over your deeds.

See how you are remembered...   **Epilogue**

❧ 475 ❧

The road narrows and twists here beneath Danesfield Hill. It is a simple matter to find a place to hide and watch the approaching traffic. If you have the code-word *Alacrity* and wish to wait for the russet-and-gold steamer, turn to **519**. Otherwise, note **passage number 433** on your **Adventure Sheet** and roll a dice to see what you encounter.

Score 1	The Constables...	**9**
Score 2-3	The Haulage Guild...	**408**
Score 4-5	A private carriage...	**136**
Score 6	The Henley locobus...	**156**

❧ 476 ❧

If you have no **Wanted Statuses**, turn to **360** immediately. Otherwise, the Constables will be likely to take a good look at you and try to match you with their list of hunted criminals. Make an INGENUITY roll of difficulty 14, adding 1 if you have a **Constables' log-book**, a **Guildsman's medallion** or a **bottle of wine**.

Successful INGENUITY roll!	**360**
Failed INGENUITY roll!	**13**

❧ 477 ❧

The colours of the steam caravan are distinctive. As you slow, a familar face appears between the shutters and then Barsali leaps down the steps.

"My friend! A damp morning but a lively sight! Oh, stop a while. Whatever your errand, it can wait for friendship, surely?"

"Alas, it cannot wait. I will return, Barsali."	**308**
"What is more urgent than friendship?"	**19**

❧ 478 ❧

"It may have been your way of living. The past does not define the future. Even the Lord God changes his mind, for while his character is changeless, his plans take account of us. Have you ever read the book of Jonah?" Father Patrick pats your hand. "But I beg you, kill no-one."

Leave the church...   **3**

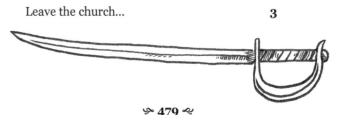

❧ 479 ❧

One evening, Chef Ramboutarde does not appear in the kitchen. You discover him groaning in his bunk and clutching his stomach. He has caught some sort of illness and the Captain insists that he is quarantined immediately - much to his frustration and anguish.

This leaves you in charge of the kitchen. How will you fare, preparing the haute cuisine that the passengers demand on a flight like this? If you have three or more levels of **haute cuisine**, turn to **443** immediately. If not, you must make an INGENUITY roll of difficulty 13.

Successful INGENUITY roll!	**443**
Failed INGENUITY roll!	**413**

❧ 480 ❧

The other customers are appalled by the sight of their friend bleeding out his life on the flagstones. They don't know whether to charge you in a mass or to run away. In the end, they opt for the latter. Lose **a solidarity point** for killing this unarmed man, but gain a point of RUTHLESSNESS.

Leave the inn...   **867**

❧ 481 ❧

Remove the **tightly-tied parcel** from your **Adventure Sheet.** The publisher retreats into his office and slams the door.

As you mount your Ferguson velosteam, it begins to rain. And it continues raining all the way back to Oxford. The lot of a despatch rider, it seems.

Return to Oxford...   **688**

❧ 482 ❧
☐

If the box above is empty, tick it and turn to **327** immediately. If it is already ticked, read on.

The channel behind Magpie Island is only just wide enough for your craft. Your mate gives a low whistle as stretching willow branches scratch along the gunwale. Very soon your boat is entirely hidden from sight. You are ideally placed to ambush river traffic.

Prepare to ambush passing craft...	**671**
Rest here and make camp...	**870**
Press on upstream...	**950**

❧ 483 ❧

The driver is far from impressed. All you have done is to warn him of your presence. An armoured shield springs up around the driver and the guards crouch into their cupolas and ready their weapons. With a crack, whizz and whistle, the first bullet passes overhead.

Fire back...	**510**
Lie low...	**300**
Make a getaway...	**noted passage**

❧ 484 ❧

In through a high window and into a dusty attic bedroom - presumably the servants' quarters when the house is fully-staffed. Down a short corridor and behind a bolted door lies a room housing a large computing engine. It seems to have just finished a computation and has wound out a long stream of closely-punched and incomprehensible code. Its hopper is empty.

Lying on a table are a series of connecting rods that can drive a small automatic telegraph mounted on the gable of the house - presumably so that the bishop or someone else can remotely access the information being calculated here - but they are currently disconnected. A machine used for punching cards with a complex keyboard is mounted opposite the engine. If you have a set of **blank punchcards**, you could use the punching machine to create your own set of punchcards. Key to that is learning from a master computationalist.

Attempt to use the punch machine...

(**blank punchcards**)	**724**
Rob the house...	**755**
Leave the place...	**343**

❧ 485 ❧

Setting off upriver from Wallingford, the green meadows of the Thameside estates are punctuated irregularly by smoking chimneys and reeking pits. Roll two dice to see what you encounter on your way.

Score 2-5	A pleasure cruiser...	**54**
Score 6-8	An uninterrupted journey...	**210**
Score 9-12	Challenged to a duel!	**278**

❧ 486 ❧

A shout rings out and a bullet whistles through the leaves beside you: the Constables have caught sight of you at the door of the cage! You quickly dash back to your velosteam and mount up, leaving the prisoners at the mercy of their captors. A quick getaway is called for!

Ride north...	**280**
Ride down the hill...	**863**

❧ 487 ❧

Goring stands beside a fine bridge over the Thames, where the river breaks through the Chiltern hills and begins to turn eastwards. A large Freight Yard stands by the wharf, straddled with gantries and cranes. It is a staging post for several long-distance routes and road-trains leave every day for the Welsh borders, Bristol and the lawless counties of Devon and Cornwall. The Telegraph Guild also maintain a small depot here servicing their towers at Woodcote and South Stoke.

Park up by the John Barleycorn...	**100**
Visit the Freight Yard...	**337**
Find a local bakery... (**Cobstone flour**)	**785**
Enter the Telegraph Guild depot...	**250**
Leave town...	**911**

❧ 488 ❧

The small town of Woodcote sits amongst cherry orchards, wheatfields and coppice woods. A few workshops have their chimneys but most of the smoke is honest woodland faggots, heating houses and cooking food. Many of the people here still live in cottages their forebears would have recognised, with simple lives tending the same common ground and the lands of the same rich families.

Enter the Red Lion...   203
Visit the telegraph station...   581
Leave Woodcote...   659

❧ 489 ❧

The steamer is packaged all about with the paraphenalia of an artist's expedition. Canvases wrapped in tarpaulin, long easels, boxes of paints, solvents and palettes are all strapped around the bodywork of the hired carriage.

"I'm painting the landscape before the age of steam destroys it for good," says the artist. "I am not a rich man." Amongst his goods are a **jeweller's loupe (ING+1)**, a **wide-brimmed hat** and a **sketchbook**. His purse contains a paltry **£2 3s**. You will now be **Wanted by the Constables** unless you possess a **mask**.

Turn to...   noted passage

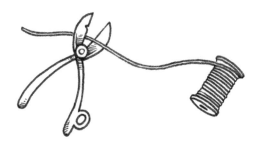

❧ 490 ❧

The grey-beard nods appreciatively as his plate of gammon and potatoes is put in front of him. He eats messily. "Can I draw you up something?" he asks. "Prettily done, I can guarantee." He is a forger. He will also pay, on behalf of his contacts, for sensitive material that you can collect.

Other items	To buy	To sell
Grantly's Membership Card	£6 10s	£3
Letter of Introduction	£15	£1 5s
Delevinne Bank Share Certificate	£8 4s	£2 10
Colonel Snappet's pocketbook	-	£5
Telegraph Guild Codebook	-	£6 2s
Major Redford's Card	-	£12
Union airship registry	-	£10
mining plans	-	£15
Title Deed to Llanfihangel	-	£24
Coal Board Accounts book	-	£7 4s

Return to the parlour...   281
Leave the Dolphin...   270

❧ 491 ❧

The manufacturer is travelling to catch a flight back to the north, where he owns several large businesses. His monogrammed luggage proves that he has certainly made a success of himself. He has **ten pounds in banknotes** and a **silk waistcoat (GAL+1)**.

Turn to...   noted passage

❧ 492 ❧

You dive into the smoke and steam and look around. A toppled wagon has spilt its load and the yard manager's office has been torn open. Take what you wish from these: a **roll of oiled silk**, **£3 5s**, **punchcards (Aramanth A)**, a **bottle of beehive stout**, a **tarpaulin**, a **brass flange joint** and a **telescope**.

Hurry away with your findings...   702

❧ 493 ❧

The road up to Gallowstree Common slopes steadily uphill. As the steamcart and escorting vehicles make their way, joined by a rag-tag straggle of bloodthirsty children and unemployed villagers, you hear a familiar sound and peer out through the slatted sides. The Captain who dealt with your arrest is riding alongside on your confiscated velosteam! How dare she?

There must be some way to escape this dreadful end. The chains around your wrists are tight, but their locks are old-fashioned and simple to pick. Make an INGENUITY roll of difficulty 14, adding 2 to your roll if you possess **lockpicks** or a **skeleton key**.

Successful INGENUITY roll!   525
Failed INGENUITY roll!   474

❧ 494 ❧

Harpsden is a tiny village nestled in its own tiny vale, a short distance from Henley. Like many hamlets in the region, it really exists to service Harpsden House on the slope of the hill.

Visit Harpsden House...	1466
Steam to Henley...	702
Ride south...	682

❧ 495 ❧

The Thames past Reading is only one of the city's waterways - the Kennet has been canalised and flows south-west through the factory town as well - but still the river in front of you is choked with traffic. Airships swing low overhead through the mist and smoke and everywhere is the smell of coke.

The massive locks here are owned by the city, not the River Guild, so a **Bargee's Badge** is practically worthless for the time being. The high tolls make a mint for the city council and despite the Guild's frequent petitions to the Crown, it looks to remain that way. A healthy trade in goods here is the consequence of the meeting of two waterways and the great Bath Road.

The cargoes on sale here are priced per unit: your craft must have a spare cargo space to buy one of them. It can be profitable to trade on the river, but you will need some capital to purchase goods and will have to know exactly where you can sell them to make a profit.

	To buy	To sell
Charcoal	£13	£12
Furniture	£20	£19
Machinery	-	£28
Pottery	-	£20
Cotton	£3	£2
Woollen cloth	-	£8
Coal	£14	£11
Beer	£16	£15
Wheat	£3	-
Malt	£8	£7
Frozen meat	-	£17
Ice	-	£12

Moor here...	663
Steam to the boatyard...	30
Head upstream towards Wallingford...	
(**8s** or **Bargee's Badge**)	305
Head downstream through the lock... (**4s**)	319

❧ 496 ❧

You eventually knock the haulier down. Your body aches from the blows he managed to land and you are breathing heavily. His mates simply drag him out into the breeze. "Always had a hot temper, our Jim. No harm meant." And that is what you must accept.

Leave the inn...	867

❧ 497 ❧

The driver is not interested in fighting you. He peers down through begrimed goggles and baulks. "The Steam Highwayman," he mutters. "I'll be lucky to live."

You may take **18s** from his purse and a **shovel**. If you are not already **Wanted by the Coal Board**, you will be now unless you are wearing a **mask**.

Destroy the coal delivery... (**explosives**)	976
Ride away...	**noted passage**

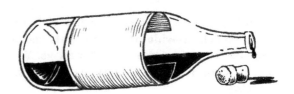

❧ 498 ❧

If you have a **Telegraph Guild codebook**, turn to **521** immediately.

The station master looks you over. "You look the sort we could use," he begins. "How can the railways ever expand and have a level playing field with all the interest the Telegraph Guild hold in parliament? Their monopoly on the optical telegraph strangles the commerce of the empire." He looks at you slyly. "We have our own computational engines - but what we need is a Telegraph Guild codebook. Beg, steal or write one yourself and we will pay well - very well. The railways are on the ascent in the capital and the Emperor believes in them. We of the Imperial Western Railway do not forget our friends."

"Where could I find you such a thing?" you ask.

"Use your head!" he replies. "Perhaps at a large Telegraph tower or from an important codesman - if you can put pressure to bear. I am sure that you are the one to do it."

"What if I cannot get hold of one?"

"The Telegraph Guild codes are very difficult and

changed regularly," he replies thoughtfully. "But it should be possible to reduce them. And that will be powerful information indeed."

"How might I do that?"

"First you will need to observe the towers - through a telescope - and record as much data as you can. Then if you feed that information into a calculating engine with the right set of punchcards, you should, theoretically, be able to crack the code."

Leave the station...   702

❧ 499 ❧

Your Aramanth punchcards are quickly processed by the machine. It is now ready to decode anything you should care to provide it with.

Analyse Telegraph Guild Codes...
    (**telegraph observations** ☑ ☑)   252
Decode the Valencia Orders...
    (**punchcards (Valencia Orders)**)   1498
Leave the machine...   **noted passage**

❧ 500 ❧

Greys Court is a grand house of chalk, flint and bricks with impressive striped gables and unmodernised Tudor windows. You will not be welcome unannounced but a **letter of introduction** may get you inside.

Knock on the door...
    (**letter of introduction**)   346
Show your sketches...
    (**sketchpad** ☑ ☑ ☑)   245
Leave the house...   158

❧ 501 ❧

You have to wait in a queue before passing through Henley bridge and emerging on the stretch of Henley Reach. Heavy timber posts sunk into the river separate the navigation channel from the width used for racing and on regatta days floating booms are strung between the poles to make the separation more permanent. On the eastern bank you can see orchards and meadows, pollarded willows being cut for basket-weaving and pillars of steam rising from harvesting engines. Roll two dice to see what you encounter.

Score 2-5   A race!   571
Score 6-8   An uninterrupted journey...   855
Score 9-12   An important person...   1025

❧ 502 ❧

The blast destroys the wagons and sets much of the coal on fire: no-one will be able to put that out easily. Smoke begins to rise from the roadside and the tarmacadam itself bubbles, boils and burns. You should get away. Gain the codeword *Bubbling*.

Turn to...   **noted passage**

❧ 503 ❧

You remember from the gossip in the Ship Inn in Marlow that the Bishop has powerful computing engines in his attic. The steam boiler may well be powering them - even while he is away.

Attempt a break-in...   1506
Talk to the servants...   404
Leave the house...   343

❧ 504 ❧

A moment after entering the wood, you are knocked off your velosteam by a heavy blow to the back of the head. Gain a **wound** immediately - and if you now have **five wounds**, turn to **999**. Otherwise read on.

You pick yourself off the ground to see a trio of brigands rushing towards you. They plainly spotted your approach and prepared an ambush with the tree branch you can see lying across the track. Your velosteam alone will be valuable to them.

Brigands	Weapons: **clubs (PAR 2)**
Parry:	11
Nimbleness:	9
Toughness:	4

Victory!   579
Defeat!   712

❧ 505 ❧

Your snare catches nothing and you leave the woods empty handed.

Turn to...   600

❧ 506 ❧

The hill is always busy with someone moving something: freight passes this way to cross Henley Bridge or to reach Maidenhead overland. Private carriages constantly ferry their insulated passengers up to London or out to their estates. Perhaps you will be fortunate enough to stop just such a vehicle. Note **pas-**

sage number 655 on your Adventure Sheet and roll a dice to see what you encounter.

Score 1	The Telegraph Guild...	198
Score 2	The Haulage Guild...	408
Score 3	A farmer...	1208
Score 4	The Atmospheric Union...	1244
Score 5	The Constables...	9
Score 6	A private steam carriage...	103

❧ 507 ❧

What inspiration or subconscious half-memory has prompted you to seek help from the gypsies? In your current state, it is harder to understand your own thoughts than to proceed with your habitual, almost mechanical actions of riding your velosteam. Weak though you are from loss of blood, dizzy and wracked with pain, you manage to coax your faithful machine towards Crazies Hill and there, at the edge of a field, stands a half-circle of four steam caravans.

You stay with the gypsies for several weeks. They reserve a caravan for you - one of Barsali's nieces and her husband forgo their space - and tow it carefully when they move ground. But the process of healing is a long one and takes a toll on their resources as well as your body: truly, Barsali must have a deep love for you.

For each **wound**, roll two dice and on a score of 11 or 12 convert it into an **intimidating scar (RUTH+1)**. Otherwise, replace it with an ordinary **scar** on your **Adventure Sheet**.

When your body has regained some of its strength you make plans to leave. Barsali tries to protest, but he recognises the power of your wanderlust, as well as your disinclination to be further in his debt.

Ride away... **546**

❧ 508 ❧

You are not a long distance from the river, but the cool water is out of sight, together with all the bothersome river patrols and passers-by. Note **passage number 433** on your **Adventure Sheet** and roll a dice to see what you encounter.

Score 1	The Constables...	9
Score 2	The Atmospheric Union...	194
Score 3	The Haulage Guild...	408
Score 4-5	A private steam carriage...	103
Score 6	A locobus...	156

❧ 509 ❧

You land squarely on top of the steamer and quickly clamber forward, swinging down into the cab and holding your weapons to the driver's throat. At once he closes the regulator and gently engages the brake, loath to make any sudden movement. Roll a dice to see what the steamer carries:

| Score 1-3 | Airship crew | 703 |
| Score 4-6 | Passengers | 592 |

❧ 510 ❧

You raise your gun and take aim at the first of the Telegraph Guild guards. Make an ACCURACY roll of difficulty 17.

| Successful ACCURACY roll! | 582 |
| Failed ACCURACY roll! | 300 |

❧ 511 ❧

At Clifton you stop for an evening meal and a drink, but your mate's loose tongue invites trouble. That night you are woken by footsteps on your counter. When you emerge from the cabin, a shadowy figure leaps ashore, clutching something to their chest. Choose one of your **possessions** randomly and remove it from your **Adventure Sheet**.

After a sleepness night watching for more burglars, you head on downstream.

Turn to... **435**

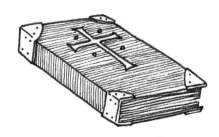

❧ 512 ❧

The bells that you won back for Parson Twinge are being refitted into St Bartholemew's belfry. The vicar smiles at his memory of Reverend Prattle's face. "We showed him, didn't we just?" You are invited to take a cup of tea and a small, a very small, piece of cake in the vicarage.

Leave the church... **867**

❧ 513 ❧

He looks thoughtful. "In the village of Stonor, near here, the villagers are forced to hire an engine to harvest their fields. If they had one of their own, they would be able to resist the unrighteous demands of their lord. Consider that. It is not glamorous work and you will not profit. But if you seek to help, consider that." Gain the codeword *Bonnington*.

Leave the church...   **3**

❧ 514 ❧

The eel-catcher continues spitting and cursing. "You didn't never have a care for an old fisherman and his bucks, ey? Well may your fine boat catch on the cill!"

He is bound to badmouth you wherever he has any sympathy: lose a **solidarity point**. You get up steam again and head on down the channel, emerging further upstream. Gain the codeword *Blasted*.

Turn to...   **950**

❧ 515 ❧

A small, wooden wharf, a few grain barges, several cottages and a low, thatched inn are all that North Stoke can offer to a traveller. The inhabitants are busy in the fields of Littlestoke Manor or Mongewell House to the north, reaping, threshing and harvesting in the summer sun.

Visit The Whistlers...	**162**
Board your boat...	
(if **moored at North Stoke**)	**959**
Head south along the road...	**615**
Head north towards Wallingford...	**860**

❧ 516 ❧

The Earl falls to the ground, incapacitated by your ruthless thrusts, entirely at your mercy. Searching his barely-breathing body, you find **ten guineas in banknotes**, £4 15s and a **silk scarf**.

Turn to...   **171**

❧ 517 ❧

The sky darkens further. Soon you are steaming along through the night, constantly on the watch for sharp turns, fallen branches or any other obstacles on the road. Your machine has settled to a whirring hum and you are able to hear the wingbeats of an owl overhead.

Then your lamp flickers once and dies. The road ahead of you is dark but something prevents you from hauling on the brakes. It only takes a few seconds for your eyes to adjust and you realise that the moonlight and starlight is more than enough to show your way. In the almost silence, two deer break through the hedgerows to your right before running alongside you for ten yards - twenty - thirty - and then leap a fence into a field.

A bump in the road jolts the lamp and water dripping onto the lime sends out another vapour. It relights and floods the road with white artificial light once more.

Ride on to Oxford...   **990**

❧ 518 ❧

The Ferguson mutters away happily as you climb the hill and skirt the Telegraph station, winding along field margins and through pasture. Kites soar above you and the sun beats down.

Soon you reach the woods near Cane End. A bulbous beech tree with a heart carved into the bark marks where you rejoin the road. You have made a considerable saving of time taking this route and it should not be too hard to retrace. Remember that when you come across the tree described above, you should add the digits of the passage number you are on together and subtract the total from the passage number if you want to take this short cut again.

Pause at Cane End...   **807**

❧ 519 ❧

Many vehicles pass on the busy road between Henley and Marlow, but you know this is the route taken by the Bishop of Barnsbury after hearing from the drinkers in the Ship Inn. You keep watch and eventually, in the dew-dripping morning, you see a russet-and-gold steamer climbing the slope towards you.

Ram the steamer off the road...	**611**
Demand the driver halt the engine...	**424**

❧ 520 ❧
□

If the box is empty, tick it and read on. If it is already ticked, turn to **488** immediately.

You come upon a steam wagon stuck in the mud. Its driver, engineer and passengers are all scratching their heads. If you want to help free the vehicle, make an ENGINEERING roll of difficulty 11. You may add 1 to your roll if you possess a **rope**, **shovel** or **grappling iron** and 2 if your velosteam has a **gas pressuriser** or **off-road tyres**.

Successful ENGINEERING roll!   **11**
Failed ENGINEERING roll!   **488**

❧ 521 ❧

"Do you have it?" asks the station master. "A codebook?"

You nod and hand it over wordlessly. Remove the **Telegraph Guild codebook** from your **possessions**.

"This will have been expensive, I am sure," says the station master. He hands you a bag of gold (**£20**) and a **letter of introduction**. "This letter will help you find advancement," he says.

Leave the station...   **702**

❧ 522 ❧
☐

If the box above is empty, tick it and read on. If it is already ticked, erase the codeword *Broadly* and turn to **605** immediately.

You recognise the boy who was herding cows on the road to Wargrave. He grins at you. "Spent my money on beer, I did," he says. "I'm a real man now. Let no-one say the Steam Highwayman ain't on the side of the little man!" Gain a **solidarity point** and erase the codeword *Broadly*.

Turn to...   **605**

❧ 523 ❧

The dog responds to your call and flops over. However, rather than getting him to drop the ball where you are, you bring him over to the hoops and he drops the ball with a roll... through a hoop. The specatators love it.

"Act of dog," calls the Viscountess again. "Play on." You gain **two hoops**.

Turn to...   **1132**

❧ 524 ❧

"You're plainly not the intended recipient," you reply scornfully. "Whatever the old man's skills as a writer, he is clearly a poor judge of character."

Bloomsbury is full of publishers. You find one rumbling with the thundering presses. Busy presses are surely a good sign? You slam open the door and insist on talking to the publisher, using your most intimidating manner. When he arrives to talk with you he is initially wary, but he takes the **tightly-tied parcel** from you, opens it and reads a few pages. "Fascinating," he says. "There could be some success in this. I will take it and see what we can do." He takes down the old man's details and you insist on seeing a telegraph message drafted out to him before you take your leave, so that at least he will be told what has happened with his book. Gain the codeword *Barrowboy*.

Taking the opportunity to rest in the big city, you look around for a short while and step into an inn called the Holly Bush - but quickly leave, finding it full of Constables. It will be a long ride back to your most recent haunts. Perhaps you should seek your fortune here in the reeking metropolis?

Remain in the city...   *The Reeking Metropolis 400*
Return to Oxford...   **990**
Return to Nettlebed...   **701**
Head for Stokenchurch...   **308**

❧ 525 ❧

The locks are old and with the **lockpicks** slipped out from your boot, you soon manage to break free. The rear door is bolted, but the jolting cart rattles the single bolt with every pothole of the ill-kept road.

Judging your moment, you shove the door upwards as a particularly large jolt shakes the cart. The door jumps from its hinges and smashes down onto the road, with you upon it. The guards leap down behind you, but you are off, running towards the trees.

The Captain on your velosteam is the first to reach you. She steers directly at you and a well-timed leap knocks her off the saddle and onto the verge. You pick up the heavy velosteam and mount up as the first gunshots ring out behind you. Too late - you are back where you belong and well on your way! Add **Cheated the Gallows** to your **Great Deeds**. Roll two dice to discover where the road leads you:

Score 2-3   Bix   **3**
Score 4-6   Sonning   **91**
Score 7-10   Mongewell Woods   **766**
Score 11-12 Deadman's Lane   **396**

❧ 526 ❧

The time has come. Enough with the landed classes, enough with the powerful and the rich, enough with the officers and the hierarchies and the control of one person by another. If by eliminating those in positions of authority, you can hasten the coming of the inevitable uprising, you will. There are many that think like you in the region, particularly in the southwest towards Goring and Reading, and your membership of the Compact for Workers' Equality has convinced you that they are willing to act in accordance with their convictions. Perhaps joining with them will allow you to speed the hour?

You have in your possession a **blunderpistol (ACC 6)**, a **sabre (PAR 3)** and a **mask**. You are also a **Member of the Compact for Workers' Equality**. Your ability scores are:

RUTHLESSNESS	5
ENGINEERING	3
MOTORING	4
INGENUITY	6
NIMBLENESS	4
GALLANTRY	2

Turn to...   **1440**

✎ 527 ✎

Sir M'Dow laughs. "Choose independently? Most of them can't even read! They've no idea about the goings-on in Parliament - let alone in the world around. I don't know what sort of radical nonsense you've been listening to, but it won't help you around here. Listen. I believe in stability - in the old ways. The people in this borough don't have steam machinery taking their jobs - and you know why? Because I won't have it. They have their ancient rights and their cottages just as their forefathers did. I'm not interested in disturbing their lives or disrupting my own estate. But in Parliament I can be a voice for progress where it's most needed. Nobody pretends that the election system is fair or proportionate, but right now it allows us to get things done. What if the Radicals got into power, with all their schemes? Destruction of communities, forcible redivision of land. Chaos and revolution! Look at France!"

"Perhaps you are right. I will convince them." **618**
"I will not campaign for you."   **583**

✎ 528 ✎

With a splash you find yourself in the green Thames, weighed down by your heavy clothes and weakened by your wounds. Even in a healthy state it would be no simple thing to escape the clutches of the river. An-

cient father Thames has no difficulty in taking you to his underwater realm - and keeping you there. Turn to the **Epilogue**.

✎ 529 ✎

The Ferryman is a square, red-rendered inn on the marketside with an oil-lantern shining over the doorway. The local beer is called Ferry and is brewed by Stacks and Co. across the river in Pangbourne.

Buy a drink... (**2s**)		133
Buy drinks for the the Whitchurch voters...		
(**£2** and **Whitchurch ballot list**)		422
Leave the Ferryman...		749
Leave Whitchurch...		693

✎ 530 ✎

You take up a position beneath a copse of Scots pine. The fragrance of their bark and needles tugs at memories - but you must focus on the present. Note **passage number 655** on your **Adventure Sheet** and roll a dice to see what you encounter:

Score 1	A private steam carriage...	136
Score 2	The Haulage Guild...	408
Score 3	The Constables...	9
Score 4	The Atmospheric Union...	194
Score 5	The Telegraph Guild...	198
Score 6	An independent haulier...	1027

✎ 531 ✎

Among the general supplies you find a **strongbox** and a leather satchel with a set of **punchcards (Selladore V)**. You may also take a pair of **goggles (MOT+1)** and **£4 15s**. It is quite a haul and of course you will now be **Wanted by the Telegraph Guild** unless you have a **mask**. What next?

Blow up the supply wagons... (**explosives**)	614
Light a flare... (**purple flare**)	684
Ride away...	**noted passage**

✎ 532 ✎

Remove the **snare** from your possessions. To lay it successfully, you should make an INGENUITY roll, adding 1 if you also possess a **net**.

Score 10 or less	505
Score 11-14	439
Score 15 or higher	356

❦ 533 ❧

You manage to enter a passenger's cabin, but are caught in the act of rifling their belongings by a crew-member. In the enclosed space you are quickly over-powered and locked up in one of the cargo holds. The Captain spits in your face. "I should have known better than to give a ruffian like you employment," he says.

Turn to...   **342**

❦ 534 ❧

The villagers are not pleased to see you. "Harsh rates?" one cries. "We thought we knew what harsh rates was! Until you scare Lord Ponsonby off and he puts an even harsher agent in. They've gone up again!"

Another chimes in. "You're too threatening by half, matey. You done scare him all the way to America. Last we hear, he's panning for gold in the Yukon, hoping to make up his fortune. And us? We're paying for his expenses!"

The barman refuses to serve you. You have no option other than to leave.

Return to the village...   **977**

❦ 535 ❧

Your mate hails you as you approach your mooring. "Here you are! Told you I'd have this finished by the time you were back." He shows you his handiwork proudly: a series of perfectly aligned crowns and half-hitches producing a firm but compressible fender.

Go aboard...   **495**

❦ 536 ❧

St Mary-le-Moor is a small, almost barn-like flint and tile building, its western end pierced by three elegant windows, recently added to the much older building. Nobody is about for the time being, although the churchyard and porch show that there is a great deal of care lavished on this place.

Draw the church... (**sketchpad**)   **1101**
Leave the church...   **28**

❦ 537 ❧

The belfry of St Bartholemew's is silent and no bells ring. Since your game with the vicar of Hambleden, even what the church possessed has been taken away from it. "Ya! So to those who have, more will be added!" rails Parson Twinge angrily. "You were no help at all!" It is no use to remind him that his own gambling began the problem.

Leave the church...   **867**

❦ 538 ❧

You are shown into a workshop where the **accounts** are taken from you by a clerk (remove them from your **possessions**). He then leaves you to wait for the response. Meanwhile you are free to look around the sacrosanct inner workings of this important telegraph station, free to peer into the hopper of the computing machine standing there quietly, powered and ready to compute.

Search and rob the workshop...   **565**
Wait for the clerk to return...   **862**

❦ 539 ❧
□

If the box is empty, tick it and turn to **767** immediately. If it is already ticked, simply read on.

The waterside presents any number of places to rest and enjoy a picnic. You spread out your coat and dabble your feet in the river while enjoying the contents of the basket: a fine pork pie, some fruit, cheese and biscuits, cold chicken, seed cake and a bottle of well-crafted amber Borris Mild, a creamy, medium-body session beer.

Return to Henley...   **702**

❦ 540 ❧

The river has brought you to Reading. A row of massive iron-framed gasholders stand on the left bank where a trio of bridges cross the mouth of the river Kennet. That way leads south-west through reading, up Blake's and County Lock and onto the long and winding Kennet and Avon Canal. The main stream of the Thames proceeds from the west, where Caversham locks straddle the river. Under the authority of the City of Reading, not the River Guild, the lock-keepers pay no attention to a **Bargee's Badge** and demand a high toll of every passing boat.

Head into Caversham Locks... (**4s**)   **495**
Return downstream towards Sonning...   **319**

✎ 541 ✎

The driver reaches a narrow stretch of the road ahead of you and manages to gain crucial yards. You are forced to give up the chase.

Turn to...   **noted passage**

✎ 542 ✎
☐

If the box is empty, tick it read on. If it is already ticked, turn to **719** immediately.

The smear of chimney and furnace smoke hangs particularly heavily over Abingdon - but when you approach, it becomes plain that the wharves and streets alongside the river are ablaze! Screams and shouts ring across the water inbetween the crashing of collapsing houses.

Help pump water to put out the fires...	735
Take advantage of the distraction to loot...	773
Try to rescue people from the flames...	665

✎ 543 ✎

The fore-wheel has a pull to the left: when you slow and investigate, you find a puncture through the thick vulcanised rubber. A repair is by no means beyond you, but you need water. Hopping over a gate you are met by the sight of something like a stone circle on a small mound. Gain the codeword *Bonehunter*.

Investigate the circle...	834
Complete your repairs and continue to Wargrave...	418

✎ 544 ✎

You pass the crossroads at the top of Aston Hill and skirt the reservoir embankment. Here, at the crest of the road, more than 700 feet up, are the unmistakeable traces of badgers on the roadside. A little trodden path continues along the verge and passes straight beneath the wire at the edge of the reservoir grounds.

Follow the badger trail... (*Brock*)	333
Ride on to Stokenchurch...	308

✎ 545 ✎
☐

If the box is empty, tick it and read on. If it is already ticked, turn to **376** immediately.

The poster reads: "The Criminal Known as Cap-

tain Coke, also Captain Coakum and James T Cook is Wanted for Theft, Brigandry, Wanton Destruction and Murder. A Reward of 500 Guineas is Offered for His Proven Death or Capture by the Atmospheric Union. Enquire at Rotherfield Greys Airship Station." Along with the writing is a mechanically transmitted printofit with its characteristic shaded squares. A cheeky, middle-aged man with several scars and a pair of red-lensed glasses grins out of the print at you.

If you wish to seek the reward, you should take the **wanted poster** and make your way to Rotherfield Greys. However, you would have to be very confident in your duelling ability before going toe-to-toe with a sky-pirate of Coke's calibre - or have a completely different plan.

Return to the bar...	2
Leave the pub...	702
Mount your velosteam and leave town...	586

✎ 546 ✎

Bolter End is little more than a crossroads with a few cottages and farmhouses dotted around it. Haybales are stacked around, awaiting transport down to a city stable somewhere. Children's voices can be heard playing out of sight.

A signpost points towards Stokenchurch and, much closer, Cadmore End, and to Lane End in the opposite direction, along the road that eventually leads towards Marlow and High Wycombe.

Ride east to Lane End... *Smog and Ambuscade* 684
Investigate Cadmore End...	28
Ride up towards Stokenchurch...	142
Take the road to Fingest...	247

✎ 547 ✎

A shiny new railway engine stands at the platform of Henley station. It resembles one of the many road locomotives in many ways, but of course it can only travel where the expensive iron rails have been laid. Nonetheless the engine-driver is enthusiastic. "This is the future! If we can only get the backing of Parliament, there'll be railways across the whole kingdom - the empire even!" If you are **Wanted by the Railway Guards**, turn to **174** immediately.

Talk to the station-master...	498
Return to Henley...	702
Buy a ticket to London...	

(**£1 8s**)   *The Reeking Metropolis 111*

❧ 548 ❧

The Viscountess surveys the field. It is still early in the game and your opponents - a quizzical, red-faced young man and a lady with blue glasses - look set to gain a leading position. The lady takes careful aim, drives her red ball across the lawn, rebounds off your black, sending it far past your next hoop, and rolls to a stop a short distance from the third hoop. She gives a satisfied smile and walks over to take a glass of champagne from a footman's tray.

Roll a dice to see how the game proceeds and what opportunities you will have.

Score 1-2 An act of dog	**1507**
Score 3-4 Ricochet!	**326**
Score 5-6 Dishonest play?	**890**

❧ 549 ❧

Spying your chance, you take the axe from your pannier and slam it through the lifting line and into the wooden frame of the mill. The lifting platform rushes down behind you, smashing onto the roadway, spilling the sacks of grain. Remove the **axe** from your possessions.

Cross the bridge into Sonning...	**91**

❧ 550 ❧

☐ ☐ ☐ ☐ ☐ ☐

If any of the boxes above are empty, tick one. If all six are already ticked, erase the ticks and turn to **1219** immediately.

The woods must swallow you now: you must leave no trace as you slip away from the scene of your crime. Where will you turn?

Towards Mill End...	**112**
To Nettlebed...	**791**
To Pishill...	**370**
To the old fort...	**401**

❧ 551 ❧

If you have the codeword *Bust*, turn to **899**. If not, but you have the codeword *Bubbling*, turn to **923**. Otherwise, read on.

A green-tunicked clerk brings you into an office where a busy woman sits shuffling punchcards and entering numbers in her book. She looks up briefly through her auto-lenses. "Are you ruthless? Do you flinch at violence or the sight of blood? The Coal Board are growing too powerful. Soon they will chal-

lenge us. Attack their wagons and disrupt their supplies. Destroy their infrastructure. Get hold of a copy of their accounts and bring it to my colleague."

"This is easily done," you reply.

"Well then. Return when you have proof that your actions can match your words."

Return to the compound...	**770**
Leave the compound...	**682**

❧ 552 ❧

"Listen," you say, leaning towards the baker and using your most threatening tones, "You really want to think about buying this flour. Better to have a delivery of expensive flour than find all your deliveries are mysteriously waylaid."

The baker is helpless to disagree. He stutters something about his livelihood, his children, his customers, then quickly writes out a **baker's contract** agreeing to pay fifteen shillings a hundredweight and you head on your way.

Leave the bakery...	**418**

❧ 553 ❧

Your careful strike sends the ball back into play, careering beneath ladies' skirts, rebounding off a deck-chair and finishing by gentling rolling your opponent's red out of line with its next hoop. Within the next few blows, you pass **two hoops** in quick succession.

Turn to...	**1132**

❧ 554 ❧

Inside the steamer is a preacher - a man of the cloth. He looks up at you with sharply focused eyes. "I have little enough wealth, my friend. And that which I have is devoted to the Lord. Will you anger Him by taking it from me?"

"I did not stop your carriage for a discussion," you reply.

The preacher smiles and grabs a sword. "It is my duty to resist you," he says, taking up the stance of a skilled fencer.

Preacher	Weapon: **rapier (PAR 4)**
Parry:	10
Nimbleness:	6
Toughness:	2

Victory!	**625**
Defeat!	**999**

❧ 555 ❧

Once you have judged you have a good lead on your pursuers, you pull aside into a small wood and dismount to clear the velosteam's intake. Frustratingly, your decision to ride off-road now means that twigs and bracken have joined the mud rammed into the grille. It takes several minutes to clear and you are just about to remount when a heavy gauntlet lands on your shoulder.

"Got you at last, sonny Jim! Now you've something to answer for!"

Turn to...   13

❧ 556 ❧

The Livingstone punchcards clatter as they flip through the machine. It pauses, almost as if taking breath. What will you instruct it to do?

Analyse other punchcard patterns...   1389
Leave the machine...   **noted passage**

❧ 557 ❧

You return the **tightly-tied parcel** to your saddlebags and turn around. Who knows whether you will find time to read it - or what the author will say if you choose to return it to him. Either way, it is a long ride back to the land of the beech-lined holloways. Perhaps you could stay here and explore the city further?

Remain in the city... *The Reeking Metropolis 400*
Return to Oxford...   688

❧ 558 ❧

The road twists down past a row of cottages and a long farm shed emitting clouds of smoke. Some sort of machinery is working inside there. You speed on past and into the cover of the wood.

From nearby comes the sound of trees falling: a drawn-out creaking followed by a crash. Idyllic these woods may look, but the timber and the underwood are both valuable commodities for someone. Roll a dice to see what you encounter:

Score 1-2	Woodcutting...	670
Score 3-4	An empty road...	807
Score 5-6	Fog!	1513

❧ 559 ❧

"So be it," replies Coke. Stunned as you are, you don't feel his blade cut through your neck, only a choking difficulty breathing and a light-headedness before you lose consciousness forever. Turn to the **Epilogue**.

❧ 560 ❧

The road towards Reading is in poor shape here: at several points it has been repaired with gravel and tarmacadam, only to slip away again beneath the heavy wheels of road wagons. You will have to ride carefully on the slopes. Roll a dice to see what you encounter:

Score 1-2	An accident...	363
Score 3-4	An uncomfortable ride...	55
Score 5-6	A road repair team...	249

❧ 561 ❧

While the passengers are ashore, you manage to slip into a cabin and look through the luggage stored in the ingenious lockers. Roll a dice to see what you find:

Score 1-3	**ten guineas in banknotes** and a **gold ring**
Score 4-5	a **gold necklace**, a **silk scarf** and a **box of cigars**
Score 6	**£15 4s** and two **silver bracelets**

Return to the kitchen...   479

❧ 562 ☙

Several cows are wandering towards you in a half-hearted way. The boy following behind them flicks a long switch of hazel to keep them moving. He sees your machine, his mouth opens and he forgets the cows entirely. "It's you!" he cries excitedly. "The Steam Highwayman!" If you wish to toss him a few coins (**4s**), gain the codeword *Broadly*.

Ride on to Wargrave... **418**

❧ 563 ☙

☐ ☐

If the boxes above are empty, tick the first and read on. If one is already ticked, turn to **656** immediately. If they are both ticked, turn to **603**.

The vicar tells you of several families in the village in desperate need of help and you seek them out and press a few shillings into their hands. "Whose are the trees lying on the common?" you ask. "There's valuable timber there."

A grey-haired father shakes his head. "We was tricked! They's common trees belong to the whole village. Two, three months ago, some chap comes up here, says he's a surveyor, looking for prime timber. Likes the look of them old oaks, so he measures them up and offers to buy them. Well, they're ready to come down and folks agree to sell the timber, so we set about felling them, me and the youngsters hereabouts, having agreed to be paid for the felling and the timber when he returns. And that's just it! We sends word we've done as he asked, and the reply is, he's no longer buying! So we'd cut 'em down without payment and then 'ad no buyer and no oaks on the common neither."

"A sad tale. I'm not in the timber business." **807**
"I'll buy the wood and pay for your work." **924**

❧ 564 ☙

The eastern end of Grim's Ditch is riddled with rabbit burrows. If you wish to try to catch yourself a coney or two, roll a dice, adding 1 if you possess a **net** or a **snare** and 2 if you have a **pair of ferrets**.

Score 1-4   No luck this time
Score 5-6   Catch **two rabbits**

Ride down the ditch... **649**
Return to the wood... **766**

❧ 565 ☙

The workshop is not a place to leave a light-fingered magpie such as yourself. After a quick look around, you lay your hands on an **adjustable wrench (ENG+1)**, a set of **punchcards (Habbukuk K)** and a **Telegraph Guild codebook**. You leave as quickly as you can, but will certainly be **Wanted by the Telegraph Guild** as a result.

Leave the compound... **682**

❧ 566 ☙

The Habbukuk punchcards reset the machine. It clears all its routines and settles into a blank state. You can now input whatever you like to have the machine design for you.

Calculate airship buoyancy... **299**
Design a stronger bridge... **612**
Leave the machine... **noted passage**

❧ 567 ☙

"Yes?" drawls an officer. "You're the one that blew up the reservoir, aren't you? Well what else have you done for us lately?" If you have the codeword *Bubbling*, read on. Otherwise, turn to **770** immediately.

When you describe your deeds pursuing and hounding the Coal Board, as you were bidden, the officer nods. "I suppose some small gratuity is in order. Here." He hands you two guineas (**£2 2s**). Remove the codeword *Bubbling*.

Turn to... **770**

❧ 568 ☙

You steam away from the little village of South Stoke on the road to Goring. The river to your right is hidden behind the muddy embankment of the Imperial Western railway line. For all the grandiose name and ambition of the company, the single line is quiet for much of the day, unable to compete with the Haulage Guild on account of massive tarrifs on coal. Will the railway ever amount to more than rich men's folly?

One other effect has resulted from the railway here: a camp of navvies at the foot of the embankment has slowly become more permanent. Shacks are being rebuilt into cottages, on the railway land. The parishioners of nearby Goring will not be pleased to have these rough neighbours settling on their doorstep.

Continue on to Goring... **487**

"Short, that dog? He bought my brother out of his own business, then sold the engines, tore down the sheds and laid him off! His wife and three of his children died next winter. You'll soon find that your friend ain't so popular round here!"

The haulier tosses the table towards you. Make a NIMBLENESS roll of difficulty 10 to avoid a **wound**, before defending yourself against the angry roadsman. If you choose to fight using a **club**, **blackjack** or **truncheon** or unarmed you may be able to knock him down without hurting him too badly. You should choose how you fight before beginning the first round.

Haulier	Weapon: **fists (PAR 1)**
Parry:	6
Nimbleness:	5
Toughness:	5

Victory using a blade!	**480**
Unarmed or blunt weapon victory!	**496**
Defeat!	**999**

As you pull out onto the road, a herd of dairy cows with swinging udders come plodding towards you, entirely filling the lane. You ride ahead of them and find yourself on a muddy cowpath. Eventually the cows let up and you are greeted by a cheery milkmaid.

"Where does this path lead?" you ask.

"Right up to his Lordship's yard," she replies.

"Hardwick House?"

"That's right. Gate's open most time."

This little-known path may prove useful: it is only just rideable on your heavy machine. Larger steam engines would certainly become stuck. Gain the codeword *Butterchurn*.

Turn back to Mapledurham...	**864**
Ride on to Hardwick House...	**460**

Several interesting water-craft are lining up in preparation for a race. They are all steam-powered but seem to have little else in common. As you watch, they churn the water and shoot forward. One races ahead, rising up out of the water on two narrow, prong-like hulls, before its boiler bursts with a massive crack!

Continue along the river...	**855**

Your Ferguson gives a final shudder and a hiss and visibly sinks on its tyres. Nothing you or any other engineer can do will get the poor mistreated machine rolling again - it has been abused and damaged far beyond its tolerance. And where does that leave you? How can you be the terror of the midnight road without your velosteam? How can you strike fear into the hauliers and nobility when you are easily overtaken by milk-carts and locobuses?

It is time to leave this life behind you and to rescue what you can of your pride. Turn to the **Epilogue** to discover how your future will unroll ahead of you.

The Aramanth punchcards set the machine whirring. It settles into a steady rhythm of calculation. What will you ask it to do?

Analyse Telegraph Guild Codes...	
(**telegraph observations** ☑ ☑)	**252**
Decode the Valencia Orders...	
(**punchcards (Valencia Orders)**)	**1498**
Leave the machine...	**noted passage**

Onboard the cruiser you find several **ropes**, a **rope ladder**, **ten guineas in banknotes**, and a **chess set**.

Leave the cruiser...	**210**

You have reached the turning to Harpsden, a short way south of Henley and not far from the river. The village and its great house are hidden from the road but the estate's white-painted gateposts and fences have lined the roadside for some miles.

Ride into Henley...	**702**
Turn off to Harpsden...	**494**

576

The prisoner is a woman in a torn dress with a wild look in her eye. "Get me out of here!" she whispers intently. "They will hang me for killing my husband!"

"You killed your husband?"

"No more than he deserved," she spits. "Now get me out!"

If you wish to free her, you will need a **skeleton key** or to make an INGENUITY roll of difficulty 12, adding 3 if you possess some **lockpicks**. If you are unsuccessful or choose to leave her, you can quietly return to your velosteam.

Successful INGENUITY roll or **skeleton key**... 368
Failed INGENUITY roll or leave her be...   313

577

You come to the junction of the Reading road and the lane to Woodcote. A hamlet here called Cray's Pond stands around the eponymous pool, which is really little more than a muddy duck-bath. Nearby is Elvenden Priory, but whether you will receive a welcome there is hard to tell. It stands a short distance to the north in its own small valley: a long, low flint-walled building with a bell-tower standing over the freshly-repaired pan-tiled roof.

Prepare an ambush here...   900
Ride to Elvendon Priory...   642
Go on to Goring...   487
Ride up the lane to Woodcote...   520
Head south towards Whitchurch...   749

578

"A lawyer? You don't dress like a lawyer," replies Lady Pomiane. "Well, if you think you can help, you're can try. Come in and take a look at the papers."

Enter the house...   352

579

Defeating the three brigands is no simple task and you are left panting and breathless. Still, with their prone figures on the ground you have a chance to turn the tables. You can loot the three **clubs (PAR 2)** if you like, along with the contents of their purses (**£4 12s**). The leader of the three also has a pair of **binoculars**, which may explain how they saw you approaching.

Leave the wood...   343
Ride further into the wood...   130

580

You are forced to ignore your machine's labouring cries for attention and you keep the regulator open. Then, just as you are climbing a hill-crest and putting your pursuers behind you, you lose power. The heavy machine skids and topples and you slide down the slope. It takes some time before you are able to right it and attempt to relight the burner. Add one **damage point** to your Adventure Sheet and gain a **wound** as a result of the fall. You also realise that the **leather satchel** containing the prototypes must be somewhere on the road behind you - but there is no chance of going back. You have lost the package and failed to complete your task. If you are still able to ride, you must make for the safety of the woods again.

If you have five **wounds**...   999
If your velosteam is **beyond repair**...   874
Otherwise...   452

581

The Telegraph station here is nowhere near as large or as important as nearby Nettlebed or Caversham. This is only a C-class tower, largely dealing in local messages. The commanding officer is unusually open and welcoming, quite against the policies of his secretive guild, but then he has to live in this small community and has his own interests.

"My boy is studying to be a Guildsman," he says. "The requirements are much stricter than they used to be. I only needed to work the old manual signalling - he needs a headful of mathematics and more."

Return to the town...   488

582

You send a trio of bullets at the guards, one after another, either wounding them or striking the metal of their cupolas so close that they believe you an incredible sharpshooter and throw down their weapons. You step out into the roadway, brandishing your weapons.

Loot the wagons...   531

583

He shakes his head. "In that case you had better leave." He takes the **Whitchurch ballot list** back and replaces it in his pocket. "If you change your mind, come and see me again."

Leave his Lordship...   460

ᔑ 584 ᔐ

South Stoke is a larger place than its northerly neighbour, but only just. It has grown considerably since the navvies arrived to build the railway. Their encampment on the side of the railway embankment is by far the liveliest part of the village, making the street of thatched cottages seem very plain and quiet.

Ride into the navvies' camp...	**1118**
Ride to the railway bridge...	**1129**
Head towards North Stoke...	**1513**
Set out for Goring...	**568**
Board your boat... (**moored at South Stoke**)	**257**

ᔑ 585 ᔐ

If you have the codeword *Burden*, turn to **534** immediately. The Fox at Ibstone is a place where the locals can drink and complain about the harsh rates they are charged by their landlord, Lord Ponsonby, who lives in Wormsley Park.

It seems that he has been steadily increasing rents. The villagers fear that he will evict them when they are unable to pay and reclaim the village as part of his parkland.

Buy a drink and chat with the locals...	(**2s**)	**51**
Leave the pub...		**977**

ᔑ 586 ᔐ

The stone bridge over the Thames shudders with the ceaseless rumble of engine wheels, day and night. That way lies Maidenhead and the busy Bath Road. On this side of the river, the road follows the river bank around in the direction of Marlow to the north-east and loops past Harpsden to the south.

Another road runs north-west: before the road into the Chilterns reaches the hills it passes along a straight, flat stretch of ground known as Fair Mile, where fashionable villas are being erected on the outskirts of town. Finally, a road leads west, straight uphill, towards the airship station at Rotherfield, where the lumbering giants of the sky are tended and fed.

Take the road towards Rotherfield...	**6**
Travel north-west up Fair Mile...	**163**
Steam north-east towards Marlow...	**126**
Cross the bridge over the Thames...	**863**
Ride south towards Harpsden...	**355**

ᔑ 587 ᔐ

You are climbing up towards an attic window when you slip and crash to the ground, letting out an involuntary yell. Crunching gravel warns of someone's approach and a voice cries out, "Stay where you are or I shoot!"

Needless to say, you are already up and running. Roll a dice to see whether the gamekeeper is lucky enough to catch you with his shot.

Score 1-3   The pellets whizz past
Score 4-6   A blast in the rear - gain a **wound**

If you have five **wounds**...	**999**
Otherwise...	**343**

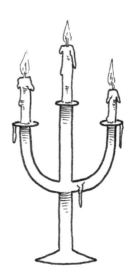

ᔑ 588 ᔐ

The Constables take a good look at you: they seem to recognise you from their set of printofit pictures. You will have to convince them quickly if you expect to get away. Make an INGENUITY roll of difficulty 15, adding 1 if you possess **Major Redford's card**. If you succeed in the roll, you can then choose the direction of your onward travel.

Failed INGENUITY roll!	**310**
Cross the bridge into Wallingford...	**270**
Ride south along the Thames...	**860**
Steam towards Nettlebed...	**698**
Head to Watlington...	**229**

❧ 589 ❧

The great Bath Road is one of the arteries of the region, pumping iron and coal backwards and forwards between the capital and the cities of the west. Whole caravans of steam wagons charge over the ancient road - a way that has been here since before the Romans straightened and smoothed it.

Prepare an ambush here...	**530**
Ride north towards Wargrave...	**418**
Take the side-road to Sonning...	**91**

❧ 590 ❧

You had agreed to help the Earl of Macclesfield preserve his estate intact after stopping his carriage on the valley road. Of course, whether you do help him or not is up to you. Remove the codeword *Burnett*.

Lady Pomiane, who claims she should have inherited part of the estate, lives nearby in Swyncombe House. When you ride up the drive late one evening, the windows are dark and shuttered, but smoke drifts from a chimney. One cracked wall of the house is supported by unwieldy timber scaffolding. Several spaniels are mooching around in the yard, but they have not caught wind of you yet.

Set the place ablaze...	**40**
Try to meet Lady Pomiane...	**321**
Leave a threatening note...	**409**

❧ 591 ❧

Just as you have given up hope, gunfire rings out. You leap to the grille to see what you can. A grappling hook scrapes past and swings the door open. Hanging from a ladder is none other than Captain Coke. He gives you a grin and extends an arm. "One good deed deserves another, matey."

"My velosteam!" you cry.

"All in hand."

You look to where a party of airship pirates are dangling from their craft, making your velosteam fast to lines and hauling it into the air with them. The Constables are kept under a constant barrage of fire from the pirates above and flee in confusion. Swinging on the foot of the ladder, you rise into the sky to the sound of throbbing propellors, rifle shots and Coke's infectious laughter!

Turn to...	**819**

❧ 592 ❧

Roll a dice to see whom you have stopped!

Score 1	A mining engineer	**469**
Score 2	A manufacturer	**491**
Score 3	A posse of journalists	**607**
Score 4	Several clerks	**20**
Score 5	A civil servant	**695**
Score 6	A travelling lady and servant	**723**

❧ 593 ❧

☐

If the box is empty, put a tick in it and read on. If it is already ticked, turn to **679** immediately.

"I've heard of you," says a rider, removing her wide-brimmed hat. "The Steam Highwayman here! I thought you worked more south-ways."

The rider insists on buying the round and pushes your coins back to you (regain **10s**). Several others come over and shoo a pair of students off the fireside table. Dandy Jim, Vicky Wren, Desdemonda Bruce and Italian all introduce themselves excitedly.

"We stay on the right side of the Constables... mostly," says the diminuitive Vicky. "Skip a few tolls, break a few speed limits, that sort of thing. Nothing like your exploits."

"Ride a Ferguson, don't you?" asks the dark man known only as 'Italian'. He has no trace of any accent. "I'd exchange my Imperial in a moment. Used to have a Humber Lampades, but the boiler blew north of Newcastle. It was always thirsty. I had taken it down to Turville, near Stonor, since there's a lady there who can work all sorts of wonders."

Soon you are all standing outside, admiring brasswork and pistons and comparing pressures and heater ignitions. Just as you are finishing your pint, a porter from St John's college comes puffing up with a **leather satchel**. It needs to be delivered to an address in Manchester post haste. The riders deferentially offer you the job first, if you would like to take it. They payment is **£10** for a safe delivery with a **£2** bonus if it is done inside two days.

Accept the job...	**17**
Let another rider take it...	**725**

❧ 594 ❧

As you fall to Coke's blade, you hear the sounds of yells and shrieks as the crew and passengers of your craft begin to panic. However, the pirates neither skin them nor throw them overboard: they are locked in the cargo hold under guard.

Coke returns to where he left you bleeding by the rail. "So, matey. You put a up a good fight. What will it be - shall I end it here for you, or will you join with me?"

"I will be a sky-pirate."	**938**
"I would rather die."	**559**

❧ 595 ❧

Northend is little more than a large farm and the cottages of several families who work the land. The farmer himself can normally be found stomping around the fields, considering how to raise productivity and prepare for hard times ahead while the going is good.

Talk to the farmer...	**264**
Take the road to Stonor...	**430**
Steam down the holloway to Turville...	**120**
Ride uphill towards Christmas Common...	**4**

❧ 596 ❧

The ball skips over the step, tumbles roughly across the gravel and buries itself in the shrubbery. It will be several more blows before you can return to the game proper, during which time your opponents are making good progress.

Turn to...	**1132**

❧ 597 ❧

The protestors are slowly convinced. They agree to join with the Compact - particularly after you give them the name of a contact to seek. They make their way off into the woods to the south as quickly as they can and you remount your velosteam, eager to put ground between yourself and the Constables before they notice the absence of their prisoners. Gain the codeword *Bargain*, as the Compact will doubtless be pleased with your recruiting. Gain a **solidarity point** too.

Turn to...	**313**

❧ 598 ❧

Wallingford has plenty of goods available. Asking around, you are directed to several shops and market stalls, though no-one wants to talk to you for very long.

Food and Drink	To buy	To sell
pork pie	2s	2s
bottle of Beehive Stout	3s	2s
bottle of wine	9s	5s
Clothing	To buy	To sell
lace shawl	£1 5s	15s
cloak	£1	-
Jewellery	To buy	To sell
locket	-	6s
pocket watch	£3	£1 18s
silver ring	-	8s
silver bracelet	-	16s
silver necklace	-	£1 10s
gold ring	-	£2 5s
gold bracelet	-	£2 8s
gold necklace	-	£3 18s
Tools	To buy	To sell
rope	4s	2s
net	6s	4s
shovel	8s	6s
adjustable wrench (ENG+1)	£1 8s	18s
welding tools	-	£1
grappling iron	12s	8s
measuring line	-	6s
brass flange joint	-	4s
high pressure valve	18s	10s
Weapons	To buy	To sell
sabre (PAR 3)	£1 5s	8s
blunderpistol (ACC 6)	£4	£2
Other items	To buy	To sell
bolt of cloth	-	15s
fine clock	-	£6 3s

Leave the market...	**270**

❧ 599 ❧

The driver hauls on the brake lever and peers down into your beam like a dazed rabbit. Only then do you realise that she is only a very young woman - perhaps it was best you didn't shoot her.

You fling open the door of the passenger compartment. Inside is a lanky aristocrat with a tall hat on his lap and a sword entangled in his cloak. He eyes your weapons:

"You have me at your advantage. A highway robber... I have use for someone like you. You can rob me now, or you can await me at the Castle. When I return I will have a lucrative opportunity to discuss with you, suited for someone of your violent talents."

"Enough of your blather. Give me your purse."	**669**
"Tell me now and I'll consider it."	**764**

❦ 600 ❧

A tall iron gallows stands at the roadside here. The chain swings freely for the time being, singing its ominous little jingle to the wind and the roads. If you have the codeword *Bernadette*, turn to **388** immediately.

Head into the nearby wood...	**401**
Ride on to Cane End...	**455**
Take the road to High Moor Cross...	**939**
Steam towards Henley...	**158**

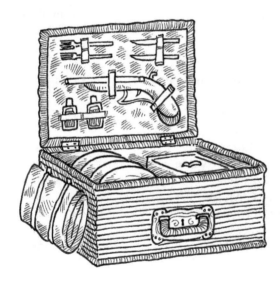

❦ 601 ❧

You wind your way through unnamed hamlets, past chalk pits and down the hill towards Stoke Row. You pass no vehicles or pedestrians, only accompanied by the hissing of your velosteam's pistons and the cry of kites above.

On to Stoke Row...	**457**

❦ 602 ❧

Your shots do little more than scare the birds away - to begin with. Then one ill-judged bullet brings down a heavy branch that knocks you to the ground. Gain a **wound** and if you have **five wounds**, turn to **999** immediately.

You must leave the wood to seek treatment for your injury.

Ride to Gallowstree Common...	**600**
Head towards Woodcote...	**488**

❦ 603 ❧

The villagers of Cane End are delighted to see you again. You are greeted by familiar faces who seem to be both better fed and healthier than when you last saw them. "Your goodness to us here has changed the village's fortunes," says the vicar. "New tools, new clothes, new work. Medicines for the unwell, woollen blankets for mothers and newborn."

"Nobody comes back here," says the widow you helped so long ago. "Nobody but you, that is. Why do you remember us?"

They have prepared a meal to celebrate your return and spread it out on the common, eating on benches and tables made of Mother Hebble's barn doors. The food is simple but good. You can enjoy their company without the need to ride on tonight and when you leave in the mist of the early morning, you can know that here at least you have changed lives for the better.

Steam to Gallowstree Common...	**600**
Ride south towards Reading...	**560**
Head northwest towards Woodcote...	**488**
Take Deadman's Lane south-west...	**396**

❦ 604 ❧

"Most wear it because they've sold out to the Guild," replies the haulier, "And because they'd rather accept a wage than earn their own living."

"Not always an easy choice," you reply. "And it hasn't been easy for me. But this badge... It tells you less about me than you think. It is a mere badge of convenience."

The haulier licks his lips, thinking of what he could do with a badge of convenience like that. If you would like to sell it, erase it from your **Adventure Sheet** and add **£2 10s** to your wallet.

Leave the pub...	**867**

❧ 605 ❧

Here at Henley market there is a multiplicity of goods on offer. You can take your time to peruse the shops and stalls, maybe not sure of the best prices, but certainly likely to see something you like.

Food and Drink	To buy	To sell
wheel of cheese	£2 4s	15s
picnic hamper	£4	-
Clothing	To buy	To sell
mask	4s	-
lace shawl	£1 5s	15s
goggles (MOT+1)	£2 15s	£1 15s
eyepatch (RUTH+1)	15s	5s
Medical	To buy	To sell
bandages	3s	-
soothing lotion	2s	-
bottle of chloroform	£2 5s	-
bottle of poison	15s	8s
Tools	To buy	To sell
rope	6s	2s
snare	3s	1s
net	8s	4s
lantern	10s	4s
shovel	9s	6s
axe	15s	6s
fishing line	2s	-
tarpaulin	6s	4s
copper pipe	8s	3s
telescope	-	£2 5s
Other items	To buy	To sell
jeweled bible	-	£4
fine clock	-	36 2s

If you have the codeword *Broadly*, turn to **522** immediately.

Head over to the auctions...   1144
Visit the stone broker... (**tally stick 712**)   1100
Look around Henley some more...   702

❧ 606 ❧

"I believe you are correct," replies the priest. "What insight you have. A desire for secret, forbidden and controlling knowledge has motivated a great deal of unclean and sinful thoughts in this place. Deeds done to learn more and to know more have made this house an altar of a kind." Increase your INGENUITY by 1.

He prays once more. As he does, the light in the lantern flickers and then burns more brightly. "That should be the last," he says. "Let's return to the sunlight."

Turn to...   329

❧ 607 ❧

The journalists are a group of lean, shabby-suited fellows who have clubbed together to buy tickets to Turkey, to report on the incredible events there. They have their travelling expenses with them (**£16**) and one of them is wearing a smart **bow tie (GAL+1)**. If you **Escaped from Gaol** or **Cheated the Gallows**, turn to **199** immediately.

Turn to...   **noted passage**

❧ 608 ❧

It takes a long time and much re-reading of the documents, but eventually you believe you can offer Lady Pomiane a solution. You point out several details and inconsistencies in the Earl's agreements that indicate his intention to deceive and to extend a twenty-year lease into outright ownership. "This should help you at the hearing, I'm sure," you tell her with satisfaction.

Lady Pomiane is very happy. "Perhaps there is more to you than meets the eye," she says. "I am not a rich woman, nor will I be when I have these farms back, but I can be a grateful one." She leaves the room and returns with a **dark cloak (RUTH+1)** and a **pneumatic manual (ENG+3)**. "These belonged to my husband. If they are of use, take them with my thanks and this money." She also presses a five guinea piece - **£5 5s** - into your hand.

You leave the house and several weeks later the rumour reaches you: the Earl lost his case and Lady Pomiane's farms were returned to her. Perhaps the Earl misjudged you after all. Gain a **solidarity point** for assisting the widow in finding justice.

Ride on...   110

✧ 609 ✧

Reading and its smog recedes behind you. The road winds uphill past Blagrave Farm, Chazey Heath and Greendean Farm. A squall of rain sends silver sheets running across the wheatfields and orchards. You shelter for a short while beneath a tree. Roll a dice to see what you encounter...

Score 1-2	An open-topped carriage...	**47**
Score 3-4	A rainbow and an empty road...	**807**
Score 5-6	A labourer heading to work...	**128**

✧ 610 ✧

You raise your mallet and swing with all of your might. The entire assembly watch as your ball ricochets up over their heads and crashes into the drinks table.

"Oh, poor show," says Major Redford, as the noise of smashing glass subsides. "That wasn't very clever."

Your opponents proceed up the lawn and although you eventually pass **one hoop**, your overexertion has left you risking defeat. It will take a bold move now to snatch victory.

Turn to... **1132**

✧ 611 ✧

You steady yourself on your velosteam and time your run down the slope. You will have to have nerves of steel and considerable skill to prevent serious damage to your velosteam. Make a MOTORING roll of difficulty 13 to ram the Bishop's steamer off the road, adding 2 to your roll if you have a **ramming beak** fitted to your velosteam.

Successful MOTORING roll!	**284**
Failed MOTORING roll!	**652**

✧ 612 ✧

It should be possible to improve upon bridge design. After all, technology has advanced but the structures commonly used are still based on ancient principles of tension and compression. Surely with the power of steam computation you will be able to produce something...

It takes the machine a long time to compute a useable answer to your puzzle. The plans it produce use suspension principles and have a lattice-work tower in the centre of the span. Intriguing - and futuristic? Would it work? Gain a **computed bridge structure**, remove the **punchcards (Habbukuk K)** and gain a point of ENGINEERING if your score is 10 or less.

Leave the machine... **noted passage**

✧ 613 ✧

The drinkers here are enjoying the local Colonial Bitter: a strong, clear brew particularly developed for freighting to South Africa and Australia. It is neither too rich nor too light but is well-hopped and fairly dry. At your elbow two customers are discussing the Earl of Macclesfield and his continuing attempts to get hold of South Coombe and Enderby farms - at any price. Another is telling his friends of how he witnessed the arrest of a trouble-maker at the last fair, who was promptly thrown into the gaol in the castle. "Be some time until he's out again! Maybe the fair next year!"

Return to the parlour... **281**

✧ 614 ✧

A few gunshots over the heads of the guards, driver and engineer convince them to flee, giving you time to set charges at crucial points along the wagons. Remove the **explosives** from your possessions and make an ENGINEERING roll of difficulty 12, adding 2 for each point of **explosives expert** you possess.

Successful ENGINEERING roll!	**662**
Failed ENGINEERING roll!	**727**

✧ 615 ✧

You open up the regulator and feel your Ferguson accelerate down the good hard road. A plume of white dust rises from the chalky surface beneath you. Ahead is the village of South Stoke where the Imperial Western Railway crosses the Thames again.

Stop at South Stoke...	**584**
Continue on towards Goring...	**487**

✧ 616 ✧

The Livingstone punchcards clatter as they flip through the machine. It pauses, almost as if taking breath. What will you instruct it to do?

Analyse other punchcard patterns...	**1389**
Leave the machine...	**noted passage**

❧ 617 ❧

If you are **Wanted by the Telegraph Guild**, turn to **429** immediately.

Christmas Common is a village of woodcutters, bodgers and craftspeople whose cottages are hidden beneath the dark trees of the high ridge. Only a short distance away, the escarpment falls to the Oxford plain, and mounted high above the village is one of the region's biggest Telegraph towers - a class A, manned around the clock, constantly sending coded messages back and forth on several channels at once. The Guildsmen have made themselves part of the village here and have brought prosperity to this once isolated community.

Investigate the Telegraph Station...	207
Observe the tower...	
(**telescope** or **binoculars**)	185
Ride south-west along the hill-top...	110
Head down Watlington Hill...	216
Take the lane to Northend...	595
Drive north-east towards Stokenchurch...	102

❧ 618 ❧

"Excellent. That list will guide you where you need to go. We don't have much time."

Leave his Lordship...	460

❧ 619 ❧

Nuffield Place is the home of the Howitz family. It is set back from the road inside its own parkland, independent and aloof from the working community of Nettlebed. If you have the codeword *Betrayed*, turn to **1493**.

Return to your travels...	836

❧ 620 ❧

"I know you," you say, remembering the badly-printed portrait on the poster you saw in the Angel. "Captain Coke. There's quite a reward for your arrest."

The man opposite you changes his face in a moment. "There is - and with reason. But you don't think yourself the one to claim it, do you?"

"I am your match."	948
"No, I am not interested in any reward."	650
"Why should I spare you?"	691

❧ 621 ❧

Once your intention is clear, the passengers begin to panic. One makes to leap down from the upper deck. Make a RUTHLESSNESS roll of difficulty 8.

Successful RUTHLESSNESS roll!	16
Failed RUTHLESSNESS roll!	29

❧ 622 ❧

"No surprises there! Those filthy anarchists will soon be squashed like vermin, and all their foul talk of revolution silenced for good. Your kind certainly don't deserve any mercy - after all the deaths of the innocent at your hands!"

You are marked as a dangerous prisoner and sent directly to Wallingford Gaol. Gain the codeword *Brand*.

Turn to...	841

❧ 623 ❧

You carefully introduce the Stiverton punchcards into the hopper and spin the reading gauge that prepares the machine for new code. Remove the **punchcards (Stiverton S)** from your possessions.

Without any further input, the engine begins to pinch, flick and read the cards with a set of spring-loaded rollers. Each turns a precise degree depending on the position of the punched holes and you can follow the mechanical reaction as control rods and cogs whirr deep inside the machine in response to each moment of code. The movements fan out exponentially through the metalwork until the whole thing clicks like a clock.

Then, as the last card is read, a wave of stillness passes over the flickering pieces and you see that the machine has been reset into exactly the position in which you found it. The punchcards have been shredded and are lying in a waste hopper beside the furnace chute.

This is not a time to remain anywhere near the Guild's engines. If this code does what you were told it would, the consequences will not be immediate but they will be powerful. Gain the codeword *Bent*.

Leave the compound...	682

❧ 624 ❧

You are recommended a business-like haulier called Jackie Jackson who is a respected member of the

Haulage Guild. She considers your proposition and makes the following offer inbetween puffs on a large meerschaum pipe; "I'll fetch your timber for you. I'll haul it here, to Nettlebed, where good building wood is in demand, for thirty shillings. Should expect to sell a full load of oak for around twenty pound, if we take the bark to the tanners too. Or I'll take it up to Oxford for you. Cost you more in haulage but we might be able to get a better price. Your choice."

"Bring it here."	(£1 10s)	**795**
"Take it to Oxford."	(£3 10s)	**865**
"I'm not ready to deal yet."		**677**

❧ 625 ❧

The preacher is an able swordsman. He parries your thrusts confidently and strikes with control, but eventually you best him. "Where did you learn to fight?" you ask as he surrenders.

"I was a man of fortune before I was a man of the cloth," he replies, "Much as you are." His pockets contain only a few coins (**13s**) but he has an impressive **pectoral cross** and two fine-looking **bottles of wine** in the coach with him.

The Preacher will certainly remember you: unless you have a **mask** you will now be **Wanted by the Constables**.

Turn to...   **noted passage**

❧ 626 ❧

The protestors acknowledge the truth in your words. "Too many people want to solve the problems of violence and control with more violence," says one woman. "Non-compliant, non-violent protest has a power too. Even martyrdom has its place."

They gather themselves, unsure of how to escape. "Head south into the woods," you recommend, "And then due east across the farmlands towards the Thicket. There are countless hiding-places there, and the Constables are somewhat loath to get in too deep."

They collect themselves and the young woman plants a grateful kiss on your cheek. Gain **two solidarity points**.

Now you yourself had better be off before the Constables realise what has happened.

Turn to...   **313**

❧ 627 ❧

You trail after the priest as he repeats his prayers in each room of the house. Books and maps of ancient cities line the hallways. An air of secrecy insulates the upper rooms. The last place Father Patrick approaches is the cellar and in the last chamber of that, beneath the dining room, he falls silent.

"What is it?" you ask.

"All created things are made to worship," he replies. "Even houses. But when they do not worship God, they honour lesser things, allowing unclean spirits in. The question is, what has been honoured here?"

"Perhaps it was money?"	**743**
"The original builders of the house?"	**971**
"Fame?"	**992**
"Knowledge?"	**606**

❧ 628 ❧

Cobstone Mill sits poised amid its yard and the smallholding on a slight rise in the crest, perfectly positioned atop Turville hill where the westerly breezes are forced upwards by the land. If you have the codeword *Brokenhearted*, turn to **643** immediately.

Talk to Miller Fursham...	**651**
Ride towards Ibstone...	**977**
Ride towards Fingest...	**867**

❧ 629 ❧

The airship crew are carrying only the little remaining of their flight pay - which you can relieve them of: **£2 9s**. However, you can also take a **box of cigars**, a **gold necklace** from one of the hostesses and an **airship officer's cap**. You will certainly be **Wanted by the Atmospheric Union** now, if you are not already.

Ride away...   **noted passage**

❧ 630 ❧

At Hambleden Lock a long weir straggles between islets from bank to bank. The lock cut is narrow and a steam crane stands beside the keeper's house, topped by a dirty cloud of steam.

On the northern bank three tall watermills stand beside their own stream, each turning a massive wheel. Lighters carrying shoddy and rags from cities along the river are unloading for the paper-makers, while along the towpath stand a row of laden wheatwagons with their engine.

The mill is emblazoned with the livery of the Imperial Northern Milling and Manufacturing Company and boasts its own C-class telegraph tower.

	To buy	To sell
Charcoal	£10	-
Furniture	-	-
Machinery	-	£25
Pottery	-	£20
Cotton	£7	£6
Woollen cloth	-	£8
Coal	£8	£14
Beer	-	£20
Wheat	-	£8
Malt	£10	£8
Frozen Meat	£15	£14
Ice	£10	£9

If you have just sold any **Wheat**, turn to **461** immediately.

Pass through the lock...
  (**2s** or **Bargee's Badge**)   855
Moor here...   390
Travel the short distance to Aston Wharf...   950
Follow the river downstream...   251

❧ 631 ❧

The strongbox contains a **gold bar**, a **gold necklace** and a sheaf of crumbling, illegible papers. What might they have been? Shares to a long-defunct company? A valuable will? It is useless to speculate: the ink has faded past reading and the paper turns to dust as you pick them up.

Turn to...   **noted passage**

❧ 632 ❧

Coke falls at your feet and his men leap for the lines to their own airship. The crew of your craft hurry over and help restrain the pirate. "We should return to Rotherfield at once," says the Captain. "This chap is worth a great deal - and you can share in the reward, too."

The airship turns about and when you disembark you are given **£12 10s** as your share for capturing Coke. "I bet you've never seen so much money," says your first mate as he counts the coins into your hand. Gain the codeword *Bernadette*.

Turn to...   454

❧ 633 ❧

Just a short distance from the main Henley road, a spring emerges from the hillside in a crystal rush. It spurts out from ferns into a cold pool. The water is sweet and this would be a good place to repair your velosteam as long as you have a filter.

If you wanted to observe the telegraph tower at the top of the hill here, there is a good sight-line from a crook in a willow tree beside the pool. Note this **passage number** on your **Adventure Sheet**.

Repair your velosteam here...
  (**pump and filter**)   180
Observe the telegraph tower...
  (**telescope** or **binoculars**)   1117
Strike out north-west across country...   518
Return to the main road...   682

❧ 634 ❧

Your final attack leaves the leader of the river pirates bleeding on the bank, but in the time you have been duelling, his gang have poled your boat out into the stream and are making off into the night. Several have guns and they begin to fire at you: it is time to get away. How fortunate that your velosteam stands on the towpath. Unfortunately you must remove the boat and any **cargo** from your **Adventure Sheet**: you will not be seeing them again.

Ride away towards Oxford...   259
Head towards Watlington...   339

❧ 635 ❧

Remove the codeword *Benign*. The ground is flinty and ridden with tree-roots. You make several excavations in likely-looking spots and late that night beneath the glow of the moon you find something glinting and golden. It is a torc and several pieces of golden finery, presumably from some long-rotted leatherwork. If you want to keep it whole, mark it as a **treasure trove** amongst your **possessions**. Otherwise this is plainly a find that anyone would value - you could note it as a **gold necklace** and two **gold bracelets**.

Return to the wood...   401

❧ 636 ❧

Turning around to Culham takes a little while, but you get the cruiser there without too much difficulty and moor it up. The lock-keeper emerges from his cottage and turns pale on seeing the cruiser. "So 'tis back," he says. "The cursed steamer! Didn't you know to leave it be? It brings death with it - death!"

He is plainly rather a dramatic fellow, but since the owner of the steamer cannot be far, you leave it moored here. Gain the codeword *Barchester*.

Sail on to Oxford...   **210**

❧ 637 ❧

Roads leave Watlington on all points of the compass. In the distance a passenger carriage approaches from Oxford. To the south and east the Chiltern hills rise suddenly like a wooded ocean's curling wave. One narrow road heads straight to the flank of the nearest hill, then climbs up to Christmas Common, marked by the vanes of a Telegraph Guild tower perched at the hill-crest. Another lane winds up a howe before rising into Britwell Hill Woods. The flat roads along the plain are far better maintained, broader and paved with slag and clinker, built to stand the heavy use of road trains and steam carriages.

Steer up the winding lane...	**110**
Ride north-east to Aston Hill...	**205**
Take the narrow road up to Christmas Common ...	**216**
Set out for Oxford...	**259**
Head for Wallingford...	**307**

❧ 638 ❧

After hours of reading by the firelight, you are forced to put the papers down. "I cannot assist you," you tell her. "This is beyond me. But I should warn you that the jealous Earl bade me to threaten or hurt you in order to get his way."

"Exactly how I would expect him to behave," snaps Lady Pomiane. "Well, if you haven't helped me, you haven't hindered me either. I will simply have to see how the case goes. In the meantime, why don't you rest here tonight? You look in need of a good meal and though the place is cold, it is dry."

Under the care of Lady Pomiane's servants you are found a room with old but rich furnishings. Resting here, any **wounds** you have will have the chance to heal and should be replaced by **scars**. In the morning you will have to ride on and leave the wrangle over the estate for others more learned than yourself.

Ride on...   **110**

❧ 639 ❧

Your reputation means that the farmer feels safe stopping for a while to chatter with you. Roll a dice to see what he can tell you.

Score 1-2	Brigands in the wood	**804**
Score 3-4	The well-digging at Stoke Row	**857**
Score 5	The arms fair	**820**
Score 6	Poachers	**893**

❧ 640 ❧

The Fleur de Lis stands in the centre of Stokenchurch, its proud sign of monarchial allegiance hanging out over the main road between Oxford and London. The landlord, a large man with a fine walrus moustache, offers beer, meals and rooms to everyone on the long journey. If you have the codeword *Beringed*, turn to **1189**.

Buy a drink... (**3s**)	**1014**
Take a room... (**£3**)	**1084**
Ask for your safe-box... (**rusty key**)	**1059**
Leave the inn...	**308**

❧ 641 ❧

The barmaid who brings you your pint of Lost City Pale Ale seems keen to chat. As you gulp at the refreshing, almost lager-like summer ale, she begins to tell you about the protestors she saw arrested at the Arms Fair. Apparently, a prison wagon took them on towards Henley.

"My kid brother's amongst them," she says. "He didn't expect that."

"He should have been prepared for it," you reply.

The beer starts with a very light nose and high carbonation, but it gathers a little more richness in a final warmth before the resiny hop finish.

Return to the parlour...	**1515**
Leave the pub...	**297**

❧ 642 ❧

The monks of Elvendon are craftsmen and builders. They keep a particularly fine garden, employing and interacting with the people of the surrounding villages, but they also retain a certain separation from the busy world. Certain brothers spend almost all of their time in prayer, worship and contemplation of the Scriptures.

When you visit, you are greeted politely but

coolly and welcomed into the square cloister garden around which the priory has been built. Although from the outside the buildings seem traditional, here you can see how much of the priory is iron-framed, supporting lightweight walls of wood, glass and wattling.

Visit the chapel...   1010
Visit the infirmary...   1017
Visit the workshop...   1060
Talk to the Prior...   1106
Leave the priory...   1131

✎ 643 ✐

Miller Fursham has run out of time. He has been forced to sell his home and livelihood to the Telegraph Guild. The sweeping sails are already coming down and Telegraph green paint has been sloshed over the gates, lintels and woodwork. In the yard, a crew are putting together a repeating telegraph frame to mount on the stump of the mill. There will be no more flour ground here.

Ride towards Ibstone...   977
Ride towards Fingest...   867

✎ 644 ✐

The evening is closing in, but on the recreation ground the Stokenchurch Warriors football team are practicing - again. You skirt the carefully-mown pitch and take the lane, turning left after the clay pit and left again at the lodge where a gated road leads into Wormsley Park. Then, headed south into the shadow of the woods, you pass a twenty-acre field still full with wheat waiting its turn under the steam-powered scythe and continue on beneath the hornbeams, ashes and beeches of Commonhill wood. A distant crow barks somewhere.

Drive through the wood and into Ibstone village... **977**

✎ 645 ✐

Janet looks at you coldly. "I'd tell you to ask him yourself, you nosy prying blighter, except I wouldn't want him going back over it. You have any idea what it's like on the peninsula? Shells screaming over, lads his age drowning in mud, gangrene claiming as many lives as the Spanish. Bleeding Anarchists. If they had kept themselves to themselves, they could have had a nice quiet revolution and our good King Charles," (and here she spits) "Might have been distracted by something like a horse-race or a pretty ankle. But oh no, they have to come out all loud and heroic and half the governments of Europe decry it and send in the troops in solidarity with King Nicolas. And that's what my boy gets for it: trench-foot, gangrene, amputation and sorrow."

"Did they pension him?"

She snorts. "Did they just. Ineligible due to misconduct."

"I can do something about that."   **790**
"I'm sorry to hear it."   **763**

✎ 646 ✐

The gamekeeper's cottage is a small, steep-roofed home with a cheery fire in the parlour. It is plainly the house of an outdoorsman: the furnishings are simple and sparse, but Mr Sands feeds you well.

"You've done a pair of work for me, you have," he says, giving one of his rare smiles as he packs tobacco into his pipe. "Let me shake your hand." You are now the **Friend of Mr Sands**. As you sit by the fire and enjoy a bottle of last winter's sloe gin together, he tells you much about his life as a gamekeeper, the secrets of the trade and the great fraternity of keepers across the land. "We all trusts one another. All has to." He even goes so far as to teach you the gamekeeper's whistle: a secret melody used by keepers and their especial friends. You may wish to use it whenever you see vermin such as foxes or weasels nailed to a post: to do so, add the digits of the **passage number** together and subtract the total from that **passage number** and turn to the resulting passage.

Mr Sands also treats any **wounds** that you might have with his particular ointment, which seems to heal them overnight without leaving any **scars**. After a good night's rest, a hearty breakfast and an early start you proceed on your way.

Ride into Woodcote...   **488**
Head towards Stoke Row...   **457**

❧ 647 ❧

"Who'sat?" he asks. "Gotta get back to Henley f' watch. Gotta keep the town safe!" He collapses where he stands.

Is he fortunate to have fallen into your hands, instead of falling into the river or being run down by a road-engine in the fog? Perhaps he might end up floating home after all. Surely the world could do with fewer Constables.

Rob him and leave him beside the road...	**331**
Rob him and throw him in the river...	**301**
Take him back to Henley...	**255**

❧ 648 ❧

You whistle the little tune that Mr Sands taught you once more and are met by the response drifting through the trees. Your friend the gamekeeper comes out to greet you. "I'm working," he says, "But I hope you've used what I've taught you wisely. If you ain't met Keeper Hodge up at Wormsley Park, tell him from me to feed his ferrets on a leaner diet. The two I got from him don't chase. They just sits and squabbles."

Return to the road...	**664**

❧ 649 ❧

The long dyke here is roughly ten feet high above the meadows and crop-fields. Hawthorn stands about its flanks but the top is worn away with countless feet walking its length. It is perfect to ride your velosteam along.

Down below the dyke there are signs of ditches either side but the sides of these have largely crumbled and fallen in with the centuries.

Ride up towards Nuffield...	**836**
Steam down to Mongewell...	**860**

❧ 650 ❧

"I'm glad to hear it," replies Captain Coke, relaxing again. "After all, money is a little thing in this world, is it not?"

Return to the parlour...	**36**
Leave the inn...	**867**

❧ 651 ❧
□

If the box above is empty, tick it and read on. If it is already ticked, turn to **673** immediately.

Miller Fursham is the last in an unbroken line of eight generations of millers who have lived and worked here. He worries about being able to pass the same livelihood onto his son. "Corn is too high and bread too low," he tells you, patting down the flour from his old-fashioned long-tailed waistcoat. "I can't get a good price for my flour from the bakers, since most of them have their prices dictated to 'em by the guilds. And now the Telegraph Guild are wanting to buy me out, to turn the mill into a telegraph station. They're offering me enough to set up my family in security, but I don't know what I'll do for work. Milling is in my blood."

"Are all the bakers set against you?"

"The village bakers have margins as small as mine - corn's so high because of the landowners. What I need is a contract with a quality baker to give me some security for prices a year on. But I'm milling every day I can, and working in the land, just to make ends meet right now."

He shows you the samples of flour he has ready to take to bakeries: if you wish to help him by negotiating a contract with a baker, you can take a small sack of **Cobstone flour**.

Ride towards Ibstone...	**977**
Ride towards Fingest...	**867**

❧ 652 ❧

Your heavy Ferguson slams into the very rear of the Bishop's steamer, right where the coal bunker absorbs the force of the blow. The driver compensates, opens the regulator and surges forward, but you are thrown off your velosteam and land with a crash on the hard road surface. Your velosteam is mangled by the attempt - gain **two damage points** and **two wounds**. If your velosteam is now **beyond repair**, turn to **874** immediately, and if not but you now have **five wounds**, turn directly to **999**.

If you somehow survive your attempt, you mount your scuffed and wheezing machine and return to the road.

Turn to...   **801**

❧ 653 ❧

Here at the Freight Yard you are confronted by the organised chaos of loading and unloading, all governed by a patented tally system in which hard, celluloid freight tags are slotted onto a set of overhead rails and spat out to various labour gangs. They in turn collect, unload and transfer the cargo at a breakneck speed - for they are paid by how many loads they handle in a day.

A few engineers are ready to share their machinery with you - for a price.

	To buy	To sell
lantern	8s	4s
adjustable wrench (ENG+1)	£2	18s
tarpaulin	6s	2s
measuring line	10s	6s
brass flange joint	8s	4s
plaster of paris	4s	2s
roll of oiled silk	£8	£5
pneumatic manual (ENG+3)	-	£8s

Return to town...   270
Leave Wallingford now...   742

❧ 654 ❧

Landlady Janet has the kitchen boy lead you upstairs to a room lit by narrow leaded windows. There is a comfortable bed, a wash-stand and a cupboard in which you can leave belongings. "You can see our garden from here," says the boy at the window glass.

At last you can rest from your days in the saddle and nights on the roadside. The boy will bring you hot water to clean yourself and down in the yard is a covered area where you can tinker with your velosteam. Write any belongings you wish to leave here in the box above and note this **passage number** before making a choice.

Repair your velosteam...	**180**
Open a strongbox...	**138**
Tend your **wounds**...	**33**
Leave the inn...	**370**

❧ 655 ❧
☐ ☐ ☐ ☐

If any of the boxes above are empty, tick one. If all four are already ticked, erase the ticks and turn to **1240** immediately.

You cannot remain here at the roadside: you must ride away before anyone comes to investigate tonight's events. Which way will you turn?

Towards Aston Ferry	**280**
On to Sonning...	**690**
Cross Henley Bridge...	**1251**

❧ 656 ❧

The villagers recognise you from your previous visit. "Kind stranger," says one. "We thought you were just appeasing your conscience - but you plainly care about us or you wouldn't have come back! We wouldn't be taking your money, but that we have the sick and ill to care for here, and the aged too. There's not many as can earn a full day's wage here in the village." Gain a **solidarity point**.

Ride off towards Gallowstree Common...	**600**
Take the Reading road...	**560**
Head northwest towards Woodcote...	**488**
Steam off down Deadman's Lane...	**356**

❧ 657 ❧

As the pirates board, you draw your own weapons and join the fight. You overpower the first few, but quickly find yourself face to face with Captain Coke himself. He is armed with a short-handled hooked blade, which hums with some sort of charge. Every time he bypasses your parry and strikes you, the blade will temporarily reduce your NIMBLENESS by 1: after the fight, return your score to its normal value.

Captain Coke	Weapon: **charged skyhook (PAR 6)**
Parry:	12
Nimbleness:	6
Toughness:	5

Victory!	**632**
Defeat!	**594**

❧ 658 ❧

If you have the codeword *Blasted*, turn to **734** immediately.

Heading downriver to Reading, you must pass through several locks, each with their attendant lock-keeper's cottages and, usually, a riverside inn. This is also a stretch along which the wealthy have built great mansions with privileged, neatened views. The owners cannot prevent the River Guild from shipping freight, coal and waste up and downstream, but when the river is quiet, this is an aristocrat's idyll. Roll two dice to see what you encounter.

Score 2-5	Airship pirates!	**90**
Score 6-8	The river is quiet....	**495**
Score 9-12	A getaway!	**341**

❧ 659 ❧

It is time to leave Woodcote, but the roads here lead every way. Some have the hardened surface of guild roads and others are merely muddy tracks. Where will you steam now?

Steer east towards Stoke Row...	**601**
Ride up Red Lane towards Wallingford...	**384**
Steam to Cray's Pond...	**577**
Head south-east towards Cane End...	**558**

❧ 660 ❧

Wooden signposts point the direction from here to other small towns and hamlets scattered over the hilltops and in the hollows.

Ride east towards Piddington...	**8**
Ride north-west towards Oxford...	**947**
Take Marlow Road towards Cadmore End...	**28**
Choose the valley road to Ibstone...	**644**
Head on to Christmas Common...	**367**
Investigate Aston Hill...	**710**

❧ 661 ❧

The Colonel of Constables laughs sharply. "An unbelievable claim! License to rob and steal in the name of the law? If you want that, you need a uniform." To convince him you will need to either drop the name of a powerful friend or bluff like you have never bluffed before, making an INGENUITY roll of difficulty 15. You can add 3 to your roll if you possess a **Constabulary logbook** and 1 if you have a **Constable's whistle.**

If you have the codeword *Ascorbic* or *Citrate*...	**667**
Successful INGENUITY roll...	**747**
Failed INGENUITY roll...	**705**

❧ 662 ❧

After lighting the fuses, you retreat to a good distance and are rewarded with a massive explosion. Scraps of cast iron and wire are flung into the trees either side of the road and a pall of smoke rises to the sky. Gain the codeword *Bolster*.

Ride away...	**noted passage**

❧ 663 ❧

You find a mooring close to Spiller's Boatyard on the southern bank and make your craft fast to some heavy piling. Your mate double-checks the lines. "So much wash along here from those heavy steamers. I'll have to keep an eye on these." He begins work on a plaited rope fender to replace the worn one at the bow. "This'll be finished by the time you're back," he promises." Note that you are now **moored at Reading**.

Go ashore into Reading...	**297**

❧ 664 ❧

The road to Woodcote turns left out of Stoke Row. You pass Basset Manor, a largely-unimproved sixteenth century brick house behind its hedge and iron railings, climb the rise through Checkendon village and pass a series of chalk-pits with a furnace and steam-crane. Beyond these, a set of posts stand with a pine marten and a jackdaw nailed up. Then shortly before you reach Woodcote itself you reach the Wallingford road which runs downhill to become Red Lane to the west and heads off into the woods to the south-east, eventually reaching Reading.

Continue into Woodcote...	**488**
Take the main road south-east...	**558**
Turn right up the Wallingford road...	**384**

❧ 665 ❧

You steer the boat cautiously towards the riverside terrace from which you can hear screams. A sheet of burning oil has spread across the river here and the mate runs to and fro on the gunwale, beating at the flames. You see a figure at a window, silhouetted against a fire. To climb up and rescue her, you must make a NIMBLENESS roll of difficulty 14, adding 1 if you possess a **rope** and 2 if you have a **grappling iron**.

Successful NIMBLENESS roll!	**200**
Failed NIMBLENESS roll!	**748**

❧ 666 ❧

The monks come tramping along the road cheerily, chatting amongst themselves in a manner far from solemn. They greet you.

"Come to the priory and join us for the evening's worship! Come and sing to your creator!"

Follow them...	**1238**
Continue on your way to Watlington...	**52**
Turn towards Wallingford...	**800**

❧ 667 ❧

"I work directly for Mrs Petty herself," you spit. "I see that name means something to you." His face has paled and he sits back from the desk. "Unless you want to upset plans far above your jurisdiction, I suggest you release me immediately."

Spluttering apologies, the Colonel releases you. Unfortunately your money and weapons are not returned so he authorises the issuing of a **sabre (PAR 3)**, a **Constable's carbine (ACC 8)** and **£4 10s** in cash. Still, you have escaped the Constables once more - and this time they will cancel any **Wanted** statuses you have in an attempt to appease Mrs Petty.

Go on your way...	**270**

❧ 668 ❧

The George and Dragon is frequented by the town's off-duty Constables, but they are far more interested in their beer and cards than any newcomer. In fact, cards are the occupation of choice here, either in the parlour or outside on the terrace, and there is an open invitation to play. If you wish to join in, make an INGENUITY roll, adding 4 if you possess a **deck of marked cards**.

Score 10 or lower	A weak hand...	**916**
Score 11-14	Three Kings...	**960**
Score 15 or higher	Royal Flush...	**730**

Drink with the locals...	(2s)	**204**
Return to Wargrave...		**418**

❧ 669 ❧

The Earl shakes his head scornfully. "All too typical. The short-term thinking of the delinquent classes. You're probably going to go and drink this all away somewhere."

You take **ten guineas in banknotes**, **£4 15s** and **pack of cigars** from him. He takes a good look at you before you go: unless you have a **mask**, he will be able to describe you and you will be **Wanted by the Constables**.

Ride away...	**171**

❧ 670 ❧

A large steam machine is chopping at timber with a repeating axe. It quickly smashes through the trunk of a young oak and the driver proceeds to climb out and switch the tool for a bark-stripper. Another machine clanks towards you: it is a man in a steam-powered carapace that amplifies his natural strength many times. You see him lift the entire tree-trunk and loop a wire cable around it. The future is here already, it seems. These two men are doing the work of a whole community.

Turn to...	**807**

∾ 671 ∾

You position your boat where you can easily steam out
and block the river traffic. Now all that you need to do
is wait - and keep your eyes open. Roll a dice to see
what appears...

Score 1-3   A River Guild barge...   **737**
Score 4-6   A private steamer...   **761**

∾ 672 ∾

Discard the **rope** from your possessions and make a
NIMBLENESS roll of difficulty 11 to leap aboard the
moving steamer.

Successful NIMBLENESS roll!   **509**
Failed NIMBLENESS roll!   **728**

∾ 673 ∾

If you have a **baker's contract**, turn to **699** immediately. If you are the **Friend of Miller Fursham**,
turn to **738**.

Miller Fursham is interested to see you again.
He is still in much the same predicament as you last
found him, squeezed by low prices paid for his flour
and high prices on the corn he buys. While you are
there, the westerly picks up and he releases the lever
that sends the mighty sails swinging.

"Hopper's empty," he admits, "But she maun
swing in the wind or it'll strip her bare. And anyways,
it tells 'em that there's still a miller at Cobstone Mill."

If you wish to take a sack of **Cobstone flour**, he
will gladly let you have one to take as a sample. You
stand together and watch the beautiful progression of
the sails, round and round. "A coal mill would grind
flour all day and night," he says thoughtfully. "The
Telegraph Guild are offering me that in exchange. But
coal ain't free and it taints the meal besides. Whereas
right now this old mill is powered by nothing other
than the breath of God."

Ride towards Ibstone...   **977**
Ride towards Fingest...   **867**

ᔟ 674 ᔠ

As the red player is about to shoot, you stumble backwards into a peering spectator, who falls in turn into the lemonade barrel with a crash. The red ball goes wild and the other guests frown and jeer. "Poor show," you hear.

On your next shot, something sharp jabs you in the ankle as you swing your mallet and your own ball trundles off uselessly into a shrub.

"What a shame," comments the red player.

Turn to... 1476

ᔟ 675 ᔠ

You describe how the directors and investors in the Imperial Western Railway make themselves rich at the expense of these men and women's labour; how their unquestioning sweat becomes the basis of profit for men who only sweat when they over-eat. Some are listening intently. Make an INGENUITY roll of difficulty 12, adding 1 for every 5 **solidarity points** you possess.

Successful INGENUITY roll! 1214
Failed INGENUITY roll! 1225

ᔟ 676 ᔠ

Patience may be under-appreciated by the rushing townsfolk and the ever-busy haulier, charging on to make another shilling, but for you patience is a discipline long-treasured. You find yourself a vantage spot, your velosteam tucked between holly and briars, and wait to see what approaches. Note **passage number 550** on your **Adventure Sheet** and roll a dice to see what you encounter.

Score 1	The Telegraph Guild...	272
Score 2	The Haulage Guild...	408
Score 3	The Coal Board...	1305
Score 4-6	A private steam carriage...	103

ᔟ 677 ᔠ

The Freight Yard is sectioned into several parts: the timber yard is busy: the industries and building yards consume countless cubic feet of wood every day, even with the increasing popularity of iron frames and scaffolds. Over at the brick bays a massive steam-crane lifts iron-framed open crates onto wagons. A furnace roars where a boiler is being re-sealed and flames flash up from the tyring ring.

Several workshops will sell you parts you may need for repairs or your own projects.

Tools	To buy	To sell
rope	4s	2s
net	6s	4s
lantern	6s	4s
adjustable wrench (ENG+1)	£1 8s	18s
tarpaulin	4s	2s
measuring line	10s	6s
brass flange joint	8s	4s
copper pipe	6s	3s
plaster of paris	4s	2s
roll of oiled silk	£8	£5
pneumatic manual (ENG+3)	-	£8s

Arrange haulage for your timber... (*Bark*)	624
Look for Jackson...	
(**tally stick 84** or **tally stick 67**)	844
Return to Nettlebed...	791

ᔟ 678 ᔠ

Two heavy dray horses are pulling a farm-wagon up the road. The wagon is piled high with produce from local farms and a ruddy, weather-hardened man sits at the reins. He looks at you suspiciously from beneath his straw hat. If you have 10 or more **solidarity points**, turn to **639** immediately. If not, but you are **Wanted by the Constables**, turn to **775**. Otherwise you simply let the farmer pass by.

Turn to... **noted passage**

ᔟ 679 ᔠ

The riders are glad to see you again. "Still getting into trouble?" asks Desdemona Wren. "How's that fabulous Ferguson of yours?"

If your velosteam is damaged, the riders will help you with repairs here. You will still need some materials but their pleasure in working on your machine means that they are happy to do the work for you. You will require a repair to remove each point of damage, so if your velosteam has **critical damage**, you must use a **high pressure valve** to repair it to merely **serious damage**, before using a **brass flange joint** to repair it to **minor damage**.

ENGINEERING score		Materials
Critical damage...	8	**high pressure valve**
Serious damage...	7	**brass flange joint**
Minor damage...	6	**copper pipe**

Return to the parlour...	725
Leave the pub...	688

❧ 680 ❧

☐

If the box above is empty, tick it and turn to **714** immediately. Otherwise, read on.

The steam carriage here has burnt through. Nothing of value is left in the blackened, twisted wreck.

Turn to...   **807**

❧ 681 ❧

"Hello," says Captain Coke warmly, swinging his airship boots off the table and shaking your hand. "I'm always glad to cross paths. How is the fearless scourge of the roads? What's new on the turnpike?"

You share stories for some hours, with much laughter and a steady flow of beer. The inn will surely gain a reputation if people talk about it as the place where the Steam Highwayman and the Sky Pirate drink.

Eventually Coke has to depart. "Come and see us in the wood again, yes? Anita is getting rather bossy and I need help keeping her in hand. As soon as you can."

Return to the parlour...   **36**
Leave the inn...   **867**

❧ 682 ❧

You have come to Sonning Bridge. The lane across the meadow climbs onto a meandering, rickety-looking wooden bridge, past a small mill poised as if on stilts and into the village on the opposite side of the river. Mist hangs in the air here, obscuring the banks and smudging the lantern light in the windows.

The bridge is too lightly-built to take heavy cargo: a single traction engine might cross here, or a farm wagon, but certainly not a long trail of freight-laden gurneys.

On this side of the river a track leads to the foot of the hill alongside a stream, while the busy road between Henley and Reading runs past along the meadows. Another side-road heads uphill to Caversham Park, the headquarters of the Telegraph Guild hereabouts.

Take the sideroad to Caversham Park...   **770**
Follow the track by the stream...   **633**
Cross the bridge into Sonning...   **690**
Head towards Henley...   **575**
Ride to Reading...   **793**
Prepare an ambush near here...   **701**
Ride towards Shiplake House...
    (*Caraway* or *Blended*)   **1091**

❧ 683 ❧

As your flight crosses the Mediterranean, you hear that bad weather is reported. Your few glimpses outside give no indication of trouble, but that evening as you are cooking the characteristically smooth flight of the airship changes into something more like a rustic dance.

A crewman comes in. "We'll be stopping at Malta," he tells the chef. "Captain says it's likely to be for a few days." Within an hour you are tethered to a mooring post at Valetta and the passengers are discussing landing and exploring the city.

Up until now you have had no opportunity to try anything in the cabins of the rich passengers. Now you will have both some time, as chef Ramboutarde and the passengers will eat ashore, and a plausible scapegoat for anything that goes missing in the inhabitants of the island. To break into a cabin and steal what you can, make an INGENUITY roll of difficulty 14, adding 2 if you possess any **lockpicks**.

Successful INGENUITY roll!   **561**
Failed INGENUITY roll!   **533**
Keep to your work...   **479**

❧ 684 ❧

Remove the **purple flare** from your possessions. You light up a flare and send a column of purple smoke into the sky. Before long, the throbbing sound of airship engines approach and Captain Coke and his crew appear over the treeline. Hanging out on a crane derrick, the indomitable pirate gives you a nod and a salute before setting his men about the task of salvaging the supplies. You will need to visit the Captain's hideout to collect your share of the booty: gain the codeword *Bragging*.

Ride away...   **noted passage**

❧ 685 ❧

Coke falls to the ground. "Now you are at my mercy," you gloat. Gain the codeword *Bernadette* and discard the **wanted poster**, if you still have it.

You may take Coke's **charged skyhook (PAR 6)** and use it as he did, subtracting a point of NIMBLENESS from your opponents for each hit. He also has a purse of **£8 5s** on him.

Taking his own belt and sash, you tie Coke firmly to your velosteam and ride off towards Rotherfield Greys, where the Atmospheric Union are based. If you are **Wanted by the Atmospheric Union**, turn to **929** immediately. Otherwise, read on.

The Atmospheric Union guards are amazed by your victory over Coke. They quickly chain him into a cell and post an armed guard. "He'll hang for sure," you are told.

"What about the reward?"

An officer hums and haws. "I suppose we can find you something." He spends some time hunting around in his office before handing you **fifty guineas in banknotes**.

"The poster promised five hundred guineas," you retort.

"Don't believe everything you read," replies the officer. "That was probably a printing mistake."

Leave the office...   **454**

❧ 686 ❧

The author is sorry to see that you have returned with his manuscript, but when you tell him of how the publisher reacted to it, he nods sadly.

"Better to keep it until the world is ready, then. Here - take this in appreciation for returning my tome." He gives you a **gold ring** and you should remove the **tightly-tied parcel** from your **Adventure Sheet**.

Return to the parlour...   **725**

❧ 687 ❧

You come alongside and leap aboard the barge, knocking a pair of rogues into the water as you do. The leader of the water-rats fires his pistol point-blank at a Guildsman, then turns, snarling, to face you.

Water Rat Captain Weapon: **sabre (PAR 3)**
Parry: 10
Nimbleness: 7
Toughness: 4

Victory!   **774**
Defeat!   **528**

❧ 688 ❧

What a mass of smoky contradiction is Oxford! The city has its own smog, formed of furnace smoke and low cloud hovering between the colleges and workshops. Countless calculation engines chatter away in ancient halls, while gowned professors mingle on the streets with industrialists, inventors, street-sweepers and labourers. The river has its part to play here too, carrying much of the freight into the city, but the Haulage Guild's power is proven largely by the vast yard from which trains of cargo wagon are towed out across the land. The University cannot dominate a city so active and various, like a beehive shared by many tribes of bees, but its influence is everywhere, providing cheap brain-power to match the century's cheap steam-power too.

Explore the city...   **808**
Enter the Eagle and Child...   **725**
Steam to the Freight Yard...   **285**
Head to the market...   **127**
Board your boat... (if **moored at Oxford**) **849**
Leave the city...   **970**

❧ 689 ❧

The protestors listen carefully as you explain how the Compact will support them, if they report in your name. "The arms trade is a deadly business, costlying the lives of many of the workers, both in the factories and on the battlefield."

"Are not the Compact themselves steeped in blood?" asks one of the protestors.

"Fire must be fought with fire."   **597**
"Their ways are not ideal - but they are
      effective."   **626**

∽ 690 ∾

□

If the box is empty, tick it and turn to **332** immediately. If it is already ticked, read on.

Dusk has turned into night as you steer your velosteam onto Sonning Bridge. The river runs quickly across the shallow gravel beds here, fanning the weed into long streamers. You dismount to lower the draw-bridge that crosses the main channel and ride across, before raising it again on the other side. Moonlight paints the water with silver patches and lights the trees as with a flare.

Ride straight to the French Horn...	**358**
Enter Sonning...	**91**
Head on your way towards the Bath Road...	**589**

∽ 691 ∾

He laughs. "Spare me? You poor fool. I would cut you to shreds if you tried to kill or capture me."

Attack him...	**948**
Leave the inn...	**867**

∽ 692 ∾

You ride hard towards Sonning, weaving around the worst potholes on the Henley road, splashing through the puddles as rain comes down around you. The lamps and bells of the Constables are never far behind you and any minute you may be met by a roadblock summoned by telegraph.

Eventually you meet the junction where the road from Sonning Bridge meets the main road. The mill beside the long, wooden roadway is still working and a consignment of grain is being hauled out of a barge. If you have an **axe**, turn to **549** immediately.

Whether you have managed to lose your pursuers depends on whether you gained enough time through the rainy dusk. Make a MOTORING roll of difficulty 11.

Successful MOTORING roll!	**465**
Failed MOTORING roll!	**13**

∽ 693 ∾

A tarmacadam lane leads along the foot of the down towards the Hardwick estate. A much less well-maintained track heads west towards Coombe Park. The main road heads steeply uphill and meets Elvendon Lane up in the woods near Cray's Pond.

Ride towards Coombe Park...	**937**
Head east towards Hardwick House...	**460**
Steam up Deadman's Lane to Cane End...	**807**
Take the road northwards...	**577**

∽ 694 ∾

Father Patrick is intrigued by your velosteam and gladly accepts the offer of a ride down to Goring. You steam off, passing Nettlebed and Woodcote and cross the river at Goring Bridge. The house he has been called to is a country pile called the Grotto, on the west side of the river, nestled under the wooded ridge where the river turns north. The owners greet you and the priest on the driveway and explain their situation.

"We bought the place last year but we're living in the grounds," says Mr Shrubham through his beard. "Too much... activity. Things moving, voices, all sorts of nasties. Were we right to call you, I wonder?"

Father Patrick nods. "The casting out of spirits is entirely scriptural," he says. "Christ plainly took it seriously."

"What equipment will you use?" asks Mrs Shrubham.

"Words of faith. Nothing more."

You accompany Father Patrick and the Shrubhams into the house. It is very quiet. They lead you to the dining room, where the glazing opens out onto a lawn and the riverside. "This room seems to be the most disturbed," says Shrubham.

Father Patrick kneels quietly for several minutes, praying under his breath. Then he strides around the room, looking about. It is hard to see what he is looking for.

"Back in my country," he says, "Many places are under the spiritual power of demons as a result of ancestral worship and repeated offerings and so on. This place has a similar spiritual atmosphere. Now you have only owned this place for a while and are unlikely to have made any agreements with the spirits here. They may even be rebelling. So we shall cast them out. It is not by saying 'In Jesus' name' in a loud voice: the authority of Christ comes by living in his manner, close to the Father. Then we can pray as he asks us to pray and command as he tells us to command."

He has reached the middle of the room. "Spirit of possession, I instruct you to leave. I forbid you place here. Begone into the abyss."

A draught seems to move through the room.

"Is that it?" asks Mrs Shrubham.

As she asks, a woman's voice chuckles somewhere on the edge of hearing.

"Plainly not," says Father Patrick.

Follow Father Patrick through the house...   **627**

❧ 695 ❧

The civil servant is an important man in a top hat, travelling with his heavy-set 'clerk', who launches himself at you directly. The speed of his assault means that he will have the first chance to land a blow!

Clerk	Weapon: **truncheon (PAR 2)**
Parry:	10
Nimbleness:	8
Toughness:	4

Victory!	**428**
Defeat!	**999**

❧ 696 ❧

As dusk falls a steam carriage approaches - but not along the Watlington road. It comes through the village of Shirburn from the direction of the castle and heads towards you. Blue and gold livery, gleaming in the low evening sun, indicates some well-to-do noble may well be the passenger.

The driver sits high on the driving step, his cap and goggles firmly fastened against the steam and breeze. They have not yet gathered speed for their onward journey: if you are bold, you could bring them to a standstill by blocking the road and calling for their surrender, relying on your RUTHLESSNESS score.

However, if you want to trust in your ACCURACY, you can fire a warning shot close to the driver before announcing your presence.

Fire a warning shot...	**753**
Block the road with your velosteam...	**845**
Let the carriage pass...	**123**

❧ 697 ❧

You have intervened at the critical moment! You block a slash at Coke's neck and he kicks out at the crewman, who stumbles over the rail and falls through the clouds with a scream. The remaining crew surrender and Coke's pirates tie them up in the hold before taking the ship in tow behind their own *Blue Devil*.

"Now I owe you my life," Coke says gallantly. "Come with us. You can have a half-share in the loot."

On the return voyage you get to know Coke fairly well. He is a fearsome Captain, punishing any infraction within his crew immediately and harshly, yet there is a charm to him as well. He is utterly ruthless towards his enemies, including anyone associated with the Atmospheric Union.

You reach his base and he tells you that he can arrange for one of his insiders at Rotherfield Greys to fetch your velosteam. He also rewards you with the promised half-share, which comes to **£40 3s**, hands you a **purple flare** ☐ ☐ ☐ and explains how you can use it. "Light this if you rob a steam carriage of some sort. We have lookouts. My crew'll come and take the heavier booty - the stuff you can't haul away on this little machine. And then pay your share, o'course." He also lets you know that he will set aside a tent for you in his woodland hideout. "After all," he says. "You saved my life. I consider the debt repaid now." You are now the **Friend of Captain Coke**.

Turn to...   **819**

❧ 698 ❧

You first steam up Crowmarsh hill, past a row of villas being built on the slope. A tall steam-crane lowers prefabricated wall sections into place: these houses will be ready in days, not months. Skirting a massive gravel-wagon and a workman's bus parked in the roadway, you increase the pressure and fly up the road.

Turn off and prepare an ambush here...	**777**
Continue on to Nuffield Common...	**836**

❧ 699 ❧

Miller Fursham is delighted to see the contract. You help him read through the longer words and he whistles at the price agreed. "I don't know how you got that offer," he says, "But I'm mighty appreciative. Thing is, I'll need it carrying. It's a long way to the bakery and there's freight to pay."

If you have **tally stick 32**, turn to **722** immediately. Otherwise, the miller invites you into his house for a meal and sup of beer while you talk through which freighters might be willing to carry his load. "The Haulage Guild - possibly. But they don't run this road to Ibstone - they stay in the valley and reach Stokenchurch through Cadmore End - so they'd be going out of their way and most likely I'd pay for it. But there are some independent-minded folks take the Ibstone lane - out of Henley and Watlington, mostly. Maybe Nettlebed."

The beer he pours you is a skillful homebrew, strong and dark like a woodland stream. "Double-malted," he says. "And then I adds a portion of caramel too. And the barm is my granddaddy's, still frothing strong. So it don't taste like their valley beer. Have another pottle there."

After another quart or so, he takes you outside to show you something. "See this old beer mug in the wall, mortared tight in? Well, that was grandaddy's. And over here between these flints is my dad's. And I'll set mine in before too long as well. If I ain't bought out."

Ride towards Ibstone...	**977**
Ride towards Fingest...	**867**

❧ 700 ❧

"A hold-out, eh? So be it!" Coke takes all of your **possessions** and **money**. The **wanted poster** he tosses into the flames of the inn fire. "Now take heed, all you," he cries to the gathered drinkers and terrified hauliers. "Challenge me not - or you'll end like this miserable slug." He stalks out.

As for you, you must find somewhere to tend your wounds and regain your strength - certainly if you would try to defeat Coke another way.

Leave the pub...	**867**

❧ 701 ❧

As dusk falls you hide yourself behind an unmanned gravel loading gantry. Note **passage number 433** on your **Adventure Sheet** and roll a dice to see what you encounter:

Score 1-2	A private steam carriage...	**103**
Score 3	The Haulage Guild...	**408**
Score 4-5	The Constables...	**9**
Score 6	The Telegraph Guild...	**272**

❧ 702 ❧

Henley-on-Thames is a bustling, busy town, full of the fashionable and glamorous weekending from London and Reading, as well as a crucial freight wharf where goods are loaded onto barges to head down the Thames. The place is water-mad: every business on the high street seems concerned with boats, whether for pleasure or business.

Stroll down to the waterside...	**539**
Visit the Angel Inn...	**2**
Visit the Freight Yard...	**458**
Visit Henley Museum... (**1s**)	**195**
Investigate the Railway Station...	**547**
Visit the Theatre...	**117**
Buy and sell at the market...	**605**
Head out of town...	**586**

❧ 703 ❧

Inside the passenger compartment are the smartly-dressed members of an airship crew. Several hostesses and a pair of officers goggle at your brusque gesture of command,. One officer draws his sabre, keen to defend the hostesses' honour.

Airship Officer	Weapon: **rapier (PAR 4)**
Parry:	11
Nimbleness:	7
Toughness:	3

Victory!	**629**
Defeat!	**999**

❧ 704 ❧

You continue to spend your days cooking in a fair degree of misery under chef Ramboutarde's obsessive control, but there are events beyond his influence in an air-voyage like this. Roll a dice:

Score 1-2	Atmospheric disturbance...	**683**
Score 3	Sky-pirates!	**875**
Score 4-6	The chef falls ill...	**479**

❧ 705 ❧

"Your own choices, your own consequences, my friend. They have led you to punishment. Take this wretch away!"

You are taken directly to Wallingford Gaol and handed into the care of the Warders there.

Turn to...	**841**

❧ 706 ❧

It will not be a difficult task to burn the sheds and operator's cabin, but it might be trickier to escape without being seen or recognised. At dusk you make your preparations and have everything ready to light. Now you must decide what to do about the members of the Telegraph Guild stationed inside.

Warn the guildsmen...   **912**
Leave them to escape...   **733**

❧ 707 ❧

It will not do to remain here beside the road too long. Inevitably trouble will come your way, so you must ride elsewhere in the region.

Head up towards Stonor...   **430**
Head to Sonning Bridge...   **682**
Ride towards Woodcote...   **664**

❧ 708 ❧

The driver merely laughs at your pathetic attempt to intimidate and accelerates towards you! You are forced to leap aside as the heavy engine smashes into your velosteam, knocking it aside into the ditch and causing **2 damage points**.

If your velosteam is **beyond repair**...   **874**
Otherwise...   **171**

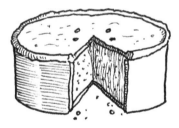

❧ 709 ❧

You are served a summer stout, chilled with river-water. "That's one of my little secrets here," says the landlord. "The old master at Mongewell always liked to sup a cold stout and now so do many round here. What do you think of it?"

The beer has a strong caramel flavour and a biscuity nose. It is not strong but it is sweet and liable to bring on an afternoon doze.

Return to the parlour...   **162**
Leave the pub...   **515**

❧ 710 ❧

The muddy, rutted road winds steeply up from the Oxford plain. At one bend, a broad, broad view of the countryside spreads out before you: pastures, wheatfields, the distant smudge of smoky Oxford. Immediately afterwards the road is plunged into the shadow of the overhanging woods.

The owners of the massive road trains that use this route have sunk concrete bollards into the roadside for winching reluctant engines up in bad weather. Heavy chains lie beside the road, locked with guild padlocks. The roadway itself is in a bad way, forcing vehicles to move slowly here. On your velosteam you will have to pick your path very carefully, dodging rain-cut channels and slippery mudslicks.

At the top of the hill, amongst the trees, is an earthen reservoir. Squabbles between inhabitants of nearby Stokenchurch and the hauliers refilling their tanks mean it is guarded by Constables around the clock, although it actually belongs to the Coal Board.

Ride south-west along the hilltops...   **288**
Head towards Stokenchurch...   **544**
Investigate the reservoir...   **379**
Prepare an ambush here...   **676**
Speed onward to Oxford...   **947**
Take the low road to Watlington...   **1000**

❧ 711 ❧

Inside this box you find a single **engraved bullet** in a soft leather bag and a pair of **duelling pistols (ACC 7)**. The tiny writing seems to be two patiently-written initials: W S. Whoever did this clearly has enviable skill - together with something of an obsession with vengeance.

Turn to...   **noted passage**

❧ 712 ❧

Once you are knocked down, the brigands waste no time in cutting your throat. You have no opportunity to bargain or escape and cannot even profit from the lesson in ruthlessness. Proceed directly to the **Epilogue**.

❧ 713 ❧

You and Captain Coke are both knocked down and the sky pirates flee. A doctor intervenes to prevent your immediate death - remove a **wound** and replace it with a **scar** - and you are chained up in the hold, quite separate from the dangerous Coke. You are now considered **Wanted by the Atmospheric Union** and gain the codeword *Bernadette* as well.

Turn to...   **342**

❧ 714 ❧

A man lies in the wreckage. He is barely breathing and may not survive being moved. If you wish to help him, make an INGENUITY roll of difficulty 13, adding 1 if you have any **bandages** or a **cloak** you can tear up, 2 if you have a **stethoscope** and 1 for each level of **medical training** you possess.

Successful INGENUITY roll!   **776**
Failed INGENUITY roll!   **789**

❧ 715 ❧

The terrified driver is not a guard or professional roadsman - he is in fact a minor cleric that the Bishop has bullied into serving as a chauffeur. No wonder he slams on the brakes and raises his hands. "Don't shoot! The Bishop's inside. Take what you want!"

The Bishop is indeed inside, his grossly fat body smeared with cream from the mashed cakes on his lap. He stammers and stutters in fear as you drag him from his luxurious compartment.

Turn to...   **765**

❧ 716 ❧

The man is a writer looking for someone to carry his latest manuscript into London. "I... I have to trust the carrier," he stammers. "I've put everything into this. I can only pay **£2** but I will write you into my next book in gratitude. It's an adventure across a whole realm, and you give me an idea for the shadowy ranger figure."

Accept the job...   **736**
Return to the parlour...   **725**

❧ 717 ❧

As you have become more notorious, the Guild is taking more and more measures to protect their goods and their reputation. An armed guard sits on the cab and another at the tail of the road train. They quickly notice you and open fire. Make a MOTORING roll to see whether you manage to dodge the bullets.

Score <9	Gain a **wound** and **two damage points**
Score 9-13	Gain **two wounds**
Score 14+	Escape the bullets

If your velosteam is now **beyond repair**, turn to **874** immediately. If not, but you have **five wounds**, turn to **999**. Otherwise you may choose how to respond.

Return fire...   **67**
Ride away...   **433**

❧ 718 ❧

You quickly steer for the woods near Crazies Hill and duck beneath low branches, jouncing over the hummocks and roots in an attempt to reach some hideaway. You will need to use all your cunning to lay a false trail: make an INGENUITY roll of difficulty 12 to lose your pursuers, adding 1 for every **possession** you discard.

Successful INGENUITY roll!   **313**
Failed INGENUITY roll!   **13**

❧ 719 ❧

You and the mate tie up beneath Abingdon bridge for the night and start early in the morning when the engine-steam still condenses on the tarpaulins and the riverside reeds. The damp and cold pass quickly and by the time you pass through Culham, the sun is up, warming the water. You pass Appleford, Clifton Hampden, Wittenham, Dorchester and Shillingford, wait for your turn through Benson Lock and arrive at Wallingford by lunchtime.

Pull in at Wallingford Wharf...   **435**
Continue downstream...   **987**

❧ 720 ❧

You leave your note and ride away from the house. However, you later hear that your threat was disregarded: Lady Pomiane faced down Lord Macclesfield in the court hearing and the case was concluded in her favour. If you killed a dog, gain the codeword *Bronte*.

Ride on...   **110**

❧ 721 ❧

If you are a **Member of the Compact for Worker's Equality**, read on. If not, turn to **768** immediately.

You give the Compact's knock and wait for the door to open. Several determined figures are waiting inside, standing around their leader at his planning desk.

Turn to...   **936**

❧ 722 ❧

Remove **tally stick 32** from your possessions.

You tell Miller Fursham about your agreement with the haulier. He jumps up and literally dances for joy. "I'm a-grinding again! Thankyou - a thousand times. What's had you spend so much o'your time on my worries, I don't know, but it seems there's still some goodness in the world." He will tell many of how you have helped him keep his family tradition alive: gain a **solidarity point**. He also promises that should you ever need his help or a hideaway from the authorities, then he will do everything he can to repay your kindness. "I'm fetching my boy in from the field and we'll take the cart down Turville now. It's corn, corn, corn for me! God send a breeze."

You are now the **Friend of Miller Fursham**.

Ride towards Ibstone...   **977**
Ride towards Fingest...   **867**

❧ 723 ❧

"Milady," you begin graciously, about to attempt something charming.

"Begone, dog!" she shouts without hesitation and draws a massive **blunderpistol** from beneath her skirts. She looses it directly at you: make a NIMBLE-NESS roll to see whether you react quickly enough to dodge the shot.

Score <13	Abdominal shot: gain **two wounds**
Score 13-15	Grazed: gain a **wound**
Score 16+	Dodge the shot!

If you now have **five wounds**, turn to **999** immediately. If you survive, however, you may take the **blunderpistol** from her, together with a **silver bracelet**, a bottle of **soothing lotion** and **£4 19s**.

Turn to...   **noted passage**

❧ 724 ❧

Discard the **blank punchcards**. To punch your own set of cards you must possess the appropriate code-word and then make an INGENUITY roll of difficulty 16. With a successful INGENUITY roll you can add the appropriate set of punchcards to your possessions - but only one set for each set of **blank punchcards** you have! A failed INGENUITY roll means that your time and **blank punchcards** have been wasted.

	Codewords needed
punchcards (Aramanth A)	*Chirp* or *Entertain*
punchcards (Habbukuk K)	*Busybody* or *Fireside*
punchcards (Selladore V)	*Collector* or *Dexter*
punchcards (Livingstone M)	*Coaxial* or *Faucett*

Return to the attic...   **484**
Leave the house...   **343**

❧ 725 ❧

Behind the leaded panes and the narrow windows, the parlour, sitting room and bar of the Eagle and Child are full with a voluble crowd, the smell of pickles and bread and roasted meat, and the scent of Oxford ale. Professors bustle past, pint pots grasped in inky fingers; students and college servants drink and eat in their carefully-observed zones; townspeople too and long-distance travellers are attracted by the reputation of the kitchen and the cellar.

Uniquely amongst the many pubs and taverns in this beer-powered centre of learning, the Eagle and Child has the reputation as the drinking-place of the despatch riders. When a telegraph just can't cope with the number of words in an academic treatise, or when the old-fashioned dons grow suspicious, the University pay for velosteamers to carry parcels across the land. A motley collection of machines are parked in the alleyway outside.

Talk to the despatch riders...
   (If you are a **Famed Lawbreaker**)   **593**
Order food and ale...   (**3s**)   **886**
Leave the pub...   **688**
Mount up and leave the city...   **970**

❧ 726 ❧

The road carries you away from the Reading smog, past a vast cemetery on one side and busy gravel pits on the other. Away on the hill stands Caversham Park, once the home of a mighty lord and now the regional headquarters of the Telegraph Guild. A vast optical telegraph stands on the high ground, smaller towers clustered around its base, all twinkling constantly as the shutters flick open and closed, transmitting hundreds of messages a minute in the complex guild codes.

Prepare an ambush here...	**701**
Head uphill to the Telegraph Guild Headquarters...	**770**
Continue on to Sonning bridge...	**682**
Ride straight on to Henley...	**702**

❦ 727 ❧

The charges detonate unevenly, destroying most of the wagons but leaving many of the supplies intact. Flames lick at the goods as you mount up and ride away.

Ride away...	**noted passage**

❦ 728 ❧

A leap... a swing... a short flight through the air... and a hard landing on the packed earth and gravel of the roadside. You tumble and roll, but still jar your leg nastily. Gain a **wound**. The driver of the vehicle does not even notice that you attempted to jump aboard and speeds off, leaving you far behind. If you have **five wounds**, turn to **999** immediately. Otherwise, you climb stiffly back onto your velosteam and prepare to ride away.

Ride away...	**noted passage**

❦ 729 ❧

"So, guildsman, eh?" asks a haulier. "What sort of cargo can you carry on that little two-wheeler, anyway? Or are you one of their... agents?" The mood at the table changes. Conversation stops while the men and women wait to see your response.

"Why I carry the badge is none of your business."	**604**
"Director Short happens to be a friend of mine."	**569**

❦ 730 ❧

The players are suspicious of your good luck. If you have a **deck of marked cards**, turn to **778** immediately. Otherwise, read on.

    The company around the table grumble and complain, not directly accusing you of cheating, but plainly feeling that something is unfair. You have a choice - if you collect your winnings of **£14 7s**, you must lose a **solidarity point** (if you have any). If you choose to laugh off the win and return the player's money to them, you lose nothing.

Return to the parlour...	**668**
Leave the George and Dragon...	**418**

❦ 731 ❧

Without a guard, it will be significantly easier to rob this engine. How will you make your attempt?

Attempt to intimidate the driver...	**758**
Ride alongside and unhitch the rear wagon...	**797**

❦ 732 ❧

You soon have your bisque ready to serve. As it is being plated up, chef comes over and gives it a taste. He spits it out. "What is this dishwater? Where is the flavour? Where did you train? Glasgow? I cannot serve this to the passengers!" He upends the hot soup over your head, giving you a nasty **burn (ING-1)**. Until you have treated this, the constant pain and discomfort will effect your concentration badly, resulting in a temporary reduction in your INGENUITY.

Turn to...	**704**

❦ 733 ❧

You light the fire and retreat, letting the occupants of the tower find their own way out. Doubtless they have an escape route planned.

    The Telegraph Guild will be puzzled by the attack, although they are likely to attribute it to the Compact for Workers' Equality, who have given an ultimatum warning that attacks on towers are imminent. Your own part in that will remain shrouded for now. Gain the codeword *Bergen*.

Ride north...	**378**
Ride south...	**589**

❦ 734 ❧

You pass through Cleeve lock smoothly, but as your boat descends through Goring lock, a sudden jar knocks you off your feet. You are thrown against the lock wall and everything goes black.

    When you awake you have been hauled onto the lockside. Your boat is broken-backed, its keel cracked by its own weight. The stern has caught on the cill of the upper doors, tilting the craft down into the water and ruining the cargo. It all seems strangely reminiscent of the old eel-man's final curse, far downstream by Magpie Island.

You are able to unload your velosteam and personal possessions, but your boat and cargo are ruined. Erase them from your **Adventure Sheet** and continue your travels. Erase the codeword *Blasted*.

Turn to...   **487**

Turn to...   **487**

❧ 735 ❧

You steam towards the burning buildings and attach your steam-pump to a canvas hose put out by the town fire-fighters. The mate oversees the pump while you jump ashore and help with the bucket chains. Little can be done to save the buildings, though, and several townspeople have perished in the flames.

"How did it begin?" you ask.

"Chimney fire," replies a soot-stained woman. "Tore through the terrace and Hampden's oil yard."

There is little more you can do here.

Turn to...   **719**

❧ 736 ❧

The author hands you a **tightly tied parcel** and even gives you the payment in advance - add **£2** to your wallet. Then you leap aboard your velosteam and fire up the burner. Your machine answers immediately: the pistons begin to whirr and thrust, your tyres bite into the gravel and you are off!

It is a long way to London - at least a day and a night's ride. You should make good time on the main road through Wycombe as long as the Constables maintain their disinterest and as long as no short-term tolls have been put in place by the Haulage Guild or any of the other road-owners. On the other hand, notoriety might force you to consider taking the smaller roads, slower though they are.

Take the main roads...   **265**
Take less-travelled routes...   **304**

❧ 737 ❧

The River Guild barge chugs along, piled high with crates and barrels. The captain will surely have some money along with him for lock tolls and there may be more to steal as well.

Threaten the crew...   **1011**
Leap aboard and attack...   **1039**
Let it pass...   **251**

❧ 738 ❧

You receive a warm welcome from the miller, who is rarely without corn to grind now. His elder son is fully engaged in the work, his daughter is learning lace-making and his youngest lad is studying for a place at Stokenchurch grammar. "Times have changed - thanks to you!" The family welcome you to their table and you enjoy an evening of good food and company, rest and good cheer.

Ride towards Ibstone...   **977**
Ride towards Fingest...   **867**

❧ 739 ❧

She looks at the tally, finds the matching stock and nods, before snapping them both in two and tossing them onto the coal pile beside one of her road engines. "That's right. One load of prime oak, hauled from Cane End to Nettlebed. Haulage paid in advance. Didn't get the best price for it, I'm afraid, since Bradley just brought in a full road train of timber before we sold. But, with the bark, I managed to make you **£22**."

She counts out the money and places the coins in your hand. "Pleasure doing business with you."

Return to the Freight Yard...   **677**
Return to Nettlebed...   **791**
Leave Nettlebed...   **944**

❧ 740 ❧

The hill is steep and your velosteam's water-gauge dips. Nonetheless you have enough to carry on until your next stop and are soon at the top of the hill, from where you have a great view of Henley and the river sparkling behind you. If you have the codeword *Bodacious*, turn to **60** immediately.

Continue up the hill...   **313**

❧ 741 ❧

Erase your last **wound** - it was merely a scratch. But with the point of his skyhook at your throat, Coke throws back his head and laughs. "It was a good fight, matey, but not good enough. Now, what'll it be? Come aboard or empty your pockets?"

"I'll join with you in the skies."   **796**
"You cannot press-gang me!"   **700**

❧ 742 ❧

The time has come to leave Wallingford. Where will you head now?

Board your boat... (if you are moored here)   **435**
Head north-east towards Watlington...   **229**
Head south-east towards Nuffield Common...   **698**
Take the road south...   **860**
Take the road towards Oxford...   **259**
Set out on the long journey to Wales...
Dark Vales and Dark Hearts 341

❧ 743 ❧

"It could be money. It could be indeed." He prays under his breath again. "But the house is not built to boast in wealth."

Turn to...   **329**

❧ 744 ❧

Your likeness has been distributed by the Haulage Guild in response to your deeds against them: the smiths, keen to share in the reward posted and emboldened by their numbers, rush over and knock you from your velosteam. A struggle, a fall and a swift knock on the head and that is all you know.

Turn to...   **961**

❧ 745 ❧

Your beer is a draught of Sparrowbeak Rye Ale: full of flavour, medium-bodied, less than 5% by volume and sensuously aromatic. At a fireside table you find yourself with company. Roll a dice to see whom you encounter:

Score 1-3   A cheerful man   **762**
Score 4-6   A Scot   **273**

❧ 746 ❧

You steam along the ridge, heading a steady north-east through the woods. Occasional coppicings and pasture hacked into the slope give you a view of the Oxford plain below, with the chimneys of Watlington smoking away. Red kites soar ceaselessly overhead, each intent on finding carrion for its chicks.

Stop at Christmas Common...   **617**
Ride on along the escarpment...   **102**

❧ 747 ❧

You choose your words carefully. "I have been in your position. The chain of command has links that bear little weight. When a leader fails to inform you of a decision that impacts you directly - is there anything more frustrating? My posting in the North country was beset with communication problems. Is it really so hard to talk honestly to the people under your command? And yet people like us, doing the daily work of the law, infiltrating dangerous extremist groups, managing troublesome civilian populations with no idea of their fragility, people like us are repeatedly undermined by leaders who don't take the time to communicate."

His demeanour has changed. He is still not quite convinced.

"I'll bet it was Wilkinson," you say, plucking a name out of thin air. "Or Green."

"Major-General Green?" the Colonel interjects. "You know that gross slug?"

"Unfortunately, yes," you reply. "A simple enough task, to inform the regional constabulary of my mission. But not simple enough for Green."

With a sigh of frustration the Colonel collapses in his seat. "What a lot of wasted time! Typical leadership!" He begins to reel off his own grudges - a long list, but worth enduring if it keeps you out of prison. Soon he comes to the conclusion that he must release you. Your money and weapons are unfortunately not returned. "More paperwork!" he rages. "How can they be lost already? The corruption in the force is astounding!" He authorises the issuing of a **sabre (PAR 3)**, a **Constable's carbine (ACC 8)** and **£4 10s** in cash to replace what you have lost. He also sends a telegraph message cancelling any **Wanted** statuses that you possess.

Go on your way...   **270**

❧ 748 ❧

You climb up onto the bank and begin to scale the rough wall, but the bricks are hot and you lose your grip. Flames rise around you - your clothes are on fire! Gain **two wounds** and a serious **burn**, meaning you must lower your NIMBLENESS and your MOTORING by 1 until it heals. You are forced to abandon your attempt and instead you dive into the river to put out the flames. If you now have **five wounds**, turn to **528** immediately.

The splash douses the flames, but you are treated to the awful sound of screams as the woman at the window burns alive. The mate hauls you aboard and puts the boat about.

Turn to...   719

❧ 749 ❧

Whitchurch sits amongst orchards and meadows low in the valley where the Thames turns eastwards on its long journey to the sea. The village is small and out-of-the-way, but some road-traffic comes this way across the river and a small market caters for local people.

Investigate the war memorial...	10
Enter the Ferryman...	529
Visit the market...	1053
Leave the village...	693

❧ 750 ❧

A drawbridge stands open in the centre of the long wooden causeway that strides across the Thames from bank to bank. Mill Island stands proud, the mill-stream quiet for now and the weir rushing. At the wharf, sacks of malt and crates of pottery produced in the village wait for shipment. Little else is produced here: the Imperial Northern dominate corn-milling at Hambleden, further downstream.

	To buy	To sell
Charcoal	-	£16
Furniture	-	-
Machinery	-	£25
Pottery	£18	£17
Cotton	-	£4
Woollen cloth	-	-
Coal	-	£12
Beer	-	£15
Wheat	-	£4
Malt	£5	£4
Frozen meat	-	-
Ice	-	-

Moor here...	972
Head through the lock...	
(**2s** or **Bargee's Badge**)	113
Turn downriver towards Henley...	882

❧ 751 ❧

You head slowly down into the Thames valley, passing an iron Henley Turpike Company post every quarter of a mile, through rich farmland. Several of the farmsteads are being rebuilt by their owners into fashionable, iron-framed mansions. It seems the age is profitable for those who own the land.

The road is open and you will be easily spotted here: your only chance to stop an engine would be to ride alongside and match speed, trusting in your MOTORING ability.

Plan an ambush here on the open road...	777
Continue on to Wallingford...	**800**

❧ 752 ❧

The crew of the *Blue Devil* come alongside and swing onto the equator walkway around your airship. Your crewmen begin to resist, but when you turn on them and join with the pirates, they are quickly dismayed. Coke himself is fighting the Captain and First Officer and you dash over towards him when you see other airmen surrounding him. If you want to see the pirates victorious, you must fight!

Crewmen	Weapons: **sabres (PAR 3)**
Parry:	10
Nimbleness:	7
Toughness:	6

Victory!	697
Defeat!	713

❧ 753 ❧

To pass a bullet close to the driver requires a steady hand: make an ACCURACY roll of difficulty 12 to succeed.

Successful ACCURACY roll!	425
Failed ACCURACY roll!	85

❧ 754 ❧

You leave your threatening letter and later hear how Lady Pomiane retracted her case. It seems she preferred not to risk what she already had to gain more. A few weeks later you steam on to Shirburn Castle to meet the Earl. He comes out to meet you, rubbing his hands.

"Well, that was a nice piece of work," he says. "Lady Pomiane won't bother me any more - and nor will anyone else round here!" He hands you a bag of coin - **£50** as agreed - and sends you off with a rather patronising pat on the back. "Don't spend it all at once!" he cries after you above your engine's noise.

Ride away... **205**

❧ 755 ❧

☐

If the box is empty, tick it and read on. If it is already ticked, turn to **449** immediately.

You creep around the darkened house, looking for portable property to take with you. There is little you can take in the attic workshop other than a coil of **ultra-tensed wire**. In the Bishop's bedroom below you find a few pieces of jewellery - two **gold rings** and a fine **gold necklace** and in a locked box lie **ten guineas in banknotes** and a **jewelled bible**.

Noise from the basement warns you that the servants are still awake and about. You had better quit while you are ahead. Gain the codeword *Bolster* if you do not already have it.

Leave the house... **343**

❧ 756 ❧

You seem to have come across someone's important medical supplies. Inside the strongbox you find a set of **false teeth**, a bottle of **cough medicine** and a tin of **white pills (ING+2)** ☐ ☐ ☐. Presumably somewhere someone is going through withdrawal symptoms - or has found a new supply.

Turn to... **noted passage**

❧ 757 ❧

The sound of several Imperial velosteams tearing over the tarmacadam towards you reaches your ears. The clanging of a brass bell as one demands a clear road - and they are upon you! You open the regulator and accelerate off up the road. Which way will you head in an attempt to lose your pursuers?

Towards Sonning Bridge... **692**
Into the woods east of Woodcote... **364**
North towards Stonor and Ibstone... **459**

❧ 758 ❧

You show yourself boldly to the driver, wearing your most ferocious grin and flaunting your weaponry. "Stop this engine before I blow blue daylight through you!" Make a RUTHLESSNESS roll of difficulty 10.

Successful RUTHLESSNESS roll! **813**
Failed RUTHLESSNESS roll! **782**

❧ 759 ❧

You manage to creep up on the wagon entirely unobserved. Within a few minutes you are at the door of the iron cage, peering through at the prisoners. Roll a dice to see who is in the wagon.

Score 1-3   A murderess **576**
Score 4-6   Protestors **779**

❧ 760 ❧

The pub here is the life of the village. You are welcomed by men and women resting after a hard day's labour in the fields. Horses are still the main form of power here and everything about the parlour has the touch of horsemanship: old brasses and tack on the walls, the smell of polish, horsehair and even horse-dung from the yard, and horseshoes over every door.

A small man called Faber works alongside the farrier here. He is a locksmith. If you have an **impression** of any sort of key, Faber will convert it for you into that **key** for a price of **£1**: for example, an **impression of a rusty key** becomes a **rusty key**. He will also sell you small tools and plaster and can open a **strongbox** for you. Note this **passage number**.

	To buy	To sell
plaster of paris	3s	-
jeweller's loupe (ING+1)	£4 5s	£3

Open a **strongbox**... **964**
Buy a drink... **(2s)** **1004**
Leave the inn... **344**

❧ 761 ❧

The private steamer that approaches is making its way upriver from Marlow to Henley. Doubtless it will have rich passengers aboard. Make a RUTHLESSNESS roll of difficulty 12 to stop it.

Successful RUTHLESSNESS roll! **1015**
Failed RUTHLESSNESS roll! **251**

762

If you have the codeword *Bernadette*, turn to **806** immediately. If not, but you are the **Friend of Captain Coke**, turn to **681** immediately. Otherwise, read on.

A short man is resting his feet on the table as he drinks beer and wolfs down battered fish tails. He cheerily offers you the plate as you take the other chair. "Nice to have company," he says. "Good to get out of the house, isn't it? Someone else can do the washing up for a change."

You share inconsequential chatter for an hour or so and you slowly realise that he is asking you more and more about your adventures on the road. If you have a **wanted poster**, turn to **620** immediately.

Eventually, he swings down his boots and leaves you alone. Another drinker sidles up and asks whether you realise you have just been drinking with Captain Coke, the sky pirate.

Return to the parlour...	**36**
Leave the inn...	**867**

763

The Crown is run by Janet Lamb, a fierce and outspoken woman unashamed of discussing politics in anyone's hearing. In such an out-of-the-way corner of the hills, however, she causes little enough trouble and is left alone.

The inn itself is a rambling building with several rooms to let under the thatch, a long stable and garage block, a brick-floored parlour and a finely kept garden. Her one-legged son Fred is always around, his hands dark with soil and grime. If you have **pension statement 4590213**, turn to **1438** immediately. If not, but you have the codeword *Betrayed*, turn to **1422**. If you have neither but you have the codeword *Bought*, turn to **1411**.

To hire a room here you must put down two pounds keep - but you must also have won the landlady's trust. Then tick the box so that you need only pay the fee once.

Buy a drink... (**2s**)	**933**
☐ Take a room...	
(**£2** and **Friend of Janet Lamb**)	**654**
Leave the inn...	**370**

764

The Earl shrugs. "Well, I wouldn't trust me right now. Listen - Lady Pomiane is taking me to court over the estate. She claims the two most productive farms in the whole region should belong to her through her dead husband's inheritance - bothersome witch. The hearing will take place in a fortnight's time. Now, what if she's unable to attend on grounds of her health? Make that happen and I'll make it worth your while - how does fifty pounds sound to you?"

"Do your own dirty work."	**669**
"I'll do it. Where can I find her?"	**833**

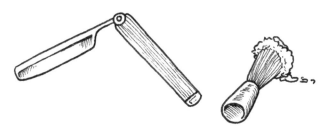

765

You rifle through the Bishop's luggage and find a **gold necklace**, a **silver ring**, a **bottle of champagne** and **£8 5s**. As you return to your velosteam, the Bishop lifts himself up from the mud and shakes his fist angrily. "You will pay for this! I will see you hanged!" Gain a **solidarity point** for punishing this false priest.

Ride away...	**433**

766

Here in Mongewell Woods, woodcutters are at work. Several tall standard beeches are being felled for building timber and the underwood of hazel coppice is being cut back in its seven-year cycle. Children gather twigs and bind them with bramble cord for faggots while their mothers drag leaves over to a wagon for fodder. As you watch, a mighty beech comes down with a crash. Countless birds, insects and small mammals have lost their homes, but in the cycle of growth and decline new trees have their chance to grow here and the wildlife is moved on to find new holes in other trees.

Investigate the Ditch...	**564**
Ride east along Grim's Ditch...	**649**
Ride into Nettlebed...	**791**
Head north...	**836**
Ride south through the wood...	**457**

❧ 767 ❧

"I say! You there!" A voice calls from a small slipper launch just coming alongside the quay. "Five pound for your picnic hamper?" If you wish to sell your **picnic hamper** to the gentleman, remove it from your **possessions** and add **£5** to your wallet.

Wander back into town...   **702**

❧ 768 ❧

As you step through the door, a bag falls over your head and you are knocked to the ground. "Who's this come larking in?" asks a voice rhetorically.

"I mean no harm," you reply through the hessian. If you have more than **15 solidarity points** or your GALLANTRY score (including any bonuses from possessions) is less than 6, turn to **201**. Otherwise, read on.

"Looks like a well-born," says the voice. "Go on lads, boots and all."

Unable to see and set about by a dozen heavy boots, you receive a hard kicking. Gain **two wounds**. The unseen assailants also take all your **money** and any **weapons** you have on you before throwing you out into the street. If you now have **five wounds**, turn to **999**. Otherwise you stagger back to your velosteam.

Turn to...   **911**

❧ 769 ❧

You add the trimmings to the bubbling butter and sauté them with the shallots before adding more cooking liquid and a little wine and straining the whole thing. It comes out a pleasing orange-pink and smells utterly delicious.

"None for you," raps Ramboutarde.

"I was only about to test it," you reply.

"I will be the judge of its flavour," replies the chef. He takes a spoon, a sip and then, for the first time, smiles. "Very good. Quite delicious. I see promise in you."

Over the next few days Ramboutarde continues to hound and push you but he allows you to look at his methods and even goes so far as to explain some of his tricks. As a result, you gain a level of **haute cuisine**.

Turn to...   **704**

❧ 770 ❧

If you are **Wanted by the Telegraph Guild**, turn to **276** immediately. Otherwise read on.

The tall hill here is topped by one of the region's Class-A telegraph towers, its flickering panels conversing constantly with Nuffield and Christmas Common to the north. Supply wagons stand in the vehicle yard, dwarfed by a mountain of coal.

In a back yard, behind the office block, a few self-interested guildsmen will sell you official supplies at unofficial prices - and buy contraband for their own profit. If you have a set of **reservoir plans**, turn to **1173** immediately.

Tools	To buy	To sell
waterproof paint	-	6s
rope ladder	9s	5s
lantern	6s	4s
wirecutters	12s	8s
tarpaulin	4s	2s
measuring line	10s	6s
brass flange joint	8s	4s
telescope	£4 10s	£3 5s
pneumatic manual (ENG+3)	-	£8
ultra-tensed wire	£2	-
blank punchcards	15s	-

Ask about doing work for the Guild...   **551**
Supply information on the Coal Board...
    (**Coal Board Accounts book**)   **538**
Head downhill...   **682**

❧ 771 ❧

You steam slowly through the streets, dodging errand-running urchins, high-collared clerks, drays, steam wagons, marketmen, hecklers and street-sweepers. Great heaps of coal stand behind fences and armed guard. Chimneys launch themselves up from street level on every side. A thick blanket of sooty smoke hangs over this side of town.

The clanging of iron on iron, the whirring of mechanical saws and the hiss of casting tell you that you are amongst the workshops and engineer's sheds. A row of painted boards name some of the businesses, but the colours themselves are dulled with smoke and grime.

Enter Richards Bros....   **155**
Enter J. Fox & Son...   **157**
Enter Dewsbury & Knight...   **173**
Return to the town centre...   **297**

❧ 772 ☙

Make a RUTHLESSNESS roll of difficulty 12 to intimidate the driver, adding 1 if you are **Wanted by the Atmospheric Union.**

Successful RUTHLESSNESS roll!	**1256**
Failed RUTHLESSNESS roll!	**1342**

❧ 773 ☙

You come alongside an unattended barge and jump into the cabin. Roll a dice to see what you can come away with.

Score 1-2	A **silver bracelet** and a **rope**
Score 3-4	A **grappling iron** and **£3 7s**
Score 5-6	Some **engineer's gauntlets (ENG+2)**

Sail on... 719

❧ 774 ☙

You knock the man's sword aside and barge him heavily into the river. He does not struggle but floats, facedown, dead.

The remainder of his crew flee back to the skiff and the crew of the Guild barge are left to tend to their wounded and weep over the slain. After doing what you can to help, the bargee thanks you. He insists on seeing to your **wounds** (convert them all into **scars**, rolling for **intimidating scars (RUTH+1)** as normal) and pressing a **malt licence** into your hand. "I'll tell the Guild of what you've done," he says. If you are **Wanted by the River Guild**, remove this from your **Adventure Sheet**. You can also gain a **solidarity point** if you currently have fewer than **20.**

Return to your vessel... 719

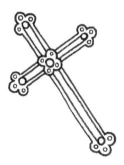

❧ 775 ☙

You let the farmer pass and wait by the road for a better prey. Sometime later, however, you hear the distinctive sound of approaching Constable velosteams. The farmer must have tipped them off to your presence!

Prepare to flee! 757

❧ 776 ☙

You manage to stop the bleeding, splint and realign the man's broken bones and lift him clear from the wreckage. He awakes, obviously in great pain, but manages to tell you his name is Tenney and his family live in Mongewell.

Take him there...	**1041**
Leave him at the side of the road...	**807**

❧ 777 ☙

You wait at the side of the road, shrouded in the falling dusk and wild clematis. Note **passage number 306** on your **Adventure Sheet** and roll a dice to see what you encounter:

Score 1	The Haulage Guild...	**408**
Score 2	An independent haulier...	**1285**
Score 3	The Atmospheric Union...	**194**
Score 4-5	A private steam carriage...	**136**
Score 6	A locobus...	**440**

❧ 778 ☙

One of the players - a slight woman with an unfocused eye - has been peering at your deck of cards. "These ain't clean," she says. "They're queer. We've got ourselves a snide toby here, we have." The players rise to their feet suddenly. Remove your **deck of marked cards** (which are thrown on the floor in disgust) and prepare yourself to fight to get away!

Card players	Weapons: **sabre (PAR 6)**
Parry:	10
Nimbleness:	4
Toughness:	6

Victory!	**418**
Defeat!	**999**

❧ 779 ☙

Inside the cage are several angry-looking young men and women, still carrying the placards and banners with which they were arrested when protesting against the Reading Arms Fair. They sit up as you approach, but are quick-witted enough to stay silent while you slip the bolt. One by one, they climb down and follow you into the woods.

"The Steam Highwayman!" whispers one in amazement. "I had no idea that you were concerned with us!"

"Continue with your noble work."	**626**
"The Compact are your real allies."	
(**Member of the CWE**)	**689**

๑ 780 ๑

At the side of the road a woman sits begging beside her crutch. She is a simple country woman but her ragged clothes and very apparent helplessness speak of hard times indeed. She raises a bowl towards you and speaks.

"Have pity on a widow, kind traveller. No husband have I, no home. I hobble on, hoping to find some rest for my aged bones."

"Have you no son to support you?"

The woman begins to weep. "I had a good boy - an honouring, hard-working son. He studied and passed his examination and the Telegraph Guild gave him a job at Wargrave. But there was a fire! He was at his station that night and weren't allowed to leave for anything. He perished that night, and with him, my heart."

If you have friends nearby and wish to take responsibility for this woman, you may be able to make amends for your past deeds.

Give her some money... (**10s**)	**847**
Take the woman to Prior Horace and	
pay for her requirements...	
(**£3 15s** and **Friend of Prior Horace**)	946
Ride on to South Stoke...	**584**
Head for North Stoke...	**515**
Speed directly up to Wallingford...	**800**

๑ 781 ๑

The heavy velosteam churns on towards the river and, despite your best efforts and the scent of scorched wooden brake-blocks, you overshoot the ferry and launch into the Thames!

The Constables are quick to catch up with you and they haul you from the river. Keen to collect their bonus for capturing your vehicle too, they drag it from the water, muddy and quiet. Note that it is now **critically damaged**.

Turn to...

๑ 782 ๑

The driver is unimpressed by your efforts and sweeps past, forcing you to jump into the hedge to escape the wheels of the steamer. Roll a dice to see whether you are hurt.

Score 1-2   Luckily unhurt
Score 3-4   A rough fall - gain a **wound**
Score 5-6   Lose a randomly chosen **item** in the hedge

If you have **five wounds**, turn to **999** immediately. Otherwise, you remount your velosteam and head away from the site of your shaming. Which way will you ride?

Turn to...   **noted passage**

๑ 783 ๑

A crowd of men and women are standing around as Constables and Atmospheric Union guards prepare the gallows. You have come to this place of execution on the day set for the death of Captain Coke.

The sky pirate is still dressed in splendour, though his clothes are torn and his face bruised. He limps up the steps but projects defiance with every movement.

As a priest blesses him, he speaks from the platform. "Do your worst!   I fear no fall - I am long overdue for my drop from the sky. Only hear this! If you seek the riches I hid away, follow the flight of the kites!"

A clank, a clatter and an in-drawn rush of breath. The trapdoor falls, Coke drops into the noose and begins to choke noisily.

You have an opportunity to shoot him down: it will require a steady hand and an accurate weapon and you will certainly earn the wrath of the Constables. Make an ACCURACY roll of difficulty 18 if you wish to try. Otherwise, you can ride away from this place of death before you are strung up yourself.

Successful ACCURACY roll!	**940**
Failed ACCURACY roll!	**927**
Ride into the wood...	**401**
Head towards High Moor Cross...	**939**
Steam to Grey's Court...	**158**
Take the road towards Cane End...	**455**

ᔓ 784 ᕗ

The crew of the barge are dispatched without mercy, but the captain of the water-rats has also been badly hurt. He grins at you. "You came just in the nick of time - the Steam Highwayman, no less? Well, the Guild'll fear you afloat and ashore now." He insists you take a share of the money captured on the barge - **£12 3s** - and you can also choose to take a cargo unit of **Machinery** if you wish, tossing any cargo you are carrying overboard if necessary.

This will soon be spoken of up and down the river and you are now **Wanted by the River Guild**.

Sail on...   719

ᔓ 785 ᕗ

The bakery in Goring is run by a family called Driver. They are mainly concerned with providing cheap, filling bread for the local people, but they recognise the quality of Fursham's so they are able to offer you a price of thirteen shillings for the hundredweight. If you accept the price, remove the **Cobstone flour** from your possessions.

Accept the price...   377
Return to Goring...   487

ᔓ 786 ᕗ

From the turning onto Patemore Lane you are presented with a long, long, even slope down from the high ground into the valley. The velosteam needs no power: it rolls effortlessly down under its own weight, governed by your gentle braking and its own stability, and once more you have cause to bless its builders. You pass isolated houses of flint and brick, bustled about with clapboard sheds for sheep, cattle and hay. Eventually the slope levels out. There ahead of you is the Crown.

Continue on down to Pishill...   370

ᔓ 787 ᕗ

The keeper looks you up and down skeptically. "What sort of woodsman would you be, then?" He shakes his head. "Beggars can't be choosers. His Lordship's pheasants are ready for the shoot, but a gang has come down from somewhere and started picking them off, ten, twelve a night, each night. I've laid traps, dug pits and more, but they keep outsmarting me. And the other night they beat my young underkeeper to a

pulp, poor lad. So you'd better be able to hold your own."

You head down to the woods and he shows you the lay of the land. The glades and undergrowth are indeed stuffed with fat pheasants. He points out the pits he has dug and several sharp man-traps prepared for the poaching gang. "They may well be armed. I certainly am," says the keeper, whose name is Mr Sands. "Don't have any mercy on 'em. Knock 'em down, scare 'em off, whatever. We're quite within our rights."

As evening falls you take up position. Your eyes accustom to the dark and your ears drink in the sounds of the woods. It is imperative that you move quietly as you patrol, so that you catch sight of the poachers before they see you. Make a NIMBLENESS roll of difficulty 11.

Successful NIMBLENESS roll!   967
Failed NIMBLENESS roll!   889

ᔓ 788 ᕗ

On your way through the twisting streets you are forced to make way for freight wagons churning up through the mud from the riverbanks. More head down towards the moorings, carrying iron stanchions and frames, crates guarded by narrow-eyed men and vast amounts of coal.

The wharves themselves stretch both sides of the river, upstream and downstream of the three parallel locks. As you watch, a massive river-barge laden with wheat is lowered from the upper river, its side-paddles smashing at the water like the hooves of an angry beast.

Board your own craft...
   (if **moored at Reading**)   535
Buy a boat...   132
Return to the city...   297

ᔓ 789 ᕗ

Despite all your efforts, you watch as the man struggles to breathe, as blood-flecked spittle rises from his lips, as his chest heaves and pauses and as he eventually falls into the stillness of death.

Bury him here... (**shovel**)   816
Rob his corpse...   822
Leave him...   807

❧ 790 ❧

"What makes you think you can do anything about it?" asks Janet. "Don't you think I've tried?"

"He's not the only one home from the war," you reply. "Tell me his details and I'll get it sorted for you."

"Lance-Corporal Alfred Lamb, Royal Oxford and Buckinghamshire Light Infantry, number 4590213." Gain the codeword *Bottle*.

Return to the parlour...   763

❧ 791 ❧

Nettlebed! High in the Chilterns, hidden from the world by the thick ranks of beeches, this bustling community is growing rich on the opportunities of the new industrial age. The old brickworks has been enlarged and clay-pits surround the town to the south and west. A tall iron mooring-post stands by an airship landing field, where an Imperial Skyways craft is currently under construction. Houses are full with families and working lodgers: the Freight Yard bustles, the town rings with the sound of metal-working. Ten miniature telegraph towers mounted on the prosperous business premises of the town wink and flicker in response to the tall A-Class signal cluster a short way north-west of town, and the streets are full with trolleys, carts and children carrying messages.

Take a look at the market...	928
Investigate the brickworks...	445
Enter the Fright Yard...	677
Visit the White Hart...	829
Leave the town...	944

❧ 792 ❧

Recognising the unique beech tree leads you to the route across the farmlands, heading south east. It is less sunny than when you originally came this way and the kites are roosting. Nonetheless, you make good time and soon emerge by the spring.

Turn to...   633

❧ 793 ❧

You approach Reading Bridge and find a queue of freight engines waiting to cross the river into the city. Speeding past them, you find a Constables checkpoint laid out across the thoroughfare. Nobody is being let in or out without identification. If you are **Wanted by the Constables**, turn to **58** immediately. Other-

wise, read on.

"What's your business, citizen?" barks a Constable as you take your turn.

"Steaming for pleasure," you reply calmly. He checks you against his wallet of printofit criminals and waves you through impatiently.

Steam over the bridge into Reading...	**297**
Head west towards Mapledurham...	**803**
Take the road north...	**609**
Ride east on the Henley road...	**682**

❧ 794 ❧

The narrowing in the road makes this an excellent spot to surprise traffic, but you are a little too close to the Constables' base at Wallingford for comfort. Otherwise, note **passage number 306** on your **Adventure Sheet** and roll a dice to see what you encounter.

Score 1	The locobus...	**440**
Score 2	The Atmospheric Union...	**1244**
Score 3	The Haulage Guild...	**408**
Score 4	The Telegraph Guild...	**198**
Score 5-6	A private steam carriage...	**103**

❧ 795 ❧

"Righto," says Jackson, putting your money into a tray. She takes a tally stick, marks it, splits it and hands you one half. Erase the codeword *Bark* and gain **tally stick 67**. "We'll get on that directly. You just head back here in a few day's time and we'll settle up. Don't lose your tally or I won't be beholden to pay you."

It is time to leave Nettlebed. Which way will you ride?

Head towards Wallingford...	**751**
Ride north...	**110**
Take the Woodcote Road...	**664**
Ride towards Bix...	**3**

❧ 796 ❧

"Well, get up then!" Captain Coke hauls you to your feet and gives a whistle. Several of his crew come in from the benches outside, blindfold you, truss you, grab your purse and all the **money** you are carrying, and then sling you over the bonnet of your own velosteam.

Faint from loss of blood and your head-down position, you quickly pass out. You come round beneath canvas. Somebody is mopping your face.

Coke's team of ruffians, brigands and thieves live for plunder. Their airship, the *Blue Devil*, is tethered beneath the treeline in an enclosed valley and the underwood is littered with machine parts, tents, a workshop and forge.

Remove one **wound** and replace it with a **scar**. Roll two dice and on a score of 11 or higher, add an **intimidating scar (RUTH+1)** to your **Adventure Sheet**. While you have been recovering, the crew have been preparing for another raid. You are not given any special treatment or ranking position, but simply assigned to the engine room as a stoker: your task is simply to feed the furnaces, hour after hour. The chief engineer and his mate haul you aboard, scornful of your injuries, hand you a shovel and tell you to get working. Within the enclosed space there are no windows and little sensation of movement. It is fearfully hot.

Turn to...   **843**

❧ 797 ☙

You carefully approach the rear wagon, doing your best to remain out of sight of the driver's mirrors. You hook your velosteam on and then clamber towards the heavy coupling. Make a NIMBLENESS roll of difficulty 12 to uncouple the wagon, adding 2 if you possess **wirecutters** or an **adjustable wrench (ENG+1)**.

Successful NIMBLENESS roll!   **854**
Failed NIMBLENESS roll!   **879**

❧ 798 ☙

The sky-pirates are well-crewed, but your craft is faster. The Captain puts about and turns the airship around. "We'll make for Rotherfield," the first mate announces. "Fee-paying passengers will be reimbursed." Of course in your case, you will be put ashore without payment. At least you have your life: you have neither been skinned alive nor tossed carelessly from the promenade deck to your death.

Turn to...   **454**

❧ 799 ☙

Jackson matches the tallies and grunts. She looks up. "That was a canny decision of yours. We got an excellent price for that timber in Oxford. One of the colleges was paying good money for new roofing." She checks the tallies once more. "I see you paid in ad-

vance for the haulage. Let's see now... That means I owe you the sale price, less my commission for finding the buyer. Here you are." She hands you **£34**.

Return to the Freight Yard...   **677**
Return to Nettlebed...   **791**
Leave Nettlebed...   **944**

❧ 800 ☙

You have reached the east end of Wallingford Bridge. There is a small Constable's hut here with an Imperial velosteam parked outside: it is not a place to remain for long. If you are **Wanted by the Constables**, turn to **588** immediately. The bridge itself crosses the often-flooded meadow on a series of medieval arches. The Haulage Guild have been proposing a rebuilding for years as the narrow roadway restricts access for their engines. Nonetheless, nothing has happened yet and so several traction engines and their wagons are parked up waiting for their turn to cross even now.

From here one road leads up towards Nuffield, another along the valley to the south and third across the low hills towards Watlington.

Cross the bridge...   **270**
Ride towards Nuffield Common...   **698**
Take the road south...   **860**
Ride north towards Oxford...   **259**
Cross the plain towards Watlington...   **229**

❧ 801 ☙

You ride beside a quarry hacked into the chalk hillside and a small row of cottages hurriedly thrown up for the labourers. Someone is making money here: nobody builds houses out of philanthropy on prime meadowland. On the other side of the road lie buttercups and clovers among lush grass: a herd of Hereford cattle are browsing at the hedge.

Prepare an ambush here...   **475**
Ride to Mill End...   **112**
Head east towards Medmenham...
                                Smog and Ambuscade 534

❧ 802 ☙

No container can resist your attempts forever. It takes hours to open the strongbox, but they are well-spent. No wonder it was heavy: the shifting contents are forty-five guineas (**£47 5s**) in gold coin.

Turn to...   **noted passage**

✌ 803 ✌
You are on the long, straight road at the foot of Chazey Wood Hill, part-way between Reading Bridge and Mapledurham. A wide meadow stretches out between you and the river, full of tall, waving grasses and head-high thistles. A clutch of farm buildings stand in the middle beneath a pillar of smoke. There is little traffic here beside vehicles from the local estates, but the road is well-kept and firm, probably paid for by the local landowners.

Plan an ambush here...	**846**
Ride to Mapledurham...	**864**
Steam towards Reading...	**793**

✌ 804 ✌
"I wouldn't go up 'eath Wood," says the farmer. "I 'eard there's some desperate brigands up there. Violent - real violent."

Turn to...	**710**

✌ 805 ✌
You make to remount your velosteam and make off. Are any of the following true of you?

If you are **Wanted by the Constables**...	811
If not, but you are **Wanted by the Haulage Guild**...	744
If not, but you are **Wanted by the Telegraph Guild**...	996
None of these...	3

✌ 806 ✌
This fellow has plainly been enjoying the Sparrowbeak Rye for several hours. His red eyes swim and he slurs as he addresses you, but as he chatters about his travels on the road you hear much of interest. He tells you how he used to see Captain Coke, the sky pirate, drinking in this very seat. He tells you of the bronze foundry at Wargrave. He tells you about the long-distance carriages that make their way to Wales from Wallingford, carrying all manner of Imperial officials, Telegraph Guild officers and nobility.

Return to the parlour...	**36**
Leave the inn...	**867**

✌ 807 ✌
Cane End is little more than a few cottages and a scrappy common on a triangle of high ground. Several felled trees lie, unsawn, at the side of the road. What could possess people to fell valuable timber and then do nothing with it?

The woods around the village are old and have been coppiced many times. One ancient and bulbous beech tree has a prominent heart cut into the bark.

Head into Valentine Woods...		**178**
Distribute some money to the poor...	(**£4**)	**563**
Steam to Gallowstree Common...		**600**
Ride south towards Reading...		**560**
Head northwest towards Woodcote...		**488**
Treavel down Deadman's Lane...		**396**

✌ 808 ✌
Oxford remains a city of contrasts. The cobbled streets are thick with mud in many areas and slum dwellings line the railway yard, the canalside and the old town walls. Yet in other places the fine college buildings, the museums and the parks have a glamour and beauty rarely seen in the land.

Go looking for Jermyn Bigod... (**clockwork bird**)	**945**
Investigate the slums...	**1107**
Trespass in the colleges...	**1093**

✌ 809 ✌
"What are you doing? You will completely dilute the soup! Get out of my way - I may be able to save this." He shoves you out of position and begins to mutter as he drains the pot and scrabbles around for the langoustine heads and shells. "What an awful so-called sous-chef! I would 'ave been better with the one who jumped!"

Turn to...	**704**

✌ 810 ✌
☐

If the box above is empty, tick it and read on. If it is already ticked, you have already made observations here and can gain little more: you must head to another Telegraph Guild tower and turn to **978** immediately.

You take up position in the branches of a tall ash tree within easy sight of the Nettlebed, Caversham and Christmas Common towers and settle yourself down for a long stint of watching. The tower has several panels, each with six, nine or twelve shutters flapping and flickering in reply to the distant observers. It takes all your concentration to note as much as you can, watching for patterns and sequences. If you possess a set of **telegraph observations** ☐ ☐, tick one of the boxes. If you do not own such an item, add **telegraph observations** ☐ ☐ to your possessions. You will need to observe the codes on three unique towers to complete your task.

Leave the tree...   **978**

❧ 811 ❧

One of the smiths in the workshop has sent a very quick message to the local Constables: when you pull out of the workshop, the sound of ringing bells can be heard along Bix lane. You had better make your escape - and quickly!

Ride towards Valentine Woods...   **364**
Ride for Oxford...   **1138**
Ride to Heath Wood...   **1354**

❧ 812 ❧

The road-train turns south and heads along the road towards Reading, following the long loop of the river Thames. Perhaps the road over the hills would reach the west more quickly, but the driver is plainly choosing to preserve his coal and water and stick to the easier steaming.

As you follow at a good distance, you can make out the details of the road-train. Roll a dice to see what you encounter.

Score 1-2   The Haulage Guild...   **408**
Score 3-4   The Telegraph Guild...   **198**
Score 5-6   The Atmospheric Union...   **194**

If you choose not to pursue the road-train, turn to **355**.

❧ 813 ❧

The driver and engineer have a momentary conference before the engineer leans over and lets out the steam with a whistle. The engine slows as it loses pressure, but you will have to be quick: others on the road may well have heard that shriek of panicked steam. Roll a dice to see what you can take from the crew and wagons.

Score 1-2   **15s**, a pair of **goggles (MOT+1)** and a **shovel**
Score 3-4   **£2 10s** and an **axe**
Score 5-6   **£1 8s** and some **welding tools**

Unless you have a **mask**, you will now be **Wanted by the Haulage Guild** as a result of your deeds.

Ride away...   **noted passage**

❧ 814 ❧

As you slip your shilling into the poor box, you hear the chink of coins. It is plainly not an empty box...

Speak to Father Patrick...   **839**
Leave the chapel...   **3**

❧ 815 ❧

You are poured a glass of Summer Blossom - a pale, well-headed ale with a low alcohol content and fresh, meadowy flavour. It is bitter, bright and resiny. The barman enthuses about it. "Triple-hopped, you see. Kent Gems to begin with, then a Burton hop called 51, and then our own from the yard to finish. You won't drink this anywhere else."

He brings you a platter of cheese and hard oat biscuits to enjoy with your pint. It would be all too easy to stay here in the sunny garden of the Cherry Tree Inn and have purely generous thoughts towards everyone, with a beer like this in your glass.

Return to the parlour...   **145**
Leave the pub...   **457**

❧ 816 ❧

Perhaps it is better to lay the man in the ground than to leave him here on the roadside, but surely he must have family somewhere who would prefer to inter him? However, in your current circumstance, burying seems the best course of action and least likely to cause a public health problem, so you dig a grave beneath the roadside beeches and lay the body in it.

Several hours later, when you have finished, you realise that you have dropped something in the grave. Remove the **fifth possession** on your **Adventure Sheet**. What a reward for doing good!

Turn to...   807

☙ 817 ❧

"So, the navvies are militarised! Excellent. You have really proven your worth to the Cause." Comrade Blewitt arranges for Compact mechanics to look over your velosteam. They repair any **damage points** and will fit one of the following customisations for you, free of charge; **ramming beak, double headlamp, muffled exhaust, reinforced boiler**.

"One more thing," says Comrade Blewitt. "As yet, the Compact has little influence in the skies, but we seek to infiltrate all levels of society. I would not charge anyone less effective than yourself with this task: hijack us an airship so that the Cause may climb above the clouds!"

He tells that if you gain control of an airship, you should bring it to the mooring post at Nettlebed. "The brickworkers there will help us take control of the station." Gain the codeword *Believer*.

Return to the parlour...   100
Leave the inn...   487

☙ 818 ❧

By some great fluke of hydrography and geology, the Thames at Henley breaks into a straight, even reach of more than a mile: it is a natural showpiece for watercraft, the best racing reach upstream of London and a fashionable hotspot. Since Henley waterside is also a busy freight wharf, where goods from Oxford and the local region are loaded onto barges bound for London, it is also busy with steam-tugs, barges, lighters, riverboys, launches and every conceivable floating invention.

You can see paddle-driven steamers, sailing barges, rowing skiffs, horse-drawn heavy-laden narrowboats and all their masters and mistresses calling, arguing and hooting beneath the narrow and much-marked arches of Henley bridge.

Moor here...   873
Trade at the wharf...   993
Turn downstream through the bridge...   501
Head upriver towards Wargrave...
    (**2s** or **Bargee's Badge**)   956
Head on towards Sonning without stopping...
    (**4s** or **Bargee's Badge**)   981
Make for Reading directly...
    (**10s** or **Bargee's Badge**)   985

☙ 819 ❧

Here in the middle of the wood, Coke has his airship, the *Blue Devil*, tethered to tall oak and beech trees. His men work in the tents and huts, sharpening weapons, dividing their booty and mending machinery. If you have the codeword *Bragging*, turn to **116**.

Talk to the quartermaster...   910
Talk to Anita, the crew's medico...   76
Go to your tent...   159
Leave the wood...   991

☙ 820 ❧

The farmer tells you about a recent trip to Reading. "Hate the place, but I gots to go there sometimes. Well, city's all preparing for some dirty great fair - selling guns and the like! Couldn't get a room for love nor money last time I was there. Foreigners come from all over to see what we makes."

Turn to...   408

☙ 821 ❧

You open the regulator and your powerful Ferguson matches speed. The driver of the Union steamer sees you approaching - you catch a glimpse of her eyes in a mirror - and accelerates. Make a MOTORING roll of difficulty 15 to match speed, adding 1 for each customisation you have made to your velosteam.

Successful MOTORING roll!   853
Failed MOTORING roll!   541

ᔒ 822 ᔒ

The man has a **dinner jacket**, a **fine top hat (GAL+1)**, a **pocket watch**, a **silver ring** and a letter addressed to Mr Tenney of Mongewell Park but no money that you can find.

Leave his corpse...   **807**

ᔒ 823 ᔒ

You tie up a little south of the village, where the railway embankment approaches the river. Across the line stands the navvies' camp. Your mate takes out his pipe thoughtfully. "I hope they don't come a-knocking," he says. "Rum lot of roughs, they is."

Go ashore...   **584**
Head back out onto the river...   **271**

ᔒ 824 ᔒ

You thrust the punt forward, lean out of the way of your challenger's quant, then swing your own pole heavily around and knock him into the water. His friends begin cheering unexpectedly. He scrambles to the bank and shakes your hand. "Well fought, that's for sure. No hard feelings then. I shall just have to ask Papa for an advance on next term's allowance." You are given the **Jousting Cup** in recognition of your prowess. Made of silver, this can be sold for **£10 10s** at any market.

Continue on your way...   **868**

ᔒ 825 ᔒ
☐

If the box is empty, tick it and read on. If it is already ticked, turn to **995** immediately.

The cruiser has been abandoned. A half-eaten meal is laid on the fine table inside and the mooring ropes are coiled neatly. The engine is at pressure and, although the paddles are disengaged, the craft is moving gently along with the current.

Loot the cruiser...   **574**
Tow it to Culham Lock...   **636**
Leave it and sail on...   **210**

ᔒ 826 ᔒ

You and your mate ease the boat into a mooring alongside a broad grain barge, overlooked by the smoky spires of Oxford city. Your velosteam is uncovered and carefully rolled ashore, its burner tested, its water tank topped up. Your mate makes everything fast and settles himself down. "Whether you be long or otherwise, I'll be waiting here," he says. "There's plenty a-doing in this old town!" Mark **moored at Oxford** on your **Adventure Sheet**.

Head directly to the Freight Yard...   **285**
Steam into the city...   **688**
Leave Oxford by road...   **970**

ᔒ 827 ᔒ

The fishermen are deep in a technical (or pseudo-technical) discussion of weights, flies, rods and lines. They chat about their successes and disappointments. You tell them about the pike by Sonning Bridge.

"Aye, he's been there many a year. No-one's caught him yet," says an angler. "I'd dear love to have that notch on my rod."

Return to the parlour...   **348**
Leave the pub...   **280**

ᔒ 828 ᔒ

You root around in the wreckage, kicking up all sorts of pungent smells with the ashes and scraps. In the control cabin of the gondola are several charred skeletons: looking around for anything to identify them, you come across a single, golden **griffin cufflink**. The crest on the gates of Hedsor House has exactly these shapes. It seems clear that the Judge's son Gregory is no more. If you return the cufflink to Hedsor you may be able to give the old man some closure at least. Erase the codeword *Abapical*.

Return to the road...   **8**

ᔒ 829 ᔒ

The White Hart at Nettlebed is a working man's pub - and a working woman's. It is full of shift-workers at all times of the day, finding what rest and refreshment they can before heading back to the furnaces.

At one table you overhear a conversation between brick-traders. One of them had been buying city dust from London, shipped up on the river to add into the clay. "But the fool of the Captain didn't know the stream and went right up the middle channel after Henley watercress fields. He had to ditch his load and now it's shallower than ever!"

Buy a drink...   (2s)   **952**
Leave the inn...   **791**

❧ 830 ❧

You finish your ale, slam down the tankard and head out to start your velosteam. This hiss of ready vapour sets your wheels immediately in motion and towns-people scatter in front of you. Note the passage number **433** and if you have the codeword *Breadbasket*, turn to **812**. If you have the codeword *Beyond*, turn to **111** immediately. Otherwise, read on.

You cross the bridge and, reading the wheel-marks in the mud, pursue the prison wagon up the hill.

Turn to... 60

❧ 831 ❧

The hedge-layers are cutting the pleachers of the over-grown hedge and twisting them into position, closing the gaps for the local landowner's sheep and letting light back into the hawthorn where it has overgrown.

On the roadside behind the occupied men, a short **billhook (PAR 2)** lies for the taking.

Continue on... 62

❧ 832 ❧

To set up a camp you will need a **tarpaulin** and an **axe**. If you have these and wish to construct a shelter here in the woods, gain the codeword *Before* and discard the **tarpaulin**.

Enter your shelter... 962
Return to the wood... 401

❧ 833 ❧

The Earl chuckles with glee. "Excellent. She lives at Swyncombe House near Eatonsfield, not far from here. Terribly old place, I'm sorry to say. Parts of it are practically falling down. Genuine health hazard. When you've done your part, come to the castle and you'll get your reward."

He knocks on the side of the carriage and the driver starts off, just missing your velosteam. Gain the codeword *Burnett*.

Head towards Watlington... 360
Head towards Stokenchurch... 710

❧ 834 ❧

The stones are massive granite megaliths, each weighing tons, arranged in a rough circle. One or two taller stones stand out like uneven canines in a ring of teeth and a rough doorway has been laid out with a long lintel laid on two other rocks.

Rabbit burrows dot the short grass. Who knows what they have discovered beneath this hallowed turf?

Dig for treasure here... (**shovel**) 135
Return to your repairs and ride on
    to Wargrave... 418

❧ 835 ❧

The washerwomen drop their baskets and call to you. They have heard about your generosity to the needy poor of Cadmore End. "Have you got something for us? Just a shilling or two? Life is hard round here."

Give them a crown apiece... (£1 5s) 881
Leave them... 901

❧ 836 ❧

You pull over at Nuffield Common. A few cottages stand around the open meadow where a horse munches on thick grass. A long gravelled driveway leads off towards Nuffield Place, just showing its chimneys and roof through walnut trees, and another track heads to the compound at the Telegraph tower. Nettlebed is only a short distance to the east, beneath smoking chimneys and the tall vanes of a windmill.

To the south of the village lies Grim's Ditch: a long earthwork stretching all the way to the Thames in a line as straight as a die. Its legendary origin is told in all the Dame schools and inn parlours: thrown up in a night by the devil to slow his pursuers. It is certainly a place where the predictable science of the modern-day seems less powerful than the rumours of the past.

Approach Nuffield Place... 619
Head to the Telegraph Guild compound... 978
Ride west down towards Wallingford... 751
Steam to Nettlebed... 791
Investigate Grim's Ditch... 564

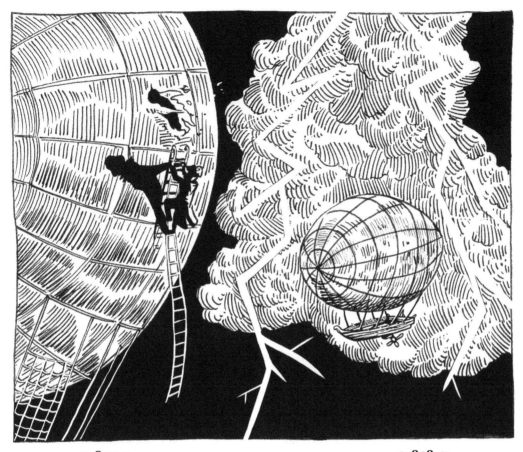

837

When your life has been as poor and bitter as your own, how else can you survive except by taking from those who have much? Wasn't that how you got hold of the velosteam beneath you, the weapons at your side and the very clothes on your back? Here in the woods and hills of the region you will be able to steal and rob and scrabble your way into some sort of security. Perhaps the likes of Captain Coke, the infamous airship pirate who has been seen in the pubs near Fingest, or the prospect of work aboard an airship at Rotherfield Greys, might help you extricate yourself from the desperate puzzle of poverty.

You have in your possession a **blunderpistol (ACC 6)**, a **sabre (PAR 3)**, a **mask** and a **deck of marked cards**. Your ability scores are:

RUTHLESSNESS	4
ENGINEERING	4
MOTORING	3
INGENUITY	5
NIMBLENESS	6
GALLANTRY	2

Turn to...   1440

838

Reading boasts shops on every street, from board-fronted alleyway dens to the vastness of Peterson's Department Store.

Clothing	To buy	To sell
mask	4s	-
lace shawl	£1 5s	15s
cloak	£1	-
dark cloak (RUTH+1)	-	£4
fur coat	£5 4s	£3 2s
engineer's gloves (ENG +1)	£3	£2 5s
engineer's gauntlets (ENG+2)	-	£5
goggles (MOT+1)	£2 15s	£1 15s
eyepatch (RUTH+1)	15s	5s
hair matches (R+2) ▢▢▢	£2	-
wide-brimmed hat	£1 10s	

Jewellery	To buy	To sell
locket	-	6s
pocket watch	-	£1 18s
silver ring	-	8s
silver bracelet	-	16s
silver necklace	-	£1 10s
pectoral cross	-	£12
Jousting Cup	-	£4 6s

nate the red kites that nest locally. "Horrible things," he says, "With their shrieking and their chick-swallowing. Will you help me some more? You'll need some carcasses - rabbit or deer - and some poison. Then if you head up to Valentine wood where they roost, we can get 'em. Oh, and I'll need you to destry their nests too."

| "Those birds need protecting, not exterminating." | 941 |
| "I'll be happy to help." | 877 |

❧ 968 ❧

You carefully steam up onto the high earthen bank above the holloway and find yourself a spot with good visibility along the roadway. Note passage number **550** on your **Adventure Sheet** and then roll a dice to see what you encounter.

Score 1-2	A private steam carriage...	103
Score 3-4	The Haulage Guild...	408
Score 5-6	The Coal Board...	1305

❧ 969 ❧

The brick and flint cottages of Skirmett are jettied out over the road, revealing their wooden frames. Several have been re-roofed with machine-cut tiles, but most show the scrappy thatch of local straw. The Hamble brook runs through the village, broadening as it flows south towards Hambleden and Mill End, where it trills out into the Thames. Here though you can step across it, or splash through it on your velosteam.

Ride towards Frieth...	896
Head south down the valley...	932
Take the lane to Turville...	57
Ride north to Fingest...	12

❧ 970 ❧

You put the smoky city behind you and ready yourself for a long ride. Wagons and carriages fill the roads and you weave between them before accelerating away.

Head north-west towards Wales...
Dark Vales and Dark Hearts 390
Ride towards Watlington...	339
Head for Wallingford...	851
Take the road towards Stokenchurch...	452

❧ 971 ❧

"I know what you mean," replies the priest. "A selfish self-honouring can be very destructive indeed. But I do not think that was the root cause."

| Turn to... | 329 |

❧ 972 ❧

An open mooring beneath the French Horn provides you with a chance to get ashore and regain your land-legs. Your velosteam needs some attention, so you and the mate oil the joints, flush the water system and start the burner carefully.

| Head into the inn... | 358 |
| Investigate Sonning... | 91 |

❧ 973 ❧

Remove **brass disc 7821** from your possessions. You toss it onto a desk in front of Comrade Blewitt, who seems to know what it means. He smiles with satisfaction. "So, you have proven yourself to Plunkett? Well our cell is a little more direct in its actions. Assassination of the nobility. Burning of their mansions to strike fear into their hearts. Theft of weapons. Radicalisation of the masses. Resistance to the guilds - particularly the Telegraph Guild. We are about to embark on a campaign against the Guild and will begin by burning their minor towers - like the D-Class tower at Wargrave. Which of these can you help us with?"

If you choose to participate in the Compact's campaign of terror, you must show initiative. Go and fulfill your Comrade's charge and return to see how your deeds are valued.

| Return to the parlour... | 100 |
| Leave the inn... | 911 |

❧ 974 ❧

"Gnah." The chef makes a sound of frustration. "Well, we cannot order more now. At least I 'ave not yet published my menu for today. I was going to serve my delicious, delicate white carrot salad. Yes, look at these disappointing chantenays. Doesn't the grocer know the difference? At least you do, my little chou-fleur." He gives your ear a playful tweak.

| Turn to... | 921 |

❧ 975 ❧

Unable to proceed for now, you and the mate moor by the riverside and continue to do your best with the engine. You put your velosteam ashore and begin to dismantle the engine, but night falls and with it, you and the exhausted mate take some rest.

You are awoken in the night by a yell and a splash. Jumping out of the cabin you see shadowy figures climbing aboard your boat and the mate splashing desperately in the Thames. River pirates have come upon you - you must fight for your life!

River pirates	Weapons: **sabre (PAR 3)**
Parry:	10
Nimbleness:	7
Toughness:	5

Victory!	**634**
Defeat!	**528**

❧ 976 ❧

The driver retreats as you lay charges along his wagons. Remove the **explosives** from your **possessions** and make an ENGINEERING roll of difficulty 12, adding 2 for each level of **explosives expert**.

Successful ENGINEERING roll!	**502**
Failed ENGINEERING roll!	**1009**

❧ 977 ❧

Ibstone straggles unevenly along the bottom of its hidden little valley like a puddle in a summer ditch. Several cottages, a larger, dilapidated house, two or three farms and a squat church make up the most of it. Then there is the Fox, a country inn standing north of the common with beans climbing its facade, and several ponds amongst the scrubby grass. On all sides the hills glower in their beech cloaks. The sky above is just as forested with cloud. There are no smoking chimneys by busy workshops here. The smell of soot is notably absent and in its place is the thin reek of woodsmoke, but if the village is a rural idyll, then the people are still poor as a result. If you have the codeword *Avatar*, turn to **1122** immediately.

Enter the Fox...	**585**
Investigate the church...	**338**
Ride up to Wormsley Park...	**134**
Head towards Turville...	**431**
Steam on to Fingest...	**867**
Ride north towards Stokenchurch...	**980**

❧ 978 ❧

The Nettlebed A-Class tower is busy and well-guarded. You will not be able to enter if you are **Wanted by the Telegraph Guild** - but you may be able to try and ambush their supply wagons here. Note **passage number 306**.

Observe the tower...

(**telescope** or **binoculars**)	**810**
Ambush the supply wagons...	**198**
Head into Nettlebed...	**791**
Ride north...	**880**
Steam onto the common...	**836**

❧ 979 ❧

The small church of St Peter and St Paul is quiet and cool. The vicar greets you nonchalantly, seeming less interested in having a visitor than in the books he is re-arranging. Shortly after you enter, he disappears through a low door.

Draw some of the features...

(**sketchpad** ☐ ☐ ☐)	**913**
Rob the poorbox...	**925**
Leave the church...	**308**

❧ 980 ❧

Commonhill wood is quiet - strangely quiet. Few birds are singing here. Perhaps the locals, starved by their harsh rates, have hunted them out. At the corner by Wormsley Lodge a gamekeeper has nailed up several foxes and a weasel. The mouldy corpses are several weeks old at least.

Ride on to Stokenchurch...	**308**

❧ 981 ❧

You steam hard and slip into Marsh Lock behind some heavy barges carrying gravel upriver to Reading. Once released on the upper pound, you set off towards Sonning, passing Wargrave without a second look and quickly reaching Shiplake Lock. Then the river's character changes again and the stream begins to twist and turn, around Hallsmead Ait and the Lynch and eventually tending westward towards Sonning weir.

Take a look at Hallsmead Ait...	**894**
Pause by the Lynch...	**935**
Continue on to Sonning...	**750**

Medical	To buy	To sell
bandages	3s	-
soothing lotion	2s	-
poison	15s	10s
false teeth	-	10s
gold tooth	-	15s
Tools	To buy	To sell
adjustable wrench (ENG+1)	£1 8s	18s
welding tools	£2 2s	£
roll of oiled silk	-	£5
pneumatic manual (ENG+3)	-	£8
calculating engine (ING+3)	£20	5s
autogauge (MOT+3)	-	£15 3s
steam fist (RUTH+3)	£18 4s	-
blank punchcards	15s	8s
nephritic solution	15s	8s
Weapons	To buy	To sell
razor (PAR-1 NIM+3)	£1 15s	18s
sabre (PAR 3)	£1 5s	8s
rapier (PAR 4)	-	£4
blunderpistol (ACC 6)	£4	£2
duelling pistols (ACC 7)	-	£10
Other items	To buy	To sell
deck of marked cards	£1 5s	5s
parasol	-	£4
box of cigars	-	£1 10s
ivory fan	-	£1 10s
revolutionary poster	1s	-
bolt of cloth	-	15s

Return to the city...	297
Leave Reading...	410

✎ 839 ✎
☐

If the box is empty, tick it and turn to **861** immediately. Otherwise, read on.

Father Patrick emerges from a pew where he is organising hymnals. "Greetings again! Christ welcomes you."

"I want to confess my sins..."	261
"How can I help the people?"	279
"Tell me your story."	361
Leave the church...	3

✎ 840 ✎
To climb the hill your Ferguson must work hard and long: it is not steep, but the slope fights against your heavy engine all the way up past the cottages, the woodside and the final nasty false crest before you reach the crossroads at Eatonsfield Shaw.

Sunlight greets you. A horse turns its head to see you steam past. Ahead is the crossroads.

Turn to... 110

✎ 841 ✎
The gaol at Wallingford is actually a series of connected cells and spaces in the walls of the inner bailey of the impressive castle. Although it serves the local Constables and their prisoners, the Warden is a member of the Wallingford Town Guard and directly appointed by the Duke of Cornwall. Since the castle is also one of the Duke's most sumptuous residences, this is also his private prison, in which various enemies of his are held alongside the local ne-er-do-wells like yourself. It has been known for centuries as Brien's Close.

Your stay in Brien's Close will not be comfortable or pleasant but you may profit from it. If you have the codeword *Brand* and are a **Member of the Compact for Workers' Equality**, turn to **1006**. If you have the codeword *Brand* but are not yet a **Member of the Compact for Workers' Equality**, turn to **1187** immediately. If, on the other hand, you have the codeword *Boorish*, turn to **1034**. Otherwise you will be thrown into a cell and left to rot.

Turn to... 1020

✎ 842 ✎
Remove the **poison** and the carcass from your possessions and remove the codeword *Bestial*. You rub the poison into the carcass and tear it into pieces, before laying several out in a glade. Within an hour, you see a kite land heavily beside the meat and begin gobbling it down. You make your way through the wood and repeat the process several times.

In the process you track the massive birds and identify several of their nests. You can complete Mr Sand's task either by climbing the trees and smashing the eggs inside or by shooting them down with a gun. Choose whether to make a NIMBLENESS roll of 13 (adding 2 if you possess a **grappling iron**) or an ACCURACY roll of 15.

Successful NIMBLENESS roll!	107
Failed NIMBLENESS roll!	34
Successful ACCURACY roll!	150
Failed ACCURACY roll!	602

❧ 843 ❧

The hours of your shift are broken by a short opportunity to sleep. You climb into a filthy hammock, just vacated by another stoker.

Soon afterwards a bell rouses you. The airship is being tossed around in the air by high winds and a thunderstorm is developing around you. The Captain has given the order to turn for home, but the airship is in serious danger.

"We're venting," shouts the chief engineer above the wind. "Get up there and seal the bag!" He hands you tools and gestures to the ratlines. As the most dispensable member of the crew, you are unlikely to be mourned if you fall. Captain Coke himself comes and grasps your shoulder.

"'Tis your moment to prove yourself, matey. Full membership of the crew if you can do this!"

The winds buffet and tug at you as you climb. Make a NIMBLENESS roll of difficulty 13.

Successful NIMBLENESS roll!	**1046**
Failed NIMBLENESS roll!	**1019**

❧ 844 ❧

Jackie Jackson is busy at her booth, still puffing on her pipe and checking her rotas. She looks up briefly. "Yes?" she says. "Can I do something for you?" If you have **tally stick 84**, remove it and turn to **799**. If you have **tally stick 67**, remove it and turn to **739**.

❧ 845 ❧

You swiftly steam your Ferguson into the roadway and face the approaching carriage.

"Stop before I blow your brains out!"

Make a RUTHLESSNESS roll of difficulty 14, adding 1 if you have a long-barrelled gun like a **carbine**, **shotgun** or **rifle**, and 2 if you have a **double headlamp**.

Successful RUTHLESSNESS roll!	**599**
Failed RUTHLESSNESS roll!	**708**

❧ 846 ❧

You must exercise your patience now. The sun warms the meadows and the hedgerows gently, so you wheel the Ferguson into the shade of a young ash to keep its boiler from overheating. Sooner or later, something will come along. If you are the **Friend of Goodman Butt**, turn to **27** immediately. Otherwise, note **passage number 306** on your **Adventure Sheet** and roll a dice to see what you encounter.

Score 1	An independent haulier...	**1027**
Score 2	The Atmospheric Union...	**194**
Score 3	A farmer...	**678**
Score 4	The Haulage Guild...	**408**
Score 5	The Telegraph Guild...	**198**
Score 6	A private steam carriage...	**103**

❧ 847 ❧

You pass the woman some coins and she thanks you profusely. But a couple of crowns cannot replace what she has lost or provide a stable future for her.

Ride on to South Stoke...	**584**
Head for North Stoke...	**515**
Speed directly up to Wallingford...	**800**

❧ 848 ❧

You power along the Wargrave road until you come to your quarry. Between the trees on the riverside lies your barge where you left it and the mate, just as you instructed him, has left the boarding ramp out. You slow, ride across and halt with a bump against the wall of the cabin. Your mate pops out of nowhere and grins. "A speedy departure, skipper?" He throws a lever forward and you churn off into the stream, a full fifty yards away by the time the Constables appear. "We'll need a new ramp," he says cheerfully. "Which way now?"

To Henley...	(2s)	**818**
To Wargrave...		**131**

❧ 849 ❧

Your craft has been shifted to the other side of the channel, but at your hail your mate re-appears on deck, waves, and begins to unmoor. Once you and your velosteam are aboard he explains. "A whole bunch of nosy kids was poking around here. They had a dirty great dog and didn't want him fouling the paint. And it's quieter this side."

Head to Oxford Wharf...	**868**
Steam downriver towards Wallingford...	
(£1 10s or **Bargee's Badge**)	**883**

❧ 850 ❧

"Ladies, gentlemen, to absent friends!" A man in Constable's livery stands and raises his mug. "Harry were never the most dutiful Constable, but he was a good friend and he was good company here. Well, he drowned in the river, and that's that."

You drain your tankard and hurry out.

Return to Wargrave...   418

❦ 851 ❧

You take the long road to Wallingford, passing through Sandford, Nuneham Courtenay, Dorchester and Shillingford. Near Benson you see a road engine pulled over at a Guild water tower, refilling its tank. If you are the **Friend of Louise Standler**, turn to **1023** immediately.

Investigate the engine...   1030
Continue towards Wallingford...   800

❦ 852 ❧

The smoke is rising from a rickety old open-roofed steambus, hired by the Stokenchurch Warriors and their supporters, who are travelling down to Henley for a game. They wave cheerily at you, holding blue scarves high and singing a song about their fearless strikers. The team themselves are a motley crew - have they any chance of victory? Gain the codeword *Bootlicker*.

Continue on...   62

❦ 852 ❧

You ride alongside and show your weapons. "Stop this vehicle!" The driver, terrified, releases the boiler pressure in a shriek of steam and the vehicle slows. Roll a dice to see what the steamer carries:

Score 1-3   Airship crew   703
Score 4-6   Passengers   592

❦ 854 ❧

The wagon falls free and quickly loses speed, swerving to the side of the road. You leap back onto your velosteam and unhitch before it too is tossed aside.

The driver and engineer look back angrily, but aside from their shouts, they can do nothing. However, unless you have a **mask**, you will now be **Wanted by the Haulage Guild**.

Turn to...   904

❦ 855 ❧

You are sailing on the Thames above the lock and the long weir at Mill End. Directly to the north is the picturesque Hamble valley and on the riverbank the road between Henley and Marlow carries a relentless stream of traffic.

Pass through the lock...
    (**2s** or **Bargee's Badge**)   630
Head upstream towards Henley...   1018

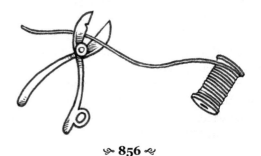

❦ 856 ❧

You ride the lane north out of Stonor and follow the twists as Balham lane climbs up the little valley to the hilltop common. Then you turn right and head downhill once more down Dolesden lane, past the farm at Dolesden and alongside the ferns bordering Great Wood.

If you have a **wanted poster** but do not have the codeword *Bernadette*, turn to **38** immediately. Otherwise, you meet a lane that leads to Turville on your right and Northend on your left.

Head towards Northend...   595
Ride into Turville...   947

❦ 857 ❧

"Stoke Row's a quiet place," says the farmer. "They had a hard time last summer when it was so dry. But they's building a new well. I heard it'll have some elephant on top - imagine that!"

Turn to...   710

❦ 858 ❧

"At least you know which end to punt from," calls your challenger. "Now, have at you!" He pushes his punt directly towards you with surprising speed, cheered on by his fellows. Make a NIMBLENESS roll of difficulty 15.

Successful NIMBLENESS roll!   824
Failed NIMBLENESS roll!   965

❧ 859 ❧

Remove the codeword *Artisan*. As you enter the yard between the tall, iron gates, there is a sudden roar of noise, a massive plume of smoke and steam and a hail of sharp-edged ironwork torn asunder by some catastrophic explosion. You dive from your velosteam for cover and a second explosion tears through the parked locomotives and wagons, knocking a massive Burley engine onto its side and ripping a tall wooden wagon into shreds.

The rain of metal and wood subsides and voices begin to cry out in the awful quiet - scalded shouts and cries for help.

Try to assist the hurt and wounded...	**1515**
Steal what you can in the confusion...	**492**
Leave before another explosion occurs...	**702**

❧ 860 ❧

You skirt the edge of Crowmarsh Hill and come to a narrowing in the road. From the west, a tree-shrouded spur of the Thames cuts into the meadows, while from the east the line of Grim's Ditch cuts straight down the hill. The embankment itself is only a few feet high here at the roadway, but it has been cut through and a tumbled-down building - presumably a defunct tollhouse - stands on the verge.

Ride north to Wallingford...	**800**
Take Red Lane towards Woodcote...	**291**
Steam south to North Stoke...	**515**
Investigate Grim's Ditch...	**905**
Prepare an ambush here...	**794**
Ride to nearby Mongewell Park...	**1037**

❧ 861 ❧

"Greetings! Christ welcomes you. I, sadly, must be on my way. I have some business down at the riverside at a house near Goring. The owners asked for an exorcism and their local priest thought I might like the practice. This would be my first English haunting. Would you like to accompany me? Otherwise you are welcome to rest here in the church."

Offer the priest a ride to Goring...	**694**
Take advantage of his absence to rob the church...	**951**
Rest in the sanctuary...	**871**

❧ 862 ❧

The clerk returns and with him an important officer in the Guild. He shakes your hand. "That's more than helpful, I can tell you. Haha - those dirty coal-grubbers will soon be shown up for who they really are." He hands you a bag of coins as a reward (gain **£14**) and notes that if you were previously **Wanted by the Telegraph Guild**, any such wrong-doing is now overlooked and you may remove it from your **Adventure Sheet**.

Turn to...	**770**

❧ 863 ❧

You pause at the foot of Remenham Hill. A massive water bunker attended by a weedy young man awaits any road trains headed uphill. Your small tank is full enough for now. The bridge into Henley arches clumsily over the Thames and a lane leads off into the fields and meadows to the north. A finger-post points the way towards Wargrave along the riverside road.

Ride up Remenham hill...	**740**
Cross the bridge into Henley...	**1251**
Follow the road to Wargrave...	**393**
Visit the Druid's Temple... (*Bonehunter*)	**834**

❧ 864 ❧

Steaming into the tiny village of Mapledurham you are presented with a vision of a past age: a row of brick almshouses, a rambling manor, a stone-towered church and a watermill surrounded by willows huddle together where the Thames bends southwards.

Visit the manor house...	**73**
Ride the cowpath... (*Butternchurn*)	**230**
Take the lane towards Reading...	**803**

❧ 865 ❧

"Oxford it is, then," says Jackson, taking your payment. "And the timber's all ready at Cane End Common, you say? I'll have one of my boys down there this very afternoon." Erase the codeword *Bark*. She take a piece of wood from a bundle on her desk, scores it in a pattern and splits it lengthways, handing you the stock and keeping the foil for herself. "That's your receipt. Come back here in a few days time and I should have a nice profit for you." Gain **tally stick 84**.

After all this business, the call of the open road is

strong. To feel the wind on your face again, free from the smog and smoke of Nettlebed's countless boilers and furnaces, you must head on your way.

Head towards Wallingford...	**751**
Ride north...	**110**
Take the Woodcote Road...	**664**
Ride towards Bix...	**3**

❧ 866 ❧
You are recognised as you approach the town and Constables block the road ahead. They prepare their weapons, giving you a moment to decide which way to head.

Skirt the town and ride north...	**378**
Cut across country and head south...	**589**

❧ 867 ❧
The village of Fingest is nestled at the foot of three hills at the very northern end of the Hambleden valley. Largely brick and chalk cottages, there are one or two bigger houses owned by the better-off families, a fine inn, the Chequers, much frequented by the hauliers who steam south or east from here, and a church with a unique double-gabled tower.

Wander through the village...	**18**
Enter the Chequers...	**36**
Steam up to Ibstone...	**400**
Head down the lane to Turville...	**947**
Ride on to Bolter End...	**546**
Take the road south to Skirmett...	**969**

❧ 868 ❧
The river above Osney Lock loops around the western side of Oxford, past the marshalling yard steaming like a volcanic pit, beside countless brick towers blossoming with dirty smoke. The river itself runs black with all the outfall and waste of the factories. Here and there a mass of cotton waste from the mills wallows, threatening to tangle the paddles or screw of any steamer. And the river is full with craft, steaming south, turning in to take the Isis Lock onto the Oxford Canal, mooring at one of the countless quays and wharfs. The pool known as Four Rivers, created where the Bulstrake Stream and the Oxford Canal meet the Thames, is a maelstrom of dodging steamers and their butties, proceeding dead slow and still thumping and colliding.

At the wharf alongside the Freight Yard, great piles of goods are loaded and unloaded by steam crane. Men and women, filthy with labour, stand ready to pluck goods ashore and tranship them. Urchins run around, garnering coppers for errands. Whatever you buy or sell here, you will need to keep a keen eye on hangers-on, pilching and 'breakages'.

	To buy	To sell
Charcoal	-	-
Furniture	-	£30
Machinery	£20	£19
Pottery	£21	£20
Cotton	-	£7
Woollen cloth	-	£8
Coal	-	£15
Beer	£12	£10
Wheat	£5	£4
Malt	-	£10
Frozen meat	-	£20
Ice	-	£15

Note that you must have a **Perkins engine** fitted to your boat if you wish to carry **Frozen Meat** or Ice. If you are unable to afford the lock tolls to travel to Wallingford, you will have to moor here until you can raise the ready money to pay for your way downstream.

Steer over to Micklewhite's Boatyard...	1194
Steam downriver to Wallingford...	
(**£1 10s** or **Bargee's Badge**)	883
Moor here and head ashore...	826

❧ 869 ❧
The strongbox has to be patiently dismantled before you can get inside it - but finally you are presented with a sheaf of **thirty guineas in banknotes** and a **locket of King Charles' hair**.

Turn to....   **noted passage**

❧ 870 ❧

Note that your boat is now **moored at Magpie Island** if it is not already.

With your boat tied up to several well-driven stakes, you and your mate are able to rest ashore for a while. He takes a liking to the little island and announces his intention to fish for eels by night. You clear a fireplace and ready a pile of firewood.

If you would like to leave possessions here, you may. Enter them into the box below and you may retrieve them when you return. Note this **passage number** before you make any further decisions.

```



```

Repair your velosteam...	180
Open a strongbox...	138
Tend your **wounds**...	33
Board your boat...	251
Cross the channel and ride to Aston...	280

❧ 871 ❧

The building is quiet and peaceful - so different to your frantic races along the region's roads. To be still, dry and warm, bathed by the light streaming inbetween the iron posts... Before you know it, you are asleep.

Then you are rudely awoken with a rough shake of your shoulder. "Citizen number?" demands a Constable's voice. If you are **Wanted by the Constables**, turn to **13** immediately. Otherwise, you had better leave this place before they begin asking questions.

Leave the church...   3

❧ 872 ❧

Deep in the woods you find the wreckage of an airship. Torn fragments of the gas envelope remain tangled in the trees, but the frame itself is burnt, twisted and collapsed. Rain-softened figures in the remains of the tail stabilisers read A711. If you have the codeword *Abapical*, turn to **828** immediately.

Leave this place...   8

❧ 873 ❧

Somehow you find a space to moor your boat between the yards, the jetties, the pleasure-cruisers, the rowing-eights, the sculling craft and the steam barges. Mark **moored at Henley** on your **Adventure Sheet**.

Go ashore...   702

❧ 874 ❧

Your velosteam is a wreck. The finely-tuned brass control machinery is twisted and unusable, the drive chain snapped, tyres shredded, boiler burst and coal-gas reservoir leaking.

Without a machine to ride, you will fall to the level of any desperate footpad, poor and insignificant. And in fact, that is what happens to you. Your glory days are behind you and after attempts to continue your way of life without your Ferguson, you drag your hungry and starving self to the workhouse, where you end your days picking oakum and breaking stones for a meagre bowl of daily gruel.

Turn to the **Epilogue**.

❧ 875 ❧

One night, the airship you are travelling on is surprised by sky-pirates. If you have the codeword *Bernadette*, turn to **798** immediately.

A crewman catches sight of the pirate's craft first: the distinctive blue cigar-shape is easy to identify. "It's Captain Coke!" he shouts. "We'll all be skinned or thrown overboard!"

As the pirate airship approaches, you see battle-scarred rogues with grappling hooks hanging from the cabling. A short and grinning figure aims a carronade at your craft. "Surrender!" he calls, "Or we'll board and scalp you all!"

Help the crew resist the pirates...	657
Side with Captain Coke...	752

❧ 876 ❧

Your beer is a pale, rather watery brew, but it sluices down quickly and, being weak, leaves you with plenty of thirst for another. It is served in a tin can, of all strange novelties. You order your second Imperishable Ale and sit chatting with the other drinkers. One wants to tell you about the city of Oxford. "You have to be mighty careful up there," advises a haulier. "Many's the time I've been ticketed for parking wrongly. Pah!"

Return to the parlour...   **934**
Leave the inn...   **360**

❧ 877 ❧

The gamekeeper nods happily. "Alright," he says. "Valentine Woods is the place, north of Lane End."

You will need either a **rabbit**, **pheasant** or **deer carcass** as well as a bottle of **poison**. When you have these, proceed to Valentine Woods to lay the lures. Gain the codeword *Bestial*.

Return to your velosteam...   **488**

❧ 878 ❧

Later that evening Ramboutarde sets you to work on the first course of the lavish evening meal he will be serving to the passengers. "Make me a langoustine bisque," he commands. "Smooth. Velvety. Fragrant. Delicious. Classic. No creativity 'ere, please."

You gently cook the langoustines and shell them - but what will you do next?

Boil the shells in water, then add this
      stock to your sauce...   **809**
Cook the shells with the shallots...   **769**
Discard the shells, of course...   **732**

❧ 879 ❧

The jolting of the wagons is too much for you to cope with. You are about to leap back onto your velosteam when a sharp movement catches your hand in the coupling. You can feel the bones in your fingers crack and shiver - then it is free.

Unhitching your velosteam clumsily with your good hand, you pull over onto the verge where you pass out from the pain. Gain a **wound** and if you have **five wounds**, turn to **999** immediately.

Turn to...   **noted passage**

❧ 880 ❧

After a rushing ride through a dark plantation of conifers you blast out into the sunshine riding through hilltop meadows. Banking through corners and churning up gravel, you speed northwards along the high hills.

Continue on northwards...   **110**

❧ 881 ❧

The women accept their coins eagerly. "Given us more than Captain Coke ever did," complains one. "No gentleman he ain't."

"What can you tell me about him?" you ask.

"Used to drink in the Chequers, occasional," replies one. "Ain't seen him for a time, tho'. Everyone knows he and his men camp out in the woods between here and Stonor - but won't let on. They guards the paths anyway."

Ride on...   **867**

❧ 882 ❧

The river flows on beneath your craft, quietly curling aside as you press on downstream. A lanky heron erupts from the riverbank where he has been hunting frogs and thumps his way to another meadow.

On the right bank, rushes mark where St Patrick's stream winds through the flat, often-flooded pastures, eventually joining the River Loddon. The stream is shallow and unsuited for heavy freight barges. Further downstream you will pass two islands - Hallsmead Ait and the Lynch - before passing through another lock and reaching Wargrave.

Take a look at Hallsmead Ait...   **894**
Pause by the Lynch...   **935**
Try to weave through St Patrick's Stream...   **227**
Pass through Wargrave Lock...
      (**2s** or **Bargee's Badge**)   **131**
Press on to Henley without stopping...
      (**4s** or **Bargee's Badge**)   **818**

∽ 883 ∾

Once through Osney Lock, you have a long journey ahead of you. If the river is clear and the locks are in your favour, you may be in Wallingford in two days. Roll two dice to see what you encounter.

Score 2-4	A rowing race...	**402**
Score 5-6	Water-rats...	**437**
Score 7	News from the west...	**467**
Score 8-10	A night-time visitor...	**511**
Score 11-12	A fire at Abingdon!	**542**

∽ 884 ∾

You find Mr Sands in his accustomed spot, whippets at his feet and a pipe in his hand. He gives a rare smile on seeing you approach. "Well, my travelling friend. The birds be well and the chicks be well. His Lordship's woods be fair full of game - thanks to you."

As you chat together he tells you more tales of the fraternity of keepers. In return, you tell him of your travels and adventures. He shakes his head in disbelief. "You keep getting yourself in trouble, that's all I know."

Return to the parlour...	**203**
Leave the Red Lion...	**488**

∽ 885 ∾

If you are the **Friend of Earl Brigg**, turn to **1128** immediately. Otherwise, read on.

The gateman takes your word when you explain that you are with Sackler's silver miners. It seems that he has seen so many strange people coming and going onto his Lord's estate that he has completely given up trying to differentiate between hoodwinkers, charlatans and real visitors. Once inside, you have a choice.

Visit Sackler at the workings...	**1098**
Visit Earl Brigg... (**letter of introduction**)	**1110**
Leave for now...	**313**

∽ 886 ∾

If you have a **tightly-tied parcel**, turn to **686** immediately. You are brought a hearty ploughman's platter, mounded with bread, pork paté, strong cheddar cheese, pickled onions, a dish of luminous piccalilli, an apple and a pint of a crisp and bubbly Director's Brew. The sharpness of the pickles suits the brightness of the beer beautifully and you chew away contentedly amongst the conversations of town and university business - builders looking for timber for a new roof needed by Christ's College, a ground-breaking paper on gas extraction by a student at Melrose College, Major Rolt's strictness in locking up several drunken undergraduates and the poor state of the sewers in Jericho. Nearby sits a grey-haired man with a pipe, sitting with a pint of beer and rustling through a sheaf of papers.

Talk to the man...	**716**
Return to the parlour...	**725**
Leave the pub...	**688**

∽ 887 ∾

You hand the money over to the waterman, whose eyes light up with delight. Now roll a dice to discover whether you have been right to trust him.

Score 1-2	The waterman disappears with your cash
Score 3-5	He brings you the **Bargee's Badge**
Score 6	He brings you a **malt licence** and a **Guildsman's medallion**

Return to Wargrave...	**418**

∽ 888 ∾

If you have **Colonel Snappet's pocketbook**, turn to **1058** immediately.

Stonor House is surrounded by a high wall and a deer park. It is not an easy place to gain entry to, but you may be able to convince the gatekeeper, the footman at the door and the family themselves if you are able to make a GALLANTRY roll of difficulty 13, adding 1 if you possess a **top hat** or **fur collar**.

Successful GALLANTRY roll...	**1220**
Failed GALLANTRY roll...	**430**

∽ 889 ∾

The cracking of twigs alerts you to an intruder and you rush towards the noise - but you have been tricked. The poachers have seen you first and prepared a tripline. You fall to the ground heavily and before you know what has happened, you receive a heavy blow to the back of the head. Gain a **wound** and if you now have **five wounds**, turn to **999**. Otherwise, read on.

You awake in the early light of day to find Mr Sands untying your hands. You have been dumped in one of his pits while the poachers went about their work.

"Thirty birds at least, last night. What a catastrophe. Something must be done," mutters Mr Sands.

He leads you to a stream where you can wash the blood out of your hair, but you had better find a way of treating your injury before it becomes a difficulty.

Turn to...   460

❧ 890 ❧

If you have the codeword *Burgundy*, turn to **1324** immediately. Otherwise, read on.

You pass **another hoop** and it is once again your opponent's strike. The lady seems to be considering her chances for shooting for her next hoop, but the line is not quite in. She shuffles around her spot, her long skirt swinging, and when you look again, the red ball seems to have rolled two inches to the left... Surely the lady has not dared to foot her ball?

"Madam, you are a cheat."   1151
Remain silent...   1132

❧ 891 ❧

The Tollman, recognising your medallion, waves you over. "You'll be looking for that lost road-train," he says. "They did come through 'ere, heading up to Nettlebed, last week it was. Engine was in fine fettle, but the driver wasn't one of your normal crew. I didn't recognise her. But engine number 502 with wagons AX67 and AX89. I've got it here in the book. Hope that helps. I got the message." Gain the codeword *Baggage*.

Return to Bix...   3
Ride west...   394
Ride towards Henley...   144

❧ 892 ❧

You push your way into the busy baker's shop and get the attention of the chief baker. "I have a flour sample," you say. "High quality. What will you pay?"

The baker shakes her head. "We're fully supplied."

You lean over the counter. "I insist you take a look."

She shrugs. You thump the **Cobstone flour** onto the polished wood. She opens the sack, smiles at the creamy colour, dips in a finger and tastes it. "Very nice. I'm paying eleven shillings the hundredweight right now."

"This is worth twice that," you reply.

"Maybe so," she answers, "But I can't sell bread in Stokenchurch at that price."

"Try the flour," you say. "This sack's yours."

She smiles. "We'll put a batch together then. Come back this evening." Remove the **Cobstone Flour** from your **possessions**.

You make your way out of the shop and find a grassy verge on which to rest. The day passes slowly but for once you are untroubled by the shoppers, the tradesmen and even the Constables. Everybody is far too busy to concern themselves with you.

Later that evening, when the bakery is empty of customers, you return to talk to the chief baker. She tears through a beautiful golden cob, revealing a creamy, springy crumb still steaming from the oven. You taste the bread together. "Fantastic, I'll not deny," she says. "I could possibly go to thirteen shillings on this one. Purely for high-end batches."

"Eighteen."

"Fourteen."

"Done."   26
"I can't go below fifteen."   42

❧ 893 ❧

"My friend Mr Sands of Hardwick Hall is having a dreadful time with a gang of poachers," says the farmer. "Up around Valentine wood, where he's the keeper. I was taking a drink in the Red Lion and he told me they took two dozen bird the other night!"

Turn to...   710

❧ 894 ❧

Several narrowboats have moored in the channel on the quieter side of the ait. They are rivermen, crammed with their families into the tiny cabins, their children running, playing, sleeping indiscriminately on the towpath, the cargo or the gunwales of the seventy-foot river-freighters.

"Any coal?" asks a bargee as you approach.

Sell the rivermen their fuel... **(coal)**   1502
Steer downriver towards Wargrave...
    (**2s** or **Bargee's Badge**)   131
Head upstream to Sonning...   750

❧ 895 ❧

You return to the place where you left your rivercraft, moored securely in a backwater wharf below the castle walls. A thin stream of woodsmoke reeks out from the chimney and your mate is sitting on the foredeck with his feet up, trying to read a badly-printed amusement page. He screws up the paper as you approach and smiles. "More adventures, Number One? Been slow here without you."

Take on cargo at Wallingford Wharf...	435
Head upstream towards Oxford...	485
(£1 10s or **Bargee's Badge**)	
Steam downriver immediately...	987

❧ 896 ☙
Here in Frieth the villagers are haymaking on the verges and the common. They are mowing the long grasses with scythes, sickles and a horse-drawn mower. A stern-looking matriarch is directing the process.

Ride to Skirmett...	969
Take the lane towards Hambleden...	932
Take the road east...	88

❧ 897 ☙
After asking around for Jermyn Bigod you come across one of his erstwhile friends. "He's gone," you are told. "Expelled from the university. They didn't say why, but it's probably because he reset the big computational engine."

Return to the city...	688

❧ 898 ☙
"Well, then. The Constables it is." You are frog-marched off by the students to the Constabulary station and handed over. Note that your boat will be **moored at Oxford**, awaiting your eventual return.

Turn to...	13

❧ 899 ☙
☐
If the box is empty, tick it and read on. If it is already ticked, turn to **567** immediately.

Several officers come out to meet you. "What a coup!" cries one. "What decision and pluck! The Coal Board are in absolute terror!"

"Without that reservoir their supply routes are completely disrupted," says another. "A very strategic choice of target."

They reward you with a **letter of introduction**, which will help you gain employment and connections with the nobility of the land, **£15** and a free customisation to your velosteam. Choose from the following: **muffled exhaust, off-road tyres, enlarged fuel tank, double headlamp, gas pressuriser, improved brakes**.

Turn to...	770

❧ 900 ☙
From your vantage point above the road here you can survey the traffic as it approaches from Goring up into the hills. However, it is harder to spot vehicles approaching from the other direction. Be careful you are not surprised by a Constables' patrol! Note **passage number 306** on your **Adventure Sheet** and roll a dice to see what you encounter:

Score 1	The Telegraph Guild...	198
Score 2	The Haulage Guild...	408
Score 3-4	A private steam carriage...	103
Score 5	An independent haulier...	1285
Score 6	A farmer...	1246

❧ 901 ☙
"Nothing for us? You're just a road-thief, out to make yourself rich. Look at you on that fancy big machine, nobody to care for or be answerable to. Some hero!" Lose a **solidarity point**.

Ride away...	867

❧ 902 ☙
The three children are amazed as you help them climb onto your velosteam. Then, as they cling tight behind you, you set off down the road at a much slower-than-normal pace. It is still by far the fastest these urchins have ever gone!

You steam into Shirburn and help them off again. The eldest boy takes charge of his little brother, who is crying with excitement and tiredness, but the girl dawdles, unwilling to let you leave. "It's easy to fool those old Constables," she says. "There's a hole in the fence by the badger's sett anyways. We swim there whenever it's hot." Gain the codeword *Brock*.

"Maggie!" A woman's shout from down the road sends the little girl flying. You raise a hand to greet the woman and remount your velosteam.

Continue on your way to Watlington...   **360**

❧ 903 ❧

An unarmed and undefended haulier is forced to halt in the roadway. When you emerge, armed and threatening, he quickly insists you take what you need from him. Roll a dice to see what you can gather:

Score 1-2   **18s**
Score 3-4   A **rope**, a **shovel** and **6s**
Score 5-6   A **pocket watch** and **waterproof paint**

Turn to...   **noted passage**

❧ 904 ❧

Roll a dice to see what you find inside the wagon.

Score 1   Beer! Take as many **Bottles of Beehive Stout** as you wish.
Score 2   Bricks, a **tarpaulin** and a **rope**
Score 3   A **picnic hamper** and two **pineapples**
Score 4   Household pottery and a crate of **cough medicine**
Score 5   Three **parasols**
Score 6   A parcel of **explosives** for quarrying

Light a flare... (**purple flare** ☐ ☐ ☐)   **684**
Leave the wagon...   **noted passage**

❧ 905 ❧

Here where the long mound of Grim's Ditch is cut by the Wallingford road, hawthorn and blackthorn hung with streamers of sheep wool stand on the grassy slope. A hollow yew tree stands amongst them in which you may leave **possessions** if you choose. Do this by writing them in the box below. When you return here you may collect them again.

```
┌────────────────────────────────┐
│                                │
│                                │
│                                │
│                                │
│                                │
│                                │
│                                │
│                                │
│                                │
│                                │
│                                │
└────────────────────────────────┘
```

Steam up along the dyke...   **649**
Return to the roadside...   **860**

❧ 906 ❧

"News of your deeds to humiliate and destroy the aristocracy has reached me," says Comrade Blewitt. "Well done. You are serving the cause admirably and many are inspired by your actions. Let me see how I can equip you further."

Comrade Blewitt shares information regarding the comings and goings of the nobility and the lords of industry - all with the intention that you waylay them on the road and kill them. "The fewer they are, the sooner our revolution will come," he says. Remove the codeword *Bolster* and gain the codeword *Brigade*, since this information may help you identify and track particularly profitable prey on the highways.

Return to the parlour...   **100**
Leave the inn...   **911**

❧ 907 ❧
☐

If box above is empty, tick it and turn to **1096**. If it is already ticked, erase the tick and read on.

The figure you saw turns out to be a beech tree, grown into a strange stunted shape as a result of half-hearted pollardings, lightning strikes and decades of decay. It looks almost like a walking man when viewed in the half-light of the woods. Someone has hung a daisy chain around it.

Steam on to Whitchurch...　　　　**749**

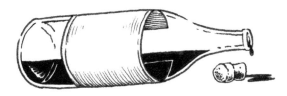

❧ 908 ❧

This box appears wooden, but it has been carefully painted to disguise its heavy iron construction. The lock is less complicated than many others, however, and before long you have it open. Inside is a **clockwork bird**, a **golden ring** and a **top hat**. Plainly you have got hold of somebody's very best hat.

Turn to...　　　　**noted passage**

❧ 909 ❧

Despite your best efforts, your boat is immobilised. After several hours' work, a passing river tug offers you a tow to Wallingford, where he knows a yard that can repair your engine. If you do not have enough money for his fee, the bargee will buy any cargo from you for **£4** per unit - regardless of what it is.

Accept the tow to Wallingford... (**£25**)　　**435**
Unable or unwilling to pay...　　　　**975**

❧ 910 ❧

The quartermaster peers through her blue-lensed spectacles. Not only is she ready to exchange coin for any manner of stolen goods, without question, but she is also able to outfit you with several possessions useful for a self-respecting sky pirate.

Tools	To buy	To sell
rope	4s	2s
rope ladder	9s	7s
adjustable wrench (ENG+1)	£1 8s	14s
heavy wrench	18s	12s
explosives	£1 4s	6s
net	6s	3s
high pressure valve	£1	9s
telescope	£5	£2 5s
Weapons	To buy	To sell
duelling pistols (ACC 7)	£12	£7
gamekeeper's shotgun (ACC 7)	-	£6
Jewellery	To buy	To sell
locket	6s	4s
pocket watch	£3	£1 15s
silver ring	10s	7s
silver bracelet	£1	10s
silver necklace	£2	£1 5s
gold ring	£3	£1 1s
gold bracelet	£3 5s	£2 2s
gold necklace	-	£5
pectoral cross	-	£16
Other items	To buy	To sell
deck of marked cards	10s	4s
parasol	-	£2
chess set	-	£2
box of cigars	-	£1 10s
ivory fan	-	£1 8s
Coal Board Accounts book	-	£8
fine clock	-	£6 5s
pair of golden candlesticks	-	£3
jewelled bible	-	£10 5s
gold bar	-	£30
ten guineas in banknotes	-	£6
twenty guineas in banknotes	-	£14
thirty guineas in banknotes	-	£22

The chief engineer of the *Blue Devil* will open a **strongbox** that you possess for a payment of **£3**. If you wish to take advantage of this, discard the **strongbox**, note this **passage number** (**910**) and turn to **964** immediately.

Return to the encampment...　　　　**819**

❧ 911 ❧

As you remount your velosteam you observe a commotion outside one of the pubs here: a group of navvies are arguing in their strange accents with the shopkeeper, insisting he has shortchanged their mate. A whistle announces an approaching Constable: it is time you were on your way.

Take the road north...   **922**
Head east towards Woodcote...   **577**

❧ 912 ❧

Once the fire has a good hold, you throw a heavy stone and successfully smash a glazed window. No sooner does a guildsman appear outside than he sees the flames licking at the foot of the tower.

"Emergency protocols!" he calls. "Destroy the codebooks and send the final transmission."

You are already on your way, but glimpses of your distinctive velosteam mean that you will now be hunted for your deeds: you are **Wanted by the Telegraph Guild** if you are not already and gain the codeword *Bergen*.

Ride north...   **378**
Ride south...   **589**

❧ 913 ❧

You settle down to make a measured sketch of some of the church's features. Two interesting brasses of knights catch your eye, marked with the dates 1410 and 1415. The square, copper-roofed tower atop the rather squat chancel makes a very interesting drawing. Tick one of the boxes in your **sketchpad** to indicate that it has been partly filled.

Leave the church...   **308**

❧ 914 ❧

The students mutter, then shout in disgust and sporting humour. "A filthy Cantabridgean! Standing at the wrong end! Tip! Tip! Tip!" Your challenger begins to push his flat-bottomed boat towards you, then readies his quant. Make a NIMBLENESS roll of difficulty 11.

Successful NIMBLENESS roll!   **824**
Failed NIMBLENESS roll!   **965**

❧ 915 ❧

You find a mooring for your boat in a backwater beneath the castle walls. The mate promises he will take good care of the boat. "Ain't no-where else for me to go, Number One," he says cheerily. "I don't much like the look of that castle and all them Constables, but the bacon and beer should be good at the Dolphin."

Ride into town...   **270**
Leave Wallingford by road...   **742**

❧ 916 ❧

The game does not go your way: aces appear magically in your opponents' hands and all you can muster are petty eights and sixes. You play on, trying to regain what you have lost, but you only find yourself further and further behind. Remove **all your money** from your wallet: if you have any hidden elsewhere, now will be the time to unearth it.

Turn to...   **418**

❧ 917 ❧

"Excellent," says the Major. "Let's show these lot how to play real croquet."

Despite his bold talk, the major is neither a bold nor an accurate malletman. He prevaricates over his shots, making several foul shots and costing you both time on the course. You, on the other hand pass your first **two hoops** cleanly, placing yourself for a smart corner. Then the Major's ball comes bouncing over a hidden divot in the turf and knocks you off into a flowerbed.

"Dreadfully sorry,"he mutters. "Misjudged the strength of that shot rather."

Turn to...   **548**

❧ 918 ❧

The younger two don't recognise your golden guinea, but the elder brother knows what it is. His eyes widen. "Come on, sis, come on Toby! Let's get back to mama and tell 'er 'oo we met!" He searches for some way to repay you. "Listen - do you want to know where we gets our peacock feathers? It's the big house over the hill in the valley there. There's a way through the wood from the road. When you sees a beech stump with a holly tree growing out of it, cross the ditch and you can get right up into the grounds without nobody seeing you."

Now that you know this, should you find a place where such a tree is described, add **17** to the passage number and turn to that passage to access the children's hidden route.

Wave goodbye to the trio...   **360**

❧ 919 ❧

It takes considerable patience and persuasion to find a haulier who will consider carrying flour from Cobstone Mill to the bakery you have struck a deal with. Nonetheless, eventually you do, and together with assurances of safe passage and a promise of a fair freight price, you get her agreement and **tally stick 32** as proof. Returning this to Fursham should provide him with everything he needs - provided you are not too late.

Return to the Freight Yard...   **360**

❧ 920 ❧

A rabbit bolts from the verge as you ride southwards. Glancing at the roadside, you see a warren with multiple entrances and fresh droppings spread around.

If you want to hunt for rabbits here, make an ACCURACY roll and consult the table below. You can add 1 to your score if you have a **net**, 2 if you have a **double headlamp** and 3 if you have a **pair of ferrets**.

Score <11	No luck!
Score 11-12...	Catch a **rabbit**
Score 13+	Good hunting: catch three **rabbits**

Continue south towards Nettlebed...   **791**

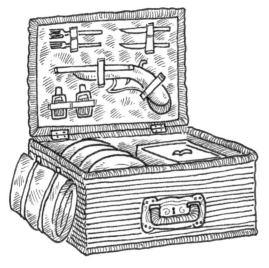

❧ 921 ❧

The airship sets off on its voyage, but you are in the kitchen when you realise that you are in flight. Most of your work in the tiny kitchen is under the chef's direct supervision, and you and the other staff are expected to work all through the day and even, if a passenger wishes, in the night. There is little opportunity to explore the craft or to look at the view - but then what did you expect?

Every mealtime must be prepped and food cooked to the very highest standard. Ramboutarde is an exceptionally demanding chef and constantly demands faster and faster preparation, even standing over you as you chop ingredients. Make a NIMBLENESS roll.

Score <10	Your knife slips! Lose a point of NIMBLENESS permanently.
Score 11-14	Your brunoise are merely acceptable
Score 15+	Impressed with your skills, Ramboutarde teaches you much: gain a point of **high cuisine** skill

Turn to...   **878**

❧ 922 ❧

You skirt a gaggle of children hopping along the street towards Goring school and feel the Ferguson warm to its work. Leaving the outskirts of the small town behind you and accelerating past an ox-cart, you head north up the winding Wallingford road. If you have the codeword *Bergen*, turn to **780** immediately.

Turn off at South Stoke...	**584**
Head for North Stoke...	**515**
Speed directly up to Wallingford...	**800**

❧ 923 ❧

You detail your pursuit of the Coal Board's wagons and assets. "Very interesting," comments a clearly-far-from-interested guildsman. "Take this money and go and do it again." Gain **£3 3s**.

| Return to the compound... | **770** |
| Leave the compound... | **682** |

❧ 924 ❧

"You'll buy it?" asks the old man incredulously. "What'll you do with all that?"

"That's my business," you reply. "Now, what would you ask for the work and the timber?"

"Well the other chap was going to pay us a sovereign between us for the felling and fifteen pound for the timber, once we'd cut it up. But we'd want the payment now see, since we ain't working that way again. You pay us now and we'll have it ready for you before the end of the week: just send someone to fetch it. If you asks around at the Freight Yard in Henley or Nettlebed you'll find someone, I shouldn't wonder."

If you agree to the old man's terms, pay him **£16** now and gain the codeword *Bark* and a **solidarity point**. If you can't afford the proposition or are no longer interested, you may simply head on your way.

Steam to Gallowstree Common...	**600**
Ride south towards Reading...	**560**
Head northwest towards Woodcote...	**488**
Take Deadman's Lane south-west...	**396**

❧ 925 ❧
☐

If the box above is empty, tick it and read on. If it is already ticked, turn to **262** immediately.

You crack open the poorbox and empty it of the coppers and silver shillings waiting inside. You will be able to find a use for the **£3 5s** - even if it is to distribute it to the people of Stokenchurch.

Leave the church...	**308**

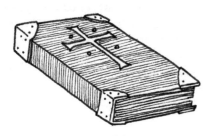

❧ 926 ❧
Coombe Park is fenced on all sides to keep the deer in and the peasants out. You skirt the fencing, coasting quietly past a gamekeeper's cottage, and head into the trees to the west of the estate.

Push on along the riverbank to Goring...	**487**

❧ 927 ❧
Your shot whistles past Coke but misses the rope. After the initial shock, the Constables come alive. "Another of his gang," shouts the officer in charge. "Arrest that pirate!" You must flee at once!

Turn to...	**310**

❧ 928 ❧
A street of workshops and market-stalls serves the people of Nettlebed for their market. Industrial goods are sold side by side with fresh produce and raw materials heaped in piles. Prices fluctuate here as massive deliveries of timber, coal and iron arrive and quickly sell out. The inhabitants have a prediliction for anything modern - including canned food - and seem scornful of the simple foodstuffs of their forebears.

Food and Drink	To buy	To sell
picnic hamper	£3 3s	£2 10s
Clothing	To buy	To sell
mask	4s	-
lace shawl	£1 5s	15s
goggles (MOT+1)	£2 15s	£1 15s
eyepatch (RUTH+1)	15s	5s
Medical	To buy	To sell
bandages	3s	-
soothing lotion	2s	-
false teeth	-	10s
Tools	To buy	To sell
rope	4s	2s
snare	2s	1s
net	6s	4s
lantern	6s	4s
shovel	8s	6s
axe	8s	6s
fishing line	1s	-
tarpaulin	4s	2s
copper pipe	6s	3s

Return to Nettlebed...	**791**
Leave town...	**944**

❧ 929 ❧
When the guards at the Atmospheric Union depot see you coming, they ready their weapons, but you make signs of peace and explain why you have come. Amazed, they shackle Coke and take him off your hands before ushering you inside to speak to the officer in charge here.

"So, you repay us with the capture of this dangerous criminal. Seeking amnesty perhaps? Well, you were never the trouble that Coke was, the dog. We'll hang him up at Gallowstree Common, where all the people can see what happens to those that cross the Union."

"What about the reward that was promised?"

"The reward? Your reward is that we shall no

longer be pursuing you for your crimes. I suggest you ponder the value of that."

Erase **Wanted by the Atmospheric Union** from your **Adventure Sheet**.

Leave the building...   **454**

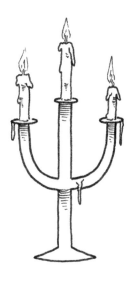

❧ 930 ❧

If you are the **Friend of Mr Sands**, turn to **884** immediately. You are served a Ground's Bitter, imported from Burton-upon-Trent by an innkeeper with ideals. "It's all in the water," he says. "You won't find any beer to match it." He fills your triangle-based glass with a slightly-burnt, roast-noted chestnut-coloured bitter, which on tasting proves to have its hop flavours kept in the background. It is malty, bitter-sweet and complex.

Beside you at the bar is a grim-faced man in the tweed and gaiters of a gamekeeper. At his feet lounge two whippets, uncollared and entirely obedient. He is just draining his own Ground's. "So you won't come out with me tonight, Edgar?" he asks the barman. "I need your muscle."

The barman shakes his head. "Your underkeeper was beaten black and blue the other night. What'll my wife say if I come home so?"

The man beside you snorts. "And all the while his Lordship's pheasants are prey to the most ruthless poaching gang I've ever seen. I need someone to help me patrol the woods - someone who isn't afeard of a tussle."

"If you need another pair of eyes, I'm with you." **787**
Finish your beer in silence...   **203**

❧ 931 ❧

There has never been a time like this to be alive. For one enamoured with machinery, steam power and mechanics, your victims are merely grit in the cogs of the workings of the vast machine of society. The machines of the airships that dock at Rotherfield Greys, the steam barges on the Thames and the computational engines hidden in the attics of the great houses are all fascinating to you. You will hunt them out, learn their secrets and build your own wonderful devices.

You have in your possession a **blunderpistol (ACC 6)**, a **sabre (PAR 3)**, a **mask** and some **welding tools**. Your ability scores are:

RUTHLESSNESS	3
ENGINEERING	6
MOTORING	5
INGENUITY	4
NIMBLENESS	3
GALLANTRY	3

Turn to...   **1440**

❧ 932 ❧

The road south from Skirmett takes you through a leafy copse full of birdsong. Nests can be seen on the branches above. If you wish to go nesting, you could pause here beside the road and try your luck in the trees.

To hunt for bird's eggs, make a NIMBLENESS roll, adding 1 if you have a **rope** and 1 more if you possess a **sack**.

Score <9   A fall from a tree! Gain a **wound**
Score 9+   Gain a nestful of **bird's eggs**

Head into the woods...
   (Friend of Captain Coke)   **235**
Continue south...   **343**

❧ 933 ❧

Landlady Janet pulls you a slim, tapering pint of Magpie Jack. It comes out of the tap chilled, thanks to the spring that runs through the cellar and cools the barrels down below. Through the beaded glass you see a fine amber-brown bitter with a lacy, large-bubbled head, looking rather like the top of a properly-made crumpet.

The flavour is strong: first the bitterness cuts through the cool and fills your mouth, then malty sweetness quickly overtaken by the body taste - a combination of mineral and malt. It brightens up your tastebuds considerably and stimulates quite an appetite.

Janet watches you sup. "You's a real connoisseur, I can see that," she says. "I do like to see someone enjoying my beer."

"I imagine people come a distance to enjoy this," you reply.

"Well, when the Constables and the like pass through I plug in the old sour cask," she says. "Amongst some I've got a reputation for the worst beer until you reach Oxford. Which suits me fine. Those vultures don't get a warm welcome here. But I know you're no friend of them either. They come a-taxing and checking on tolls but they don't stay long."

"How long have you run this place?" you ask politely.

"Well, Mr Lamb had it from his folks some thirty year ago and he's been gone these twelve years now. My lad Fred will take it over. I was scared I'd lost him in the war, but he made it back, thank God, cut up though he is. But I ain't hoping for grandchildren so maybe some other sort will have it then."

"How did he lose his leg?"	**645**
"Excellent beer."	**763**

✥ 934 ✥
Here at the Carriers there are amusements and even music as well as beer and food for the traveller. A small crowd stands around the dartboard, including a woman who looks like a nun, and a musician is setting up to perform later in the evening.

Buy a drink... (**2s**)	**876**
Leave the inn...	**360**

✥ 935 ✥
If you have the codeword *Benefit* or , turn to **1252** immediately. If not, read on.

A fire amongst the woods on the Lynch betrays that there are people camping here. When you ap-

proach, they run out to hail you. They are an extended family who have lost their village to strip-mining in the West, making their way to London to seek their fortunes together. "Can you take us to the city?" asks the eldest. "We'll fit aboard somehow, and pay our way."

Carry them to London... (**butty boat** or **enlarged cabin**) *The Reeking Metropolis 301*	
Offer them work on your estate... (*Best*)	**1260**
Steam upstream...	**750**
Steam downriver to Wargrave... (**2s** or **Bargee's Badge**)	**131**

✥ 936 ✥
In the back room of the John Barleycorn you find yourself face to face with Comrade Blewitt, the regional commissar. He oversees the 'interventions' and activities of the Compact between here and Henley.

If you are the **Friend of Captain Coke**..	**955**
If you have **brass disc 7821**..	**973**
If not, but you have the codeword *Bergen*...	**989**
If not, but you have the codeword *Boosting*...	**817**
If none of these...	**949**

✥ 937 ✥
Coombe Park stands aloof and severe within its haha, thick hedge and deer-fencing. A track leads into the park and beyond the house, running north-west. The driveway leads up to the house and down towards Whitchurch.

Seek an audience... (**letter of introduction**)	**312**
Leave the park down the front drive...	**749**

✥ 938 ✥
"I'm glad to hear it," replies Coke. "We need bold and resourceful crew." He has his shipboard medico, a thin, fierce woman he calls Anita, patch you up. Remove one **wound** and replace it with a **scar**. Roll two dice and on a score of 11 or higher, add an **intimidating scar (RUTH+1)** to your adventure sheet. Then you are sent straight to the engine room to stoke the furnaces of the *Blue Devil*.

Turn to...	**843**

❧ 939 ❧

A small E-Class telegraph tower stands on the green at Highmoor Cross. No guildsman is manning it: there is probably only a single, part-time officer assigned to the post. The grass on the common is long and the cottages unkempt. The men are away at war and children working in the towns.

Enter Valentine Wood...	**401**
North to Nettlebed...	**791**
East towards Stoke Row...	**296**
West to Grey's Court...	**158**
To Gallowstree Common...	**600**

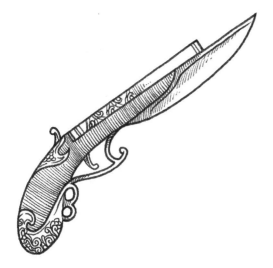

❧ 940 ❧

The crash of your gun is almost instantaneous with Coke's fall from the gallows. As the Constables, priest and crowd dive to the ground, confused and terrified, unsure of how many rescuers they face, you urge your velosteam forward and haul Coke aboard. Still choking, he can do little more than hang on, the torn noose -rope still looped about his neck.

You open the regulator fully and accelerate up the road towards High Moor Cross. Shouts and cries ring out and the Constables mount their own Imperials behind you - but you have a good lead and you know these roads and lanes better than anyone. Weaving, twisting, turn through fields and bumping over tree-roots, down almost impassably-steep slopes, you leave your pursuers in the distance. Captain Coke begins to laugh.

"I owe you my life, matey. Ride me on to Hambleden vale and I'll lead you through the woods to my crew. You're an adventurer after me own heart."

You are now the **Friend of Captain Coke**. He gives you a **purple flare** ☐ ☐ ☐ and explains how you can use it. "Light this if you rob a steam carriage of some sort. We have lookouts. My crew'll come and take the heavier booty - the stuff you can't haul away on this little machine. And then pay your share, o'course." He also lets you know that he will set aside a tent for you in his woodland hideout. Remove the codeword *Bernadette*.

Turn to...	**235**

❧ 941 ❧

Mr Sands looks at you incredulously. "Them kites is just poachers like these wretches is poachers." He stomps off brusquely.

Return to your velosteam...	**401**

❧ 942 ❧

The survey team are reading the lie of the land with theodolite, tripod and long measuring lines. They are quite absorbed in their work and pay little attention to you - or to some of their belongings, strewn about on the roadside.

Steal a **telescope**...	**1054**
Leave them be...	**62**

❧ 943 ❧

The river runs due south and you press on against the current. The chimneys and towers of Wallingford stand over the horizon beneath their streams of smoke. From the river you can see the long causeway bridge, built centuries ago and constantly under repair. The town walls run down to the river as well, encircling much of the town, but Wallingford has swollen with prosperity. A large Freight Yard stands on the south-western corner, where behind massive coal bunkers, locos and their wagons begin the long journey into the West.

Continue upstream to Oxford	
(**£1 10s** or **Bargee's Badge**)...	**485**
Steam to Wallingford Wharf...	**435**

❧ 944 ❧

Roads lead in all directions from Nettlebed. The main road to Wallingford continues to climb north-west for a while and runs east towards Bix through dense woods on the opposite side of town. A well-used track heads towards the Class-A Telegraph Tower at Nuffield Hill and another road runs north towards Watlingon and south across the common to Highmoor Cross.

Take the north road...	**880**
Steam directly to the Telegraph Station...	**978**
Steer south...	**345**
Head south-east to Bix...	**426**
Ride uphill on the Wallingford road...	**836**

☙ 945 ❧
☐ ☐ ☐

If any of the boxes above is empty, tick one and read on. If they are all ticked already, turn to **897** immediately.

You go around the city asking if anyone knows of Jermyn Bigod. Plenty of students have heard of him, but none can give you details until you come across a group of drinkers in the Black Boy. "He's upstairs," says one.

Bigod is a thin, undernourished fanatic. He lives to punch code and to stretch what modern computational engines can do. At first he is suspicious, but when you give him the **clockwork bird** (remove it from your **possessions**), he agrees to see if he can hack the Constable's records and remove the charges against your name. This is the sort of challenge he enjoys: programming a message into the Telegraph system that will query secret records, alter them and then check their changed state.

Bigod will give it his best shot but makes no promises. Roll two dice to see what results from his programming.

Score 2-3   A disaster: the Constables will hunt for you harder than ever!

Score 4-5   Partly successful: remove one **Wanted Status** from your **Adventure Sheet**

Score 6-12 A flawless routine: remove all **Wanted Statuses** from your **Adventure Sheet**

Return to the city...	**688**

☙ 946 ❧
You gently lift the old woman onto your velosteam and make your way to Elvendon Priory, where you are sure she will be welcomed and cared for. Once there you speak to the Prior and he sighs. "We are so limited in our ability to care for the poor. But we shall do what we can. The money you give will help somewhat, but this woman has lost what coin can never find for her again. We will find some occupation for her here and what comfort we can, I pray."

Before you leave she thanks you and asks why you have shown her such care - but the honest answer would bring her only more sorrow. You leave in silence.

Leave the priory...	**577**

☙ 947 ❧
In Turville you can see the thatched cottages typical of the hamlets and villages hiding in every hollow of the hills. A few, however, have been re-roofed with new-fangled machine-cut tiles - a sign of the changing times. Among them is a fine, white-washed pub standing at the junction of the road to Turville and beside that is the forge, shutters folded back and ringing with the sound of work. From here lanes and roads lead in all directions, bringing prosperity to this place for refreshing both man and engine.

Park by the forge...	**340**
Enter the Bull and Butcher...	**405**
Ride up the holloway to Christmas Common...	**120**
Head towards Ibstone...	**444**
Take the lane to Stonor...	**430**
Steam on to Skirmett...	**969**
Leave for Fingest...	**867**

☙ 948 ❧
Captain Coke draws his weapon and leaps up from the table, just as you ready your own. He is a skilled and determined fighter: you will be hard pressed to defeat him. He fights with a short-handled hooked blade, which hums with some sort of charge. Every time he bypasses your parry and strikes you, the blade will temporarily reduce your NIMBLENESS by 1: after the fight, return your score to its normal value.

Captain Coke	Weapon: **charged skyhook (PAR 6)**
Parry:	12
Nimbleness:	6
Toughness:	5

Victory!	**685**
Defeat!	**741**

❧ 949 ❧

Comrade Blewitt looks you up and down briefly, then waves dismissively. "I have no tasks for you now. But Comrade Plunkett has need of recruiters. You can find him at the Three Guineas. Now go. The committee has things to discuss."

Leave the inn...   911

❧ 950 ❧

You have arrived at Aston Wharf. A small warehouse stands beside a jetty stacked with bales of hay and other farm produce. The crew of a flat-bottomed river ferry are busy steadying a steam-wagon before making the crossing to the northern bank.

If you wish to moor here, mark **moored at Aston** in the mooring section of your **Adventure Sheet** and turn to **280**.

Steer east downriver...   251
Steer west upriver...   630

❧ 951 ❧

With the priest out of the way, you look around to see what you can carry off. A **pectoral cross** hangs on the wall by the vestry and the poorbox contains **17s**.

Leave the church...   3

❧ 952 ❧

You enjoy a strong stout with a sweet flavour. It is nicknamed Tarwater here. As you drink, you listen to the chatter and complaint of the other drinkers. "Them at the brickworks are not happy. Their piecework rates are being cut - it's 200 bricks a shilling now!"

"You're telling me. Isn't it my own wife over there? There isn't enough money in this town for us all to get by."

Return to the parlour...   829
Leave the inn...   791

❧ 953 ❧

Monsieur Ramboutarde comes over. "Eh? Address me as 'Chef'. So now I have to look myself? Why would I give you a job if I have to do it myself anyway? Is that how you will cook for me?" He rummages for a moment. "You fool!" He grasps one of the hard green apple-ish things and knocks you on the head with it. "What is this if not a chayote? Get into the kitchen

and prepare your station. You can begin with vegetable prep." He rummages a bit more. "Zut alors! Chantenay carrots? These English grocers are all idiots - like their cooks!"

Turn to...   921

❧ 954 ❧

You are given a punt and long punt pole: your challenger takes the same. You have been forced to participate in the ancient student ritual duel of punt-jousting. The punt itself is a flat and unstable craft, easily capsized, and the pole or quant is unwieldy and long.

Stand on the counter...   914
Stand inside the punt...   858

❧ 955 ❧

"I have heard you have fallen in with that Captain Coke," remarks Comrade Blewitt. "He is no friend to the cause. Perhaps you mean to undermine him - or to infiltrate his circle? It would be better if he were behind bars. Unless you split from him, you can do nothing more for us."

Return to the parlour...   100
Leave the inn...   911

❧ 956 ❧

Upriver of Henley you pass through Marsh Lock with its wooden walkways over the weir and turn south into a stretch bordered by watercress meadows. Several scrub-covered islands split the flow and you will have a tricky time finding the channel unless you know the river well.

Stay close to the Berkshire bank...   1036
Steer towards the Oxfordshire bank...   1016
Try to stay in the middle...   1026

❧ 957 ❧

You dismount and rub your tired backside before settling down to wait. The Ferguson is reliable, fast and tough - but riding it day and night has set an ache into your bones. Note **passage number 550** on your **Adventure Sheet** and roll a dice to see what you encounter.

Score 1	A private steam carriage...	**136**
Score 2	The Haulage Guild...	**408**
Score 3	The Constables...	**1184**
Score 4	The Coal Board...	**223**
Score 5	The Telegraph Guild...	**272**
Score 6	An independent haulier...	**1027**

❧ 958 ❧

You chat to the hauliers and find one prepared to carry Fursham's flour to the bakery where you have negotiated a better price. He nods and then marks up a tally stick - the wooden reminders much used by the often-illiterate hauliers. "Take this up to Cobstone and give it him," says the haulier. "This should be good business for us both." Gain **tally-stick 32**.

Return to the Freight Yard...	**458**
Head into Henley...	**702**
Leave town...	**586**

❧ 959 ❧

You find your boat where you left it, beneath the willows at North Stoke. It takes some time to heat the boiler before you can send power to the screw and bring her out onto the river itself. In the meantime, you chat with the mate who has been living aboard while you adventure on dry land.

Steam towards Mongewell Park...	**31**
Head upriver towards Wallingford...	**943**
Sail towards South Stoke...	**271**
Continue on to Reading...	
(**8s** or **Bargee's Badge**)	**658**

❧ 960 ❧

You do well - but not so well as to draw attention to yourself. One of the Constables laughs as his mate is forced to hand over his **truncheon** and **Constable's whistle** in addition to the **18s** you have won. "You're a good hand," he grudgingly says. "Mayhap the match for Barrymore, even."

"Barrymore?" you ask.

"Earl Barrymore plays in Henley," he replies. "At the theatre, most Friday nights. But high stakes, you know. Guineas and carriages and the like."

Return to the parlour...	**668**

❧ 961 ❧

You awake inside a swaying carriage, chained to the wall. Cautiously looking out, you find yourself on the road to Goring and after several hours' journey, you recognise the Freight Yard.

A haulier opens the door and grunts. "Awake, then. Well now you'll see what we've prepared for the likes of you."

You are bundled out and blink in the daylight. Your velosteam has been brought along and stands a short distance away, but most of the yard is taken up with a crowd of hauliers.

"Which one will it be?" asks the haulier. "Right or left?"

You are dragged forward into a circle and your wrist clamped down onto a block. Then, with a blur, a heavy blade is swung down and your hand falls into the mud.

They cauterise the stump with hot tar and then send you off on your way. Remove 2 points from your NIMBLENESS and MOTORING scores and add **lost a hand** to your notes on your **Adventure Sheet**. You are, at least, no longer **Wanted by the Haulage Guild.**

Turn to...	**911**

❧ 962 ❧

Your camp in the woods is as you have left it. The tarpaulin flutters a little where the wind has tugged at it, but it is quickly tied down. You walk around it and check for wind-gaps and rain leaks before hunkering down for a rest.

You may leave possessions here, writing them into the box below. You should also note this **passage number** before making your choice.

Repair your velosteam...	180
Open a strongbox...	138
Tend your **wounds**...	33
Leave the camp...	401

❧ 963 ❧

You look around for the gamekeeper's cottage, sure to be nearby, and give the keeper's whistle. After a short while the Wormsley Park keeper appears. He introduces himself as Hodge and shakes your hand. "Any friend to the profession is a friend to me," he says. "Can I help you at all?"

If you have any **wounds**, Hodge will treat them for free with his favoured ointment. Remove them and replace them with **scars**. He is also willing to sell you a **pair of ferrets** for a guinea (**£1 1s**).

Ride on to Stokenchurch...	308
Return to Ibstone...	977
Take the track through the woods to Christmas Common...	617

❧ 964 ❧

These strongboxes are meant to be proof against lock-picking and brute force, but patience and persistence are tools of considerable power. Roll a dice to see what the opened strongbox reveals.

Score 1	Turn to...	869
Score 2	Turn to...	908
Score 3	Turn to...	802
Score 4	Turn to...	756
Score 5	Turn to...	711
Score 6	Turn to...	631

❧ 965 ❧

Unsteady and barely moving fowards, you are hit squarely in the chest by the heavy end of the student's quant, knocking you into the water with a splash. Any **paper items** among your **possessions** (such as **letters**, **books** or **tickets**) will be ruined. The students haul you out and stand you before your victor.

"Now, that skiff cost me thirty guineas! Pay up or I'll hand you over to the Constables."

Give him the money... (**£31 10s** or **thirty guineas in banknotes**)	868
Unable or unwilling to pay...	898

❧ 966 ❧

The Guildmembers recognise you from your attacks on their convoys and quickly prepare to take you captive. After all, there is quite a reward on your head. Now you are on their ground, not in the open woods of your territory but in the busy, confined yard and you have no choice but to fight!

Guildsmen	Weapons: **clubs (PAR 2)**
Parry:	10
Nimbleness:	8
Toughness:	7

Victory!	360
Defeat!	961

❧ 967 ❧

Your patience and nimbleness allow you to move through the wood as silently as a phantom. Long after midnight, you see a procession of four poachers approaching the wood up a hedgerow and you quickly find Mr Sands and silently point them out.

"Let's have them," he says with a grim smile.

You position yourselves and once the poachers are in the wood, Mr Sands lets fly with his shotgun, aiming for the legs. One poacher falls and the others flee. You give chase and the unwary gang head straight for a series of pits: one tumbles in, head-over-heels, another screams as a toothed man-trap closes on his shin and the fourth gets away.

"Excellent," says Mr Sands. "He can go and warn anyone else that the easy pickings are done around here." He pays you **15s** for the night's work and offers you some of the poacher's pickings - a single fat **pheasant**, a **razor (PAR-1 NIM+3)**, a **snare** and a **pocket watch**. Finally, he tells you of some further work he has. It would involve helping him extermi-

❦ 982 ❧

The quiet willows slip by as you steam downstream. You catch sight of a disused quarry on the Berkshire bank, below the Henley road, and see the smoke of a wanderer's fire in the woods behind Marsh Lock. You have to wait for some time before being allowed into the pound: the lock-keeper insists on waiting for another boat to conserve water.

Steam into Henley...	**818**
Pass straight on by...	**501**

❦ 983 ❧

A cough and a choke from your engine tell you that something is wrong. The flywheel is turning erratically and as your mate lets the pressure out of the boiler, it becomes clear that this is a serious issue. A cracked casing has sent the shaft bearings out of alignment and the continual running of the engine has worn several components into useless iron. The mate shakes his head. Make an ENGINEERING roll of difficulty 11 to fix it, adding 1 for each of the following you possess: **wirecutters**, **welding tools** or a **brass flange joint** (which you should discard if you use).

Successful ENGINEERING roll!	**719**
Failed ENGINEERING roll!	**909**

❦ 984 ❧

The inn-keeper gives you a funny look: he is certain that you are not the same person that paid for the safe-box, but since you have the key, he can hardly deny you access. He fetches a metal-bound strongbox. Inside you find a **catling knife (PAR 1 NIM+2)**, **£3 18s** and **ten guineas in banknotes**.

Replace items in the strongbox...	**1059**
Return to the parlour...	**640**

❦ 985 ❧

You set off from Henley, carefully steering between the frail rowing eights that have come out for their practice, each with a capped crew entirely focused on their stroke and utterly oblivious to working river traffic. The trip to Reading will take you through four locks, with tolls to pay at each one, and along a considerable stretch of the Thames. Roll two dice :

Score 2-5	Trouble in the dusk...	**1012**
Score 6-8	A uninterrupted journey...	**495**
Score 9-12	A River Guild check...	**1001**

❦ 986 ❧

You creep through the rank grasses, the teasels and the low shrubs to the edge of the reservoir's bank. The brick retaining wall is shattered and cracked and only a small muddy pool sits at the bottom of the once-brimming tank.

The hillside beneath the reservoir shows just how forceful the torrent of released water was: the clay has been stripped away, exposing the chalk bedrock, tumbling beeches and hornbeam into a torn and splintered heap at the foot of the hill.

Return to the road...	**544**

❦ 987 ❧

You leave Wallingford behind you and steam south. Dairy cows splash in the shallows on the western bank, looking up nonchalantly as you chug past. Clouds flit across the sky.

Steam towards Mongewell Park...	**31**
Moor at North Stoke...	**383**
Sail towards South Stoke...	**271**
Continue on to Reading...	
(**8s** or **Bargee's Badge**)	**658**

❦ 988 ❧

Two men are at work digging the well. They drill and hammer through the stone, hauling it up to the surface by hand. They're glad of the chance to stop and chat.

"We've been at this most of the year," says the elder. "And it's good work too. Once this is dug, the village'll have water all year round - no more trusting in unreliable springs."

"Who is paying you to do it? And why is the shelter decorated like this?"

"Ahh," replies the well digger. "'Tis the Maharajah of Benares - a good and kind ruler far off in India. Took pity on us when he was told the story of a boy beaten for drinking the last of the water in the cottage. And that's remarkable because that boy was myself."

"We're almost two hundred feet down now," says the other well-digger. "The surveyor chap said we might have to go to three hundred to reach water."

Return to the village...	**457**

❧ 989 ❧

Comrade Blewitt makes a steeple of his fingers and peers over them at you. "You did well to destroy that Wargrave Tower. The people there fear us and the Telegraph Guild are learning that they cannot take their power for granted." He takes a box of **explosives** from the supplies. "Here - I'm sure you can think of something interesting to do with these."

Return to the parlour...   100
Leave the inn...   911

❧ 990 ❧

Constables guard the road to Oxford, checking the identities and business of everyone entering the city. If you are unknown to them you will be able to steam past their checkpoint: if you are **Wanted by the Constables**, read on. Otherwise, turn to **688** immediately.

The checkpoint is manned by a young Constable who is clearly struggling to match the numbers in his ledger with the identity papers, cards and registrations with which he is being confronted. You may be able to hoodwink him: if you want to enter the city, make an INGENUITY roll of difficulty 13, adding 1 if you possess a **Guildsman's medallion**. On the other hand you can simply turn your velosteam around and head across the plain.

Turn around...   970
Successful INGENUITY roll!   1171
Failed INGENUITY roll!   13

❧ 991 ❧

The road runs north up Hambleden Vale, skirting Great Wood where it crawls down the hillside to your left, smoking here and there with what are undoubtedly charcoal-burners' fires. The valley bottom is a series of meadows owned by the Bishop of Barnsbury.

Head into the woods...
  (**Friend of Captain Coke**)   235
Continue on up the valley...   969

❧ 992 ❧

"The house does smack of a desire for reputation, of which we should all be careful. But something else is at stake."

Turn to...   329

❧ 993 ❧

Coming alongside the busy brick-built wharves is no easy task here, but once tied up you spring ashore and set about finding the best prices you can for the various cargoes.

	To buy	To sell
Charcoal	£13	£12
Furniture	£30	£26
Machinery	-	£25
Pottery	£18	£17
Cotton	-	£4
Woollen cloth	-	-
Coal	-	£12
Beer	-	£15
Wheat	-	£4
Malt	£5	£4
Frozen meat	-	-
Ice	-	-

Return to the river...   818

❧ 994 ❧

"All correct? Good - now go and prepare your station. The first meal we shall serve is my famous white carrot salad." The chef rummages in the boxes. "Idiot! How can I make my white carrot salad with orange carrots? Don't you know the difference between chantenay and satin carrots when you see them? Are you colourblind? Go and practice your brunoise!"

Turn to...   921

❧ 995 ❧

As you approach the cruiser, a man emerges from the cabin. He is plainly the worse for drink. "Get away," he shouts. "I'm doing fine!" He grabs a blunderpistol and waves it in your vague direction. "Everything's fine here."
Sail on...   210

❧ 996 ❧

You realise that something is wrong when you try to fire your velosteam's burner: the friction lighter has been removed. Dismounting, you realise that the smiths have left the workshop. Smoke is seeping from beneath a doorway... a pungent, purple smoke. A couple of breaths and you fall to the floor...

Turn to...   15

❧ 997 ❧

The Chilterns are left behind and the road stretches out towards Oxford ahead of you. Through Postcombe, Tetsworth and Milton Common you ride. If you have the codeword *Bolster*, turn to **1115**.

Turn to...   **990**

❧ 998 ❧

Your attempt to open the box fails and you are unfortunate enough to have broken one of the **items** you were using (for example **lockpicks** or any possessions granting an ENGINEERING or INGENUITY bonus). Remove the broken item from your possessions.

Try again...   **116**
Leave the **strongbox** for now...   **noted passage**

❧ 999 ❧

Total your **wounds** and **scars**. If the total is 20 or greater, you are unable to recover from this latest defeat and you must turn to the **Epilogue** immediately, leaving your body at the roadside.

If you have fewer than 20 **wounds** and **scars** and you have friends hereabouts, this is the time to call on them for aid: if you have bolt-hole prepared, perhaps you will still be able to reach it before your day is done.

Retreat to the hillfort...	*(Before)*	**75**
Ride towards Shiplake House...	*(Blended)*	**48**
Call on Mr Sands...		
(Friend of Mr Sands)		**37**
Steam to Cobstone Mill...		
(Friend of Miller Fursham)		**246**

If you are unable to choose any of these options then your time as a road-pirate is over. Without friends or a hideout in which to recuperate, you can never hope to weather the inevitable failures and defeats of life in this drastic and heartless age. Turn to the **Epilogue**.

❧ 1000 ❧

The Ferguson sings breathily as you tear down the hill and along the fine, straight road. Watlington is not far: the chimneys of the town are sending wood and coal smoke up into the dusk. You pass three children carrying baskets who wave and cheer as you steam by.

The road here is well-used, but presents you with little cover from which to ambush travellers. None-theless, if you are confident in your MOTORING ability, you might be able to out-race an engine on the straight here.

Prepare an ambush here...	**696**
Turn around and approach the children...	**293**
Continue on to Watlington...	**360**

❧ 1001 ❧

An armed patrol cruiser chugs towards you. The River Guild work hard to keep the river free from trouble-makers and piracy - otherwise what benefit would their members gain from all their tolls? If you are **Wanted by the River Guild**, read on. If not, turn to **495** immediately.

When they catch sight of your craft, the cruiser accelerates and a patrolman hails you through his loudspeaker. "Prepare for an inspection! We will board and search you."

Slip over the side...	**1067**
Hide on board... (**secret compartment**)	**1112**

❧ 1002 ❧

You are drawn a fine bitter with a foamy top and a bright colour. The flavour has led to its nickname: Meadowsweet Ale. If you are the **Friend of Miller Fursham**, turn to **348** immediately. Otherwise, read on.

"I hear the miller at Cobstone Mill has sold out at last," says one of the drinkers. "Just struggling to make ends meet and unable to resist the Guild's offer. Shame, since there's been a mill there for three hundred year."

Gain the codeword *Brokenhearted*.

Return to the parlour...   **348**

❧ 1003 ❧

The anglers crowd around you. "What a catch!" says one. "A good stone or more."

"That's nothing," says another. "When I was up at Sonning last I caught a twenty-pounder, fat as butter."

There is always a bigger fish - or a fisherman with a bigger mouth.

The innkeeper offers to buy your **large pike** for **£2**. He will put it on the wall with the others, if you like.

Return to the parlour...   **348**

❧ 1004 ❧

The beer here is brewed with spring water, local hops and barley malted in the stables. It bears the grand name of Shire Prince and is served in a heavy tankard. It has a red colour, a golden head and a fine, building flavour with bready notes, treacly undertones and a bright hoppy finish. The landlord refills your tankard as it falls back to the table. "We only drink quarts here," he says. "A day's work needs as much."

You ask about the routes to Maidensgrove and are told how to approach the village from Pishill in the north and Bix to the south. "It's easy to miss the track, see? Past the old chapel at Pishill and behind the sand bunker from Bix."

Now that you know the route, you will need to add 50 to the passage numbers in which you see these landmarks mentioned in order to find the secret way up to Maidensgrove.

Return to the parlour...	**760**
Leave the inn...	**344**

❧ 1005 ❧

"How fast can you get this parcel to Oxford?" asks the manager of the Freight Yard. "I need it done quickly. Payment of two pound on delivery to the yard there."

If you want to take the job, you will need to keep track of the number of passages you use between this and your destination. Do this on your **Adventure Sheet** or notepaper and gain the **urgent parcel**.

Turn to...	**337**

❧ 1006 ❧

When you are released into the common holding cell, a woman approaches. "We heard about your interrogation," she says. "You peached on us."

"What do you mean?"

She narrows her eyes. "You know what I mean."

If you are a **Member of the Compact for Worker's Equality**, you have now lost that status. Remove the codeword *Brand* as well.

Turn to...	**1020**

❧ 1007 ❧

The navvies soon come round to your way of thinking. "We'll unionise and join this here Compact," commits one man, to the cheers of his fellows. "Let's do something right!" Gain the codeword *Boosting*.

Leave the camp...	**584**

❧ 1008 ❧

The gravel spits out from beneath your tyres as you brake hard and then skid to a stop on the wooden platform of the ferry. The ferryman is already turning the winch and you move steadily across the stream.

A minute later, the Constables appear on the now-receding jetty, halt and begin to shout at the ferryman, who turns to you and feigns deafness. "Awful quiet at the moment," he says. "Though I can pick out that blackbird yonder in the peace. I'm just crossing to get my lunch from the missus, so don't you worry about any fare."

Turn to...	**112**

❧ 1009 ❧

The charges go off prematurely, before you have completed the task or got away to a safe distance. The blast and the massive lumps of coal knock you about terribly: gain **two wounds**. If you now have **five wounds**, turn to **999** immediately. Otherwise you must climb back onto your velosteam and make off.

Turn to...	**noted passage**

❧ 1010 ❧

The chapel is a vaulted, metal-framed building, reminiscent of an airship's gasbag envelope. When you ask one of the monks, he grins. "It is an airship frame. We are preparing to launch an airborne hospital. The Prior will tell you about it."

Then a group of monks enter to sing God's praise in an ancient song.

Try to rob the chapel...	**1185**
Listen to the music...	**1238**
Return to the cloister...	**642**

❧ 1011 ❧

The Guildsmen are not trained to deal with violent attack and you will undoubtedly be able to frighten them into submission. Make a RUTHLESSNESS roll of difficulty 11, adding 1 if you are **Wanted by the River Guild**.

Successful RUTHLESSNESS roll!	**1052**
Failed RUTHLESSNESS roll!	**1072**

❧ 1012 ❧

As night falls, you hear arguing voices somewhere ahead. As you strain to hear over the throbbing of your steam engine, two sudden flashes of gunfire echo across the river. All falls quiet.

Stop and investigate the gunfire...	**1159**
Steam on through the night...	**495**

❧ 1013 ❧

The gates to Mongewell Park are open, presumably expecting a returning carriage, so you steam up the drive towards the house. However, when you approach, a woman appears on the steps with a gun. She seems to recognise your hat.

"You blackguard!" she cries. "Kill my father and rob him too?" She fires her rifle and proves to be an excellent shot! Roll a dice to see what ensues.

Score 1-2	Gain a **wound**
Score 3-4	Your velosteam receives a **damage point**
Score 5-6	A **wound** and a **damage point**

If you now have **five wounds**, Susan Tenney will capture you and hand you over to the Constables: turn to **13**. If your velosteam is **beyond repair**, turn to **874**. Otherwise, you must turn about and speed away!

Turn to...	**860**

❧ 1014 ❧

You are served a pint of beer called Toothy Dog. It is fiercely alcoholic and a wild ride of flavours: caramel and berries, toast and warm spice, then gingeriness and a light finish. It seems popular with the long-distance hauliers here. They are discussing the best place to sell 'used' jewellery.

"I know that chap at the compound at Christmas Common buys just about everything," says one drinker. "And then the Richards brothers down in Reading will buy pieces to melt down."

"That gypsy chap Barsali pays the best prices," says another.

Return to the parlour...	**640**
Leave the inn...	**308**

❧ 1015 ❧

The crew of the steamer let out the steam pressure with a whistling shriek and the boat slows alongside. Roll a dice to see who is aboard.

Score 1-2	A courting couple	**1024**
Score 3-4	An angry man	**1048**
Score 5-6	A picnicking party	**1071**

❧ 1016 ❧

Despite the narrowing of the river, it becomes clear that this is the main navigational channel. A heavy coal barge coming downriver towards you could not have come from any other direction. You are soon approaching Wargrave.

Steam on to Sonning... (**2s**)	**471**
Steer for Wargrave wharf...	**131**
Moor at the quarry... (*Breaker*)	**1485**

❧ 1017 ❧

In the infirmary you meet Brother Hume, the order's herbalist and healer. "I am always ready to pray and to act," he says. "Healing requires our readiness to be obedient to God's way, not simply the anointing of the flesh or the speaking of words." Brother Hume would appreciate a donation to cover the cost of the medicines he will use.

	To buy
Heal a **wound**...	**15s** - replace with a **scar**
Treat a **fever**...	**10s**
Treat a **burn**...	**8s** - replace with a **scar**
Treat a **toothache**...	**6s**
Treat a **bite on the neck**...	**4s**

Donate medical supplies...	**1332**
Return to the cloister...	**642**

❧ 1018 ❧

If you have any **furniture** as cargo, turn to **1032** immediately. If not, but you do have any **wounds**, turn to **1038**. Otherwise, read on.

You steam around the long riverbend, keeping to

the left bank and avoiding a string of heavy grain-barges and their steam-tug destined for the capital, far downstream. A stray cow looks up from its long drink and meets your eye before returning to whatever was occupying its thoughts.

Stop at Henley...	**818**
Continue on towards Wargrave...	
(**2s** or **Bargee's Badge**)	**956**
Press on for Reading...	
(**10s** or **Bargee's Badge**)	**985**

❧ 1019 ❦

At the widest point of the bags where the lines are at their hardest to grasp, you slip and scrabble and slip again. Rain is soaking the canvas and the oiled silk and you have neither harness nor safety line. One too many times, your tired hands lose their hold and you plunge through the air like an unmourned Icarus. There will be no further chances for you. Turn to the **Epilogue**.

❧ 1020 ❦

You are not permanently kept in the same cell throughout your imprisonment. Disorganisation and over-crowding means that you are moved several times and, when you return to your cell, you find yourself sharing it with another inmate. If you have a **bite on the neck**, turn to **1033**. Otherwise, roll a dice to see what happens to you.

Score 1-2	Gaol fever!	**1043**
Score 3-4	Make a friend...	**1051**
Score 5-6	Make an enemy...	**1065**

❧ 1021 ❦

You accelerate onto the grassy verge and pull past the road trains. However, just as you need to get ahead, a ditch cuts through the bank. You must make a MOTORING roll of difficulty 13 to pass it unscathed, adding 1 if you possess **off-road tyres**.

Successful MOTORING roll!	**990**
Failed MOTORING roll!	**1031**

❧ 1022 ❦

It turns out that the officer is a keen artist - or he professes to be. He looks through your sketchbook scornfully. "You need to spend much more time looking at your subject and worry less about 'getting the right shape'. Your proportions are all wrong. All wrong." He remounts his velosteam, still laughing, and motions for his Constables to follow.

Wait for something else to ambush...	**957**
Head on towards Bix...	**3**
Ride to Watlington...	**5**
Steam off to Hambleden...	**343**

❧ 1023 ❦

☐

If the box above is ticked, turn to **1030** immediately. Otherwise, read on.

As you approach you recognise the Master Brewer from Wethered's in Marlow. Louise Standler is watching as her crew water up the engine. She turns at the sound of your approach and waves.

"Well met, friend," she says.

"Not in the depths of the brewery today, then?"

"We've just delivered a full load of our brew to the Oxford inns - and aren't they glad of it! We're cutting down on the river deliveries nowadays but still have to deal with the guilds." She nods towards the water tower. "You wouldn't believe how much they charge for access to these."

"I would," you reply with a grin. "It can be very dangerous for guildsmen out here. Danger money increases the cost of this infrastructure significantly."

She smiles in reply. "I am glad to see you still alive - although somewhat scarred. I've been telling everyone I can about how you helped keep Wethered's going. It won't be forgotten." Note that you are now the **Brewer's Friend** on your adventure sheet. You must leave the brewer and her team to their work and you ride on to yours.

Steam on to Wallingford...	**800**

❧ 1024 ❦

A young couple are out enjoying the river. The man gets up and looks for something with which to defend his fiancee's honour, but loses his balance and collapses. He is unable to resist you: you may take a **silver necklace**, **£4 18s** and a **silver ring**.

Turn to...	**251**

❧ 1025 ❧

☐

If the box above is empty, tick it and turn to **1056** immediately. If it is already ticked, read on.

The traveller is a nobleman with a large entourage on a long steam-yacht. He is far too well-protected to rob - but maybe you will cross his path ashore.

Turn to...   **855**

❧ 1026 ❧

The river here is surprisingly shallow and the current unpredictable. If you have a **strengthened screw** you will pass through: turn to **131** immediately. Otherwise you will come aground and be forced to jettison one of your **units of cargo**, if you have any aboard.

Turn to...   **131**

❧ 1027 ❧

The approaching vehicle has none of the livery of the Haulage Guild or any other big business: it is a man or woman trying to make their own living as an independent businessman, finding what contracted work they can. The engine tows three wagons of goods.

Threaten the driver...   **1089**
Let the road-train pass...   **noted passage**

❧ 1028 ❧

Susan Tenney greets you warmly. She thanks you again for the rescue of her father. "Many a passer-by would have left him there at the side of the road, or robbed him. You are a genuine good Samaritan." She tells you of the business on her estate, the difficulties with poachers and robbers in the woods towards Nuffield House and the hopes for improving the local villages. "But what have I to complain about?" she asks. "I have much to be thankful for."

After a stroll around the garden, she tells you that she intends to pay a visit on the Viscountess Bell-Happing at Fawley Court. "She's a dreadfully sly sort of person," she says, "Always match-making and scheming. But she gives the most marvellous parties - and there are always the most fabulous croquet matches. I'm sure I could get you an invitation."

Accompany her to Fawley Court...   **104**
Board your boat...
    (moored at Mongewell Park)   **31**
Leave the house...   **860**

❧ 1029 ❧

The mate shovels more coal into the furnace and you open the regulator. Your boat surges forward heavily and you round the riverbend to see men and women defending themselves from the roof of a pleasure steamer. Several gentlemen are attempting to fight off the sky-pirates with swordsticks and sabres but the pirates are grabbing women and bundling them into their nets. You have a split-second to choose your side: ally with the passengers or with their ruthless attackers.

Help the sky-pirates...   **1057**
Help the gentlemen...   **1103**

❧ 1030 ❧

The steamer is an independent operator - prone and vulnerable here. Will you choose to rob them, or to continue on your journey? Note **passage number 171**.

Threaten them...   **202**
Steam on by...   **800**

❧ 1031 ❧

The front wheel dips into the ditch, catches and the rear of your speeding velosteam rises up, up, up and over, launching you onto the road. The engine drivers swerve and the left-hand machine pulls ahead. You, however, land with a crunch. Gain a **wound** and a **damage point**. You must also remove one **customisation** if you have any. If your velosteam is **beyond repair**, turn to **874** immediately. If not but you have **five wounds**, turn to **999**. Otherwise you pick yourself up, dust yourself down and remount your damaged machine. Hopefully you will be able to afford repairs in Oxford.

Ride on...   **990**

❧ 1032 ❧

The cargo seems to have been unevenly stowed and it is causing your boat to travel unevenly through the water, consuming more coal and more water than it should. Clambering forward, you see that the problem lies with the stack of furniture which has shifted as you have sailed.

The reason is soon apparent. A teen-aged girl lies asleep in a nest she has made within the furniture stack. When she awakes, she gabbles fearfully about running away from an abusive father. She wants to be an acrobat in the circus and wants to reach Reading.

Put her ashore at Henley...	918
Take her directly to Reading... (10s)	1045

❧ 1033 ❧

The bite you suffered from the madwoman - or vampire - becomes infected in these awful conditions and you succumb to a dangerous fever. The guards are uninterested and unwilling to allow a doctor to see you. You experience a week of strange, sweaty fever dreams, hallucinations and fears. In your visions you are continually brought back to the view of an abbey overlooking a stormy coast. A ship approaches from the wave-wracked sea and is driven into the harbour and smashes into the quay. Something leaps ashore... You watch, again and again as the scene replays itself.

The fever eventually abates and the bite heals, but leaves a nasty **scar**. Remove the **bite on the neck**.

Turn to...	1077

❧ 1034 ❧

You remember that the woman on the locobus told you about her uncle Max, imprisoned here for causing trouble in the town. You find him when you are moved to one of the common cells - a jolly man, despite his circumstances. "Oh, I'm always giving them gyp," he says, "The Constables, the Town Guard, they just throw me in here on any excuse now. I stay as long as I want."

"What do you mean?" you reply.

"Oh, it's not too hard to get out, if you know how."

"Help me to escape."	1080
"I shall serve my term."	1020

❧ 1035 ❧

In one of the tea-breaks you climb onto a brick stack and begin to tell the workers about the struggle for power, the rightful ownership of the means of production and the evils of the capitalist classes. Some young hot-heads are immediately convinced, but you will need to have strong arguments if you want to politicise this very self-reliant workforce. If you have the codeword *Arithmetic* or *Clavicle*, turn to **1270** immediately. Otherwise you must make an INGENUITY roll of difficulty 15, adding 3 if you have a **revolutionary poster** and 2 if you have more than **20 solidarity points**.

Successful INGENUITY roll!	1061
Failed INGENUITY roll!	791

❧ 1036 ❧

Your boat comes to halt with a thump as the bow fender strikes against a willow tree. This channel is far too overgrown to pass through.

Turn to...	956

❧ 1037 ❧

If you have a **fine top hat**, turn to **1013** immediately. If you are the **Friend of Susan Tenney**, turn to **1028**. Otherwise, read on.

Mongewell Park stands on the riverside with its own lake and gardens separating it from the road to Wallingford. Iron gates guard the estate and a sleepy gatekeeper sits waiting by the entrance.

Ask to see the Lord of the Manor...	
(**letter of Introduction**)	1076
Return to the road...	860

❧ 1038 ❧

The river is peaceful here. For once the stretch below Henley is quiet and willow leaves dip and trail in the stream. You moor up and take a swim before resting on deck. When you wake, you are feeling refreshed. Remove one **wound** without converting to a **scar**.

Stop at Henley...	918
Continue on towards Wargrave...	
(**2s** or **Bargee's Badge**)	956
Press on for Reading...	
(**10s** or **Bargee's Badge**)	985

❧ 1039 ❧

The crew resist you with their boathooks and clubs. You will have to cut them down!

Crew	Weapons: **clubs (PAR 2)**
Parry:	8
Nimbleness:	6
Toughness:	5

Victory!	**1052**
Defeat!	**528**

❧ 1040 ❧

☐

If the box above is empty, tick it and read on. If it is already ticked, turn to **1066** immediately.

"Are you looking for work?" asks the Coal Board Director. He leans back in his canvas seat and judges you carefully. "You'll know we're no friends to the Telegraph Guild and their monopolies? Well one of our engineers has come up with a way to hash their clever mechanics. They use punchcards to code all their messages and those codes run through their mechanisms like a song in a bird's throat. We've a new code that, once it's in their system, will slowly set their telegraphs out of alignment. With every message, they'll become increasingly inaccurate. And it spreads out from one tower to another, inside the messages they send."

"Like a mechanical disease."

"Exactly. Now what we need is someone to introduce this disease into their system. Take these." He hands you a pack of **punchcards (Stiverton S)**. "Infiltrate the Guild. Buy your way in, if you need, with these faked-up documents." He also gives you a **Coal Board Accounts book**. "Introduce the code into one of the Guild computational engines and it will do the rest."

Leave the compound...	**308**

❧ 1041 ❧

You lift the wounded man onto your velosteam and make your way towards Mongewell Park - the large, gabled house at the riverside upstream from North Stoke. There you have no problems convincing the gateman to let you in. He gasps in recognition at 'The Master!' and waves you through.

At the house you meet Susan Tenney, the daughter of the man you have rescued. She orders her servants to carry him into the library, where beside a roaring fire, she tends to him on a brocaded silk chaise-longue.

You are much celebrated. She is plainly a woman of standing and a strict social code but she recognises your best characteristics and takes a liking to you. "Without your selflessness," she says, "I would be an orphan. Mama died when I was young and papa is all the family I have. He and my people here."

Once her father is resting and stable, she shows you around the grounds. A fine lawn runs down to the riverside. "I love the river," she says. "Don't you find the sound of running water captivating? Come and visit me again - and if you do, moor here."

You are now the **Friend of Susan Tenney**.

Leave the house...	**860**

❧ 1042 ❧

Attempting the manoeuvre, you lose control of your velosteam and the machine twists, kicks and rolls onto the roadside. Roll a dice to see what you suffer.

Score 1-2	A **wound** and a **damage point**
Score 3-4	**Two wounds**
Score 5-6	**Two damage points**

If your velosteam is **beyond repair**, turn to **874** immediately. Otherwise, the Constables will haul your broken body from the wreckage and process you.

Turn to...	**13**

❧ 1043 ❧

In prison conditions like these, one thing you cannot avoid are the ever-present lice. They hop and crawl into every possible crevice and joint, bite you while you sleep and while you wake. The discomfort is far from their worst consequence, however.

The guards are constantly engaged in a half-hearted struggle against gaol fever - epidemic typhus - which is forever breaking out in one cell or another. Several prisoners awake one day with the tell-tale sores and are quarantined in one of the largest cells. You soon join them.

Gaol fever has an almost certain progression. Rashes, fevers, intolerance of light, inflammation of the brain, delirium, coma and death. You see the youngest and frailest of your cellmates succumb first and, despite your own strength, soon lose much of your ability to cope or observe. If you have any levels of **medical training**, turn to **1087** immediately.

You survive the gaol fever but at a terrible cost. Your body is weakened and wracked by the infection: remove 1 from your NIMBLENESS, INGENUITY and MOTORING skills.

Turn to...   1077

❧ 1044 ❧
You join a posse of green-coated codesmen on their walk to the inn and fall into conversation. They are naturally wary but eventually open up under the influence of beer and gin and tell you many details about their lives in the guild.

"Oh it seems very glamourous and secret to a youngster," says one. "But what do I know of the messages I send? Very little. The high policy of the land coming through on a 111, why that's double-coded. Everything I can read is prices in Reading, what freight's being shipped in Southhampton, who needs coal in Stoke-on-Trent."

"It ain't all coded hard," says another. "I mean private messages are open enough normally."

"That's true. How you met your wife, ain't it Lou?"

A dark-haired man smiles shyly.

Leave the men...   487

❧ 1045 ❧
As you steam along, the girl devours the food you put before her and chatters away noisily. How will she fare in the city? What hope has she of surviving in the ruthless dens, alone and penniless?

It is not your concern...   495
Give her money... (**£4**)   1099

❧ 1046 ❧
Despite everything the storm can throw at you - despite the wet lines, the slippery surface of the varnished silken bags, the gusting winds and the insistent rain, you climb to the vent and seal it up with needle and thread, sailmaker's wax and oilcloth. Your fingers are torn and bloodied but when you climb back down to the deck, Coke claps you on the back. You see why his crew have such trust in him.

"We'll make it home now! Well done indeed."

You are allowed to collapse into your hammock once more and when you awake you have been carried ashore and laid in a tent. Remove one of your **wounds** and replace it with another **scar**. You are

also now the **Friend of Captain Coke** and a valued member of the crew. Your velosteam has been returned to you - although not your possessions or money - and you will be allowed to come and go as you please.

Turn to...   819

❧ 1047 ❧
If you are **Wanted by the Constables**, turn to **1268** immediately. Otherwise, read on.

As you leave the inn, the landlord gives you a nod. "No-one'll touch your room," he promises, "Except the cleaning lady."

Turn to...   308

1048
The passenger gets up and challenges you. "How dare you!" he cries. "You have no right to threaten me!" He draws his sword.

Angry man	Weapon: **sabre (PAR 3)**
Parry:	8
Nimbleness:	5
Toughness:	4

Victory!   1068
Defeat!   528

❧ 1049 ❧
You quietly make your way behind a storage shed and climb onto the roof. From there you must make your way down through a skylight without being seen to access the supplies. Make a NIMBLENESS roll of difficulty 12, adding 1 if you possess a **rope** or a **grappling iron**.

Successful NIMBLENESS roll!   1083
Failed NIMBLNESS roll!   15

❧ 1050 ❧
☐
If the box above is empty, tick it and read on. If it is already ticked, turn to **1239** immediately.

The servant stares at you, making up his mind. "Come then," he says eventually.

You are led to a stable on the outskirts of the village where a young man is bleeding from a deep sword-thrust to his abdomen. He has plainly been there for some time and as you move him to better get at the wound, fresh blood begins to flow.

"Who did this?" you ask.

"My master," replies the servant.

You clean and tend the young man's body, noting the marks of hard usage - the marks of the lash, scarred hands and heavy bruising. "He has been treated badly - and now with a sword?"

A figure darkens the doorway. "Do not bother yourself with the cause of his injuries. Rest assured they were the consequence of his own choices - as all we experience is." A smartly-dressed nobleman, glamorous from the buckles on his boots to his powdered hair, smiles mockingly down at you. "Let me know this. How soon will he be able to work?"

"This wound will weaken him permanently," you reply. "And it may be months before he can lift or drag anything of any weight."

"How unfortunate. His family will struggle without his wage." The nobleman disappears, but you are too busy with bandages and bloody rags to watch him go.

Turn to...   1062

❧ 1051 ☙

☐

If the box above is empty, tick it now and read on. If it is already ticked, turn to **1113** immediately.

The prisoner locked into your cell is a notorious murderer - violent, dangerous and unpredictable. You notice the guards and other prisoners avoiding him and treating him with a fearful respect. For much of the time he is chained, but after discovering that he has a surprisingly polite and gentle nature, you help him to loosen the chains so that he can take them off at will.

His name is Horace Konig and he appreciates your friendship. Exchanging stories about your adventures and histories, he becomes keen to share his talents with you and trains you in razor-fighting. After much practice, countless exercises and trials of speed and strength, you come to match him in his abilties. Add 1 to your NIMBLENESS score.

Shortly after this he is taken from the cell to his execution. You hear the crowd's roar on the morning of his hanging through the barred window of your cell.

Turn to...   1077

❧ 1052 ☙

The crew surrender and you may rifle through their boat. If you have a **cargo crane** fitted, you may steal some of their units of cargo: they are carrying **malt**, **wheat** and **furniture**. You may also take **4s** and a **Bargee's Badge**.

You will now be **Wanted by the River Guild**.

Turn to...   251

❧ 1053 ☙

The people of Whitchurch keep a weekly market to trade their produce. There are also a few shops in which more specialised equipment and supplies can be purchased.

Food and Drink	To buy	To sell
bottle of wine	10s	8s
bottle of champagne	£1 5s	18s
bottle of whisky	£1 10s	£1
pork pie	3s	2s
picnic hamper	£3 3s	£2 10s
Clothing	To buy	To sell
mask	4s	-
silk scarf	-	15s
cloak	£1	-
dark cloak (RUTH+1)	-	£4
fur coat	£5 4s	£3 2s
top hat	-	£1 5s
Tools	To buy	To sell
grappling iron	12s	8s
fishing line	1s	-
jeweller's loupe (ING+1)	£2 2s	£1 12s
binoculars	£3 15s	£2
telescope	£4 10s	£3 5s
Weapons	To buy	To sell
sabre (PAR 3)	£1 5s	8s
rapier (PAR 4)	-	£4
blunderpistol (ACC 6)	£4	£2
duelling pistols (ACC 7)	-	£10
Other items	To buy	To sell
parasol	£6	£4
box of cigars	£1 19	£1 10s
ivory fan	£4	£1 10s
fine clock	£10	£6 3s
pair of golden candlesticks	£6	£2 14s
gold bar	-	£30

Return to the village...   749
Leave Whitchurch now...   693

❧ 1054 ❧

It should not be too hard to whip the **telescope** away from under the surveyors' noses. Make an INGENU-ITY roll of difficulty 12 , adding 2 if you have a **fishing line** or a **grappling hook**.

Successful INGENUITY roll!	**1097**
Failed INGENUITY roll!	**62**

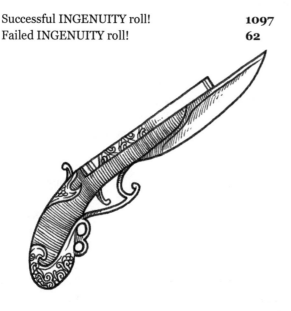

❧ 1055 ❧

"A picnic? Why yes, that does look like a delicious outdoor repast." The officer beckons his men over. "Look at this! What a lovely way to spend your leisure time! I'm sure our friend here won't mind sharing a meal with the gallant Constabulary." In no time the laughing Constables have emptied your **hamper** (remove it from your **possessions**) and remount their velosteams, wiping crumbs and beer-foam from their lips. "Be careful of robbers in this region, citizen," says the officer before steaming off down the road.

Wait for something else to ambush...	**968**
Head on towards Bix...	**3**
Ride to Watlington...	**5**
Steam off to Hambleden...	**343**

❧ 1056 ❧

The important traveller is a businessman on his way to the arms fair at Reading. He has chartered a steam yacht and is enjoying the luxury of travelling the river in style. A numerous crew, including guards, will keep him safe.

Board and attack!	**1078**
Let him pass...	**855**

❧ 1057 ❧

With your help, the passengers and crew are quickly overcome. They are certainly no match for someone ruthless enough to attack men and women in such unfair circumstances. The pirate captain grins as you walk between the wounded and the cowering. "Go on, mate, take your pick. But choose quickly as my crew are hungry for plunder!"

You take **£4 2s** in coins and can choose two of the following: **ten guineas in banknotes**, a **silver necklace**, a **swordstick (PAR 2 GAL+1)**, a **top hat** and a **fur coat**.

Once you have chosen your loot, you clamber back onto your boat and steam off downstream. If you are not already, you will now be **Wanted by the Constables** and **Wanted by the River Guild** for your deeds.

Sail on to Reading...	**495**
Turn back the way you came...	**305**

❧ 1058 ❧

You have at last reached Stonor House, where you know Colonel Snappet imprisoned Professor Benner after torturing him for his secrets. Will you find him dead or alive here? Will he have any understanding of who and where he is, any recognition of old friends?

The house is owned by the Stonor family, close friends of the dead Colonel and allies in his nefarious deeds. For the part they have played in imprisoning the professor they have surely earnt a dreadful reward.

Break in and look for the professor...	**1075**
Ambush and coerce the owners...	**1090**
Bluff your way in...	**1102**

❧ 1059 ❧
☐

If the box is empty, put a tick in it and turn to **984** immediately. If it is already ticked, read on.

The innkeeper will keep the safebox hidden away for you as long as you give him no grounds to report you to the Constables. You may place any items into it that are pocket-sized or made of paper, together with any money you might not wish to carry around, but larger items such as tools, guns larger than a blunderpistol or large pieces of clothing will not fit. Write anything you want to deposit in the box below, erase anything and add it to your **possessions** if you wish to take it out.

"Now you owe me five shilling for that," says the innkeeper as you hand the box back. You must pay him **5s** or surrender the **rusty key**.

Return to the parlour...   **640**

✦ 1060 ✦
In the workshop, monks and laybrothers are intent at work on a pair of massive airship engines. When you ask how this relates to their vocation, they grin and reply, "Worship can take many forms! Are you joining in?"

Help the monks...
    (ENGINEERING skill of 8+)   **1124**
Return to the cloister...   **642**

✦ 1061 ✦
"There's a lot at risk if we rise up," says one young man. He is quickly hushed by his peers.

"Don't just think of yourself," they say. "There's a whole nation at stake - and many worse off than us!"

You have the brickworker's allegiance. The comrades of the Compact will be pleased to hear this. Gain the codeword *Blown* and a **solidarity point**.

Leave the brickworks...   **791**

✦ 1062 ✦
After washing at a pump you are approached by an old stable-hand who wants to thank you. "The boy didn't deserve that. He was only trying to protect his sister's honour."

"What do you mean?"

He looks at you, goggle-eyed. "Her wedding to a man in the village and milord Monsberg insisted on his rights - his drat de segneur. And then ran the boy

through when he picked up a hay-fork."

"Does no-one resist him, then?"

"He's the lord of the manor on this side of the village, and up the river too. And he's a fearful swordsman."

The Viscount Monsberg of Coombe Park is a harsh man but within his rights to punish his own serfs and tenants. Surely behaviour this vile cannot go unpunished, however. Gain the codeword *Brimming*.

Challenge the Viscount...   **1141**
Carry the grudge...   **529**

✦ 1063 ✦
Note that your boat is now **moored at Shiplake House**.

You clamber onto the old jetty and see about getting your velosteam shore without wetting it. If you have the codeword *Blended*, turn to **1073** immediately. Otherwise, you head up to the house to see how work is proceeding.

Turn to...   **1091**

✦ 1064 ✦
You find a bitter guildsman selling everything he can lay his hands on. "I'm being invalided out without a pension," he say, "So it's only natural I should try and set a bit by for myself, ain't it?"

Tools	To buy	To sell
adjustable wrench (ENG+1)	£3	-
tarpaulin	4s	-
skeleton key	£7	-
jeweller's loupe (ING+1)	£4	-
lockpicks	£1	-
autogauge (MOT+3)	£30	-

Leave the compound...   **487**

❧ 1065 ❧

The guards open the door one day and haul you out. "That cell's getting fumigated for our next guest. You're in with neighbour Adams."

Neighbour Adams turns out to be an angry and frustrated man, often weeping with rage and self-pity, utterly ruined by his confinement. He conceives an anger at you, his new cell-mate, and tries to murder you in your sleep. Wakened by his hands on your throat, you somehow beat him off, but your crushed windpipe will take a long time to recover. Remove 1 from your NIMBLENESS score.

Turn to... 1077

❧ 1065 ❧

If you have the codeword *Bent*, turn to **1082** immediately. If not, read on.

The Director is busy. "Still looking for employment? We're looking for mercenaries in Wales. The brigands are organising and we need someone to lead an expedition to wipe them out!"

Return to Stokenchurch... 308

❧ 1067 ❧

You quietly slip over the side and into the cold, cold river. It will take considerable strength and stamina to keep yourself at or below the waterline while the patrolmen search your boat. Make a NIMBLENESS roll of difficulty 12.

Successful NIMBLENESS roll! 1109
Failed NIMBLENESS roll! 1120

❧ 1068 ❧

You knock the man to the deck and rifle his pockets. He is carrying **£7 4s**, a **silk scarf** and a **gold ring**.

Turn to... 251

❧ 1069 ❧

The grounds of the ruined Reading Abbey have been taken over for the Imperial Arms Fair: a massive convention of manufacturers, traders and dealers in weapons. Buyers come from as far as the Confederacy and even Japan to see the most up-to-date machines for killing and exerting power. Two great halls have been built, Paxton-style, to house the displays, the war machines and the demonstrations and to keep the public out. Admittance is strictly controlled.

Outside a small group of protestors are being corralled by guards. They are nervous and outnumbered, but ready to pay the price to bring people's awareness to the evils of the weapons trade. One calls out to you: "They took some of us away towards Maidenhead! Free them, Steam Highwayman!"

Return to Reading... 270

❧ 1070 ❧

A group of villagers are discussing how they would like to climb out of the poverty trap. "It's labour," says one. "If we had our own steam engine, we could use it to harvest the common fields. But as it is, it takes everyone so long to do that we ain't got any time to pursue anything else. There's no way to earn any extra and our rents to the big house take everything we can make."

"So you want an engine?" you ask.

"Aye. But we can't afford to buy one." Gain the codeword *Bonnington*.

Turn to... 430

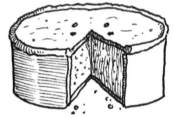

❧ 1071 ❧

A group of young men and their lady friends have been enjoying a picnic. You can take **£2 3s**, a **silver bracelet**, a **pocket watch**, a **bottle of champagne** and a **picnic hamper**.

Turn to... 251

❧ 1072 ❧

The crew are not scared of you. They laugh and the man at the tiller steers towards your boat, ramming you with a heavy thump and knocking you into the water.

You drop your **weapons** instinctively: they will sink straight to the bottom. In addition, any **paper** items such as tickets, cards or letters will be ruined. By the time your mate hauls you back on board your boat, the laughing guildsmen are far downstream.

Turn to... 251

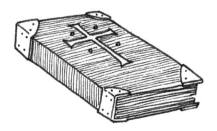

❧ 1073 ❧

Welcome to the comfort of your own stately home. After visiting, sneaking into and being thrown out of countless great houses across the region, now you have a drive up which you can steam with complete confidence; a garage in which your velosteam will be maintained by your own groom; a butler to welcome you and keep the riff-raff out. You have your own study for quiet retreats, your own four-poster bed for sleep. How many nights have you spent asleep under the stars on a mattress of tree-roots, waking with dew-soaked clothes and shiver through your bones. No more!

It has taken a long time to attain this goal. Your prestige and wealth have brought this far, but without ruthlessness and daring, that would amount to nothing. What will life have in store for you now? Note this **passage number**. You may leave items here in perfect safety - including sums of money.

Repair your velosteam...	180
Open a strongbox...	138
Tend your **wounds**...	33
Head to your boat...	
(moored at Shiplake House)	471
Ride toward Henley...	702
Steam towards Sonning Bridge...	682

❧ 1074 ❧

You climb onto a crate and begin to address the workers on the subject of the struggle of all the working classes against the privileged and powerful. Perhaps they, the navvies, enjoy some degree of stability and comfort. Can they enjoy this while mill-workers and farm-labourers are mercilessly exploited? Can they consider their own prosperity the greatest good and wink at the injustices across the Empire? Make an INGENUITY roll of difficulty 13, adding 3 if you possess a **revolutionary poster**.

Successful INGENUITY roll!	1007
Failed INGENUITY roll!	1225

❧ 1075 ❧

That night you climb into the deer park and make your way to the house. There are lights on and a party in progress - all the better to cause a noisy distraction, although you will have to be careful with all the people milling around.

You check the outbuildings but see no sign of any prisoner. If he is kept in the house itself, it will most likely be in a cellar or an attic. Where first?

Enter the cellar through the coal chute...	1142
Climb up to the attic...	1209

❧ 1076 ❧

A footman carries the letter into the house. After half an hour, he reappears with the letter and returns it to you. "Miss Tenney is not in need of your services," he says shortly. "Though if you are looking for work, she suggests you try the Freight Yard at Wallingford."

Leave the house...	860

❧ 1077 ❧

Eventually your sentence is served. The guards hoist you out from your cell, shabby, dirty and blinking in the light - but still unbowed by circumstance. You may remove all your **Wanted statuses** and you are issued with a **convict's pass**, but your other possessions and money will not be returned to you. However, something has motivated the guards to keep your velosteam in a shed and you find it in the same condition that you left it. Now it will be your choice to continue in the way of life that the Constables interrupted, or to find a new way of making a living.

Turn to...	270

❧ 1078 ❧

As your boat comes level, you launch yourself up the side of the steam-yacht and knock the first guard into the water. The others react quickly - you must fight them at once!

Crew	Weapons: **clubs (PAR 2)**
Parry:	7
Nimbleness:	5
Toughness:	8

Victory!	**1094**
Defeat!	**1086**

❧ 1079 ❧

With a final swipe you slash the face of the pirates' leader. The others, surprised by the ferocity of your defence, leap for the lines still hanging from the airship as it moves away. You are left to collapse, exhausted, to the deck of the steamer amongst the dead and wounded.

"You have saved us all," says a thin young man. "What a hero!" The remaining steamer crew and passengers do what they can for you, mopping your brow and giving you **bandages** and a **bottle of whisky** to help with the pain.

The steamer captain is also hurt, but he hobbles over to see you. "The owner is an important man in London. If you take him this, he'll surely show his appreciation." He gives you a **crested envelope**.

Return to your boat and steam on...   **495**

❧ 1080 ❧

"Can do," says uncle Max. In the middle of the night, when most of the inmates are asleep, he takes you to an old chimney built into the wall and proceeds to gently remove several bricks and an iron grille that blocks the flue. "Up we go," he says.

You climb through the soot and mess of fallen birds' nests and emerge low on the battlements of the curtain wall. "Got to look sharp," says uncle Max. "Follow me!"

"I must find my machine," you insist.

"Fair enough. Likely to be in one of the sheds in the outer bailey."

Together you descend on tough ivy stems and search the sheds. There, as he said, is your velosteam in much the same condition as you last saw it. He grins. "Now your turn. Give me a lift out of here?"

You ready the machine and wheel it towards the main gate, waiting until the dawn laundry-cart comes through. Then, at a rush, you kick the velosteam into life and power through, laughing at the guards left behind you, uncle Max clinging on behind. "Take me up to Christmas Common," he says. "I'll make my way from there." Add **Escaped from Gaol** to your list of **Great Deeds**.

Turn to...   **617**

❧ 1081 ❧

The haulier brightens up a little. "Well, since I see you don't intend to hurt me, maybe I'll make it back home alive. Let me tell you - there's plenty of Guild engines on the route to Oxford if you want to rob somebody. They ain't got my overheads!"

Turn to...   **noted passage**

❧ 1082 ❧

The Director claps you on the back. "Well done indeed," he says. "The Executive Board have heard about what you did and are commending me. The Chairman himself has come to hear about the endeavour. I will introduce you."

He leads you into an inner parlour where a man in dusty black is drinking sherry. He does not get up when you enter but turns and you see the milky-white pupils of a blind man.

"Ah, our young adventurer," he says in his creaking, raven-like voice. "Give me your hand."

His palm is dry and hard like the claw of a bird.

"Leave us, Regional Director," says the Chairman. "I wish to ask this resourceful young blade a few questions."

He asks you about what you saw inside the Telegraph Guild Compound at Caversham: the details of the computational engine, the staffing, the faces and voices of the officers you met - but nothing seems to surprise him. In fact he continually nods as though it was all known to him previously.

"I shall tell you that I myself punched those cards you delivered," he says. "The damage they will do to the Guild's infrastructure and reputation is not immediate, but it should be undetectable for a time. The world is changing, you see, and what people like the Guild and even our good Director here do not want to admit is that revolution will come. The people are becoming educated, enabled, empowered by technology and will certainly rise up. Whether they succeed or fail in their attempts to overthrow the hegemony of privilege and the monopolies, someone must make a profit from the business. And the Coal Board must emerge on the right side of history. I am no especial friend to the nobility, nor to the wretches in the factories and fields, but I do not wish the Telegraph Guild to grow. They look to the past and hold this nation back. They even blindly hold themselves back."

He pauses. "As for you. you will be rewarded." He hands you a wrapper containing **thirty guineas in banknotes**. "Do not find yourself on the wrong side," he warns you. "Madame History is severe."

Leave the offices...   **308**

☙ 1083 ☙
You manage to remain unnoticed by the guildsmen and lower yourself down into the shed. You have a brief window to grab what you can and get away. Roll a dice to see what you find.

Score 1-2   a **velosteamer's helmet (MOT+2)**
Score 3-4   a **strongbox**
Score 5-6   **welding tools** and **titanium alloy**

Leave the compound...   **487**

☙ 1084 ☙
The landlord takes your money and leads you through to a room at the rear of the inn, overlooking the yard. Here you can rest, leave belongings and plan your ambushes on the unwary travellers of the road. If you wish to leave anything here, write it into the box below and you will be able to collect it on your return. Note this passage number before proceeding.

```



```

Tend to your wounds...	**33**
Open a strongbox...	**138**
Return to the parolour...	**640**
Leave the inn...	**1047**

☙ 1085 ☙
Considering that your birthright was wealth and privilege, disregarding all that for the benefit of the common man may seem idealistic to some. However, it was a moral necessity for you: there was no way to remain part of a parasitical, controlling class and to retain any self-respect. Now you will do what you can, whenever you can, to convince the rich and powerful to fulfill their responsibility to society - by force, guile or gallantry. The likes of the Tenneys of Mongewell Park, the Earls of Macclesfield at Shirburn Castle and the Monsbergs of Coombe Park are all families of privilege who must play their part in improving the lives of the poor - or pay a heavy toll.

You have in your possession a **blunderpistol (ACC 6)**, a **rapier (PAR 4)**, a **mask** and a **letter of introduction**. Your ability scores are:

RUTHLESSNESS	4
ENGINEERING	3
MOTORING	3
INGENUITY	4
NIMBLENESS	4
GALLANTRY	6

Turn to...   **1440**

☙ 1086 ☙
You are handed over to the Constables, barely breathing but still able to receive their punishment. This is how they like their prisoners best - unable to resist.

Turn to...   **13**

☙ 1087 ☙
The little medical education you have allows you to do what you can for your cell-mates and yourself. There is no treatment you can offer, least of all within the gaol, but you make the prisoners as comfortable as you can, beg and argue through the bars for willow-bark, clean water, candles and clean cloths.

Many of the prisoners die. You survive, weakened and greatly disturbed by the suffering you have observed. Eventually the guards re-open the cell, remove the final bodies, and marvel at your emaciated figure.

Turn to...   **1077**

☙ 1088 ☙
You are recognised by the poor of the city - if not by face, then by your mighty Ferguson velosteam.

"Steam Highwayman," cries one woman, "Help us! Look around you at our squalor!"

Vow to help the poor of Oxford...	**1127**
Leave them...	**688**

❧ 1089 ❧

The night is falling and you will undoubtedly shock the driver with your sudden appearance. Make a RUTHLESSNESS roll of difficulty 9 to halt the wagon.

Successful RUTHLESSNESS roll!	**1425**
Failed RUTHLESSNESS roll!	**1342**

❧ 1090 ❧

Note **passage number 430**. A careful watch allows you to notice all the comings and goings of the family of Stonor House - Lord Stonor, his wife and daughter. When the steam-carriage returns, late in the evening, you step out into the roadway to make your challenge. Make a RUTHLESSNESS roll of difficulty 15.

Successful RUTHLESSNESS roll!	**1114**
Failed RUTHLESSNESS roll!	**782**

❧ 1091 ❧

If you have the codeword *Blended*, turn to **1073** immediately. Otherwise, read on.

The foreman doffs his cap when you enter the hallway. The house rings with the sound of chisels and hammers as masons and panellers work hard to get the place ready for you to move in. You and the foreman discuss progress on the construction works. If you are **moored at Shiplake House** and have a unit or more of **furniture** as cargo, remove it and tick the boxes below.

❑ A delivery of building stone (*Bought* or *Clapper*)
❑ ❑ Two units of **furniture** shipped by river
❑ **£108 13s** for wages

If all the boxes are ticked, gain the codeword *Blended* and turn to **1073** immediately. Otherwise, you must continue to exercise patience.

Head to your boat...	
(moored at Shiplake House)	471
Ride toward Henley...	355
Steam towards Sonning Bridge...	682

❧ 1092 ❧

A strong smell begins to emanate from your saddle-bags: it is the fish you have been carrying with you all this time. It has begun to rot: you must remove it from your **possessions** before riding on.

Carry on up the road to North Stoke...	515
Ride straight through, heading north...	860

❧ 1093 ❧

You park up your velosteam and take a stroll into the colleges. After only a few steps, a burly porter prevents your entrance. "No visitors!" he barks. "Closed for examinations!"

You return to find a parking fine notice attached to your velosteam.

Rip it off...	688

❧ 1094 ❧

The rich arms-trader is at your mercy. You can take his **pocket watch**, his **hamper** and **twenty guineas in banknotes**. Note that you will now be **Wanted by the Constables** if you are not already.

Steam away...	855

❧ 1095 ❧

Barsali recognises you as you fly past. "Constables?" he shouts. "Don't worry - I'll slow them down." He drags his caravans out to block the road and then sets to work 'mending' their roadwheels. Your pursuers will not find your trail so easily.

Turn to...	308

❧ 1096 ❧

You find a man in a shabby coat, his arms stretched out like a scarecrow with woodland birds on his sleeves and hat. They fly off as you approach. "You got anything to eat?" he asks. If you have any **food** or **drink**, turn to **1145** immediately.

Ride away...	749

❧ 1097 ❧

Gain a **telescope**. It folds neatly inside itself and has its own brass lens-cap to match. Taking the leather case would be a little more tricky as the chief surveyor is still wearing it.

Continue on the road...	62

❧ 1098 ❧

☐

If the box is empty, tick it and read on. If it is already ticked, turn to **1452** immediately.

You find Sackler at the workings and there have your suspicions confirmed. He looks very busy and has hired a few men to labour for the day, but the whole procedure is an elaborate ruse to milk money from the too-credulous nobleman. There is no silver and precious little lead.

He smiles greasily at you. "You don't have to tell anyone this. We could go into partnership... This could be worth a lot of money to you. Say... a hundred guineas?"

Accept the offer...	1121
Force Sackler to split the profits with you...	1148
Go straight to Earl Brigg...	
(letter of introduction)	1110
Leave the place...	313

❧ 1099 ❧

She takes the money gratefully and tears come to her eyes. You sternly warn her to be wise - to make it last - to find a way of making more that will not put her at risk. Gain the codeword *Bonny*.

Put her ashore...	495

❧ 1100 ❧

The stone broker takes the **tally stick** from you (remove it from your possessions) and looks through his ledger. Roll a dice to see how much your legitimate business has earned you.

Score 1-2	**£10 14s**
Score 3-4	**£25 6s**
Score 5	**£30 18**
Score 6	**£35 7s**

The broker pays you in coin, of course.

Return to Henley...	702

❧ 1101 ❧

☐

If the box above is empty, tick it now and read on. If it is already ticked, turn to **28** immediately, as you have already drawn this building!

Taking your pencil in hand, you make a fair stab at reproducing the proportions of the western windows, the open-structured wooden porch and the decorated bell-hanging on the eastern end. In all it makes a charming set of sketches. Tick one box in your **sketchpad**.

Leave the church...	28

❧ 1102 ❧

To arrive with an air of sufficient aplomb and entitlement, you must make a GALLANTRY roll of difficulty 13, adding 1 if you possess a **top hat** or **fur coat**.

Successful GALLANTRY roll...	1220
Failed GALLANTRY roll...	430

❧ 1103 ❧

"Steer alongside!" you call to the mate. Then, at the moment the gap looks leapable, you spring onto the long roof of the steamer and draw your weapons! One pirate falls to your first blow and splashes into the river: they were not expecting a rescue!

Sky pirates	Weapons: **sabres (PAR 3)**
Parry:	8
Nimbleness:	5
Toughness:	10

Victory!	1079
Defeat!	528

❧ 1104 ❧

Your stake is soon lost and you retreat from the table to the jeers of the other players. Lord Barrymore is particularly scathing.

Turn to...	702

❧ 1105 ❧

You ready your weapons and throw open the door of the steam carriage. "Surrender all your valuables," you cry, "Or your life's blood!" Make a RUTHLESSNESS roll of difficulty 10.

Successful RUTHLESSNESS roll!	1168
Failed RUTHLESSNESS roll!	1139

❧ 1106 ❧

If you are the **Friend of Prior Horace**, turn to **1247** immediately. Otherwise, read on.

The Prior is able to give you a short amount of time. He is busy administrating the business of the priory, taking charge of the spiritual well-being of his flock and managing the interaction of the order with the temporal authorities.

Make a donation to the order... (**£10**)	1282
Give a gift... (**jewelled bible**)	1382
Ask about the hospital airship...	1307
Return to the cloister...	642

❧ 1107 ❧

In the slums of Oxford you come across countless beggars and desperate children. One manages to take a coin from your pocket and dash away down the street. Roll a dice to see what he took:

Score 1-2	A florin - **2s**
Score 3-4	A crown - **5s**
Score 5-6	A double guinea - **£2 2s**

If you have more than 20 **solidarity points**, turn to **1088**.

| Leave the slums... | 688 |

❧ 1108 ❧

You return to the quarry and show the foreman the lease. "Mister foreman," you say triumphantly, "Call back your quarrymen. Tell them to get cutting and I'll see that they're paid." Remove the **quarry lease** from your possessions and gain the codeword *Breaker*.

In a short time, the men are back from their villages and the steam-crane is working again. The ringing sound of iron on stone sings out over the valley.

The quarry will produce a fine stone for public buildings and large houses. To profit from this business, you will need to return periodically to pay the wages - the foreman tells you that you can expect to need to pay **£15** at a time. A broker in Henley will sell the stone for you and keep the profit. It looks like you have set up in an honest trade at last.

| Ride north... | 863 |
| Head south to Wargrave... | 418 |

❧ 1109 ❧

The cold water chills you through but you are able to keep your head above water. Your mate hauls you back on board as the patrol-boat steams away, then insists you head into the cabin and warm yourself. In spite of the warm steam-stove and dry clothes, you

find you awake later in the night with a **fever (NIM-1 ING-2)** (note it on your **Adventure Sheet**). You will suffer a reduction of 1 from your NIMBLENESS and 2 from your INGENUITY until you can find some way to lift it.

| Turn to... | 495 |

❧ 1110 ❧

Remove the **letter of introduction** from your **possessions**.

When you are brought to see the Earl you immediately explain about the unscrupulous scoundrel you met in the Flowerpot. "It is very clear to me," you explain, "That he means to fleece you." The Earl narrows his eyes. To convince him you can either make an INGENUITY roll of difficulty 13 or a GALLANTRY roll of difficulty 12.

| Successful INGENUITY or GALLANTRY roll! | 1229 |
| Failed roll! | 1137 |

❧ 1111 ❧

Remembering the song of the one-armed veteran in the John Barleycorn and the other tales of suffering you have heard from the men of the Oxford and Bucks Light Infantry, you are resolved to find the records that reveal who was in command, that dreadful day in Valencia when hundreds were ordered needlessly to their deaths. You will need to break in at night, using equipment to open the doors or climb the walls, then avoid numerous armed guards and get inside the document store. A set of punchcards of the correct sort will be needed to access the records and translate them from their coded format. Only then will you have the information to understand what happened that dreadful day.

Try to unlock the doors...	1195
Scale the walls...	1204
Return when better prepared...	270

❧ 1112 ❧

After hearing some clumping and banging overhead, your mate gives his knock on the panelling and you slide out. "Looks like money well spent, skipper," he says. "But I wasn't able to stop'em confiscating some of our cargo." Remove one unit of cargo from your **Adventure Sheet**.

| Steam on... | 495 |

❧ 1113 ❧

Your cellmate introduces himself as Simon Shackles - a clerk who managed the Duke of Cornwall's investments in shipping and air-freight. "I was making him all sorts of money," he complains, "Left, right and centre. But one bad investment and the whole thing came crashing down and I took the blame." He explains his methods in detail and you listen carefully to the workings of the stock exchange, the ways in which traders out-manoeuvre and trick one another, the great need for a risk-taking temperament and above all, luck. Gain the codeword *Bullring*.

Turn to...   1077

❧ 1114 ❧

The terrified driver hauls on the brake lever and you tear open the door. Inside is Lord Stonor's terrified daughter and her chaperone. You grip the young lady's arm, pull her onto the gravel and brandish your weapons. "We are going to have a little chat with your father," you tell her."

A few minutes later you stand outside the house. "Lord Stonor!" you cry. "A simple, fair exchange. Give me Professor Benner and I will return your daughter. Otherwise this drive will run with her blood."

Lord Stonor sees that you are serious. Initially he tries to talk, to discover who you are, how you know about the Professor, to make some sort of deal, but then he realises that the old man is worthless to him anyway. The Professor is brought up from the cellar, shambling, half-mad, coughing consumptively and still in chains. You release the girl, who runs to her father and scoop up the old man before he falls to the ground. "Take me to Elvendon Priory," he says indistinctly. "The monks there know me."

Turn to...   1122

❧ 1115 ❧

You come across a family on the road. They used to be in service with a noble house in the region but since the destruction of their owner's estate they have struggled. The father carries his youngest daughter, dead.

"We're looking for hallowed ground where they'll let us lay her to rest," he says. "But then we must be moving on to Oxford. There'll be some work for us there, surely."

Turn to...   990

❧ 1116 ❧

At the close of the evening you come out marginally ahead. As well as your **ten guineas in banknotes** you receive **£4 8s** in small coins. The Earl has most of the rest of the money on the table and it seems that his games normally go that way.

Leave the theatre...   702

❧ 1117 ❧
☐

If the box above is empty, tick it and read on. If it is already ticked, you have already made observations here and can gain little more: you must head to another Telegraph Guild tower and turn to **633** immediately.

Peering through your lenses and noting down every pattern and sequence you can see, you barely notice the darkening sky until the telegraphists at Caversham light oil lamps behind the shutters. Hours have passed and you have pages of notes. If you possess a set of **telegraph observations ☐ ☐**, tick one of the boxes. If you do not own such an item, add **telegraph observations ☐ ☐** to your possessions. You will need to observe the codes on two more towers to complete your task.

Leave the tree...   633

❧ 1118 ❧

You arouse a great deal of interest riding into camp on your fine Ferguson velosteam. Few of the labourers have ever seen anything like it and they are all machine-mad. They have recently finished building the embankments, cuttings and bridge that carry the Imperial Western Railway over the river here and will soon be moving on, but some of the younger men have begun settling into families with the local girls and are in their own negotiations of staying or going.

Several clever mechanics and machine-men work here, including one older man known for his inventiveness and skill with intricate mechanisms. Hearty food sells for a good price too: the navvies are paid well for their work and will not be satisfied with 'cheap country stuff'.

Food and Drink	To buy	To sell
wheel of cheese	-	**£3**
pork pie	-	10s

Clothing	To buy	To sell
mask	4s	-
engineer's gloves (ENG +1)	£3	£2 5s
engineer's gauntlets (ENG+2)	-	£5
velosteamer's helmet (MOT+2)	£8	£6 12s

Tools	To buy	To sell
rope	4s	2s
shovel	8s	6s
adjustable wrench (ENG+1)	£1 8s	18s
explosives	£1 4s	-
grappling iron	12s	8s
telescope	£4 10s	£3 5s

Talk politics with the navvies...	**1361**
Leave the camp...	**584**

✎ 1119 ✐

The foreman is happy to see you. If you can pay him **£12** for the men's wages, he will give you **tally stick 712**, to take to the broker in Henley. There you will be able to collect your profits.

Ship a load of stone...	
(moored at Temple Coombe quarry)	1343
Go aboard your barge...	
(moored at Temple Coombe quarry)	131
Ride north...	**863**
Head south to Wargrave...	**418**

✎ 1120 ✐

The river is an unpredictable and fickle friend: the Thames may carry you and your cargo without complaint for most of the time, but now there is no doubt who has the mastery. You only just manage to keep afloat but many of your possessions are swept away. For each item on your **Adventure Sheet**, roll a dice and on a score of 5-6 you must discard that item.

Eventually the mate drags you back on board. "Bad news, skipper. I couldn't stop them from confiscating the cargo." You will need to remove any **cargo** from your **Adventure Sheet** as well.

Turn to...	**495**

✎ 1121 ✐

"Excellent, excellent," says Sackler. "Now I haven't got the cash here, oh no, not all of it." He hands you **five guineas in banknotes**. "That's a start. Now I'll give you a cheque for the rest. Changeable at any bank, mmm?" He also gives you **Sackler's cheque**.

Turn to...	**313**

✎ 1122 ✐

You bring the sad news of Andrea Rathbone's misery and death to her parents. They are heartbroken, but when you tell them of how you pursued and punished Ennis, they have some light return to them.

"He will do no more evil to girls like Andrea," you tell them.

"But others will..." says her father. "Oh, 'tis a wicked world."

They thank you. The story of your persistent vengeance will hopefully do much to shake the nobility's belief in their untouchability. Will it strike fear into the hearts of wrongdoers? Either way, your reputation will be greatly increased by this. Gain **two solidarity points** and remove the codeword *Avatar*.

Turn to...	**977**

✎ 1123 ✐

Your play is exceptionally sharp tonight - and undoubtedly luck (or trickery) is on your side. The hands fall your way one after another and Lord Barrymore puts into his pocket to try and extricate himself. Soon that money is gone too and, as he calls for more wine, it seems that the show down below is drawing to a close. You have won a total of **forty guineas in banknotes** and **£8 12s** in coin. Barrymore pores over the cards. "If you were noble," he says slowly, "I might have something to say about this conduct. But one does not bandy accusations with the servant classes." He draws his rapier and puts the point to your throat. "Return the money."

"Never. I am your match."	**1183**
"Of course, my Lord."	**1150**

✎ 1124 ✐

You settle down to help tune and improve the engines. The brother in charge details what he wants you to do. "I've seen that velosteam of yours outside. Do you know that you can get a gas pressuriser for that? If you do, we can use those parts to finish these engines."

If you have the **gas pressuriser** customisation on your velosteam and want to sacrifice it for the monks' project, erase it from your **Adventure Sheet** and turn to **1154**. Otherwise you will simply be able to tinker with the engine in much the same way as any other half-skilled engineer.

Return to the cloister...   **642**

❦ 1125 ❧
You roll your velosteam into the path of the approaching wagons and display your weapons. "Stand and deliver!" you roar. Make a RUTHLESSNESS roll of difficulty 11, adding 1 if you are **Wanted by the Atmospheric Union**.

Successful RUTHLESSNESS roll!   **1162**
Failed RUTHLESSNESS roll!   **782**

❦ 1126 ❧
The paymaster is a shallow man, impressed by two things: rank and money. Make a GALLANTRY roll of difficulty 17, adding 1 to your roll for each guinea (**£1 1s**) you offer him.

Successful GALLANTRY roll!   **1181**
Failed GALLANTRY roll!   **270**

❦ 1127 ❧
You make a clear and public vow to help change the conditions in these slums - but what lasting effect can you hope to have? How will you, a mere road-thief, overturn the centuries of injustice and oppression and see the meek inherit the earth? Gain the codeword *Barnet*.

Turn to...   **688**

❦ 1128 ❧
The Earl greets you warmly. "I can't thank you enough for ridding me of that leech!" he says. "I'm still landscaping the workings, but maybe I think I can turn them into an oriental garden. I've been offered some excellent plants - exclusively from Japan, you know?"

You can stay with the Earl for as long as you like. He has a suite at your disposal and offers you the use of his garage to mend your machine. You may leave items here if you please, writing them in the box below and collecting them on your return. This is also a safe place to leave any money. Note this **passage number** before making any further decisions.

Tend your wounds...   **33**
Mend your velosteam...   **180**
Leave the house...   **313**

❦ 1129 ❧
The railway bridge is a fine brick structure, much like the one at Maidenhead, but because it crosses the river obliquely it has a skew to its arches. From underneath the courses run almost diagonally, neither in line with the arch or the ground, but this gives the construction its great strength. The navvies nearby have only recently finished work here and the broad-gauge tracks are fresh and free of weeds. If you have the codeword *Boosting*, turn to **1430**.

As you stand looking at the view, a pillar of steam rises in the distance, announcing the approach of a railway train.

Return to the roadside...   **584**

❦ 1130 ❧
"Come out and talk face to face," you say. "You are a privileged man. Consider the men you have commanded - the many who died when you lived. Don't you have a responsibility for them? For their families?" Make a GALLANTRY roll of difficulty 10.

Succesful GALLANTRY roll!   **1157**
Failed GALLANTRY roll!   **1139**

❦ 1131 ❧
The gate swings shut behind you. Which way will you turn?

Towards Goring...   **487**
Towards Woodcote...   **520**
Towards Whitchurch...   **488**

❧ 1132 ☙

The guests quieten as the game enters the closing phase. Your opponents are playing well and have only a few more shots to complete the course.

Distract your opponents...	**674**
Joke with the guests...	**1469**
Insist upon silence for your shot...	**95**

❧ 1133 ☙

A well-placed shot will bring the road-train to a halt: you know that these Atmospheric Union locomotives are fitted with a deadman's handle and that as soon as the driver loosens their grip, the machine will slow and stop. Make an ACCURACY roll of difficulty 12.

Successful ACCURACY roll!	**1162**
Failed ACCURACY roll!	**1221**

❧ 1134 ☙

As the game was being set up you noticed that several of the pitch-edge flagpoles were weakly staked. Now you prepare to use them to your advantage. A heavy blow with your mallet sends the hard black ball directly at the nearest post, knocking it out of the ground and ricocheting back into play. The post topples, tips your partner's blue through the nearby hoop, cuts your opponents red and yellow off from the centre post and guides your ball gently through the hoop and back to your feet. The guests applaud and the Viscountess cheers. "That's how to play croquet! Take your follow-on, finish them!"

Another shot, much simpler, means that you have now passed another **two hoops**.

Turn to...	**1132**

❧ 1135 ☙

"So what have you done about it all?" asks a deserter angrily. "Is that officer still living?"

"She's dead," you reply.

The old soldiers are quiet for a while. "Maybe she'll meet some of our boys on the other side," one says grimly. "They'll be pleased to see her."

Leave them...	**102**

❧ 1136 ☙

The haulier pulls over without resistance and watches glumly as you rifle through the wagons. Roll a dice to see what you find:

Score 1-2   Several **bottles of wine**, **£1 2s** and a **shovel**

Score 3-4   An **adjustable wrench (ENG+1)** and a **box of cigars**

Score 5-6   A **strongbox**

Turn to...	**noted passage**

❧ 1137 ☙

"What nonsense!" exclaims the Earl. "You can't just come up here making accusations like that! Get off my land this instant, do you hear?" Remove the code-word *Botanical*.

Turn to...	**313**

❧ 1138 ☙

You will need to out-run the Constables. Mounted on their powerful Imperial velosteams, they may not have your Ferguson's responsiveness or manoeuvrability but they do have straight line speed. You will need to milk every ounce of power from your engine - or provide a truly tempting distraction. Make a MOTORING roll of difficulty 12, adding 2 if you have a **strengthened boiler** and 1 for each **£2** that you discard on the road.

Successful MOTORING roll!	**688**
Failed MOTORING roll!	**13**

❧ 1139 ☙

The officer is trained for war but unprepared for an ambush. He is not scared of a fight but he was hoping for a relaxing period of leave. Your appearance has surprised and frustrated him.

Officer	Weapon: **sabre (PAR 3)**
Parry:	8
Nimbleness:	5
Toughness:	3

Victory!	**1168**
Defeat!	**1272**

❧ 1140 ❧

The gate to the compound is open, and as you turn in and put your foot down, several armed Constables and guards in the Coal Board black and yellow appear from the outbuildings. Their guns are levelled and ready - it would be folly to resist.

Turn to... **13**

❧ 1141 ❧

You make your way directly to Coombe Park, a short distance from Whitchurch. Forcing your way past the gatehouse and up the steps to the front door, you call out a challenge. "Monsberg! Vengeance is come!"

He steps outside. "I have no need to dignify your desire to die on my blade," he says, "But I will hurt you to teach others not to interfere." He immediately takes up a trained swordsman's posture.

Viscount Monsberg	Weapon: **rapier (PAR 4)**
Parry:	14
Nimbleness:	10
Toughness:	4

Victory!	**1245**
Defeat!	**1190**

❧ 1142 ❧

Gain the codeword *Bursting*. A box of matches and a candlestick allow you to proceed and in one bay you find the barely-sleeping, shallow-breathing wreck of a white-haired man, chained to a wall beside a drawing board. His hair is long and lank, his eyes wild and his fingers... His fingers are crippled by the tearing out of his nails.

You wake him gently, but he still starts and shrinks behind raised arms. "Hussssh," you say. "You shall be free once more."

He shivers and sniffles. "Free? I have not the strength to live again."

"I will tend to you," you reply.

"It is too late," he replies. "Light or dark make no difference to me now. I do not feel the cold or the heat." He puts out his hand into the candle flame without flinching and you see that he is quite correct.

"I cannot leave you here," you reply.

The chain is attached to a spike in the wall. With an bar from the wine cellar opposite, you lever the rotten iron out of the wall and gently lift the prisoner from his rotten bed of straw. He seems to weigh less than the manacles around his wrists.

A low door unbolts to allow you up steps into the yard. The moonlight and the clean night's dew bring a clean shock to the old man, and he begins to weep. "I did not think to see the stars again," he says. "Can you take me away from here? Get me to the priory. They are good people there."

"Which one?"

"Elvendon. Take me there."

Turn to... **1356**

❧ 1143 ❧

"Rather late to take a joy-ride, is it not?" The officer is of the sarcastic type. His corporal, who has flicked through the printofits of wanted criminals, shakes his head. The officer continues. "There are dangerous types on the road here. Where are you travelling? We will escort you to your destination."

"I'll remain here. Your men need refreshment."(**£1 2s**)	**968**
"I am travelling to Stokenchurch."	**308**
"I am on my way to Mill End."	**112**
"I am heading for Henley."	**702**

❧ 1144 ❧

If you have a **quarry lease** or the codeword *Breaker*, turn to **1179** immediately. Otherwise, read on.

Amongst the cattle auctions, the furniture sales and the arguments over grain prices, a landowner is trying to sell the lease for Temple Coombe Quarry on the road to Wargrave. He has several interested bidders.

Bid high...

(**£42** or **forty guineas in banknotes**)	**1317**
Leave the auction...	**605**

❧ 1145 ❧

Remove the **food** or **drink** from your **possessions**. The shabby man wolfs down the food and sits happily on the leaf-litter. He is an animal-charmer and tells you of how he gains the trust of animals through gentle, soothing melodies and calm movements. Gain a level of **animal friendship**.

Turn to... **749**

❦ 1146 ❧

The paymaster is uninterested in your attempt to have justice for Fred Lamb. "What you need to understand," he says drily, "Is that there is a protocol for these things. This is a purely military matter."

Offer the man a bribe...	1126
Threaten him...	1156
Leave the office...	270

❦ 1147 ❧

The Bay of Biscay. The Cape of Finisterre. Porto. Lisbon. Then, after a stop of a few days, Funchal. The airship is prepared for the long oceanic flight. The navigators hope to find a tailwind, or the band of still air known for centuries as the Doldrums. Then, with luck and skill, they will make landfall in Puerto Rico, refuel once more and be in Belize within a week.

One evening, two nights out across the Atlantic, you return to your cabin after dinner to see the small but unmistakeable signs of someone searching through your possessions. Unlike some of the passengers with trunks and trunks laid down in the cargo section beneath the coal, everything you have with you is in this room, together with Alphaea Harpsden's emerald jewellery. The question is, where did you decide to put the jewellery?

Behind a panel in the cabin wall...	1277
Inside the Captain's safe...	1306
I kept it with me at all times...	1319

❦ 1148 ❧

You draw your weapons and grab Sackler by the throat. "If you don't give me an even share, I'll tell the Earl all about your little scheme," you say. He struggles to breathe and nods.

"Come back in a week or so and I'll have your share ready," he replies.

Turn to...   313

❦ 1149 ❧

You sneak into the castle grounds by night and follow the laundrymaid's directions to Uncle Max's cell. The door opens, squeaking noisily, yet you are still forced to enter the cell and shake Uncle Max awake. He seems neither surprised nor excited to be rescued, but follows you back out the way you came, over the wall and into the alleys of the town. "Any chance you could lend me a few bob?" he asks. Remove the codeword *Boorish* and gain the codeword *Burdensome*.

You will have to return the keys - but if you possess any **plaster of paris**, you will be able to make an **impression of Wallingford gaol keys**.

Turn to...   270

❦ 1150 ❧

You count out the **forty guineas in banknotes** and the **£8 12s** and push it across the table. Lord Barrymore laughs scornfully. "A coward and a cheat," he says.

Your reputation will suffer for this. Lower your RUTHLESSNESS score by 1.

Turn to...   702

❦ 1151 ❧

Silence suddenly descends upon the lawn. The guests are in shock - did you just accuse a lady of cheating in public? If you have a RUTHLESSNESS score of 8 or higher, or 15 or more solidarity points, turn to **1504** immediately. Otherwise, read on.

The lady's partner walks up to you as strikes you in the face. "How dare you!" he cries. "My wife is no cheat and you are nothing but low-born scum."

The insult has been given. The croquet lawn is cleared to become a duelling green. You must fight!

Croquet player	Weapon: **rapier (PAR 4)**
Parry:	9
Nimbleness:	5
Toughness:	4

Victory!	1497
Defeat!	999

❦ 1152 ❧

The explorer collapses, clutching his bleeding side. "You've bested me. Take my gold, take my equipment, just don't take my journals." You may rob him of **£7 2s**, a **lantern**, a **rope**, a **shovel**, a pair of **binoculars**, a **silk scarf** and a handwritten book labelled **Travels of a Gentleman**. You will now be **Wanted by the Constables** unless you have a **mask**.

Turn to...   **noted passage**

❧ 1153 ❧

You enter the Flowerpot and drift into the rear parlour. After some eavesdropping and putting two and two together, you identify the driver and guard of the private carriage. You slip into a seat next to them and drop a few hints about the way they might supplement their pay while preserving their own skins should they see any threatening figures on the roads.

Make an INGENUITY roll of difficulty 10, adding 1 for each **£1** you give the pair to convince them.

Successful INGENUITY roll!	**1160**
Failed INGENUITY roll!	**1177**

❧ 1154 ❧
☐ ☐

If either of the boxes above are empty, tick one and read on. If they are both ticked, turn to **642** immediately.

The parts are carefully stripped from your velosteam and used to improve the efficiency of the big engines. It seems that they are just what was needed. "Perfect!" says the monk in charge. "Thanks very much."

You have learnt a lot in the process: roll two dice and if the score is greater than your unimproved ENGINEERING ability, you may add 1 to that skill.

Return to the cloister...	**642**

❧ 1155 ❧

Bumping over ruts and roots, you charge through the woods down lanes and tracks with the sound of Constables' bells behind you. A fallen tree blocks the way - will you ride the up the steep side of the holloway or can you ram the blockage out of the way before your pursuers catch up with you? Make a MOTORING roll of difficulty 13, adding 2 if you have a **ramming beak**.

Successful MOTORING roll!	**628**
Failed MOTORING roll!	**13**

❧ 1156 ❧

You lean over the desk and look the paymaster in the eye. "I am sure that if you take another look at the case, there may be factors you have overlooked."

He licks his lips nervously and eyes your weapons. "You would do nothing here. There are armed men all around..." Make a RUTHLESSNESS roll of difficulty 14.

Successful RUTHLESSNESS roll!	**1198**
Failed RUTHLESSNESS roll!	**1207**

❧ 1157 ❧

The officer steps down. "I am proud of serving as a soldier," he says. "If you are truly taking money to the families of my soldiers, then I am not ashamed to contribute." He fishes in his pockets and takes out a bag of coins (**£2 8s**).

Ask him about his war service...	**1228**
Leave him by the road...	**1197**

❧ 1158 ❧

You are waiting in the bushes when the charges blow with a muffled thud and a sudden water-spout. The ground shakes and the earthen retaining wall cracks. A sudden torrent of water streams out, widens, roars and tears down the hillside: gain the codeword *Bust* and a level of **explosives expert**.

A spotlight flashes on and the bright limelight beam sweeps the compound, then picks you out. You will have to be very quick to escape now! Make a NIMBLENESS roll of difficulty 12.

Successful NIMBLENESS roll!	**1176**
Failed NIMBLENESS roll!	**1201**

❧ 1159 ❧
☐

If the box above is empty, tick it and read on. If it is already ticked, turn to **1172** immediately.

The mate steers you into shore where you find two bodies in a clearing beneath the beeches. They are both noblewomen and both dead. Beside them you find a pair of **duelling pistols (ACC 7).**

Steam on through the night...	**495**

❧ 1160 ❧

☐

If the box above is empty, tick it and read on. If it is already ticked, turn to **1186** immediately.

The driver and guard look at one another, then wordlessly nod in agreement. "We should hope to recognise you," they say. "Give us fair warning, and no blood to be spilt."

It looks like you have recruited accomplices in your robbery. Gain the codeword *Blarney*.

Return to the parlour...   (2s)   **348**
Leave the pub...   **280**

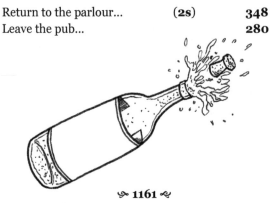

❧ 1161 ❧

A short walk brings you to the State Office, where you ask for Gill and are shown into his wooden cabinet. He seems to be more important than a simple clerk.

"I'll take these off your hands," he says. Remove the **emerald jewellery** from your **possessions** - in return, he gives you **£15** and writes a cheque for Alphaea. "I'll send this to her myself," he says guardedly. "But I suggest you head down to find Mr Mawkins."

Turn to...   **1445**

❧ 1162 ❧

You are free to pick through the supplies intended for the Atmospheric Union base at Rotherfield Greys. Roll a dice to see what you find.

Score 1   A **strongbox**
Score 2   A **roll of oiled silk** and six **bottles of champagne**
Score 3   Some **welding tools** and **copper pipe**
Score 4   Some bars of **titanium alloy** and a **net**
Score 5   three **picnic hampers** and a **pineapple**
Score 6   **waterproof paint** and a **rope ladder**

You will now be **Wanted by the Atmospheric Union** unless you have a **mask**.

Turn to...   **noted passage**

❧ 1163 ❧

A rickety steam-wagon with a cattle-carrying compartment built onto its rear chassis splashes through the puddles. A driver - probably the owner of the cows - and a younger fireman are fighting to keep the machine moving. It seems that their pressure is low.

Ask them about cattle markets...   **1169**
Offer to help them with their engine...   **1178**
Let them pass...   **noted passage**

❧ 1164 ❧

It is not an easy business to match speed with the engine, particularly after the driver notices you coming alongside and begins to weave the road-train across the tarmac. You will have to keep the velosteam very steady while leaning across to unpin the wagon. Make a MOTORING roll of difficulty 13.

Successful MOTORING roll!   **1162**
Failed MOTORING roll!   **1249**

❧ 1165 ❧

Airship crew smoke like chimneys when they are aground and the fine tobacco helps them warm to you. A pat on the shoulder, a joke and a laugh and refilled drink all show that you are convincing them. It may be an expensive way to win friends and influence people, unless you have stolen the cigars in the first place.

Turn to...   **1495**

❧ 1166 ❧

The Captain falls to your blade and the First Officer cowers. "Now do as I say - or you will follow him."

Message the Compact...   **1196**
Fly into the west...   *Princes of the West 551*

❧ 1167 ❧

"Oi! What are you doing?" A Telegraph Guild apprentice emerging from the pub catches sight of you approaching the carriage. He draws his sabre: you must fight!

Apprentice   Weapon: **sabre (PAR 3)**
Parry: 7
Nimbleness: 4
Toughness: 4

Victory!   **280**
Defeat!   **15**

ᔐ 1168 ᔑ

The officer is at your mercy: you can now rob him of his **regimental key**, **£3 5s** and a **gold ring**, as well as his weapon. He shivers, clutching at his wounds.

Ask him about his war service...   **1228**
Leave him by the road...   **1197**

ᔐ 1169 ᔑ

You wave to the farmer, who looks up in surprise and slows the wagon. He smiles as you approach. "Filthy weather. Nobody out to rob?"

"Going far?" you ask.

"That's right. We'd be droving these beasts otherwise, but I want to keep 'em fat if I can."

"Where are you heading?"

"Wycombe, most like. Fair prices there for prime beef. But maybe I'll go as far as Smithfield, if I can get coal cheap somewhere between here Piddington."

"This will get you a good price for coal."
    (Guildsman's medallion)   **1188**
"I hope you get your price."   **noted passage**

ᔐ 1170 ᔑ

The explosion sends a colossal tower of water into the air, but when the smoke and steam subside, you see that the reservoir itself is still holding. The guards and watermen are rushing around, distracted for the time being, so you are able to make a quick getaway in the opposite corner of the compound and remount your velosteam.

Turn to...   **710**

ᔐ 1171 ᔑ

The Constables are simply distracted and you take the opportunity to slip past on your velosteam. One looks around, frowning, but he is quickly bothered by a freighter trying to get an entry stamp on his pass.

Ride into Oxford...   **688**

ᔐ 1172 ᔑ

The gunfire proves to be a gang who have waylaid a traveller here in the mist. On your approach they flee into the dark, leaving a stripped corpse and no sign of their presence.

Return to your boat and head on upstream...   **495**

ᔐ 1173 ᔑ

You bring your set of plans to the officers of the Guild and describe how you found the weak spots in the Coal Board's construction. "Very well," says a bored officer, "But why didn't you blow them then and there? I suppose we'll have to find someone more committed." They take the **plans** (remove them from your **possessions**) and give you a reward of **£5** for your deeds.

Turn to...   **770**

ᔐ 1174 ᔑ

You settle down at the fireside and begin to talk with the deserters. After hearing of their difficulties, hiding here in the woods, you explain what you discovered by decoding the orders you found in the regimental headquarters.

"Orders always come down the chain," says one soldier. "Someone told her to send us in on the attack. That's how it works."

Another shakes his head. "If that was the case, then why were we sent by ourselves? Why wasn't there any support? I say she was just looking to move the line forward and get herself a commendation."

Leave the men...   **102**

ᔐ 1175 ᔑ

Earl Brigg is known as a keen lawnsman and his first shots are cool and tidy. You manage to rebound together and he sets you up to take both of your balls through the second hoop in a single bound. "Well done," he says calmly. "But let us keep our heads." He is a completely different character on the sports pitch to the easily-swayed spendthrift you see on the estate. Note that you have now passed **two hoops.**

Turn to...   **548**

‹ 1176 ›

The wire fence rattles and shudders as you grasp at it, but before the gunshots start behind you, you are over and down with a thud! You race for your velosteam and head off into the night.

The Coal Board will not take this lightly: they will certainly be looking for you now, if they are not already. Add **Wanted by the Coal Board** to your **Wanted Statuses** if you do not already posses it.

Ride down Aston Hill...	**710**
Head for Piddington...	**8**
Head South towards Ibstone...	**977**

‹ 1177 ›

"Just who do you bleeding think you are?" asks the guard, picking up his shotgun. "We don't deal with the lowdown likes of you!" The others in the parlour eye you uneasily - you will have to beat a retreat to avoid a brawl.

Leave the pub...   **280**

‹ 1178 ›

You offer to help the farmer and his boy repressurise the underslung boiler built beneath their cab. Make an ENGINEERING roll of difficulty 10, adding 1 if you possess a **wrench** of any kind and adding 2 if you have a **high pressure valve.**

Successful ENGINEERING roll!	**1271**
Failed ENGINEERING roll!	**noted passage**

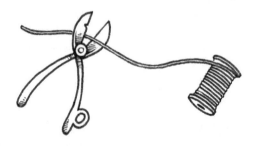

‹ 1179 ›

The main focus of today's auction is the sale of a house on the river below Shiplake Lock. The local nobility have all sent their agents to bid - mostly to prevent one another from getting their hands on it. In the end it sells for a vastly inflated price to an industrialist to whom money is no object, much to the disgust of the locals.

Return to the market...   **605**

‹ 1180 ›

If you have the codeword *Charity*, turn to 1203 immediately.

The Mother Superior looks at you sternly. "I know your reputation," she says. "Violence I abhor and the way of the Cross is the way of service - yet you can help us. Some months ago I despatched a team of sisters to London, to serve the communities of Bermondsey where there is great need. I have not heard from them since. Go and find them and bring me word of my sisters."

Leave the Convent...   **88**

‹ 1181 ›

The paymaster's eyes glint as he pockets your money. "I believe that, on reflection, there may have been a mistake in the young man's pension calculation." He turns to his ledgers, writes out a new form and hands you **pension statement 4590213**. Remove the codeword *Bottle*.

Leave the office...   **270**

‹ 1182 ›

The recipient of the parcel is the female driver of the colossal road-engine. In her goggles and cap, her features are hidden but there is something familiar about her. Is it her air of self-possession at the controls of the mighty machine, or is it the whisper of auburn hair that escapes her hat? She leans down from the driving plate to take the **urgent parcel** - remove it from your **possessions**.

"We needed these," she says, without telling you any further details, and flicks down a double-guinea (**£2 2s**). The massive machine shudders and slowly heads off through the gates.

Return to the city...   **688**

❧ 1183 ❧

"So. I must teach you a lesson."

As you draw your weapon and stand, the performers onstage stutter and stop. The musicians cease playing and then, in a moment of inspiration and a flurry of whispers, the conductor leads them in the Duellists' Mazurka.

Lord Barrymore	Weapon: **rapier (PAR 4)**
Parry:	11
Nimbleness:	7
Toughness:	3

Victory!	**1205**
Defeat!	**1086**

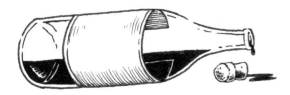

❧ 1184 ❧

The sound you have heard is a trio of fast-moving Constabulary velosteams. They are patrolling the region on the lookout for suspicious characters, thieves, deserters and highwaymen. If you are **Wanted by the Constables**, turn to **1219** immediately. Otherwise, read on.

When the Constables approach, you make a great show of nonchalance and surprise. They halt on the roadway and a goggled officer approaches you.

"What is your business here, citizen?"

"I am sketching..." (**sketchpad** ☐ ☐ ☐)	**1022**
"A picnic!" (**picnic hamper**)	**1055**
"Riding for pleasure, officer."	**1143**

❧ 1185 ❧
☐

If the box is ticked, turn to **1265** immediately. Otherwise, read on.

You stay in the chapel until all the monks have departed, giving the impression that you are devoutly persisting in prayer. Eventually the coast is clear and you are able to take the **gold cup** and a **pair of golden candlesticks**. You had better depart immediately.

Make your getaway... **1131**

❧ 1186 ❧

"We ain't doing this again," says the guard. "Questions was asked last time. It isn't worth the risk. We could lose our jobs - or get strung up." Any money you attempted to give them is returned and they pointedly ignore you. You will have to leave to avoid a scene.

Leave the pub... **280**

❧ 1187 ❧

When you are thrown into the common holding cell, a ragged but wild-eyed enthusiast approaches you.

"Comrade! We heard of your brave stand against the Constable. You even identified with the Compact in your interrogation. Now we will induct you into the Compact in truth as well as in name."

"But in prison, what difference will it make?"

"Nobody stays here forever, comrade! And we are as strong inside these walls as anywhere outside!"

"Where can I find you once I am released?"

"When we break out, you mean? You can find cadres in Goring and Reading. Wherever you see the drink called Vlaada Original advertised, the Compact is near."

Note that you are now a **Member of the Compact for Workers' Equality**.

Turn to... **1020**

❧ 1188 ❧

Remove the **Guildsman's medallion** from your possessions. The farmer catches it and smiles. "Now that will get me good coal indeed. I won't ask how you got hold of this." He and his engineer restart the locomotive. "I'm much obliged. Maybe I'll see you up in town." Gain the codeword *Baron*.

Turn to... **noted passage**

❧ 1189 ❧

The landlord recognises you as the trouble-maker who brought the Constables down about his ears. Parts of the building are still blackened ruins and he blames you! He pulls out a blunderbuss and fires it in your direction. Roll a dice to see what occurs.

Score 1-2	**two wounds**
Score 3-4	**one wound**
Score 5-6	Just a scratch

Whatever the outcome, you are no longer welcome here! If you now have **five wounds**, turn to **999**.

Turn to...   **308**

❧ 1190 ❧

As you fall to the gravel, the Viscount laughs with scorn. "You underestimated my skill with the blade. Now physician, heal thyself!"

You are dragged away by his servants and indeed given water and bandages: remove one **wound** immediately and convert it to a **scar**. However, you are still very weak and must find a place to rest and regain your strength.

Turn to...   **937**

❧ 1191 ❧

The driver is far from happy. "What you playing at? I ain't a bad man! I'm just doing my job. I don't set the fares, but I'll get the sack for this. My goodness - I can't just carry them all for free - fair's fair, matey?"

He opens up the mechanical till and gives everyone their fare back. A few try to claim they bought returns and then 'remember' the real state of affairs when you loom over them, but the short-lived joy of a free journey may be less satisfying than they think. Gain the codeword *Brilliant*.

Turn to...   **noted passage**

❧ 1192 ❧

"Oh, it's only you again," says the wharfmaster. "No problem here, carry on."

Turn to...   **630**

❧ 1193 ❧

You have no problem stopping the locobus. The driver trembles and a lady on the upper deck faints, or pretends to, crying "'Tis the Steam Highwayman!"

The upper deck is really the place for the poorest passengers. Downstairs, several of the better-off look fairly uncomfortable, but plenty of those aboard realise that they have nothing to lose.

Take from the downstairs passengers
    and give to the upstairs...   **1199**
Collect everyone's money and share it out...   **1222**
Give some of your own money to the
    poorest-looking... (**£1 10s**)   **1211**

❧ 1194 ❧

Steve Micklewhite and his company are well-known for their inventiveness and the quality of their repairs. They can offer you several customisations for your boat, including a **Perkins engine**, which will allow you to carry **ice** or **frozen meat** as cargoes.

	To buy
Fit a **Perkins engine**...	£20
Mount a **strengthened screw**...	£10
Purchase a **butty boat**...	£25

A **butty boat** is an unpowered craft that you can tow behind your own, increasing your cargo capacity by three units.

Return to the wharf...	868
Steam downriver to Wallingford...	
(**£1 10s** or **Bargee's Badge**)	883
Moor here and head ashore...	826

❧ 1195 ❧

Late at night, when the bailey is still and the ramparts are silent, you cut the gas-line to the lamp above the door to the headquarters and kneel down to get to work. If you have a **regimental key**, turn to **1261** immediately.

To successfully open the door, you will need to make an INGENUITY roll of difficulty 13, adding 3 if you possess a **skeleton key** and 1 if you possess some **lockpicks**.

Successful INGENITY roll!	1261
Failed INGENUITY roll!	1269

❧ 1196 ❧

Using the airship's onboard telegraph you show a pre-arranged coded message beneath your gondola. A reply from Nettlebed mooring post is not long in coming: the red flag is raised! The brickworkers have seized control, as Comrade Plunkett hoped. You set a course and soon are standing on the foredeck as a crewman hooks the mooring line. Plunkett is there.

"Proud comrade!" He is in high spirits indeed. "You have excelled! The Compact cannot be stopped now. I have recommended you to the highest level of the organisation: they have informed me that henceforth you will be known as **Comrade 74**!" (Mark this on your **Adventure Sheet**.)

Plunkett has also arranged for your velosteam to be collected from Rotherfield Greys. He has had it refueled and serviced (remove any **damage points**) and has fitted a new **customisation** (choose from **muffled exhaust**, **off-road tyres**, **enlarged fuel tank**, **double headlamp**, **gas pressuriser**, **improved brakes**).

The Atmospheric Union will certainly be after you now. If you are not already, you are now **Wanted by the Atmospheric Union**. Perhaps a time of lying low will be needed - or a change of appearance.

Head out of Nettlebed...   **944**

☙ 1197 ❧

You mount your velosteam and head off into the night. The officer is only the first of your many victims. Rest, healing for your cuts and refreshment for your body is now in order. Where will you head to find shelter?

To Pishill...	**370**
To Stokenchurch...	**308**
To Henley...	**702**
To Nettlebed...	**791**
To Wallingford...	**270**

☙ 1198 ❧

A velosteamer's grip is no brush of a moth's wing. You grab the paymaster by the throat, lift him from his seat and squeeze.

"I see your position," gasps the paymaster. "Compelling! I may be able... to help..."

You drop him and he scurries about, writing out a docket and making entries in large ledgers. He hands you **pension statement 4590213** nervously and sidles to the edge of the room.

You leave unobstructed, but he will report you and you are now **Wanted by Wallingford Town Guard**.

Turn to...   **270**

☙ 1199 ❧

You climb onto the step of the lower cabin and hustle the passengers off. "Now turn out your pockets!" You collect around four pounds from the passengers and begin to share it out amongst the upper-deckers who have come down to take a more comfortable inside seat.

"What are you doing?" asks one woman. "Am I rich because I have to travel inside? I'm only inside because of my bad neck! She," and the woman points to an upper-decker "Has plenty of money, she's just too tight to shell out for a dry seat!"

The passengers are quickly in uproar. You tell the driver to head off and to leave the original downstairs passengers at the roadside, but he is far from happy with that. "They paid for their tickets. What will my manager say?" You wonder whether he will simply return and pick them up again when you are out of view. Have you really done anyone a favour by getting involved like this?

Turn to...   **noted passage**

☙ 1200 ❧

Wandering through the boulevards and alleyways, you come to the Pearl Quarter. Here the lanes are close together, brackish drains cut through the land and plank bridges cross them unevenly. A jeweller's shop stands at the side of the road.

Enter the shop...	**1445**
Return to the hotel...	**1323**

☙ 1201 ❧

You make a dash for the fence, but whichever way you turn, the spotlight seems to predict your every move. Turning this way and that, you are quickly outpaced and surrounded. Dark figures of guards appear and a blow to the head sends you into unconscious captivity.

Turn to...   **13**

☙ 1202 ❧

You have once again encountered the Wallingford locobus. Some of the passengers recognise you from your previous meeting. If you have the codeword *Boorish*, turn to **1227** immediately. If not, but you have the codeword *Burdensome*, turn to **1248**. If you have the codeword *Brilliant*, turn to **1242**. If you have none of these, simply read on.

"It's you again," says one passenger. "You was robbing us last time! Robbing the poor! Well, we ain't having it, I tell you!" He picks up a cabbage and launches it at your face.

His aim is good and his arm is strong and you are knocked clean off your velosteam. By the time you have picked yourself up, the locobus is chugging off down the road again.

Turn to...   **noted passage**

✎ 1203 ❧

You tell the Mother Superior of the demise of the Bermondsey Mission. She shakes her head sadly. "It is my responsibility. I did not choose a leader amongst them of sufficient character. They were not ready for this task." She thanks you and gives you a small token of her appreciation: a **St Katharine's Brooch**. "You will be surprised what doors this opens for you," she says.

Leave the convent...   **88**

✎ 1204 ❧

To climb the walls and break in through a window, you will need to make a NIMBLENESS roll of difficulty 13, adding 1 if you possess a **grappling iron** or **rope** or 2 if you have a **rope ladder**.

Successful NIMBLENESS roll!   **1261**
Failed NIMBLENESS roll!   **270**

✎ 1205 ❧

Lord Barrymore's lesson teaches you both much about sword-fighting: you tiptoe along the rail of the boxes, leap the heads of cowering audience, swing on drapery and slide on banisters. Add 1 to your NIMBLENESS score.

With a slow inevitability your fight is drawn onto the stage itself where, at last, Barrymore is at your mercy. He sinks to his knees.

"Your day is done, Barrymore."   **1234**
"I shall not kill you over money."   **1253**

✎ 1206 ❧

Your shot resounds with a heart crack, clipping the red ball and sending it directly towards the umpire, who shrieks and dives beneath the cake table. Your black, meanwhile, ricochets off towards the portable sun-shelter and severs three guyropes that are holding the rickety structure in place. As the sun-shelter collapses onto the pitch it launches a tent-peg through the air directly at Major Redford, striking him squarely in the chest.

Your catastrophic attempt would be funny if so many of the guests weren't hurt or seriously inconvenienced. You had better make a sharp exit.

Turn to...   **62**

❧ 1207 ❧

Your attempt to frighten the paymaster backfires. He calls for help and several soldiers burst in. You will have to fight them to get away!

Soldiers	Weapons: **sabres (PAR 3)**
Parry:	12
Nimbleness:	9
Toughness:	6

If you defeat the soldier you must nonetheless flee - and you will now be **Wanted by the Wallingford Town Guard**.

Victory!	742
Defeat!	705

❧ 1208 ❧

A farmhand is steering a wagon piled high with baskets of strawberries, heading to Maidenhead and the markets there. "Them codesmen in the galleries there pay good prices for these berries," he says. "And I'll sell at least half at the World's End. Take in a show before heading back this way. They have some fancy American beers there too."

Turn to...   **noted passage**

❧ 1209 ❧

A small window in a high eave is standing open. Marks of nesting birds indicate that it opens into an unused room. Make a NIMBLENESS roll of difficulty 12 adding 2 if you possess a **grappling iron**.

Successful NIMBLENESS roll...	1335
Failed NIMBLENESS roll...	430

❧ 1210 ❧

The castle is an important seat of Imperial Authority in the region. Not only does it house the town gaol and the headquarters of the Town Guard, but it is the garrison of the Royal Oxford and Buckinghamshire Light Infantry. Is this a place for an outlaw like yourself to be spending any length of time?

Attempt to free Uncle Max... (*Boorish*)	1231
Break into the Regimental Headquarters...	
(*Benediction*)	1111
Visit the Regimental paymaster... (*Bottle*)	1146
Return to the town...	270

❧ 1211 ❧

When the passengers realise that you are giving money, not taking it, they become competitively needy, telling you of their desperation, their ill parents, their lack of prospects, the cabbage-fly in their gardens. How does such a craven display of need and greed affect you? When the locobus sets off again, you see the passengers arguing and snatching at the few shillings you gave. Angry voices rise on the breeze. If you have fewer than **six solidarity point**, gain one now.

Turn to...   **noted passage**

❧ 1212 ❧

The airship is making progress. However, its vast number of controls for handling the gas bags, the steering, the altitude and the engines were designed for a team of skilled pilots and specialists. Will you be able to coax the craft the short distance to Nettlebed? Make a MOTORING roll of difficulty 16.

Successful MOTORING roll!	1196
Failed MOTORING roll!	1258

❧ 1213 ❧

You fight off the attackers and find Mr Knapp has run back to the hotel. He is shaking and shivering. "I want to leave this terrible place," he says. "I will re-book for the first flight back."

In the morning you travel out to the airfield again and board the craft that will take you back to England. It must travel directly over the high alps and there, once again, Mr Knapp's bad luck comes into play.

You are taking a short rest when the airship lurches and awakens you. The sky outside the port-hole is a uniform cloudy white - until you glimpse, shockingly close, the rock of the mountainside merely yards away. You dash out onto the deck just as a jutting rock tears into the lower bulge of the gasbag, venting the precious helium and bringing the airship crashing onto the snow and rock.

The wind is rising: the airship is driven against the mountain and collapses. The heavy furnace falls with a crash, pulling the upper superstructure with it. A faint shout of terror reaches your ears where you lie in the snow, desperately scrabbling for a solid surface to cling to.

The lower gondola is left on the ledge with part of

the massive envelope frame, now twisted out of shape, but the fore-cabin, the bridge and the engine room have all disappeared down the mountain in the white fog and wind. You can see a few other figures: passengers, mostly, including the unfortunate Mr Knapp.

You do your best to keep the survivors alive and motivated, but two slip away that night in the cold and their despair. As for the rest of you, you huddle in the cabins of the torn gondola trying to keep a fire alight and waiting for the weather to clear.

When the morning comes, you are stranded on an island of rock and snow above a sea of mist. The sun shines brightly and there in the distance is an airship.

Your rescuers are Swiss airpolice. They collect the survivors from the ledge, heal your **wounds** (convert them into **scars**) and fit you out for a return to England. Mr Knapp is once more put into your care. He says very little, but as the chartered airship approaches Rotherfield he turns to you gratefully.

"You saved my life at least twice on this ill-fated flight," he says. "Which was your job. I shall never fly again. I'm sure you will also think twice before taking to the air." You are paid **£20** for your work.

Turn to...   **454**

※ 1214 ※

"It's true," says one hot-head. "We've done all this work and been paid and that's enough for the likes of them! But they're still making a profit on the railway - on our digging and our rail-laying. We should all have a share!"

The navvies decide to do something about it in a demonstration. They will not be so easy for the Railway to employ again. Gain the codeword *Befriend*.

Leave the camp...   **584**

※ 1215 ※

You are not welcome back to the card table here at the Theatre. In fact, the players are surprised that you dare to show your face around here.

Leave the theatre...   **702**

※ 1216 ※

If it took you more than **13 passages** to reach this passage since collecting the **urgent parcel,** read on. If you were able to complete the task in **13 or fewer** passages, turn to **1182** immediately.

You look for the recipient of the parcel you were given at Goring, but are told that she has already set out for Birmingham. "Won't be back for a while." Remove the **urgent parcel** from your possessions. "We'll keep it for you here."

Return to the Freight Yard...   **285**
Leave the yard...   **688**

※ 1217 ※

"Tell me what bothers you," you say to the passengers. "And please, consider something more important than bus fares."

"I'll tell you," says one woman. "The Wallingford Guards! Always pushing people around. My uncle Maximilian was thrown in the gaol for weeks - and all he did was complain that the fair was going to be cancelled! They called him a troublemaker and locked him up!"

The passengers agree. "It's true," says another. "If you want to be a-helping us everyday folks, go and do something about her uncle Maximilian!" Gain the codeword *Boorish*.

Let the locobus drive on...   **noted passage**

※ 1218 ※

"I know who you are and what you plan," you tell the dockers. "I have come to bring you these." You take the **emerald jewellery** from its pouch and hand it over. "You have guns? Good - buy more. The military have a shipment of carbines just like this: you will need many more to overpower them."

The dockers are speechless. Their leader regains some self-control and thanks you, promising to hand the jewels over to his own commander. As for you, you stroll out of the docks freely.

Return to the hotel...   **1323**
Go to find a replacement for the jewels...   **1445**

❧ 1219 ❧

☐

If the box is empty, tick it and turn to **1263** immediately. If it is already ticked, read on.

Three Imperial model velosteams burst into view over the crest, each bearing a driver and an armed sharpshooter. They have your scent and are accelerating fast! This will be a ride to test you. Which way will you turn?

Towards Pishill...	**1368**
Into Heath Wood...	**1354**
Towards Cobstone Mill...	**1155**
Make for Oxford...	**1138**

❧ 1220 ❧

You hoot your horn rudely at the gateway and wave impatiently at the gatekeeper, saying brusquely, "I'm expected man, clear the road at once!" It does the trick and you are inside the park, steaming between the close-cropped wood-pasture.

At the door you dismount your Ferguson and introduce yourself as a cousin of Lord Fanbury - one of the richest and most influential members of the cabinet as well as a forward-looking technologican. You are welcomed and greeted and taken to meet the lady of the house. If you have the codeword *Botanical*, turn to **1236** immediately.

"We're honoured to have you - an unexpected privilege," she says. "Any Fanbury is a friend of ours. My husband is out on the estate, but will return later to dine."

You spend much of the day making the house your own, treating the servants with rude disregard that convinces the Lady Stonor of your truly blue blood far more than the wild lies you tell about your pretended relationship with Fanbury. When Lord Stonor reappears, he is far more interested in making a good impression on you than caring to check your credentials and speaks incessantly of his own successes, ambitions and abilities.

Later that night, when the family and even the hard-working servants are asleep, you creep from your luxurious chamber.

Look for valuables to steal...	**1255**
Investigate the attic...	**1335**
Delve into the cellar...	**1142**

❧ 1221 ❧

Your shots go wide and only serve to enrage your opponent. Bullets whizz towards you in response - much more accurately than your own! Roll a dice to see whether you are hit!

Score 1	Receive **two wounds**
Score 2	Gain a **damage point**
Score 3-4	Receive a **wound**
Score 5-6	Escape unharmed

If your velosteam is now **beyond repair**, turn to **874** immediately. If not but you have **five wounds**, turn to **999**. Otherwise you will have to remount your velosteam and make yourself scarce.

Ride away...   **noted passage**

❧ 1222 ❧

It takes time to get everybody off the locobus, to collect their coins in a puddle of silver and copper on a cloak laid on the grass and then to threaten those who are obviously hiding more to turn out their pockets. In the end, when everyone has received an average share, including the driver, a few have lost a lot, most have gained a very little and a fortunate few are far richer than when they set out.

"This ain't fair!" protests one passenger. "The only reason I was carryin two pound was because I was on the way to market to buy leather for me business. It's all I've saved for the last month!" Is he telling the truth? Are any of the arguing, fussing passengers? In the end you are forced to give up and the locobus moves off. Some passengers will bully their way back into receiving what they had and some will be disappointed.

Ride away...   **noted passage**

❧ 1223 ❧

If you are unable to get the engines of the airship working, how would you ever hope to fly it into the hands of the Compact? Perhaps you have avoided a dreadful catastrophe. You slip aground again, leaving the airship bobbing against its lines, and make your way to your velosteam. You will need to make another attempt after having improved your MOTORING ability if you wish to succeed.

Turn to...   **68**

❧ 1224 ❧
A maid turns you away from Alphaea's room. "She's preparing for the wedding," she tells you. "Go away!"

Turn to...   **1323**

❧ 1225 ❧
"Oh, give over," says a large chap in a bowler hat. "You're just trying to stir up trouble here. Get out before we throw you out."

Turn to...   **584**

❧ 1226 ❧
You launch yourself off the deck of the airship and your **winged harness** unfolds behind you, each vane and feather perfectly aligning to allow you to travel down, down, down. You land in a cornfield not far from where you left your velosteam at the edge of the airfield. Climbing back on board, you have a chance to reflect on how close you came to your end.

Steam away...   **68**

❧ 1227 ❧
At the front of the locobus you see the woman who complained to you about her uncle Maximillian. She certainly recognises you. "Hello," she says. "Well, some freedom fighter you are. My uncle Max is still in gaol! What has this trumped-up character done about it, folks? Absolutely nothing! What a waste of space."

The passengers mutter and jeer. The driver starts up his engine and they steam off. Lose a **solidarity point**.

Turn to...   **noted passage**

❧ 1228 ❧
"Did you serve in Spain?" you ask the officer, after a glance at his medal ribbons.

"I did," he grunts. "What is it to you?"

"Then you know of what happened to the Oxford and Bucks Light Infantry?"

He grimaces. "A catastrophe. A slaughter. They are reforming the regiment now in Wallingford, but recruits are hard to find. Particularly for a cursed regiment."

"It wasn't a curse, but the folly and stupidity of the commanders," you reply. "I want to know who gave the orders that sent those men across the plain at Valencia to their deaths."

He shakes his head. "I don't know. But the records will show. Go to the garrison in Wallingford. Everything is recorded there. Everything."

The officer has nothing more to say: you leave him with his servants.

Turn to...   **1197**

❧ 1229 ❧
You explain what you know of Sackler's scheme, how you distrust him and the tiny, nay, miniscule, chance of finding silver in Berkshire.

"You really think he's a con-man?" asks Earl Brigg, disappointedly.

"I am sure of it," you reply.

"I knew it. I knew it all along," says the Earl angrily. "What a fool I have been. I should have trusted my instincts. Now you are a truly trustworthy sort of person - I'm a very good judge of character and I've seen that right off. Help get rid of this blackguard."

The Earl rousts out his gamekeepers, footmen and grooms and together you head over to the workings and confront Sackler and his workmen.

"Sackler!" shouts the Earl. "Get out of here and stop ruining my estate!"

"My Lord Earl," says the wretched prospector. "We are really very close to a good production of silver to show you: I have a small ingot here that we refined just today! This is the crucial stage. Another hundred guineas will see us minting wealth, milord."

The Earl pauses. "Just another hundred, eh?"

You jog his elbow firmly. "It's all lies." You call to the servants. "We're breaking up this camp. Give them a beating for their temerity!"

The men of the estate have been waiting for a little leadership. They charge the burly miners and half-pay workmen, who are less than keen to hold their ground, considering that they have been earning a few shillings a day simply by appearing busy. A few are beaten but the rest flee. The canvas and wooden structures are knocked down and thrown into a bonfire. Sackler is beaten, kicked and taken down to the river, where he is ceremonially ducked by the butler.

The Earl breathes a sigh of relief. "That leech would have sucked me dry," he says. "Thankyou." You are now the **Friend of Earl Brigg**. He also has his butler give you a bag of coin (**£10 10s**) and a **letter of introduction**. He invites you to read in his library, where you can gain a level of **legal knowledge** or **genealogy**.

Head on your way...   **313**

❧ 1230 ❧

Comrade Plunkett and his band of revolutionary anarchists are still waiting for you to hijack an airship for them. It will be a daring act indeed, but if you wish to try to take control of this airship you must act immediately, making your way to the bridge and preparing your weapons, however you smuggled them aboard.

Head to the bridge...   1326
Continue with your work...   1304

❧ 1231 ❧

You discover that Uncle Max is well-known to the servants and washerwomen of the gaol. He is a nuisance, boring people with his interminable stories, borrowing money recklessly and flirting with the laundrymaids. Everyone wants rid of him, so it is not hard to convince an under-warden to lend you his keys for an hour - for a price.

Bride the under-warden... (£4)   1149
Return to town...   270

❧ 1232 ❧

A crowd of villagers are making their way from one village to another, celebrating the harvest. When they see you, they hail you as a local hero and insist that you join their celebration. Much beer and cider is drunk, great pies are served, dancing and games go on by bonfire-light late into the night. If you have an **odd number** of **solidarity points**, gain one now.y6=

Continue down the lane...   867

❧ 1233 ❧

The Flight Engineer puffs on a cigar. "I love a smoke," he says. "Can't get a puff aloft. Against regulations. Used to work on Serpents back when they were flown, but I've been seconded to the Confederated State Air Fleet for the past few years. Learnt a thing or two there, I can tell you."

Return to the lounge...   80
Head outside...   454

❧ 1234 ❧

One final thrust finishes Lord Barrymore and you stalk off the stage. The audience are terrified - you will certainly be **Wanted by the Constables** now if you are not already. Gain the codeword *Bloodied*.

You leave the theatre and mount your velosteam: it is surely prudent to put some distance between you and your deeds now.

Turn to...   757

❧ 1235 ❧

The Constables handcuff you as you lie on the straw of the yard. "I knew we'd find the Steam Highwayman here," says an officer, flicking cigar ash onto the ground. Gain the codeword *Beringed*.

Turn to...   13

❧ 1236 ❧

Lady Stonor recognises you immediately. "You are no Fanbury," she says. "I shall not forget your face!" As quick as a flash, she leaves the room and slams the door closed. Footsteps come running - several servants and footmen, grabbing weapons as they come. You must flee! What folly inspired you to return here?

You leap for the window and kick out the glass. A servant swings at you with a heavy beater's stick, but you dodge and dive out onto the gravel. Your velosteam is still standing there, so you leap aboard and open the regulator, kicking up white dust and stones in your pursuers' faces.

Turn to...   430

❧ 1237 ❧

The Captain does not hesitate to cut you down. The crew only do the minimum to staunch your wounds before clapping you in irons, removing all your **money** and **possessions** and locking you in the brig. It will be a long flight back to Rotherfield Greys, where you will be handed over to the Constables to pay for your crimes. Note that you are now **Wanted by the Atmospheric Union** on top of any other record you might have.

Turn to...   13

❧ 1238 ❧

The songs rise and swell. Hymns in six-part harmony, solo offerings of carefully-practiced and totally devoted worship and simple choruses expressing great truths are all sung by the monks. They seem to take great delight in their music.

Return to the cloister...   642

❧ 1239 ❧

You assist the servant in administering aid to a wealthy traveller whose carriage has been involved in an accident. Roll a dice to see how you are rewarded.

Score 1-3   **£4 4s**
Score 4-5   A **gold ring**
Score 6   A **letter of introduction**

Turn to...   **529**

❧ 1240 ❧

Your movements have become predictable and the Constables have anticipated your return to the region! As soon as you move off down the road, you become aware of approaching pursuit vehicles - Imperial velosteams, most likely. You will have to accelerate and try to out-run them. Which way will you turn?

Cross the river at Sonning...   **441**
Head into the woods...   **718**
Ride for Aston Ferry...   **137**
Make for your barge...
     (moored at Temple Coombe Quarry) 848

❧ 1241 ❧

You bow to the tall lady and proffer the second mallet. "Will you allow me the honour," you ask, "Of playing in your colours?"

She sees the burnt rose pinned to your breast and smiles. "I must. Though I warn you - you will need to play fast and hard to keep up with me."

The lady is not joking. From the first winning toss (with a two-faced coin?) she wolfs around the course, cannoning and roqueting your opponents fiercely. You are the last to pass through the **first hoop**.

Turn to...   **548**

❧ 1242 ❧

The passengers recognise you. "Oh yes," they say. "It was your clever idea to get the driver to give us all our money back. Well now the company's put the fares up again. And who's fault is that?"

You are unable to answer that query. The locobus sets off again.

Turn to...   **noted passage**

❧ 1243 ❧

The First Officer looks at you strangely. "Is that a joke?" he asks. "Rum sort of joke. Don't you know how fast they are?" He puts down his drink and heads off.

Turn to...   **1346**

❧ 1244 ❧

Some of these Atmospheric Union vehicles carry armed guards, so you had better make your choice carefully as you prepare to hold it up. The vehicle will have to pass beneath an overhanging branch, so you do have an opportunity to swing aboard on a rope. Otherwise you will have to trust in your ruthless reputation, as the enclosed driver's cab is bullet-proof.

Swing aboard... **(rope)**   **672**
Block the road...   **772**

❧ 1245 ❧

The Viscount Monsberg lies dead at your feet. Who knows what chaos of inheritance will ensue now. Will his heir be of his character - or someone awed by the punishment you have meted out on the dead man at your feet? Gain **two solidarity points**, remove the codeword *Brimming* and gain the codeword *Broken*.

Turn to...   **937**

❧ 1246 ❧

A rusted and almost-clapped out farming engine makes its way towards you. The driver is oblivious to your ambush.

Several labourers sit on the long wagon trailed behind, resting in the freshly-cut hay and sharing a flagon of cider. There is nothing to steal from these travellers.

Turn to...   **noted passage**

1247

The Prior is glad to see you. "Welcome back," he says. "Come and take rest. I am sure that you have been characteristically busy. You will have burdens to lay down."

You spend some time in conversation but the Prior never asks a direct question about the way in which you have spent your time since he last saw you. He shares his concerns for the oppressed and the needy in the land, particularly in the north of the country where rebellion has destroyed so much.

Return to the cloister... **642**

1248

☐

If the box is empty, tick it and read on. If it is already ticked, turn to your **noted passage** immediately.

"It's you!" cries a female passenger. "You saved my uncle Max!" She leaps down from the locobus and flings her arms around your neck, planting a sloppy kiss on your cheek. "I'm so grateful!" In her gratitude, she gives you a **pork pie** and tells all the other passengers about your heroism. Gain a **solidarity point**.

Turn to... **noted passage**

1249

The driver opens the regulator and swerves hard against your velosteam: you are taken by surprise and knocked down! Your prey escapes and you must roll a dice to see how you fared.

Score 1 Receive **two damage points**
Score 2 Gain a **damage point** or lose a **customisation**
Score 3-4 Receive a **wound**
Score 5-6 Escape unharmed

If your velosteam is now **beyond repair**, turn to **874** immediately. If not but you have **five wounds**, turn to **999**. Otherwise you will have to remount your velosteam and make yourself scarce.

Turn to... **noted passage**

1250

The engines respond sluggishly but you read the revolutions on the rear propellors increasing slowly. Despite a wind from the north-west, the airship begins to move. Away with the automatic mooring line release and you can churn slowly forward into the night.

The door to the bridge is thrown open. A wild-eyed officer has escaped from his cabin. "What the blazes are you doing?" he cries, drawing his sabre. You must fight!

Airship Officer   Weapon: **sabre (PAR 3)**
Parry: 10
Nimbleness: 7
Toughness: 4

Victory!   **1212**
Defeat!   **342**

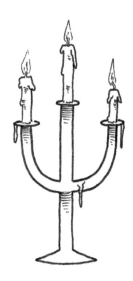

1251

If you have no **Wanted Statuses** or **Major Redford's Card**, turn to **702** immediately. Otherwise the Constables will want a good look at you before you are allowed into Henley. Make an INGENUITY roll of difficulty 15 to fool them into letting you through, adding 1 if you possess a **top hat**, 1 if you have a **cloak** of any kind and a further 1 if you have an **eyepatch**.

Successful INGENUITY roll!   **702**
Unsuccessful INGENUITY roll!   **13**

1252

Now that the migrants have moved on, the Lynch is quiet. The sour smell of rain-soaked fireplaces and occasional pieces of litter let you know that someone once camped here.

Steam upstream...   **750**
Steam downriver to Wargrave...
(**2s** or **Bargee's Badge**)   **131**

❧ 1254 ❧

Is there something in Barrymore's eye that has moved you to pity? Or have you simply reflected on the pettiness of the cause? Either way, you leave him to live and stalk out of the theatre un-opposed.

Turn to...   702

❧ 1255 ❧

A grand house like this is full of booty for a ruthless thief. Roll a dice to see what you find.

Score 1-3   Lord Stonor's pocketbook containing **forty guineas in banknotes**
Score 4-6   Miss Stonor's jewellery box with a **gold necklace**, three **gold rings** and a **sapphire pendant**

You risk awaking the family and the many servants with every extra moment you creep around the house. Can you afford to stay any longer?

Leave the house...   1273
Look around some more...   1284

❧ 1256 ❧

Before you come into pistol range, the Atmospheric Union carriage screeches to a halt. Roll a dice to see what the steamer carries:

Score 1-2   Airship crew   703
Score 4-6   Passengers   592

❧ 1257 ❧

You are left for dead on the Hungarian pavement, bleeding out your lifeblood far from home. Whatever possessed you to take this employment? Whatever called you to travel such a long way from your own climes? Whatever plans or intentions you had for your future will remain unfulfilled. Turn to the **Epilogue**.

❧ 1258 ❧

The massive craft overwhelms your attempt to control it. It quickly begins to lose altitude at the mercy of the wind and you risk your own destruction along with it. If you have a **winged harness**, turn to **1226**. Otherwise this foolhardy endeavour may prove to be the worst and final decision of your adventure as the Steam Highwayman.

A sharp gust brings the nose down. You are too slow to correct it and the controls become sluggish and limp. Somewhere, a cable has snapped and without crew to help you, you are at the mercy of the wind.

Down, down, down, increasingly steeply, until a rending noise announces the twisting of the metal structure and shudders beneath your feet transmit the distortion in the frame. A sudden drop indicates that a bag has blown and a fireball bursts into the bridge.

Your Icarus flight has ended in a fiery comet and your skeleton will not even be recognisable in the ashes. Turn to the **Epilogue**.

❧ 1259 ❧

"You're right, it was fast. Fastest things in the sky with those big old engines. All very well, but there's no mod cons at all - only a bucket and not even a lid to that. They don't know how to design a real elegant cruiser, the Italians."

Turn to...   1418

❧ 1260 ❧

You go ashore to discuss terms with the head of the family. He listens and considers your proposal. After all, there are the cottages on the edge of Shiplake House grounds with their gardens that need tenants, or they will crumble and decay. And there is still much work to be done completing the house and staffing it. "And we'll pay low rents?"

"Offset by your work," you reply. "You must have some skills."

"I was a market gardener," he replies.

"Head gardener, then," you respond. "I've wanted to build some greenhouses. You can lay out the plans and your youngsters can learn the trade."

He shakes your hand and agrees to the business. They will pack up your belongings and cross over to Shiplake on their raft, taking up residence on your estate in the next few days. "I think this'll suit us much more than the city," he says, musing. The family name is Mudge. Gain the codeword *Benefit*.

Steam upstream...   750
Steam downriver to Wargrave...
        (**2s** or **Bargee's Badge**)   131

❧ 1261 ❧

Inside the hallway is quiet and still. Faded battle standards hang from the high ceiling. You make your way to the records office on the first floor and take your bearings.

Long shelves of boxed punchcards line the record office: to find the correct orders amongst them would take the trained clerks some time, let alone a burglar like yourself. Several stacks of **blank punchcards** stand on a desk - you may take a set if you wish. A small computational engine stands waiting by the head clerk's desk, its hopper ready to receive the various inputs needed to translate code or identify records. If you are unable to run the device, you will have to look for the records yourself.

Look for the records manually...   **1293**
Sneak out...   **1280**

≈ 1262 ≈
The first day's work wears you out: a long shift of ten hours has left you physically exhausted. You are permitted to climb into the narrow hammock slung in the rear equipment store and try to sleep.

A clang, a shout and a rush of steam announce that something has failed. Mrs Betting calls and you wrest yourself out of the hammock and back to the room - how long have you slept?

One of the regulators has failed. Mrs Betting wipes it and scowls. "Dry! That was your job. Get over here and fix it - now! We're losing power." Make another ENGINEERING roll, adding 2 if you possess a **steam fist** or a **mechanical hand**.

Score 13 or lower   Gain a **wound**
Score 14-16   Gain a **burn (NIM-1)**
Score 15-18   Fix the regulator

If you now have **five wounds**, turn to **999**.

Turn to...   **1313**

≈ 1263 ≈
With the sound of Constables catching you fast, you take any path at random through the woods, dodging between massive beech boles, frightening deer into the undergrowth and bumping over outcrops of sandy bedrock. Before long you are headed up a steep slope on a path that you realise you have never taken before and the sound of your pursuers is far behind.

Here on an isolated hilltop is the village of Maidensgrove, sheltered by its coppices and wheat-stoks, unreachable by any tarmacadamed road. You roll up to the village pub and dismount in the sudden sunshine, where an old man nods in greeting.

"Well met, traveller. What a fancy machine indeed."

Turn to...   **760**

≈ 1264 ≈
Not to be out-done, you prepare a trick-shot of your own. It will take some skill to set up! Make a NIMBLENESS roll, adding 3 if you have a steam fist or a mechanical arm.

Score <11...   **1206**
Score 11-16...   **1134**
Score 17+...   **610**

≈ 1265 ≈
Since your last attempt, the monks have been forced to remove all of their gold and valuables. Perhaps they have been prompted to sell them and give the money to the poor? Anyway, the chapel is now furnished with simple wooden decorations and the communion cup, the patten and the offering plate are plain pottery.

Return to the cloister...   **642**

≈ 1266 ≈
You tear away and head for Grim's Ditch. The long earthwork and its paths will lead you out of the wooded hills quickly and away from your pursuers.

Out in the open, you hear the throbbing of propellors. The Constables have signalled in an airship. Shouts carry on the wind and gunshots begin to pepper the grassy bank and whine over your head. They have every advantage except speed. If you drive straight into the wind you may be able to escape them. It is all a question of power. Make a MOTORING roll of difficulty 14, adding 1 if you possess a **strength-**

ened boiler.

Successful MOTORING roll!	**259**
Failed MOTORING roll!	**13**

❧ 1267 ☙

The First Officer tells you of life in an airship crew. "If you've a good captain then the officers are all on good terms. Last flight I says to the skipper, 'Cruise, I'll be glad to be back,' and he says 'Yes indeed, Cruise.' That's how you speak to another officer on your flight - but it ain't ever used aground or with any officer you're not flying with."

"And is it really as glamorous as the tales tell?"

"Well, I was in Paris for the King of France's birthday ball and that was pretty glamorous. Flight to Singapore was a laugh too."

Return to the lounge...	**80**
Head outside...	**454**

❧ 1268 ☙

As you prepare to leave your room in the early morning, you hear the approach of an Imperial velosteam. The Constables have been informed of your presence here. Looking out of the window, it is clear that they have surrounded the inn. To escape and get to your velosteam you will have to take them by surprise.

You climb silently down the stairs and creep through the scullery to a rear door. Men are plainly waiting on the other side, talking in hushed voices. But your velosteam is just beyond them. It is now or never.

You crash through the door, knocking one man down and drawing your weapons. You must overcome the other Constable quickly!

Constable	Weapon: **truncheon (PAR 2)**
Parry:	8
Nimbleness:	6
Toughness:	3

Victory!	**1288**
Defeat!	**1235**

❧ 1269 ☙

The lock is far too complex for you to pick. Since the door will not open to your cleverness, you must scale the building or leave.

Try to climb in through a window...	**1204**
Sneak back out...	**270**

❧ 1270 ☙

"Don't say any more," says a forewoman. "We've all heard of how you armed the workers. Rest assured, we're ready to seize control of production on the word - and not until then." Gain the codeword *Blown*.

Turn to...	**791**

❧ 1271 ☙

The cattlewagon moves with a much smoother and steadier motion now. The farmer is very grateful. "I'll reach London at this rate. This beef is worth much more there. Look out for me in town," he says. Gain the codeword *Baron*.

Turn to...	**noted passage**

❧ 1272 ☙

The officer pauses with his blade at your throat. "I should run you through," he says, "Although I rather pity you, somehwy. Do I know you?"

"I also fought the anarchists in Spain."	**1289**

❧ 1273 ☙

You make your way out of the house as silently as you can, but a creaking stairway gives you away. Somebody calls out after you: you dash for your velosteam and the open road. Gain the codeword *Bursting*.

Turn to...	**430**

✖ 1274 ✖

"Not scared?" leers a massive docker, reaching for a crowbar. "Let's see about that."

Docker	Weapon: **club (PAR 2)**
Parry:	8
Nimbleness:	6
Toughness:	7

Victory!	**1364**
Defeat!	**1381**

✖ 1275 ✖

"You can't possibly think that!" cries the Flight Engineer. "Did you not see those pictures of the *Presteigne* in flames? That would have never happened with coal!"

Turn to... **1346**

✖ 1276 ✖

You pour the chloroform onto a gauze and then hang that over the ventilators into the crew cabins. That should keep them asleep while you go aloft. Next you quietly pay out the mooring line and unhook the ground lines: the big airship rises quietly towards the stars.

Turn to... **1250**

✖ 1277 ✖

The thin box-wood panelling has been split apart with a knife and the case with the **emerald jewellery** is gone: remove it from your **possessions**. Somebody must have observed you hiding it or suspected that you had it with you - but who? You cannot arrive at the wedding empty-handed but thankfully you have a little time. The airship will not arrive at San Juan for another three days. Where will you start?

Talk to the crew...	**1362**
Search the passengers' cabins...	**1379**
Search the crew's quarters...	**1399**
Look in the cargo hold...	**1413**

✖ 1278 ✖

The Captain is aground after bringing in a flight from Marrakech against contrary winds and Spanish pirates. "We sailed around the peninsula of course, but those anarchists are bold, bold fellows." He slurps at his gin and lights up a cigar. "Never had so much trouble since I was flying Dangerfields over Bermuda. And they were well-named, let me tell you! Steering linkages ran through the officer's mess, right underneath the dining table!"

Return to the lounge...	**80**
Head outside...	**454**

✖ 1279 ✖

The cabins are still largely intact. You stuff your pockets with up to three of the following: **ten guineas in banknotes**, a **gold necklace**, **£8 2s**, a **box of cigars**, an **ivory fan** and a **clockwork bird**.

The First Officer calls you together. "We will tow it to Aberdeen," he announces.

Your airship approaches at a signal and you help attach the towing lines. After a few hours' preparations, the airship is ready to be towed. You return to the engine room and later that night the abandoned craft is brought to the airship station on the hills above Aberdeen. Your own airship flies on.

Turn to... **1370**

✖ 1280 ✖

You close the door to the dusty records office and make your way to a window cut through the curtain wall. Can you force it open without alerting anyone? Make an ENGINEERING roll of difficulty 10.

Successful ENGINEERING roll!	**270**
Failed ENGINEERING roll!	**1303**

✖ 1281 ✖

It is a thankless task, continually oiling, wiping, recalibrating and checking gauges, heaving coal, hauling on the fuel lift and pumping up water. Nonetheless, you are fed well and sleep peacefully in the satisfaction of a day's work well done.

Turn to... **1313**

❧ 1282 ❧

The Prior receives your money gladly. "We are always happy to accept money as a gift," he says. "There are many needs around us, and while the brotherhood are mercifully able to support ourselves, many in the villages near here are struggling. There are widows as a result of this dreadful war and cripples besides. And then somebody stole our communionware recently and it would be nice to replace that."

Return to the cloister...   **642**

❧ 1283 ❧

The change in subject jars but the other officers quickly agree with you. "Quite right. This newfangled nonsense - far too finickity for mounting aft the bridge. Fine machinery's all very well but you have to trust it to the class of people who can actually understand it."

Turn to...   **1470**

❧ 1284 ❧

To continue your way around the house you must be delicate indeed: make a NIMBLENESS roll of difficulty 11.

Successful NIMBLENESS roll!   **1315**
Failed NIMBLENESS roll!   **1301**

❧ 1285 ❧

The approaching haulier is not a member of any guild and is unlikely to be armed. Make a RUTHLESSNESS roll of 13 to stop him.

Successful RUTHLESSNESS roll!   **1136**
Failed RUTHLESSNESS roll!   **782**

❧ 1286 ❧

Shortly after your arrival into Stokenchurch, you spy the returning Warriors football team on their brightly-painted bus. Their expressions, however, are far from bright.

"How was the match?" you ask, cheerily.

"It was a slaughter!" shouts the striker angrily. "An eight-nil slaughter! Goalie couldn't lay his hands on his own buttocks!"

"Pipe down," shouts another. "It ain't his fault. You know Harry's never played in goal before."

"We need new management," says the striker mournfully. "We won't get anywhere with our current leadership. Just more slaughter."

"We don't just need a new manager," returns the goalie. "We need new boots. Mine is falling off. You try saving goals while yer feet is flapping around!"

Erase the codeword *Bootlicker*.

Offer them a contribution towards their
    boots and kit... (**£5**)   **1482**
Wish them better luck...   **308**

❧ 1287 ❧

You wind up through the paths towards the crossroads at Eatonsfield Shaw. Out of nowhere, a fast Constabulary monobike bursts onto the road alongside you. The rider leans out and struggles with his carbine. You must knock him off the road! Make a MOTORING roll of difficulty 12, adding 2 if you have a **ramming beak**.

Successful MOTORING roll!   **110**
Failed MOTORING roll!   **1042**

❧ 1288 ❧

You dash the Constable to the ground, knocking over an oil lamp that spills onto a heap of straw and sends up a sheet of flame. Your velosteam is ready, so you release the emergency pressure valve and start the machine before lighting the burner. You are quickly on the road, but pursued! Gain the codeword *Beringed*.

Turn to...   **1219**

❧ 1289 ❧

"Blow me down," replies the officer. "A veteran, come to this. You must be desperate indeed." He bids his driver and valet help patch you up - remove a **wound** and replace it with a **scar** - and then tosses you a small bag of coins (**15s**). "Report to the Regimental Headquarters in Wallingford," he says. "Re-enlist. The war effort still needs you."

Your assault has not succeeded, but at least you

are not lying on the road, bleeding out your future in hot, red liquor. You mount your velosteam and make for a nearby pub to try to recover.

Turn to... **763**

❧ 1290 ❧

The steward is not able to give you much help at all. "That man with the bowler hat is always poking around," he says, "But I would not try anything with him. I know he carries a knife!"

Search the passengers' cabins... **1379**
Search the crew's quarters... **1399**

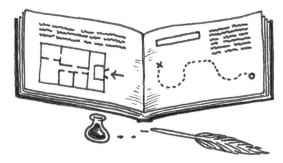

❧ 1291 ❧

The Captain and First Officer quickly regain their self-control. "You blackguard scoundrel," cries the Captain. "Number One, take command of the ship while I deal with this rogue!" He draws his rapier from his side, forces you back through the hatch onto the upper deck and proceeds to attack!

Airship Captain	Weapon: **rapier (PAR 4)**
Parry:	12
Nimbleness:	8
Toughness:	3

Victory! **1166**
Defeat! **342**

❧ 1292 ❧

If you want to convince the others to overpower the officer, unite behind you and take control of the airship, you will need to impress them with your leadership. Make a GALLANTRY roll of difficulty 17, adding 1 for each 5 **solidarity points** that you possess. If you are unable to convince them, you will still be able to loot the cabins.

Successful GALLANTRY roll! **1320**
Failed GALLANTRY roll! **1279**

❧ 1293 ❧

It will be a simple matter of luck as to whether you find the records in the time you have available. Each box is labelled by date, but there are also coded references to the rank of various officers and the protocols in which they were processed. Roll a dice.

Score 1-2	**1321**
Score 3-4	**1314**
Score 5-6	**1302**

❧ 1294 ❧

You have got the engineers onto one of their favourite topics. "I quite agree," says one, spitting with vehemence. "Welsh coal burns strongest and cleanest. Let the navy burn any grubby Kent or Durham stuff."

Turn to... **1418**

❧ 1295 ❧

Your ability impresses Mrs Betting, who shows you much of the workings of the engine room and patiently explains the job. Roll two dice, and if the score is greater than your ENGINEERING ability, you may add 1 to it permanently.

Turn to... **1313**

❧ 1296 ❧

You draw your weapons and prepare to fight. The wharfmaster blows a whistle and several private guards rush over.

Guards	Weapons: **sabres (PAR 3)**
Parry:	10
Nimbleness:	7
Toughness:	6

Victory! **630**
Defeat! **1086**

❧ 1297 ❧

Your Aramanth punchcards are quickly processed by the machine. It is now ready to decode anything you should care to provide it with.

Analyse Telegraph Guild Codes...
  (telegraph observations ☑ ☑) **252**
Decode the Valencia Orders...
  (punchcards (Valencia Orders)) **1498**
Leave the machine... **noted passage**

∽ 1298 ∾

Something about your manner fails to impress the officers. Perhaps you seem a little too brash for their effete, white-jacketed company. Or maybe you have struck the wrong tone of swagger. Whatever it is, they are sure to give you a grilling before accepting you as one of their own.

Turn to...   **1372**

∽ 1299 ∾

Your ride to Stokenchurch takes you past a trio of steam caravans parked by the side of the road. If you are the **Friend of Barsali**, turn to **1095** immediately. Otherwise, you must make a MOTORING roll of difficulty 10 to dodge the wagons and get away.

Successful MOTORING roll!   **308**
Failed MOTORING roll!   **1042**

∽ 1300 ∾

The vehicle approaching is clearly an Atmospheric Union steamer, possibly carrying rich passengers. Do you feel ready to attack it here on the main road to Oxford? Note **passage number 171**.

Attack the steamer...   **1244**
Let it pass...   **710**

∽ 1301 ∾

The first intimations of your attacker are his shadow and his breath: he is very close when he lands a heavy blow on your head. The dark house becomes even darker and you tumble into a deep cavern of unconsciousness.

Eventually you are able to open your eyes - or one eye, as the other is bruised and crusted with blood. Manacles and chains are on your wrists and a short tug reveals that they are themselves stapled into the wall of the cellar.

Opposite you is an old man, wheezing and panting for breath. His white hair and sallow skin tell of countless sorrows, but worst of all are his bloody, nailless hands and his wild, roving eyes. Is he recogniseable to you at all?

He does not respond when you greet him quietly, but mutters and raves, making a rough music with his constant babble. He is quite mad and very near the end of his squalid existence. There is nothing that you can do for him, chained, bloody and bruised as you are.

Unable to stay awake much longer, you slip back into confused darkness and are only vaguely aware of being dragged from the cellar and handed over to the Constables. Gain the codeword *Bursting*.

Turn to...   **13**

∽ 1302 ∾

High on a top shelf are several boxes relating to the disaster at Valencia. You shuffle through them to find the order cards that relate to the attack across the plain and remove the crucial cards. Gain **punch-cards (Valencia orders)**.

Return to the records office...   **1261**

∽ 1303 ∾

The window cannot be forced or cajoled open and you have to take the long route back through the bailey. However, as you slip out of the door you are spotted and a cry goes up. A dash towards the supply sheds brings you face to face with a guard, who draws his weapon and attacks!

Guard	Weapon: **sabre (PAR 3)**
Parry:	9
Nimbleness:	3
Toughness:	5

Victory!   **270**
Defeat!   **1086**

∽ 1304 ∾

Oiling pistons is tedious work. Every hour or so you also put in a stint hauling Welsh coal from the fuel lift to the furnace bunkers. Make an ENGINEERING roll to see how the flight develops for you.

Score<15...   **1262**
Score 15-18...   **1281**
Score 19+...   **1295**

❧ 1305 ❧

A steam-wagon in the yellow and black livery of the Coal Board is shuddering and churning its way down the road. Whether it is defended or not, you cannot tell at this distance. You could challenge the driver, depending on your RUTHLESSNESS to intimidate, ride alongside and board using your MOTORING ability or ready your gun, if you have one, and shoot first.

Challenge the driver...	**1338**
Ride alongside and board...	**1360**
Open fire!	**1352**

❧ 1306 ❧

Nothing seems to have been taken from your cabin, but the search puts you in a nervous mood and you go to ask the Captain to check his safe for the jewels. He sends a brusque response through his steward, but an hour later he comes to you in person, ashen-faced.

"I am dreadfully sorry to have to tell you that my safe has been robbed. Several things are missing - important documents and a large amount of money - and the jewellery with which you entrusted me."

"This is utterly unacceptable! The Union are liable!"	**1401**
"I demand you show me the safe."	**1408**

❧ 1307 ❧

"Ah yes, the airship. Quite a project," says the Prior. it will be a medical craft that we can take to places where there is no healthcare - a mobile, flying surgery. But we need help: we must recruit another doctor to assist Brother Hume. He is busy collecting medical supplies. And finally, our most able engineers are working on making the engines more efficient - you could speak to them. Can you help with any of these?" Gain the codeword *Birthright* if you do not already have it.

"I know of a willing doctor." (*Camberwell*)	**1393**
"I will be your doctor." (four levels of **medical training**)	**1374**
"When I can help, I will return."	**642**

❧ 1308 ❧

"I knew it," she replies. "Do not fear. My brother Macauley is the one who will cause a fuss, but I will not. It is enough for me to have received you as a messenger from that world to which I can never return, from my uncle and my home in Harpsden. There is a man in the Pearl Quarter called Macauley. Go there and buy me some of his jewellery. It is nothing like as precious as the emeralds you were given, but it looks it." She gives you **£15** to make a purchase for her.

Leave her...	**1323**

❧ 1309 ❧

"This is all nonsense," says the wharfmaster. You are grabbed by her guards and held until a team of Constables are fetched. Note that your boat is **moored at Mill End** and your mate will wait for your return - should you ever return.

Turn to...	**13**

❧ 1310 ❧

"Unusual idea," comes the reply. "First person wearing that cap I've ever heard say that. I thought everyone found Cairo perfectly enthralling."

Turn to...	**1491**

❧ 1311 ❧

The figure at the bridge recognises you immediately and drops the bridge. You speed across, then risk a look back to see the rope winding around the drum again and the drop-leaf raising up to let a barge through. The Constables are forced to wait, despite their rage and cries, and you rumble over the wooden slats and onto the hard, dry land of the northern bank.

Turn to...	**682**

❧ 1312 ❧

You beat the Captain down but his horrified crew quickly overpower you, throw your weapon overboard and clap you irons. They lock you in the brig and you will not be going aground in Belize, but will be taken directly back to Rotherfield on the return flight and handed over to the Constables. Remove all your **money** and **possessions** and note that you are now **Wanted by the Atmospheric Union**, on top of any other crimes.

Turn to...	**13**

❧ 1313 ❧

The airship sails on through the night. In the early morning, the lookout spots something unusual and everyone comes on standby. Roll a dice to see what happens:

Score 1-2	Attacked by sky pirates!	**875**
Score 3-6	A flying wreck	**1330**

❧ 1314 ❧

You have spent hours poring through the records and to no avail. Suddenly, you realise that someone has entered the room: an early clerk has arrived for work! He dashes out into the corridor and raises the alarm. You must make a break for it!

Try to open the window...   **1303**

❧ 1315 ❧

A cat could not walk more silently than you. You reach the service staircase. Which way will you proceed?

To the cellar...	**1142**
To the attic...	**1335**

❧ 1316 ❧

As you prepare to mount up, hands grab you and bundle you off into a monk's cell. After some hours of enforced solitude, the door opens and you see several Constables all too happy to see you.

Turn to...   **13**

❧ 1317 ❧

The auctioneer hands over the **quarry lease** rather suspiciously. You are not the buyer he expected.

The quarry is most easily reached from Wargrave, as the turning is unmarked and easily missed. If you take the lease there, you will be able to take possession.

Return to Henley...   **702**

❧ 1318 ❧

The man looks very confused and quickly takes stock. "I don't believe I know you," he replies and leaves the room.

The young blond captain laughs. "Did you just char that steward? How very odd."

Turn to...   **1491**

❧ 1319 ❧

Of course the pouch with the jewellery is still hung inside your shirt beneath your arm. Nobody can take it from there without waking, warning or warring with you.

But the case, left in your tiny closet, has plainly been moved. And since nothing else has been taken, it seems that somebody on board knows of the jewellery. And wants them.

The next day, as you stroll on the equator walkway around the balloon, Louis Gill approaches you. You met him at dinner one day - a small, unremarkable man seemingly married to his bowler hat. He is clerk travelling to Belize to return to his work in the State office. He addresses you directly, since nobody else is in earshot.

"Have you considered to whom you are carrying your cargo?" he asks. "Alphaea Harpsden is a rich heiress, to be married to one of the most ruthless businessmen in the state - in the Caribbean. What need has she of further gewgaws for her neck?"

"How do you know my business?" you reply, grasping his lapels.

"These are significant people," he responds calmly, not even noticing your fist and his bundled jacket front. "They are watched by many. Only let me say this: the great wealth you bring her will not remain in her keeping for long. When the plantations are seized, the estates burned and all her treasures stolen, the emeralds will be used by the revolutionaries to bedeck their own Cleopatras, or sold to buy gunpowder and shot."

"Is the colony doomed, then?"

"It certainly is. I will be surprised if a month passes before the population are in all-out revolt. Your gems are being thrown away. Find a better use for them. Sell them to me - I offer you fifty guineas, now - or take them to a man I trust when we land. Mawkins, in the Pearl Quarter. He will replace them with a counterfeit that you can offer to the happy bride."

"And what will you do with them?"

"Endeavour to buy what peace I can. Buy time. Bribe people - use them as a lure and a snare and do everything in the power of the Confederated States to keep Belize from an apocalypse of flame. Not everyone in our country believes in the right of one man to own another and many believe that reform is long overdue in the Caribbean states. I represent a very powerful group of such people."

"And you would buy them?"

"The money will simply allow you to assuage your conscience however you see fit."

"They are worth far more than that," you reply.

"I know. But what are they worth around the neck of a doomed woman? Ignore the crisis, return to England condoning the cruelty of the plantationeers by your nonchalance and learn, in a few months time, of the slaughter and fire. Or do what you can now."

"Here, take the jewellery."   **1341**
"I can use them wisely without your advice."   **1348**

❧ 1320 ☙

The other airmen are more than happy to follow you. "The officer? Let's scrag 'im and throw 'im overboard," says one rough engineer. Note that your velosteam is **left at Rotherfield Greys**. If you do not have *The Great North Road*, you must convince the crew to bide their time and turn instead to looting the cabins.

Overpower the officer...   *The Great North Road 673*
Loot the cabins...   **1279**

❧ 1321 ☙

Box after box after box of punchcards reveal no reference to the battle at Valencia. You are running out of time in which to search. If you choose to look again, roll a dice. Otherwise you may slip out while the coast is clear.

Score 1-3   **1314**
Score 4-6   **1302**
Leave the office...   **1280**

❧ 1322 ☙

You begin to explain your right to sell the wheat, despite not being a member of the cartel. The wharfmaster listens skeptically. Make a GALLANTRY roll of difficulty 13, adding 1 if you have a **malt licence** and 1 if you have a **Bargee's Badge** or **Abbey Ribbon**.

Successful GALLANTRY roll!   **1270**
Failed GALLANTRY roll!   **1309**

❧ 1323 ☙
☐ ☐ ☐

If any of the boxes above are empty, tick one. If all are already ticked, turn to **1406** immediately.

Your room in the most fashionable hotel in Belize is paid for by the Harpsden family. Alphaea is staying in her own wing of the same hotel and many of the wedding guests are too. You have a little time before the great celebration and are at complete liberty to spend it as you will. Note this **passage number**.

Tend any wounds or illnesses...   **33**
Head into town...   **1475**
Speak to Alphaea...   **1419**
Take the gems to Macauley...
    (**emerald jewellery**)   **1406**

❧ 1324 ☙

Your opponent shuffles his feet and for a moment, it seems that he have footed their ball. Then his partner rushes over. "Don't you know what happened last time someone cheated the Steam Highwayman?" you hear. "He almost died!"

The gentleman apologises profusely. "Terribly sorry - terribly, terribly sorry. Must have caught the ball on my trouser cuff." He turns pale and loses his composure. You are easily able to pass the next **two hoops** without any interference.

Turn to...   **1132**

❧ 1325 ☙

The steamer is an interesting, three-wheeled design. It may be a rich nobleman travelling between his estates or simply a few middle-class travellers who are sharing a fare between towns. Note **passage number 171**.

Attack the steamer...   **103**
Carry on with your journey...   **710**

❧ 1326 ☙

"Gentlemen," you say, drawing your weapons, "That will do nicely. I will now be taking command of this airship." Their eyes goggle in amazement. Make a RUTHLESSNESS roll of difficulty 16.

Successful RUTHLESSNESS roll!   **1350**
Failed RUTHLESSNESS roll!   **1291**

❧ 1327 ❧

The steward apologises quickly and ducks back out. The officer beside you chortles. "Told him, didn't you? Got to keep the staff in their place: fore and aft we run the craft. Now, what were we talking about?"

Turn to...   **1429**

❧ 1328 ❧

"You are missing something expensive? It was certainly one of the passengers," he says. "Most likely that bowler-hatted spy. The crew would not dare - they would be skinned and their families indentured. No, rest assured that it is somewhere hidden in a cabin."

Search the passengers' cabins...   **1379**

❧ 1329 ❧

"You took them!" you cry out. "It was too much temptation for you - I should have kept them with me!"

"How dare you try to besmirch my honour!" replies the Captain, spitting with rage. He draws his sword and attacks you!

Airship Captain	Weapon: **rapier (PAR4)**
Parry:	12
Nimbleness:	8
Toughness:	4

Victory!	**1312**
Defeat!	**1237**

❧ 1330 ❧

The engine crew crowd onto the after deck and peer through the cloudy night. "It's a floating wreck," says one. "Could be salvage money in it for us..."

"Belay your chatter," calls the First Officer. "Volunteers to board the wreck! Six airmen, two engineers."

Volunteer to join the boarding party...	**1345**
Keep out of trouble...	**1358**

❧ 1331 ❧

Macauley returns to the store-room where you are chained with a fistful of banknotes. "What are these?" he rages. You sold my sister's inheritance for a measly few guineas! Disgusting. I am amazed that my uncle was so foolish as to trust a miserable piece of humanity like yourself."

Remove the **guineas**, all your **money** and **weapons** from your **possessions**. You are then hauled aboard an airship to be sent to England for trial. The flight back will not be as comfortable as Sir Roger's ticket made the one here. Your confinement in the cargo hold beside steam pipes and cotton bales sees you suffering with cold one moment and heat the next - receive a **burn** (NIM-1) from the boiling pipes.

Turn to...   **13**

❧ 1332 ❧

To donate medical supplies, remove the item you can give from your **possessions** and tick the relevant box on the list below. When you have ticked all the boxes, turn to **1355**.

☐ **soothing lotion**
☐ **cough medicine**
☐ **bandages**
☐ **catling knife**
☐ **pink pills (NIM +2)** ☐ ☐ ☐

Return to the cloister...   **642**

❧ 1333 ❧

"Excellent," he says. "Come with me."

He leads you to a safe in his dressing room, removes a beautiful set of **emerald jewellery**, and hands it over to you carefully. It must be worth a fortune. In its case and velvet bag it fits beneath your outer clothing without a sign. "Now Alphaea will love these, I know, and I want her husband to know what sort of people she comes from. Take the Atmospheric flight to Belize from Rotherfield Greys. They'll store your velosteam until you come back. I'll make sure there's a cabin reserved for you and I'll think about how to thank you while you're away. Keep them hidden, but if anyone tries to take them off you, I know you're able to hold your own. Don't pull any punches for the sake of decorum!"

Sir Roger's staff serve you a good dinner and fine wine and when you leave, late that night, he shakes your hand once more. "Good luck! Enjoy the flight!" Gain the codeword *Balance*. He also has his housekeeper see to any **wounds** you may have: remove them and replace them with **scars**, testing for **intimidating scars** in the normal way.

Leave the house...   **494**

♔ 1334 ♔

When you tell the officers about how you turned the navvies against the Imperial Western Railway, they laugh and rub their hands with glee. "Getting far too powerful," harrumphs one fat Colonel-of-Signals. He hands you **£15** in coins. Erase the codeword *Befriend*.

Turn to...   **617**

♔ 1335 ♔

The attic of Stonor House contains a large number of crates covered in dust. Each contains steel and brass components packed in straw. It looks like a dismantled calculating engine. In one small casket you find a set of **punchcards (Selladore V)**.

Leave the house...   **1273**
Continue to explore...   **1284**

♔ 1336 ♔

The wharfmaster nods and waves her hands. "I see, I see. I thought you were just an opportunist trying to undercut the cartel. Next time, mention this conversation." Gain the codeword *Bespoke*.

Turn to...   **630**

♔ 1337 ♔

The punchcards clatter through the machine, which processes them in lightning speed. It seems that the regiment have invested in the most up-to-date computational engine available. What will you ask it to do?

Identify the location of the Valencia Orders... **1302**
Reconstruct missing information...
    (torn manifest)   **228**
Write a piece of music...   **1511**
Return to the records office...   **1261**

♔ 1338 ♔

You step out into the road and grin your wickedest grin. "Stop your wagon or you won't see Henley again!" As the wagon approaches, you see the flash of a gun muzzle from the roof. Make a RUTHLESSNESS roll of difficulty 11.

Successful RUTHLESSNESS roll!   **1383**
Failed RUTHLESSNESS roll!   **1342**

♔ 1339 ♔

With the Lord of the Manor dead and his heir not yet come into inheritance, there is no-one to respond to your letter. You are not given it back.

Leave the house...   **937**

♔ 1340 ♔

You are welcomed aboard. Your cabin is comfortable and clean - a little sparse, but then weight is the prime consideration for every design and activity on board a long-distance airship like this.

The other passengers are nobility, the families of the well-to-do, rich travellers, ladies and gentlemen. You manage to keep up appearances and in the course of the flight learn a good deal about their business - without giving too much of your own away. Several are taking the flight with you all the way to Belize.

"I am going to inspect my plantations," says one woman. "They've been in the family for years - it was mostly cotton for a long time, but I had several switch to rice. And cane of course. But I've been hearing reports of troublemakers amongst the slaves and I'm not convinced my manager is being decisive enough: if he's not able to keep control I'll put one of my other men in charge."

The one thing you hear on everybody's lips about the Confederate State of Belize is the slave unrest. Apparently there was an uprising some thirty years ago which was put down in a very bloody manner. As the capital of the Confederated Caribbean states, Belize has a significant military presence, but although the officers are American or European, the vast majority of the troops are a mix of indigenous, ex-slave and levied soldiers. Their reliability is rather dependent on their pay and their treatment.

A Major in the Confederate forces is aboard. When you ask him about the military situation he snorts. "The men are utterly unreliable. Need to keep them busy. But as soon as we get a sniff of the ringleaders, we'll make an example of them. That's the way to keep things in order. We've got a shipment of repeating carbines coming in: I'm to train the garrison. I tell you, no-one in the Caribbean has ever seen such things."

Turn to...   1147

❧ 1341 ❧
You hand over the **emerald jewellery**: remove it from your **possessions**. In return, Gill hands you **fifty guineas in banknotes**. "Remember," he says, "When we arrive in Belize, Mawkins in the pearl district can arrange a counterfeit for you to give to the bride. I advise you not to stay too long in the city: whether I succeed or fail, there will be bloodshed and suffering aplenty."

Turn to...   1373

❧ 1342 ❧
The driver is totally unimpressed by your attempt to seem frightening! The vehicle accelerates towards you and then, to make matters worse, shots ring out! You dive for cover, but you must roll a dice to see whether you or your velosteam are hit.

Score 1   Receive **two wounds**
Score 2   Gain a **damage point**
Score 3-4   Receive a **wound**
Score 5-6   Escape unharmed

If your velosteam is now **beyond repair**, turn to **874** immediately. If not but you have **five wounds**, turn to **999**. Otherwise you will have to remount your velosteam and make yourself scarce.

Turn to...   **noted passage**

❧ 1343 ❧
The quarrymen set to work and before long you are able to fill your boat with as many units of **stone** as you are able to carry. This is not a standard cargo and can only be sold in places where there are large building projects being undertaken, like in the capital, or used for a project of your own.

Unmoor...   131
Return to Wargrave...   418

❧ 1344 ❧
The water slops and shimmers as it reflects what little moonlight breaks between the the clouds. You wait until you are sure you have the patrolling guards' patterns worked out and prepare your charges - remove the **explosives** from your possession.

Quickly scuttling out of hiding, you lower the charges and their waterproof fuses into the water. The cords you use allow them to hang directly against the brickwork: if you have prepared them correctly, you should be able to crack the massive wall. The power of the shock-wave rushing through the water should do the rest. Make an ENGINEERING roll of difficulty 12 adding 2 for each level of **explosives expert** you possess.

Successful ENGINEERING roll!   1158
Failed ENGINEERING roll!   1170

❧ 1345 ❧
The two airships bump gently together and the First Officer leads your boarding party across on a quickly-retracted gangplank. After a search, it is clear that the abandoned craft is mainly intact and in working condition. Has it escaped from a tether or been raided by pirates? Either way, you have an opportunity.

Steal what you can from the cabins and hold... 1279
Convince the boarding party to turn pirate... 1292

❧ 1346 ❧
You have failed to impress the airship officers and they leave you without saying any more. Their suspicion will prevent you from being able to slip aboard and your ignorance of their work and manners mean that you would never succeed in maintaining the charade.

Return to the airfield...   454

❧ 1347 ❧

After a long wait you are taken inside the house to meet the Viscount. He has just been enjoying a meal with friends and licks the last drop of wine from a glass as he enters the room. "I know you," he snarls. "The moral doctor. Come to try and punish me? Me!" He draws his sword.

Viscount Monsberg	Weapon: **rapier (PAR 4)**
Parry:	13
Nimbleness:	9
Toughness: `	3

Victory!	**1245**
Defeat!	**1190**

❧ 1348 ❧

Gill shakes his head. "I will see you again - I know it. Don't imagine that everything is the way it seems in Belize. Appearances can be very deceptive."

You push him aside and return to your cabin. The jewels will not leave your side until you arrive.

Turn to...   **1373**

❧ 1349 ❧

A rare steam-carriage comes to collect you for your return flight. Is the scent of oil, coal-gas and steel dissimilar to that of your own Ferguson, thousands of miles away in a shed at Rotherfield Greys? How many days since you were in that well-worn saddle?

As the carriage pulls away into the dusk, an explosion rocks the city and flames leap up.

"That's the garrison," says the driver, entirely unperturbed.

"Is it the revolution?" you ask.

"A revolution," he replies. "Will it be the one we need? We've had so many revolts. Once I've taken you to the airfield, I'm heading up to Ladytown to take my family into the jungle and wait it out."

It seems that the inevitable pressure of cruel exploitation has burst at last in Belize. Whether it will bring about a more just, more fair society or one even more brutal, you will not be able to answer.

Turn to...   **1484**

❧ 1350 ❧

The crew are terrified into submission, but the captain quickly sees an opportunity. "I never liked working for the Union anyway. If you'll be our Captain, we'll turn pirate! With the Steam Highwayman to lead us, we'll be the terror of the skies! Captain Coke will have nothing on us!"

This will go down in legend: add **stole an airship** to your **Great Deeds**.

Hand the airship over to the Compact...	**1196**
Fly into the west...	*Princes of the West 551*

❧ 1351 ❧

When you board, the Steward looks at your ticket and mutters to himself. "I'm afraid there has been a mistake," he says. "This should be a Third-Class cabin." He leads you onboard and brings you to a narrow room at the rear of the lower gondola. A narrow porthole will give you a view aft.

The flight is long and not very pleasant. Your cramped conditions and the disdain of many of the other passengers are discomforts that you are soon able to cope with - after all, how do they compare to an outlaw's life on the road?

Once it is known that you are travelling on to Belize, you gain the interest of a thin gentleman with a predilection for showy, striped clothes. He tries to find out what your business there is.

"Are you a gun-runner? No. Or perhaps a person of finance? You're carrying paper money, or drafts on a bank, or jewels? I could well expect that the people there will be in need of money for their endeavours. Revolutions are always expensive."

"Revolutions?" you ask innocently.

"Yes. Of course you know about the situation there. Ninety percent of Belize's population are slaves. I'm not saying there's anything wrong with that, but the Confederated States Government have been remarkably short-sighted. Even some small concessions in the way of living standards, some token rights, would have staved this off entirely. Now I doubt there is anything they can do to prevent it."

"Is the difference between rich and poor that stark?"

He looks at you uneasily. "You'll see for yourself. The landowning class do not need any help to stay rich. So, why are you travelling there yourself?"

"I'm no longer quite sure," you reply.

Turn to...   **1147**

❧ 1352 ❧
You aim carefully down the road, watching the silhouette of your target over your gun's sights. Make an ACCURACY roll of difficulty 12.

Successful ACCURACY roll!	**1383**
Failed ACCURACY roll!	**1221**

❧ 1353 ❧
Susan Tenney is sharp and excited. She puts aside her glass of sparkling wine and doesn't touch it for the length of the challenging match. Her blue ball moves ahead and you pursue her, but a mean blow from your red opponent leaves you making up time. You have passed **one hoop.**

Turn to...	**548**

❧ 1354 ❧
The long straight down Hambleden valley should be perfect for putting distance between you and your pursuers, but when you arrive there, the cows are out, moving between their pasture and the evening milking. Make a MOTORING roll of difficulty 12 to clear them, adding 1 for each level of **animal friendship** you possess.

Successful MOTORING roll!	**130**
Failed MOTORING roll!	**1042**

❧ 1355 ❧
Brother Hume thanks you. "You have given much. I pray that God will give much to you in turn." He also teaches you about the use of the equipment you have brought him: gain a level of **medical training** and roll two dice: if the total is greater than your INGENUITY score, increase it by one.

Return to the cloister...	**642**

❧ 1356 ❧
The prisoner lies across your lap, his stinking rags reeking more than the smell of your gas and oil and the leafmould of the woods. Your ride brings you to Elvendon Priory and you hand him over to the monks, who go to wake the herbalist. Your own exhaustion overcomes you and sleep arrives while you sit in a high-backed chair.

The morning brings a bowl of steaming porridge and a grave monk. "What of the old man," you ask. "Does he..?"

The monk shakes his head. "His body was tormented beyond bearing. What evil intention could have done such a thing! He died an hour ago."

In death, the man's body seems even smaller than when you bore it here. Small, frail and delicate. The monks will bury him in their graveyard.

You have rescued a man only to see him die. Did he die a better death free than in that cellar? Did your intervention hasten his end, and would that have been a good thing? The monks are unwilling to discuss it further and you must be on your way once more.

Turn to...	**1131**

❧ 1357 ❧
Since Lord Ponsonby's flight from the region and the change in Estate manager, the house has been shuttered and quiet. The peacocks still strut around, but goodness knows who feeds them.

Return to the village...	**977**

❧ 1358 ❧
The boarding party return without enthusiasm. "Nothing there for us," one says. "Burnt-out cabins, gas leaking away. Incredible it's still floating. Must have been pirates."

Turn to...	**1370**

❧ 1359 ❧
"One of these days I'll settle down with a nice reliable woman in a cottage somewhere in the country," slurs a quickly-decomposing officer.

"No you won't. You'll die young and famous."	**1444**
"Sounds ideal."	**1346**

❧ 1360 ❧
Your velosteam should be a match for any vehicle on the road! You gauge your moment carefully, then launch off alongside your target and steer for the driver's position. Make a MOTORING roll of difficulty 11.

Successful MOTORING roll!	**1383**
Failed MOTORING roll!	**1249**

1361

The navvies are a proud, unified tribe. What affects one of them affects them all, and this makes them able to negotiate good wages from their employers. However, you talk to some of their decision-makers about the other labourers in the region's farms and factories who do not enjoy their solidarity.

"What concern is that of ours?" asks one man.

Stir up unrest against the railway...	**675**
Recruit them for the Compact...	
(Member of the CWE)	**1074**

1362

You talk to the steward - the member of the crew with the best idea of what is going on around and about the airship. Make a GALLANTRY roll of difficulty 12, adding 1 if you want to give him a **bottle of wine** or 2 if you give him a **bottle of whisky**.

Successful GALLANTRY roll!	**1328**
Failed GALLANTRY roll!	**1290**

1363

"Aha! The Steam Highwayman! I've been looking for you!" The passenger you have surprised is a high-ranking Constable, glad of the opportunity to make his name with your capture. However, he is fat and slow and you have a fair chance of turning the tables.

Constable	Weapon: **sabre (PAR 3)**
Parry:	9
Nimbleness:	6
Toughness:	6

Victory!	**1437**
Defeat!	**13**

1364

The dockers flee in terror as you knock down their leader. Whistles and shouts announce the arrival of watchmen and you quickly make your way back to the safety of the hotel.

Turn to...	**1323**

1365

Remove the codeword *Balance*. A long, slim Atmospheric Union skyship is moored on the centre of the airfield: it is the long-distance flight to Belize stopping at Lisbon, Funchal and San Juan. Fifty passengers are booked aboard a flight known for its luxury and decadence. Your cabin has been booked and your ticket paid for by Sir Roger Harpsden and all that remains is to board the ship and enjoy the journey. It may be worth packing a selection of possessions that will help you get along in high society: if you wish for more time before making the flight, turn to **454**. Otherwise, make a GALLANTRY roll.

Score 9 or lower	**1351**
Score 10-14	**1340**
Score 15 or higher	**1378**

1366

The measurements you take of the reservoir will allow someone to calculate its capacity and the strength of explosive needed to break it open, giving weight to their threats. Whether they do or not, you do not have to take direct responsibility for that destruction. Gain a set of **reservoir plans**.

Sneak back out...	**544**

1367

"What the devil do you mean?" asks Macauley, turning red in the face. "You were employed expressly to prevent them being stolen or lost! And now you mean to tell me that you've been too busy enjoying a cruise to protect my sister's inheritance. How dare you! I'll have you arrested!"

Taken off-guard, in unfamiliar surroundings and without your weapons to hand, you are swiftly arrested and put in irons. Macauley plainly has the ear of the powerful in the city. Your belongings are searched. If you in fact possess the **emerald jewellery**, turn to **1392**. If you do not, but you have at least **fifty guineas in banknotes**, turn to **1331**. Otherwise, read on.

Since there is no sign of the gems amongst your possessions, there is nothing Macauley can do. There is no direct record of you having the jewels and you cannot be proven the thief. Needless to say, you are not given a first-class cabin on your return, but are bundled up into the cargo hold in irons and flown back to England without delay.

The flight is cold, uncomfortable and degrading. Not only do you catch a **fever (NIM-1 ING-2)** from your confinement but you also have far too much time to think over your mistakes. This might have been one of the Steam Highwayman's greatest adventures, but you are thrown off the airship at Rotherfield Greys without the least ceremony.

At least your velosteam will be where you left it in the care of an under-engineer at least and the roads and woods are the allies they always were.

Turn to... **454**

❧ 1368 ☙
You tear along the lanes, banking hard at the bends and cutting the grassy corners at junctions. Your Ferguson was made for this, but you will still have to ride carefully to keep ahead and upright. Make a MOTORING roll of difficulty 12 to outrun your pursuers and lose them before you reach Pishill.

Successful MOTORING roll! **370**
Failed MOTORING roll! **1042**

❧ 1369 ☙
You lay out the necklace, earrings, pendants and bracelets, the rings and the tiara. They make quite a sight. Alphaea Harpsden shakes her head in wonder. "So generous. Dear uncle Roger. Yet do I need them?" She sighs. "There is a man in the Pearl Quarter called Mawkins. He makes jewellery - but nothing like this. I want you to take this to him, sell it, bring me the money and buy me something much simpler."

"After bringing it all this way, you want me to sell it?"

"Yes. The money can help me. I will keep this," she says, and takes a simple emerald pendant, "To remember how someone far away cares for me. But the rest I have no need of."

"Where shall I sell the rest?"
"There is a man who came on the same airship as you," she says. "A clerk called Gill at the State Office. I know he will buy them."

Take the emeralds to Gill... **1161**

❧ 1370 ☙
At Reykjavik the airship is moored overnight and in the early morning, heavy winches bring it down to the ground for unloading, hand-to-hand. With every crate and sack tossed down the chain, ballast is heaved on board in the form of coal, water or return freight, and all the time the engineers alter the trim to keep the craft under control. "Try doing this in high winds!" says Mrs Betting. "This is nothing."

The crew are given only a few hours' shore leave and then you must depart once more. During your time ashore you have the chance to visit the famous workshops of the Icelandic mechanics and look at some of their wares.

Tools	To buy	To sell
adjustable wrench (ENG+1)	£2 5s	-
explosives	£1 4s	-
welding tools	£2 2s	£1
skeleton key	£5	£1 10s
jeweller's loupe (ING+1)	£3	£1 12s
telescope	£5	-
lockpicks	6s	2s
pneumatic manual (ENG+3)	£13	-
calculating engine (ING+3)	£25 4s	
autogauge (MOT+3)	£16 10s	-
steam fist (RUTH+3)	£15	-
ultra-tensed wire	18s	10s
nephritic solution	15s	8s

Turn to... **1386**

❧ 1371 ☙
Ponsonby laughs when he recognises you. "I don't have any money," he says. "Look!" He turns out his pockets. "If you were going to kill me, you would have done it already. But it won't help the villagers. My manager has instructions."

Turn around... **noted passage**

❧ 1372 ☙
A young captain and several officers are laughing as one of them regales the others with a tale of shooting a giraffe from low altitude on a flight to Durban. "Then we had to hoist the thing up, of course, and the chef insisted on serving us all a giraffe steak. Not that pleasant, I have to say. Went bad in no time but we'd dropped all manner of ballast to take it on. When we reached Durban I had it stuffed."

"Well, Higgins, it's a good thing you didn't shoot an elephant."

"Elephant tastes even worse, let me tell you. But we had plenty of champagne aboard to swill out the flavour of the savannah - not as good as this stuff. Though after a while it does tend to give your teeth a tingle." He looks your way. "I say, what are you drinking there? That looks refreshing."

"Just water. Must keep my head clear." **1486**
"Markovitz and tonic water." **1456**
"Neat London gin, of course." **1477**

❧ 1373 ❧

The flight continues across the wide, blue sea. You arrive in Puerto Rico behind schedule and the crew hurry to refuel and refill the water tanks. The gas pressure is equalised and after only a few hours, the airship is on its way to Belize City.

The final stretch of the flight across the sparkling Caribbean sees the passengers break out into the careless indulgence of the irresponsible rich. Cocktails are served at all hours, music and dancing, games, dressing up and all manner of illicit rendezvous and trysts are carried out in the liberated atmosphere of sun and warmth. Perhaps you also enjoy the release of a luxury flight with your expenses paid. Or perhaps you have your own concerns about arriving in Belize.

Turn to...   **1455**

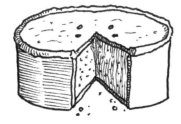

❧ 1374 ❧

Prior Horace is impressed by your offer and gladly accepts. "To put your skills to the service of God and the poor - now that is admirable." He initiates you into the order as a layperson and you are prepared for your flight.

Together with a team of eight other monks, you spend several weeks travelling the country dispensing healthcare, teaching about cleanliness and hygiene and treating the sick. In the course of your journey you become close with the brothers, hear much of the goings-on in the land, see first-hand the wounds of rebels in the north, the suffering of factory workers in the cities and the abject poverty of the peasantry. You are able to do much good but there is a bottomless well of need that could absorb all the charity and all the generosity of a thousand flying hospitals.

When you return at last, Prior Horace greets you. "I have heard of all your deeds. Well done. Rest now and recuperate after all you have given. But ponder this, too. You have rare skills. Will you join our order permanently and help us to heal the people of this land?"

"I must be on my way."   **1388**
"I will join you."   **1409**

❧ 1375 ❧

You have had the misfortune to come across someone who lives, as you do, by their wits and by the sword. Will you be able to come out victorious in an even match?

Officer	Weapon: **sabre (PAR 3)**	
Parry:	10	
Nimbleness:	7	
Toughness:	5	

Victory!		**1427**
Defeated!		**999**

❧ 1376 ❧

Despite your best efforts, your target manages to stay ahead of you on the narrow road and soon you reach a downhill stretch. To pursue them further will take you towards inhabited areas and run the risk of a run-in with the Constables. You turn and halt your velosteam as the vehicle gets away. At least without armed guards it is unable to harm you.

Turn to...   **noted passage**

❧ 1377 ❧

You are shown to a dirty and badly-dressed Telegraph Officer, who begins to rant about the encroachment of the railway on the Telegraph's patents. "They need teaching a lesson! I tell you where they're vulnerable - the workmen - slaves almost - who do all the hard work for them. They've got to be paid off - or something. They're still finishing that bridge down by South Stoke - if we can stop that, then their whole expansion will suffer."

Leave the compound...   **617**

❧ 1378 ❧

Your manners and aplomb quickly win you regard amongst the other passengers and the Captain himself welcomes you aboard. "I hope you enjoy the flight," he says, "And find your cabin comfortable. I will be giving a little dinner tonight - would you be so good as to join me and a few others? I have a very fine case of de Pelet that I'd like to share with some who are able to appreciate it. My First Officer, lamentably, is a beer drinker."

The other First Class guests are almost alarmingly well-to-do. An opera singer and her diminutive husband, an officer in the Confederate Army, several plantation owners and a Portuguese nobleman returning to his estates are all invited - along with yourself - to dine with the captain in the sumptuous dining room at the very front of the ship. They presume that you are some sort of government agent and refrain from too many questions. However, one begins to talk about a wedding in Belize City. His friend Jack Acreage is marrying a beautiful young heiress.

"Is that the Harpsden wedding?" you ask.

"Why yes," he replies. "Jack's done very well for himself. She brings several fine plantations with her and considerable investments in shipping - sea and air."

"And is it a love match?"

He laughs. "From all I've heard, far from it. But a woman must be wed and a man must have a wife. Mistresses and go-to-women are all very well for a chap, but you can't get yourself an heir that way."

Turn to...   1147

❧ 1379 ❧

Your search of the passenger's quarters does not go well. You are soon challenged by another passenger and, despite insisting that you are searching for stolen property, are accused of thievery yourself. You only narrowly escape being thrown in the brig.

Give up the search for now...   1373

❧ 1380 ❧

A frail old woman dressed in widow's black is travelling to stay with her family. The last thing she expected was to be robbed on the way. If you choose to let her pass now, turn to your **noted passage** immediately.

Otherwise she strangely leaps at you with her bare hands and claws at your face! You will have to fight her off - but you may wish to use your bare hands (**PAR 0**) or a blunt weapon if you have one.

Widow	Weapon: sharp nails (**PAR 0**)
Parry:	11
Nimbleness:	11
Toughness:	3

Victory with a blunt weapon or hands!	1433
Victory with a bladed weapon!	1426
Defeat!	999

❧ 1381 ❧

You are beaten to a pulp and all your **money** and **possessions** are taken from you. A pair of patrolling watchmen find you and return you to your hotel. They find you **three bandages** and have you taken to your room.

Turn to...   1323

❧ 1382 ❧

"This is interesting," says Prior Horace. "Thank you very much indeed for bringing this to us." He leaves you in his study for a moment while he steps outside to speak to a brother.

Leave the study...   1316

❧ 1383 ❧

The driver and guard of the Coal Board wagon quickly surrender. They are not looking to get hurt for a petty wage. "If we was paid fairly, then maybe the Board would find us rather more in a fighting spirit," says the driver unhappily. "But then we ain't paid enough to put up against the Steam Highwayman." You may rob them of **£2 5s**, a **shovel**, some **dungarees (GAL-2)** and a **lantern**, but the rest of their cargo is heavy vehicle anthracite coal and far too bulky to steal by yourself. You will now be **Wanted by the Coal Board** unless you were wearing a **mask**. You also gain the codeword *Bubbling*.

Turn to...   noted passage

❧ 1384 ❧

To convince the guard that you are an official engineer, you must make intelligent-sounding comments as you poke around the engine house, making an ENGINEERING roll of difficulty 12 - or carry a **pneumatic manual** to refer to.

Successful ENGINEERING roll or possess	
a **pneumatic manual**...	1397
Failed ENGINEERING roll!	710

ᕼ 1385 ᕽ

You lie in wait in the shadows where trees overhang the driveway to the house. It is only a matter of time until Lord Ponsonby rides out in his steam carriage.

Eventually he does. You step out into the road and show your weapons. Note **passage number 550** and make a RUTHLESSNESS roll of difficulty 15.

Successful RUTHLESSNESS roll!	**1403**
Failed RUTHLESSNESS roll!	**782**

ᕼ 1386 ᕽ

On the return flight you settle into the routines of your duties and shifts. The constant noise and heat are becoming bearable, while certainly still unpleasant. Make an ENGINEERING roll to see how the remainder of your flight passes.

Score <16	Scalded: gain a **burn (NIM-1)**
Score 16-17	Find a **silver ring** on deck
Score 18+	Save a crewman's arm: gain a **solidarity point**

Rotherfield Greys is soon in sight: the airship docks and you are paid off. "You weren't completely useless," grunts Mrs Betting grudgingly as she hands you **£3 10s**. You have also gained a great deal of knowledge about the workings of aerial steam engines: gain a point of ENGINEERING permanently.

Turn to...   **454**

ᕼ 1387 ᕽ

On the door of the compartment is a golden parliamentary crest and inside you discover a politician with his wife - or possibly mistress. He has spirit though and draws his swordstick.

Politician	Weapon: **swordstick (PAR 2 GAL+1)**
Parry:	10
Nimbleness:	8
Toughness:	3

Victory!	**1443**
Defeat!	**999**

ᕼ 1388 ᕽ

"Well, you have given much," replies Horace. "Return whenever you wish." You are now the **Friend of Prior Horace**.

Leave the Priory...   **1131**

ᕼ 1389 ᕽ

Livingstone M punchcards are powerful meta-calculators. Feeding them into the machine allows it to print out a shadow impression and a set of rules, which you realise will allow you to create your own punchcards, if you have access to a punch machine. In this instance, it looks like a set of Aramanth A cards... You now have an ability many would covet. Gain the codeword *Busybody*.

Leave the machine...   **noted passage**

ᕼ 1390 ᕽ

Through your carefully-focused lenses you can see that the engine is undefended and that the three metal-framed wagons beside are stuffed full of supplies - largely massive timber spars used for building the frames of the telegraphs, as well as cables of wire. In the driver's cab you can see a cloth-capped driver and a fireman shovelling coal, but neither seem to be armed.

Swing into the passing driver's cab... (**rope**)	**1404**
Intimidate the driver...	**1424**
Ride alongside...	**1412**

ᕼ 1391 ᕽ

Do you remember Comrade Plunkett's final order? He desired you to hijack an airship for the Compact and bring it to Nettlebed mooring post. If you want to try and complete this dangerous mission now, you have two ways to go about it: you can either try to sneak aboard an airship that is being prepared for take-off and overpower the crew, relying on your ENGINEERING and MOTORING skills, or you can impersonate an Atmospheric Union captain and take control once in the air, depending on your GALLANTRY skill and ability to bluff.

Attempt to sneak aboard...	**1405**
Impersonate a captain...	
(**airship officer's cap**)	**1423**
Leave the lounge...	**454**

ॐ 1392 ॐ

The **emerald jewellery** is discovered in your baggage and Macauley has proof of your attempted thievery. Remove it from your **possessions**, along with any **money** or **weapons**. "What a poor show," he scoffs. "You didn't even manage to hide it well."

He has you shipped back to England in chains in the hold of a returning airship. Once there, you are handed over to the Constables.

Turn to...   **13**

ॐ 1393 ॐ

You explain how you have convinced a doctor to come and help the monks. Prior Horace claps his hands with glee. "That is the most helpful of all," he says. "I am grateful - so grateful. It will not be long before we can send out our helpers, then." You are now the **Friend of Prior Horace**.

Return to the cloister...   **642**
Leave the priory...   **1131**

ॐ 1394 ॐ

To convince that you are a nobleperson out joyriding, with every right to go where you like, you must either possess a **fur coat**, a **top hat** or make a GALLANTRY roll of difficulty 12.

Successful GALLANTRY roll or possess
    a **fur coat** or **top hat**...   **1397**
Failed GALLANTRY roll!   **710**

ॐ 1395 ॐ

"I don't set a great store by my own happiness," says Alphaea. "But I will have what I need and I will be able to do much more for the colony, for the slaves and even, perhaps, for the man I have married than I ever could before. We may grow to love one another and that must suffice for me. All people change, and I fear that unless he changes, he may not enjoy his wealth for very long."

"The rebellion is coming sooner than you think," you reply. "You have very little time and stability left to you. This place is illusory - a dream of privilege floating on a sea of suffering."

"You do not know what I think or what I plan. You have played your part in this story and mine is still to play. Goodbye, Steam Highwayman."

Turn to...   **1349**

ॐ 1396 ॐ

You catch sight of a patrol of Constables headed your way. They can do you no good, so you quickly check the pressure in your boiler and prepare to head off. If you are **Wanted by the Constables**, turn to **306** immediately.

Ride towards Reading...   **793**
Head for Woodcote...   **488**
Steam into Goring...   **487**

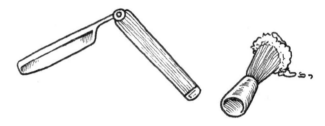

ॐ 1397 ॐ

Looking around the compound you gain a very good idea of the reservoir's capacity, the supplies and needs of the engine house and some weak spots in the retaining embankment. How will you choose to use this information?

Attempt to destroy the reservoir by night...
    (explosives)   **1344**
Leave the compound...   **710**

ॐ 1398 ॐ

The drinking and story-telling will continue far into the night. Some Captains will be carried to their cabins and others will sleep in the rooms behind the lounge here, waited on by patient bosuns and stewards.

"I think I've had too much to drink."   **1346**
"Let's have some more champagne!"   **1444**

ॐ 1399 ॐ

If you have fifteen or more **solidarity points**, read on. Otherwise, turn to **1479** immediately.

The crew are initially very wary but one of them recognises who you are. "It's the Steam Highwayman, mates," he says. "He's for the likes of us, don't you worry."

You explain what you're looking for, but it does not turn up. "It ain't us, mate," says one. "It'll be one of your guests up front."

That is as far as you are able to investigate for now. The crew promise to keep their eyes and ears open but they are unable to help you pinpoint the thief.

Turn to...   1373

❧ 1400 ❧

Is terrifying people for a living beginning to take a toll on you? How much longer can you continue threatening and stealing? Whether you can answer this or no, you must now make a RUTHLESSNESS roll of difficulty 12 to stop the steamer.

Successfull RUTHLESSNESS roll!   1428
Failed RUTHLESSNESS roll!   782

❧ 1401 ❧

The captain shakes his head sadly. "I know we are," he says. "I can offer you **fifty guineas in banknotes** for the loss - perhaps you will be able to find something to replace them in Belize City? I know that there are skilled jewellers in the Pearl Quarter."

"What an insulting offer!"   1408
"I will take the money."   1449

❧ 1402 ❧

The businessman you find inside the steam carriage is not keen to fight, but he will in an attempt to maintain his self-respect. He splutters and sidesteps and dodges and waves his sword ineffectively, like one who barely knows how to use it. He could still hurt you, though.

Businessman	Weapon: **rapier (PAR 4)**
Parry:	8
Nimbleness:	4
Toughness:	2

Victory!   1451
Defeat!   999

❧ 1403 ❧

Ponsonby - who is driving his own steam carriage - comes to a halt and you approach him carefully. When you are close enough to haul him down from his seat, you look him in the eye belligerently.

"Give me your money."   1441
"I can reach you any time I please."   1420

❧ 1404 ❧

The beech branch is broad and steady: you creep along it and tie a firm bowline in your rope, judging the distance you will have to swing and the time to launch yourself to land on the driving platform of the wagon.

The engine passes beneath you, the exhaust fumes billow around you and you sail down in a cloud of smoke and steam, careering into the fireman and sending the driver reeling. They are quickly on their feet and struggling with you for control of the engine!

Engine crew	Weapons: **shovels (PAR 2)**
Parry:	8
Nimbleness:	6
Toughness:	4

Victory!   1436
Defeat!   999

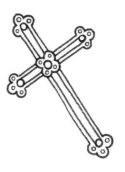

❧ 1405 ❧

Under the cover of darkness you approach an airship that you have seen being prepared for takeoff. The crew are resting in their cabins before the morning's flight. If you have a **bottle of chloroform**, turn to **1276** immediately. Otherwise you climb aboard and proceed to creep down the corridor, jamming the doors of the cabins with whatever you can find.

Once that is done, you head to the engine room to check the furnaces. They are still hot and can quickly be stoked back into life. You will not need a great deal of pressure to steam to nearby Nettlebed, but managing the entire ship by yourself will be a challenge. Make an ENGINEERING roll of difficulty 12.

Successful ENGINEERING roll!   1250
Failed ENGINEERING roll!   1223

❧ 1406 ❧

Macauley is sat in a chair in your sitting room. "Here you are," he says. "The wedding is this afternoon at two. I need the gems now."

"Here they are." (**emerald jewellery**)	**1488**
"They were stolen from me."	**1367**

❧ 1407 ❧

You recognise Professor Challing from the Henley Museum - and she recognises you as well. "Oh hello," she responds chirpily. "What are you doing here?"

"I'm robbing you."	**1417**
"I was hoping to bump into you. I have some questions."	**1421**

❧ 1408 ❧

The options are few: the captain himself has taken the gems, a member of his crew with access to the safe has opened it or another passenger - a safe-cracker - has done the job. You have some time to find the jewels again and to punish the thief.

Accuse the captain...	**1329**
Talk to the crew...	**1362**
Search the passengers' cabins...	**1379**
Search the crew's quarters...	**1399**
Look in the cargo hold...	**1413**

❧ 1409 ❧

And so it is. Your past of theft, threat and murder dissolves in your memory with the daily business of helping, healing and protecting the weak. You still use your skills to protect the brothers aloft, to help maintain and fly the airship and to learn what you can of their faith, but violence is no longer a recourse.

This is the end of your adventure, for you never return. The legend of the Steam Highwayman will fade. Turn to the **Epilogue**.

❧ 1410 ❧

Your money on the bar will certainly attract airship officers. Who they will be is a mere matter of chance: so many crews fly through here in their VA8 freighters, their Hoffpunkt cruisers, the big double-baggers called Bumblebees. Roll a dice to see who you meet.

Score 1-2	A Captain...	**1278**
Score 3-4	A Flight Engineer...	**1233**
Score 5-6	A First Officer...	**1267**

❧ 1411 ❧

"Colonel Howitz is dead," you tell Fred and Janet.

"Good," replies Fred quickly. "No grand parade for her, I hope." He shakes you by the hand. "You're plainly someone who ain't scared of blood or of getting things done. Did you ever take the King's shilling?" Gain a **solidarity point**.

Return to the parlour...	**763**

❧ 1412 ❧

You burst out from hiding with a roar of steam and flame from your vents and slam down onto the road beside the freight wagon. The driver, terrified by your appearance, opens the regulator and the road train surges forward. You must make a MOTORING roll of difficulty 12 to get alongside and wrest control, adding 1 if you possess a **reinforced boiler** or **off-road tyres**.

Successful MOTORING roll!	**1436**
Failed MOTORING roll!	**1376**

❧ 1413 ❧

In the cargo hold you look around for hiding places, but the range of possibilities is far too great. The jewels and their pouch could be inside one of any number of boxes, trunks, crates and bales. You are looking for a needle in a haystack.

You don't find the jewels, but you do come across five shillings (**5s**) in loose coins and a fluttering paper which turns out to be a **Delevinne Bank Share Certificate**. Will you turn thief now, while hunting for your own stolen property?

Talk to the crew...	**1362**
Search the passengers' cabins...	**1379**
Search the crew's quarters...	**1399**

❧ 1414 ❧

Your shots richochet of the wagon's metal-work, alerting the Constables. Unperturbed, they unholster their own carbines and begin firing back. One bullet whizzes through your **hat** if you are wearing one, ruining it completely (or close over your head if not!). Prudence is the better part of valour here.

Ride north...	**280**
Ride down the hill...	**863**

❧ 1415 ❧

"Get down and surrender your valuables," you cry, wielding your weaponry threateningly. A doctor climbs down from the passenger compartment carrying his bag. If you are the **Friend of Dr Smollett**, turn to **1489** immediately.

"I don't think I have to do what you say," says the doctor. "Let me see what I have here..." He rummages in his bag and springs on you with a heavy-bladed knife used for amputations.

Doctor	Weapon: **catling knife (PAR 1 NIM+2)**
Parry:	8
Nimbleness:	5
Toughness:	2

Victory!	1474
Defeat!	999

❧ 1416 ❧

You must aim carefully to knock down the guard before he catches sight of you. A successful shot is sure to cow the driver and bring the steamer to a halt. Make an ACCURACY roll of difficulty 12.

Successful ACCURACY roll!	1428
Failed ACCURACY roll!	1221

❧ 1417 ❧

"Rob me?" The Professor is quite upset. "Really? I... I don't know what to say. I feel quite betrayed and that is the truth. Here, take my purse and your so-called friendship with it." Her purse contains **£6 4s** and you are no longer the **Friend of Professor Challing**.

Turn to...   **noted passage**

❧ 1418 ❧

"I'm thinking of transferring to the Telegraph Guild," says an officer. "I've heard they offer real career progression."

"Why on earth would you want to do that?"	1359
"Seems fair to me."	1346

❧ 1419 ❧
☐

If the box above is empty, put a tick in it and read on. If it is already ticked, turn to **1224** immediately.

Alphaea Harpsden is very happy to see you. She has a strong resemblance to her uncle Roger and plainly cares for him deeply. "How is he? He and my aunt raised me until I was sent here when I was eleven. I haven't seen him since. But Harpsden and the woods are still in my heart. Dear Uncle Roger. And now to send me what he has."

She quickly works out that you too are a lover of the woods and villages of the Chilterns. She manages to get you to tell her of your adventures on the midnight road, through her innocent openness. You are a very long way from home.

"Here are the gems." (**emerald jewellery**)	1369
"I do not have the jewels."	1308

❧ 1420 ❧

Lord Ponsonby laughs. "Are you trying to scare me? You don't know my estate or my house and yet you want to pretend to be some sort of assassin!"

If you have a **peacock feather**, turn to **1460** immediately. Otherwise, Ponsonby flings down a purse of money (**£3 1s**) and laughs. "You can take this - but it will be the villagers who pay. I'll simply tell my estate manager to increase their rents."

Make a getaway...   **noted passage**

❧ 1421 ❧

"Well, it's very nice to bump into you," replies the Professor. "Now what did you want to ask?"

You spend a short while quizzing her about the local archaeology. She is particularly interested in the Saxon earthworks in the region, such as the popularly-named Grim's Ditch and the much more ancient fort in the wood near Gallowstree Common. If you have the codeword *Before*, gain the codeword *Benign*.

Turn to...   **noted passage**

❧ 1422 ❧

You tell Janet and Fred what you have found out about the battle at Valencia.

"It weren't a battle," says Fred angrily. "It were a slaughter. And not for any purpose but to fertilise the fine fields of Spain with my mates' blood. If you know who's to blame, I say kill 'em. Let 'em pay for it."

Return to the parlour...   **763**

❧ 1423 ❧

You swagger into the officer's lounge with your hat rakishly over your eye in the manner you have seen so many of the pilots affect. The main thing is to keep your cool. No-one has a reason to suspect you - yet. The fact that these crew travel so far and so frequently is, of course, in your favour. Nobody is surprised to see an unfamiliar face.

After ordering a drink you take a look at the flight board and see the destinations of the day's departures. Several look promising. A younger officer raises his glass cheerily and you respond in kind. You must make a GALLANTRY roll to attempt the manner of a travel-weary, bon-vivant airship Captain.

Score 11 or lower...	**1298**
Score 12-15...	**1448**
Score 16 or higher...	**1462**

❧ 1424 ❧

You prepare yourself and put on your most aggressive, intimidating impression before stepping into the road and levelling your weapons. Make a RUTHLESSNESS roll of difficulty 10 to convince the driver to halt.

Successful RUTHLESSNESS roll!	**1436**
Failed RUTHLESSNESS roll!	**782**

❧ 1425 ❧

The driver halts the vehicle without complaint and watches dejectedly as you approach. He leans on his shovel and groans. "First tolls to the Guild for use of the road, then Gammage overcharges me for the coal. I can't afford water for the tank from the Haulage tanks so I hose it up from the pond and block my filter. And now a highwayman."

He has **3s** and a **pork pie** on him. His wagons are carrying bricks, brushwood, straw and beer.

Rob him...	**noted passage**
Offer him some money... (**10s**)	**1081**

❧ 1426 ❧

The old woman has a surprising amount of blood in her and before long it is running over the road in a slick, crimson stream. When word of your deeds get out, you will be reviled by the common people. Lose **two solidarity points**. However you do get what you came for: a **silver necklace**, a **lace shawl**, a **locket** and **£7 12s**. As there is no-one left to give a real description, you will not be **Wanted by the Constables** as a result of this robbery - unless you are already, of course.

Turn to...   **noted passage**

❧ 1427 ❧

At last the officer is down. You tear his jacket from him and rifle through it, finding a **pocket watch**, **ten guineas in banknotes** and **4s**. That is all. Since he is breathing his last, you are unlikely to be described accurately and will not become **Wanted by the Constables** - unless you already are, of course.

Turn to...   **noted passage**

❧ 1428 ❧

Roll a dice to see who is inside the compartment.

Score 1	A man and wife...	**186**
Score 2	An artist...	**489**
Score 3	A woman in white...	**322**
Score 4	A young nobleman...	**70**
Score 5	A military officer...	**1375**
Score 6	A senior Constable...	**1363**

❧ 1429 ❧

"Tell me more," says the officer in front of you. "What do you fly?"

"Bumblebees mostly. And VA8s."	**1359**
"I've been on Serpents all this year."	**1470**
"Dangerfields over Bermuda."	**1418**

❧ 1430 ❧

The navvies have set up a row of obstacles across the tracks here at the bridge. They are manning the barricade night and day, preventing any rail traffic from passing. One recognises you and waves.

"There'll sure be response to this," he says, "But we're ready for them when they come!"

Leave the bridge...   **584**

If you have the codeword *Betrayed*, turn to **1442**. If not, but you have the codeword *Bought*, turn to **1450**. Otherwise, read on.

The veteran is still here, still drinking. He grimaces as he shifts himself in his chair uncomfortably. "To think that the blighter who sent us all to our deaths is probably sitting at their table, quaffing wine and enjoying themselves without a second thought for what we went through. Who will give us justice?"

Return to the parlour...	**100**
Leave the inn...	**487**

She falls silent for a moment. "A moralising assassin," she chuckles, her throat gurgling with blood. "Leave me to my regrets, my conscience and my torment. You have done enough."

Have you done enough? She still lives and now that you know a little more of her story, perhaps you cannot condemn her as the bitter veterans did. People will hear about this, and your punishment of Colonel Howitz will not go unremarked: gain **two solidarity points** and remove the codeword *Betrayed*.

Turn to...	**360**

You knock the old woman roughly down and she stays down, sobbing in desperation. Her scratches smart and sting terribly. You can take a **silver necklace**, a **lace shawl** and a **locket** from her as well as **£7 12s**. You will now be **Wanted by the Constables** unless you are wearing a **mask**.

Turn to...	**noted passage**

The Constables are very interested in your comings and goings. If you are **Wanted by the Constables**, turn to **310** immediately. Otherwise, read on.

Make for Oxford...	**990**
Ride towards Watlington...	**360**
Head towards Wallingford...	**800**
Make for Aston Hill...	**710**

The man is taken aback. "Well, I, err, don't quite know how to answer that. But you're quite right to ask. Uncle Roger did say that he was going to be sending someone careful. I tell you what - let me bring you to the hotel and once you're settled and satisfied, I can introduce you to Alphaea and you can hand over the, err, items, directly. How say you?"

"That will suit me well."	**1323**
"I no longer have them. They were stolen."	**1367**

The driver and engineer of the Telegraph Guild steamer are at your mercy. They glumly surrender and allow you to take whatever you want from their supplies. Most of it is heavy lumber, building supplies and bulk food packages, but there is some portable property aboard. Roll a dice to see what you can take.

Score 1-2	**£2 4s** and three **wheels of cheese**
Score 3-4	**£3 8s** and a **pocket watch**
Score 5-6	**£4**, a **rope** and a **net**

Of course the Telegraph Guild will be incensed to hear of this robbery. Unless you are wearing a **mask**, the crew will describe you and you will be **Wanted by the Telegraph Guild**.

Destroy the road train... (**explosives**)	**614**
Set off a flare... (**purple flare**)	**684**
Ride away...	**noted passage**

The Constable collapses heavily. You look through his tunic and his compartment and find **£5 14s**, a **Constable's logbook** and a **strongbox**. You will certainly be **Wanted by the Constables** as a result of this attack, regardless of any attempt to hide your identity.

Turn to...	**noted passage**

You call maimed Fred over and show him the paperwork. "I don't read," he says. "What is it?"

"Your pension entitlement," you reply. "Full disability payment. Eighteen shillings a week. To be collected from Nuffield Telegraph Guild Station."

"Eighteen bleeding shillings won't get me my leg back," he snarls. Remove **pension statement 4590213** from your **possessions**.

Janet comes over. "I appreciate it," she says. "The money will help. And it proves they value what he gave - even if it is an insult to think that his leg and his manhood is worth less than a pound a week to them." You are now the **Friend of Janet Lamb** and you can also gain a **solidarity point**.

Turn to... 763

Turn to... 763

❧ 1439 ❧
"Unforgiveable? If it is so, then I am no better alive or dead. A lifetime of guilt and an eternity of punishment. Kill me now."

"Receive what you ask for." 1473
"I cannot kill you." 1432

1440 ❧
Your velosteam responds immediately to the opening of the regulator and you steam into the road. The driver of the engine responds immediately, throwing on the brake and swerving to a stop. How will you proceed? To threaten the occupant will demand a high RUTHLESSNESS ability, but may avoid violence. Otherwise you can appeal to the passenger's common sense with your GALLANTRY or attack and take them by surprise.

Threaten the passenger... 1105
Talk them into surrendering their money... 1130
Take them by surprise... 1139

❧ 1441 ❧
If you have the codeword *Burden*, turn to **1371** immediately. Otherwise, read on.

Ponsonby spits. "You have been put up to this by those disgusting villagers," he says. "Trying to frighten me. Well, you can have this money." He tosses down a purse containing **£6 5s.** "But assure yourself that the villagers will bear the cost." Gain the codeword *Burden*.

Make a getaway... **noted passage**

❧ 1442 ❧
You return to tell the veteran of what you discovered by decoding the orders. "Colonel Howitz? Why would she have done that? It don't make any sense at all to me," he says. "She was probably seeking a promotion. She knew there was guns trained on the plain. Some clever-clever plan. Well - the world without her would be better, if you ask me. Her family should know our pain. And she deserves to die."

Return to the parlour... 100
Leave the inn... 487

❧ 1443 ❧
Once you have defeated the politician, you can take his weapon, the contents of his wallet (**twenty guineas in banknotes**) and his companion's **fur coat**. Unless you were wearing a mask, he will be able to describe you and you will find yourself **Wanted by the Constables** if you are not already.

Turn to... **noted passage**

❧ 1444 ❧
You have certainly given every impression of being a genuine Atmospheric Union airship captain. Wherever you learnt all this, or the ability to bluff so wildly, you will go far with such a reputation. Before long you find a friendly, impressionable young captain who is willing to take you aboard in the fly-seat as a supernumary officer. Once on the bridge it is only a matter of time before you can strike.

Bells ring indicating that pressure has been reached. The Captain sends a series of messages down his internal wire-controlled telegraph and you hear the thump of cables falling to the turf. Shouts of the deckmen mix with the rising thrum of the propellors and you see the grass of Rotherfield Greys falling away.

Up, up she rises. The flight engineer keeps a steady eye on every gauge, watching as the increasing altitude is matched by an expansion in the lifting gases. The windspeed is favourable and the captain steers west.

Hijack the airship... 1326

❧ 1445 ❧

You come across a workshop with the name Mawkins written over the open front. Inside, a wizened man is huddling over a tiny anvil. A small forge adds to the tropical heat. He looks up as you enter and sees your interest in the gems at his fingertips.

"Pretty, ain't they? Look just like emeralds - but much cheaper. Most can't spot the difference."

	To buy	To sell
jeweller's loupe (ING+1)	£4 6s	-
emerald jewellery	£15	-
sapphire pendant	-	£30
pearl earrings	£4 3s	-
pearl necklace	£10 5s	-

Return to the hotel...   1323

❧ 1446 ❧

"Lies!" responds Sir Roger. "You have sold them to a nefarious colleague! I shall call the Constables immediately!" He hauls a broadsword down from above the fireplace and attacks you! If he successfully hits you, his weapon will cause you **two wounds** at once, although its weight and size does slow the wielder somewhat.

Sir Roger Harpsden	Weapon: **broadsword (PAR 4, NIM-2, 2 wounds)**
Parry:	9
Nimbleness:	7
Toughness:	4

Victory!   1467
Defeat!   1086

❧ 1447 ❧

The passengers quickly surrender: afloat on the middle of the river, they feel even more vulnerable. Roll a dice to see what you can steal.

Score 1-2   a **grappling iron** and **£2 6s**
Score 3-4   an **ivory fan** and **15s**
Score 5-6   **£2 1s** and a **gold necklace**

You will now be **Wanted by the Constables**, unless you possess a **mask**.

Turn to...   305

❧ 1448 ❧

You have managed to assume some of the manners and behaviour of airship crew, but nobody is quite sure who you are. You finish your first drink quickly and have the barman pour you another glass of Markovitz and tonic water. A friendly young Captain, drinking heavily, wants to chat. He tells you about his recent trip to Serbia.

Turn to...   1456

❧ 1449 ❧

The captain continues to mumble apologetically and fetches **fifty guineas in banknotes** with which to pay you. Exactly what you decide to do with the money is now up to you. Either way, the flight continues on over the wide, wide sea.

Turn to...   1373

❧ 1450 ❧

The veteran is pleased to hear of his ex-commanding officer's death. He spits on the floor. "Good! So there is some justice in the world. I hope she suffered. My, how I suffered out there on the plain, praying to die before the anarchists got their hands on me. I wept and I screamed and when it got dark, the stretcher-bearers came and got me and took me off to that fly-ridden field hospital. I hope she suffered."

Gain a **solidarity point** for righting this wrong.

Return to the parlour...   100
Leave the inn...   487

❧ 1451 ❧

The businessman quickly surrenders and you can take his **top hat**, **pocket watch** and **£8 19s**. Unless you were wearing a **mask**, he will be able to describe you and you will find yourself **Wanted by the Constables** if you are not already.

Turn to...   **noted passage**

❧ 1452 ❧

You return to the workings where Sackler had his den, but there is no sign of the man. Heaps of spoil cover the parkland and half-built sluices and dams spill dirty, stagnant water over the sward. He will not be returning here. Lose the codeword *Botanical*.

Turn to...   313

✒ 1453 ✏

You ready your weapons and step out into the road like so many times before. The driver does not even wait for you to speak, but slows down and cowers behind the controls. Colonel Howitz jumps down. "Who dares stop me on my own land?" she asks. "I'll run you through!"

Colonel Howitz	Weapon: **sabre (PAR 3)**
Parry:	10
Nimbleness:	7
Toughness:	5

Victory!	**1463**
Defeat!	**999**

✒ 1454 ✏

You hand the **wedding bouquet** to Sir Roger with his niece's greeting - remove it from your **possessions**. He is overjoyed to hear your account of the celebration. "How very good of you," he replies. "Now, let me see what I can give you in return."

Choose two of the following: **twenty guineas in banknotes**, a **lock of King Charles' hair**, a **broadsword (PAR 4 NIM-2, 2 wounds)**, a **pneumatic manual (ENG+3)** and a **jewelled eyepatch (RUTH+1 GAL+1)**. Roll two dice: if the total is greater than your GALLANTRY score, mixing with these members of high society has refined your manners considerably and you may add 1 to your score permanently. Gain the codeword *Bearclaw*.

Leave the house...	**494**

✒ 1455 ✏

Belize City stands on the low-lying delta of the Belize river. Wide boulevards bordered by massive mature hardwoods and long veranda-wrapped houses radiate outwards grandly from the opera house, the garrison, the State Office and the cathedral. Towards the edge of the city you can see the ramshackle shanties of the poor and beyond, the vast plantations that bring the city its wealth.

The airship is skilfully steered in to its mooring mast and hauled down on capstans turned not by coal and steam but by the far cheaper muscle of men. As you walk down the gangplank, a man steps up to meet you.

"Welcome to Belize. Name's Macauley. You've got something for me, I think."

"Here you are." (**emerald jewellery**)	**1488**
"How do I know who you are?"	**1435**

✒ 1456 ✏

"Ever been to Cairo?" asks the young Captain. "Markovitz always makes me think of Cairo. We had to put up there for a month when the rains were bad. I mean the Union found me a nice spot with a young Greek lady. We drank Markovitz in the morning and Sangria in the afternoon."

"I've never been to Cairo."	**1346**
"I hate Cairo. Such a turgid place."	**1310**
"I haven't been since the Revolution."	**1429**
"Do you know that charming place on Ibrahim Street?"	**1495**

✒ 1457 ✏

"Must I? Is that my punishment? Or do I await another, much more terrible, beyond the grave? I have not slept in weeks, nor felt any rest. Nor do I long for death, when torment must await me."

"If you gave the command in error, you must seek forgiveness."	**1432**
"It is your time to die."	**1473**

✒ 1458 ✏
□

If the box above is ticked, turn to **1478** immediately. Otherwise, read on.

Sir Roger Harpsden shakes your hand warmly and waves you into a deep chair. "I've heard you're someone I can trust. My niece is getting married in Belize City. She's a dear thing and I want to send her my wife's set of emeralds, but I need someone who can take them by airship. Will you do it? I'll pay for your flight, first-class, and arrange for her brother, Macauley, to meet you at the airfield and collect the emeralds. I can't travel all that way and I know you can protect them. Will you do it?

"Of course I'll help."	**1333**
"I can't busy myself with your problems."	**494**

❧ 1459 ❧

The crack of your gunshot rings out through the parkland. Colonel Howitz jerks, attempts to stand, and topples out onto the roadway. Her driver slews round and climbs out, putting himself behind the steamer.

Your cold-blooded vengeance is complete and without risk to yourself. This stroke of punishment cannot blot out the suffering of hundreds of families or bring the dead soldiers back from Spain, but it will send a clear message to the rich and powerful and once your name is attached to it, you will be both feared and respected. Gain **two solidarity points**, remove the codeword *Betrayed* and gain the codeword *Bought*.

Turn to...   360

❧ 1460 ❧

"I know every inch of your land," you tell Ponsonby, twirling the feather under his nose. He recognises it - and what it means. It means that you have been able to enter his estate secretly and unopposed - and that you really can harm him here.

"I suggest you leave," you tell him. "I'm sure you have other houses - other places to go. And you won't need to bother with knocking the village down if you're going to be living elsewhere."

He has turned quite pale. He doesn't reply, but speeds off at once.

Later, when you have returned to the village you hear how Ponsonby has indeed moved out and decided to hire a new Estate Manager - one who has immediately lowered the rates in line with the other estates nearby. It seems that he did not like the threat of your appearance by night, unannounced. Remove the codeword *Burden* if you had it and gain the codeword *Blouse*. Also gain **two solidarity points** for protecting the villagers from their wicked landlord.

Turn to...   977

❧ 1461 ❧

You subdue the huntress eventually and knock her knife away into the bushes. She slumps, panting, against the muddy wheels of her carriage. She is not carrying any money, but you may take her fine **Leboutier hunting rifle (ACC 10)** and the **deer carcass**.

Turn to...   **noted passage**

❧ 1462 ❧

The assembled officers don't take a second glance at you: you wear the upper-class snobbery and hauteur of an airship Captain as though you were born to it.

"Come far?" asks another officer.

"Not too far - a short hop across the pond from Belize, then transferred up from Hastings."

Turn to...   1477

❧ 1463 ❧

The Colonel collapses, coughing blood. "Where is the strength in my arm?" she splutters. "No sleep, no rest, no strength. Kill me and put me out of my misery."

"You deserve no less."   1473
"What misery can you know?"   1480

❧ 1464 ❧

The doors of Harpsden House are shut and bolted. No-one responds to your approach. The family have plainly gone away.

Return to the village...   494

❧ 1465 ❧

She shakes her head. "Blind? I have lived here since I was a very small girl. I know what is coming and I know just how much it needs to happen. But this is my place, the situation I have been tasked with. I shall not run away and I shall not do nothing, either. We all have our parts to play. Farewell, Steam Highwayman."

Turn to...   1349

❧ 1466 ❧

If you are the **Friend of Susan Tenney, Lord Brigg** or **Lord Dashwood**, turn to **1458** immediately. Otherwise read on.

The Harpsdens of Harpsden House are a noble family known for staying aloof from the money-grabbing schemes of many another clan. Their estate is not large but they are very wealthy indeed. If you want to connect with them, no mere letter will do: you must know the right people.

Return to the village...   494

❧ 1467 ❧

Sir Roger falls to the ground, badly wounded. You may take his **broadsword (PAR 4 NIM-2, 2 wounds)** if you wish, as well as a **gold ring** and a **cloak**. You had better leave before his servants and the Constables arrive. Gain the codeword *Baroche*.

Make yourself scarce...   757

❧ 1468 ❧

The steward helps you to your cabin, where you rest for the remainder of the flight. Under the steward's careful ministrations your **wounds** begin to heal: replace one **wound** with a **scar**.

Turn to...   1373

❧ 1469 ❧

You attempt to lighten the atmosphere - after all, this is simply a party game, isn't it? Fooling around with your mallet, you manage to flick a cream cake onto a fat man's lap, which sets the guests laughing. Your partner wants you to take the game more seriously. "I can still shoot the hoop," you reply, and indeed you pass **a hoop** with your next shot.

Turn to...   1476

❧ 1470 ❧

"I flew a Marcozzi once," mentions a First Officer. "Some Italian chappy had brought it up to Hastings and died. I had to return it to the Neapolitans."

"What slugs those Marcozzis are."	1243
"I'm sure you made record time."	1259

❧ 1471 ❧

As the Colonel's steam-carriage approaches, you ready your gun and carefully take sight. If you miss, you will need to make off, fast. Make an ACCURACY roll of difficulty 14.

Successful ACCURACY roll!	1459
Failed ACCURACY roll!	306

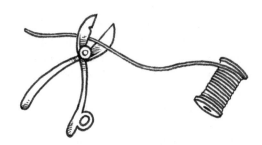

❧ 1472 ❧

Your next shot must be carefully considered. A direct blow will simply move the yellow further ahead, but a glance might ricochet yours off into the lead. Make a NIMBLENESS roll of difficulty 12.

Successful NIMBLENESS roll!	553
Failed NIMBLENESS roll!	1132

❧ 1473 ❧

You finish the job and leave Colonel Howitz's body lying at the roadside. Remove the codeword *Betrayed* and gain the codeword *Bought*. You may take a **box of cigars**, **£9 12s** and a **cloak** from her corpse if you wish and you can also gain two **solidarity points**.

Leave the place...   360

❧ 1474 ❧

The doctor does not fight for long. After you land a couple of hits, he steps back and surrenders. "Alright, alright, take my money. There are people who depend on me, you know. This world has seen enough brutal death and punishment already."

You can take his wallet containing **£5 2s** and a **stethoscope** as well as his **catling knife (PAR 1 NIM+2)** as normal. Note that you are now **Wanted by the Constables** if you are not wearing a **mask**.

If you have the codeword *Birthright* and would like to ask the doctor about volunteering for the monk's airship, turn to **1481** immediately.

Turn to...   **noted passage**

❧ 1475 ❧

You spend some time walking the streets of Belize, keeping to the shade of the giant trees as best you can. They bring you down to the port and the creekside, beneath the shadow of the old fort. The Pearl Quarter, where they make jewellery from the bounty of the countless atolls and lagoons along the coast, is a short walk away. If you have the **emerald jewellery**, read on. Otherwise, turn to **1200** immediately.

With your nose for trouble, you find your way into a warehouse where several men and women are unloading crates from a barge. One is dropped at your feet and several repeating carbines slide out from their straw and sacking. Immediately, the men and women move towards you threateningly.

"I am friend. I bring a contribution to
the cause."   **1218**
"You cannot scare me."   **1274**

৵ 1476 ৵
If you have now passed six hoops, turn to **1500** immediately. Otherwise, read on.

The yellow player shoots their final hoop and knocks the post with a crack and a jingle of the tiny bell. The game is not over, however, until both red and yellow complete the course. You and your partner have a few strokes left. How will you play?

Attempt to knock your partner's blue ball on... **1492**
Clear the red off the lawn...   **1508**

৵ 1477 ৵
That was exactly what the most rambunctious and self-aggrandising airship Captain would have said. You will fit in quite well here if you carry on like that.

Offer round some cigars... (**box of cigars**) **1165**
Tell a story about awful passengers...   **1429**

৵ 1478 ৵
If you have the codeword *Baroche* or *Bearclaw*, turn to **1464** immediately. If you have the **wedding bouquet**, turn to **1454**. Otherwise, read on.

Sir Roger is intrigued to find that you have returned. "Have you not delivered the jewels yet?" he asks. "The date is fast approaching."

"I will take them very soon."
    (**emerald jewellery**)   **494**
"I have put them in safe-keeping."   **1446**

৵ 1479 ৵
The crew do not take kindly to your attempts to search their quarters. They resist, violently, and you receive **two wounds** before an officer appears and intervenes.

If you now have **five wounds**, turn to **1468**

immediately. Otherwise you are forced to put aside your jewel hunt for now until you have recovered.

Turn to...   **1373**

৵ 1480 ৵
"Do you feel remorse for all your crimes?" gasps Colonel Howitz, clutching at her wounds. "Or are you hardened to their deaths? How many have you killed? Thirty? Fifty? My mistakes cost the lives of three hundred and twenty men, the freedom of eighty-two more and left almost two-hundred maimed for life."

"Why did you order the attack?"

"Intelligence. Planted by the anarchists. I was told that they were out of ammunition for their weapons. It was then or never. Do you think I would throw away the lives of the very men I commanded?"

"Your folly is unforgivable."   **1439**
"You must find a way of living with it."   **1457**

৵ 1481 ৵
"I know I've just robbed and wounded you," you say to the doctor, "But would you be interested in joining a flying hospital currently looking for medical staff?"

He looks at you as if you are mad. "Are you serious? No! I have people to look after in my own practice. And what would I owe you?" He spits at you - a most ungentlemanly reaction.

Turn to...   **noted passage**

৵ 1482 ৵
The goalie brightens up. "That'll help," he replies. "Here, take this scarf." He hands you a blue and white **Warriors scarf**. "The wife knitted that. We'll see you at our next match." Gain a **solidarity point**.
Turn to...   **308**

৵ 1483 ৵
The Colonel does not seem to go out much. You lie in wait, observing and waiting, until you are sure that the Colonel is in the vehicle. It is an open-roofed machine, expensive and powerful, bought with the wealth that keeps people like this in power and privilege while the common man is forced to enrol for a shilling a day and a grave in a far-off field.

Shoot the Colonel without warning...   **1471**
Stop the carriage...   **1453**

❧ 1484 ❧

The return flight is a sombre one. Many of the passengers reflect on their narrow escapes from the revolutionary uprising. You keep to your cabin, mostly. Any **wounds** you were bearing have time to heal - replace them with **scars** on your **Adventure Sheet** and by the time you return to Rotherfield Greys in the pouring rain of the late summer evening, the hot land of Belize could not seem further away or less real.

Turn to...   **454**

❧ 1485 ❧

You bring your barge alongside the jetty at the quarry and prepare to go ashore. Your mate smiles. "A lovely mooring, cap'n" he says. "Won't nobody find us here."

Note that you are now **moored at Temple Coombe quarry**.

Turn to...   **1119**

❧ 1486 ❧

"Clear-headed? Alcohol has been scientifically proven to bring clarity and insight once aloft," replies the Captain. "That water has been dripping through muddy channels in these awful hills, picking up all sorts of ugly homunculi on the way. You'll make yourself ill."

Another bare-headed officer approaches. He has two gold bars on his shoulder over his blue epaulette. How will you address him?

"Can you give me a lift to Europe?"	**1346**
"Hello, Cruise."	**1318**
"This is an officer's lounge. Get out!"	**1327**

❧ 1487 ❧

If you have now passed **six hoops**, turn to **1500** immediately. Otherwise, read on.

Your partner is a hoop ahead: the blue ball quickly reaches the post, setting it a-jingle, and only you and the red have yet to finish the course. The red player cannot quite get a clear shot, so they knock your black hard, putting a the post between you and your next hoop. How will you respond?

Try to jump the post...	**1509**
Rebound off a heavy chair...	**1490**

❧ 1488 ❧

The wedding proceeds with a stately glamour. Alphaea Harpsden, heiress and beauty, is resplendent in her white gown, the green jewels at her neck admirably complimenting her pale complexion and her auburn hair. Her groom, Jack Acreage, is a broad-shouldered, tower of a man, some years older than her but plainly quite a match. The cathedral is full of the great and good of Belize, the surrounding Confederacy and, far down the nave, many of the slaves and workers who have been granted a rare half-day's holiday to observe the specatacle.

How far you are from the misty haunts of your own territory. The tropical heat of the day is combatted in various ways by the guests and the populace and when the evening comes the city is far more alive than it was at two o'clock in the afternoon. You are asked to go to see the bride one last time before you leave.

Turn to...   **1494**

❧ 1489 ❧

It is indeed Dr Smollett on his way to assist a suffering patient. "I wondered when would come the day," he said. "I had always suspected that you were behind the ruthless robberies around here. Well, if you have decided to continue pursuing that path, who am I to oppose you." He sadly hands you his wallet, containing **£5 15s** and climbs back into the carriage. Your are no longer the **Friend of Dr Smollett**.

Turn to...   **noted passage**

❧ 1490 ❧

The iron chair is not as heavy as it looks: your blow knocks the chair and its occupant to the ground and your black is lost in crinoline and petticoat. The red knocks the post firmly: you have lost the match.

"Quite a game!" says Viscountess Bell-Happing. "I do hope you'll come again!"

Leave the house...   **62**

✤ 1491 ✤
The young captain wanders over to join his own officers in a discussion. You are swept up by an enthusiastically technical group of officers who are discussing how they have tuned their engines to get the greatest power. "Coal is the only way," says one. "I've heard they're using gas in Germany but I hate to think of what damage a leak could cause."

"Gas is perfectly safe. Much lighter too."	**1275**
"Welsh coal. It has to be Welsh coal."	**1294**
"Rotary pistons are a lot of rubbish."	**1283**

✤ 1492 ✤
A careful jab sends your black into the blue, cannoning it forward to hit the post. Your black, however, hits some stone or uneven patch in the lawn and rolls off sideways into the grass. The red player is swift to take advantage and passes their final hoop. The yellow, rather than knock you off, rolls into a blocking position.

Turn to...   **1487**

✤ 1493 ✤
This is the home of Colonel Howitz - the commander who sent so many soldiers to their needless deaths. Some form of justice is due: you will need to get face to face with the Colonel, whatever you decide to do.

Ambush the Colonel's steamer...	**1483**
Leave the house...	**836**

✤ 1494 ✤
Alphea Acreage visibly no different from the unmarried woman she was. Her husband is nowhere to be found and she has returned to her suite at the hotel. She smiles as you are chaperoned in.

"Thank you for everything you've done," she said. "These lovely gems are much more to me than money or glamour. They remind that somewhere, far away, I am loved for myself, and they will always remind me of that. Take my best regards to Uncle Roger. Oh, and this as well." She hands you her **wedding bouquet**.

"Will you be happy, married to this man?"	**1395**
"Are you really so blind to reality here?"	**1465**

✤ 1495 ✤
A tipsy officer is telling a long story about how, when flying from Marrakech, a female passenger tried to seduce him. "And what did I do?"

"Reminded her that you had other duties."	**1398**
"Went along with it, of course!"	**1359**

✤ 1496 ✤
☐
If the box above is empty, tick it and read on. If it is already ticked, turn to **1167** immediately.

The Telegraph Guild wagon is unguarded for now so you can attempt to unlock the doors, rifle the baggage compartment and steal anything you can lay your hands on. Roll a dice to see what you find, adding 1 if you possess **lockpicks** and 3 if you have a **skeleton key**.

Score 1-2	a **shovel** and a **bottle of wine**
Score 3-4	some **engineer's gloves (ENG+1)**
Score 5	a **pneumatic manual (ENG+3)**
Score 6+	**punchcards (Aramanth A)**

Leave the wagons...   **280**

✤ 1497 ✤
You cut the man down and leave him, his blood bright on the turf. "I hope this teaches you to play fair," you say to the lady with a bow. She blushes and sees to her husband.

Your partner takes you by the arm. "I think you're taking the game a little too seriously. Come and sit in the shade."

"Too seriously? This is croquet!"

This game is postponed indefinitely, but the guests will think twice before playing you again. Gain a point of RUTHLESSNESS and the codeword *Burgundy*.

Leave the party...   **62**

❧ 1498 ❧

Remove the **punchcards (Aramanth A)** and the **punchcards (Valencia orders)** from your **possessions**.

As you feed the second set of punchcards into the machine, it hesitates, almost as it if is wondering whether it should be telling you this information. Then, after a grinding of gears, the printing pad begins to flick back and forth across an unrolling spool of paper.

The Oxford and Buckinghamshire Light Infantry Regiment were in an entrenched position south of the city of Valencia, occupied by radical anarchists in rebellion against their government and monarch.

Colonel Howitz ordered the men of A, B and C companies to mount an independent assault across the open ground. Approximately 80% of the men were captured, badly wounded or killed.

Howitz retained rank but was given a period of leave and currently resides at Nuffield Place, a short distance from the regimental headquarters. Gain the codeword *Betrayed* and remove the codeword *Benediction* if you have it.

Turn to...   **noted passage**

❧ 1499 ❧

Recognising the uniform of the driver and guard, you lean out of your hiding place and give the signal you agreed with them in the pub. The steamer immediately coughs, slews round and grinds to a halt.

As you dash up to the door of the passenger compartment, the driver and guard look at you anxiously. "Remember - you promised no blood. We've kept our side of the bargain."

Turn to...   1428

❧ 1500 ❧

Your final shot knocks the post with a loud clack and the guests cheer. It has been quite a game and you should be proud of your success! Who was your partner?

Major Redford...   324
Earl Brigg...   374
The tall lady...   379
Susan Tenney..   316

❧ 1501 ❧

You are given a warm welcome by the museum staff. "Welcome back! The professor left instructions that you should be allowed free entry to the museum! She is out on a dig at the moment - it could be one of several we ave underway." You are refunded your shilling (**1s**) and invited to look around.

Eventually you find the cabinet housing your donation. It is accompanied by a long written description and the note 'Donated Anonymously', which may give you some satisfaction.

Return to Henley...   702

❧ 1502 ❧

The rivermen need coal for their steam engines and their cooking stoves. They have come down the Grand Union from Leicestershire and are slowly making their way towards London. They will pay you £12 for a load of coal and be mightily glad of your help. If you choose to sell it, remove it from your adventure sheet.

Steam upstream...   750
Steam downriver to Wargrave...
    (**2s** or **bargee's badge**)   131

❧ 1503 ❧

Parson Twinge decks you out in ecclesiastical garb and you steam down to the Hambleden vicarage for the game. The Reverend Prattle is initially concerned, but he is ready to play you for the Fingest bells. You settle down to the card table.

If you have a **deck of marked cards**, turn to **43** immediately. Otherwise you must make an INGENUITY roll of difficulty 13 to make the most of your hand.

Successful INGENUITY roll!   43
Failed INGENUITY roll!   86

❧ 1504 ❧

Nobody dares contradict the Steam Highwayman - you are too well known and too feared for that. But the lady turns bright red and complains of feeling unwell in the sunshine. She receives much attention, sympathy and help, while you are given dirty looks and scorn. The game is over, you must lose a point of GALLANTRY as a result of your behaviour and will have to leave the party.

Turn to...   62

❧ 1505 ❧

If you are **Wanted by the Coal Board**, turn to **1140** immediately. Otherwise, read on.

A keeper's lodge, a fine brick engine-house for the steam-pump and several outbuildings face the road. Beyond them you can see the neatly-trimmed grass embankment rising to the height of the reservoir wall. However you are not left with any chance to explore for yourself: a guard armed with a short repeating carbine approaches and asks your business.

"I am an engineer, come to inspect the tank."	**1384**
"How disgustlingly rude! Don't you know who I am?"	**1394**
"Oh, sorry. I thought this was public."	**710**

❧ 1506 ❧

To break into the manor will not trouble you too much, but it will be considerably easier with some equipment. Make a NIMBLENESS roll of 11, adding 1 if you have a **rope**, and 2 if you have a **grappling iron**.

Successful NIMBLENESS roll!	**484**
Failed NIMBLENESS roll!	**587**

❧ 1507 ❧

Your next shot is ready to pass a hoop and head out into the open space. It looks certain to give you a lead. Then you become aware of a snuffling around your feet and a foolish auburn spaniel bounds towards the ball.

"Get it off the lawn!" yells Major Redford. "Or I'll shoot it myself!"

Polite commotion ensues - no-one is quite sure whose the beast is, but it noses the red, yellow and blue in turn before taking your black in its jaws and toddling off towards the summerhouse.

Viscountess Bell-Happing raises a gloved hand. "Act of dog," she says. "The black must be played from where it lies."

Chase the dog...	**353**
Wait for it to drop the ball...	**398**
Call the dog...	**412**

❧ 1508 ❧

The red ball must be stopped! The angles are almost right... You swing your mallet and your black passes through **a hoop**, knocks the red into the yellow and both under a table, and drops a few feet from the post. "Excellent play!" says your partner.

Turn to...	**1487**

❧ 1509 ❧

A careful chip sends your black skipping over over the post and squarely through the hoop. If you have now passed **six hoops**, turn to **1500** immediately. Otherwise, read on.

Sadly, despite your efforts and skill, you have been beaten. Your partner has disappeared: after all, they finished some time ago and may consider you a dead weight. You find another drink but nobody wants to talk and after a little longer in this effete, silly company, you return to your velosteam and the road.

Leave the house....	**62**

❧ 1510 ❧

Leticia Forebury has not been here at Mapledurham for some time: you are told that she is spending the season in London.

Leave the house...	**864**

1511

You instruct the machine to create a piece of music. It pauses, the whole mechanism quivering, before launching into an energetic and rhythmic calculation. The printer clatters and a ream of sheet music, all mechanically impressed, flops out.

At a quick glance, it looks like a symphony in five movements. The opening melody is stark, brave and somehow sad. How will it sound when it is played? Gain the **calculated symphony**.

Leave the machine...   **noted passage**

᭝ 1512 ᭝

The explosion rocks the house and collapses one exterior wall, but it is not a complete success and you realise as you watch from Hanger Wood that Lord Burgess, his family and servants are all unharmed. This will do little to terrify them. Remove the codeword *Bother*.

Steam up to Ibstone...	**400**
Head down the lane to Turville...	**947**
Ride on to Bolter End...	**546**
Take the road south to Skirmett...	**969**

᭝ 1513 ᭝

You quickly leave South Stoke behind you and steam between fields of wheat and turnips. The road almost hums with the warmth of the sun. If you have a **large pike**, turn to **1092** immediately.

Carry on up the road to North Stoke...	**515**
Ride straight through, heading north...	**860**

᭝ 1514 ᭝

Fog drifts across the hillside and you tilt your lantern down towards the road. Suddenly a shape looms up at you: a private steam carriage is leaning into the ditch here.

Investigate the carriage...	**680**
Ride straight on towards Reading...	**560**
Pull over at Cane End...	**807**

᭝ 1515 ᭝

You throw yourself into the rescue effort and manage to extricate several trapped people from the rubble and burning timber. Your selflessness does not go unnoticed: gain a **solidarity point**.

Return to town...   **702**

᭝ 1516 ᭝

The Three Guineas stands amongst the marshalling yards of the Imperial Western Railway, serving the working men of the Freight Yard, the marshalling yards and the foundries. Once through the smoke-stained doors with the tarnished handles, you come into a noisy, open parlour. Eyes flicker at your road-stained clothing, then look away hurriedly. On one side of the room a frosted glass door reads 'The Venture Lounge'. A pair of men with red neckerchiefs sit at a table beside it, drinking lemonade. If you have the codeword *Bargain*, *Chosen* or *Driven*, turn to **189** immediately.

Order a drink... (**2s**)	**641**
Enter the Venture Lounge... (if **Member of the Compact for Workers' Equality**)	**124**
Leave the Three Guineas...	**297**

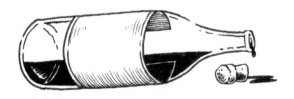

Epilogue

So your days on the lawless road are over. Before calculating a final score to enter on the Roll of Honour, you can discover what follows your story in this book by using the table below. Did you finish your tale in ignominious execution, pain-wracked suffering or wealth and respect? Did you ever take the time to plan for your future - or was the excitement of the present enough for you?

	Dead	Alive
Money in purse...	0 points / £	1 point / £2
Money in bank account...	0 points / g	1 point / guinea
Scars	-	-3 points / scar
Wounds	-	-10 points / wound
Codeword *Best*	-	30 points

	Dead or Alive
Ruthlessness...	2 points / point
Engineering...	1 point / point
Motoring..	1 point / point
Ingenuity...	1 point / point
Nimbleness...	1 point / point
Gallantry...	2 points / point
Solidarity Points...	5 points each
Wanted status...	10 points each
Friendships...	10 points each
Great Deeds...	20 points each
Famed Lawbreaker....	50 points
People's Champion...	100 points

	Who?
100 points or fewer...	**Laughing Stock**
101-150 points...	**Trouble Maker**
151-200 points...	**A Character of Repute**
201-250 points...	**A Generation's Hero**
251-350 points...	
351 points or more...	**Never Forgotten**

Who?

The Guilds do not remark upon your disappearance from the highways and holloways of the region. If anything, other far more successful robbers quickly become greater threats to the road trains than you ever were. The few imprints you left in the minds and hearts of the people are ultimately as transient as the marks of your velosteam's tyres in the mud, distorted by the sun of the day and washed away with the first rain.

Laughing Stock

There were things you did that may live on - but really only in jest. That time you fell in the river and ruined all your weapons? The run-in with the fat Constable who nonetheless arrested you? And then, as is the way with jokes, they pass and your name and reputation fade away.

Trouble Maker

It was a considerable impact you had on the region but your absence leaves most people breathing a sigh of relief: your unpredictable and unreliable nature scared the commoners and bemused the rich. You become a byword for wasted talent, spoilt efforts and trouble. Ferguson is frustrated by your continued association with their velosteam models and sales suffer as a result. Eventually the company is forced to declare bankruptcy - are you proud of what you have achieved?

A Character of Repute

When you arrived in the region there were many who remarked upon your manners, your ruthlessness and guile. Now that you have disappeared you are still a favourite topic of conversation in the inns, parlours and dining rooms. Your motivations and plots are speculated over and many wonder where you ended up...

A Generation's Hero

The tales of the Steam Highwayman have become famous across the land in your own time: many young people take you as their model, in morals, manners and in fashion. The tricorne becomes the hat of choice for the dashing and independent-minded as they mimic your style. The Ferguson velosteam sells a hundred thousand models. For years to come, deeds of valour, daring and ruthlessness will be falsely attributed to your secretive activity and eventually you become a figure of speech as well a figure of legend.

Never forgotten

This is the real legacy of the Steam Highwayman: your story is never forgotten by those whom you have encountered and never ignored by those to whom it is told. You characterise the best of the spirit of independence and restitution; your deeds become popular songs, a stage-play and one day, a moving picture. More than this: your efforts to help the needy and the poor produce countless stories of gratitude and hope. Urchins, widows, apprentices, tramps, maids and old men tell how you came into their lives and rescued them. The rich, the guildsmen, the powerful and the self-important shiver at the mention of your name - and who can tell whether the Steam Highwayman will return again?

ROLL OF HONOUR

Date:	Points:	Fate:	Memorable Adventures	Reader's Name

Acknowledgements

Your promise and your word to me
Have been fulfilled Lord, gracefully.
So let this book reflect what's true:
I wrote this book to honour you.

Thanks and appreciation to my wife and best friend

Cheryl Anne Adamos Noutch

whose constant support and encouragement has enabled the entire project.

Also to:

Ben May; illustrator. Ben, your way of visualising my world has given me so much satisfaction and pleasure. I'm proud to be sharing your art along with my stories and consider it an honour to have your pictures flying the Steam Highwayman banner.

Daniel, Ellie, Bea, Ali and Andrew Kesson; proofreaders and backers 3. Thanks for your constant support and interest in my writing and my work. May God bless you - and fill your children with bold creativity!

Jon, Charlotte, Gwendolen and Joshua Winn; proofreaders and backers 157. Thankyou once again for enjoying my books! I hope that this beautifully-covered once replaces the old proof copy on your shelves - but don't throw that away! It'll be a vital collectible one day!

Jemimah and Peter Reid; proofreaders. Thank you so much for reading through my proofs so diligently. Your help was really significant in getting the proof ready enough to use.

Kevin Abbotts; proofreader and backer 2. It's so good to have you aboard the Ferguson once again, Kevin. Thanks for your tireless help with the proof.

Mark Lain; proofreader and backer 5. Thanks for your support and encouragement, Mark. I wish you every success with your own **Destiny's Role** gamebook series!

Ruth, Noah, John and Aidan Noutch; proofreaders and backers 225. Thanks for the help proof-reading, talking over ideas on the phone and everything else. Enjoy the adventure!

Jessica Noutch; proofreader. Thanks, Jess, for always

remaining interested in my work. It's been great to talk about Steam Highwayman with you from the start.

Dave Morris; Thanks for your support and interest as the project has grown, Dave. After all, if it weren't for travels in Old Harkuna twenty years past, who would be here?

benjebobs; backer 1. May the open road bring you to pies and places to use pies, Ben. Thanks for your comments and your encouragement as the project has grown.

Simon Hedley; backer 4. I hope *Steam Highwayman* makes a proud addition to your collection, Simon - and I hope that your adventures in the page are as exciting as in gamebooks of yore.

Rob 2.0; backer 6. Thanks for returning to pledge once again, Robert. I hope you enjoy the continued adventures astride your velosteam!

Peter Fuchs; backer 7. Welcome aboard, Peter! I wish you smooth riding, sleepy constables and unsuspecting nobility wherever you choose to ply your secretive trade.

The Creative Fund; backer 8. This project was supported by The Creative Fund on Kickstarter.

Matthew Lockman; backer 9. Matthew, it's great to have your support and interest. May your boiler never burst!

Pete Bounous; backer 10. Thanks for your pledge, Pete! I'm so glad that you came across *Steam Highwayman* and I hope the adventure recalls some of the best of what you love about gamebooks.

Zacharias Chun-Pong LEUNG 梁振邦 ; backer 11. Thanks for returning to pledge again. May your wounds all convert to intimidating scars!

Colin Oaten; backer 12. Colin, thank you for your support for my gamebooks. I hope you enjoy the adventure and the world of *Steam Highwayman*.

Jack Noutch; backer 13 and WANTED CRIMINAL. Thank you, bro, for all of your contribution. I hope your poster doesn't get around!

Ser Inncubus; backer 14. Adrian, thanks for joining the *Steam Highwayman* campaign. I hope that you find what you are looking for on the midnight road!

Robert Langston; backer 15. Welcome back, Robert! Thanks for continuing to pledge and support my writing. More steam to your boiler, sir!

Michael Phillips; backer 16. Great to have your help and your enthusiasm for the project, Michael. May you find friends and allies in every watering hole and never be served sour beer.

Serena Lee; backer 17. Thank you so much for your pledge, Serena. It means a lot to have your support in my passion project.

Josh Bruce; backer 18. Thanks for your pledge, Josh. If you have any mechanical difficulties with your velosteam, I know you're the man to get them fixed.

Derek Devereux Smith; backer 19. Derek, thanks for your support. I'm really pleased you found the project and hope you enjoy taking your place astride the velosteam of justice.

Martin Ellis; backer 20. From one Steampunk Martin to another, let me offer my sincere gratitude for your help in getting *Steam Highwayman* moving!

Ranger Tim; backer 21. Thanks, Ranger Tim, for coming back and continuing to support the project. May you always out-steam your pursuers and overtake your prey!

David Robertson; backer 22. David, thankyou for your generous pledge and your interest! May California cower before the approaching adventurer!

Robertson Sondoh Jr; backer 23. I really appreciate your pledge for another *Steam Highwayman* volume - and hope that you've enjoyed the first! May your students always hearken to your wise teaching.

Anton Ducrot; backer 24. Thanks for your support and friendship over the last six months, Anton. It's been great to share. I wish you every success with **Flytrap Factory**

and your own Kickstarter projects!

Daniel Shaw; backer 25. Dan, thanks for your continued and faithful support for my work. I hope *Smog and Ambuscade* is well-thumbed by now - you'll enjoy this one even more.

Neil Taylor; backer 26. Grea to have your support, Neil. I hope you find the world of *Steam Highwayman* as enthralling as I do.

Campbell; backer 27. Oh distant friend - thankyou for your support from afar. Let the denizens of New Zealand hear the legend and the roar of the velosteam.

Gábor Joe Telekesi ; backer 28. Thanks so much for your pledge. It's great to be sending my writing off to Hungary again, with your help.

Graham Hart; backer 29. Enjoy your new copies, Graham. Thankyou for your generosity.

Danny Fuerstman; backer 30. Great to have your support, Daniel. Best wishes.

Nicodemus; backer 31. Thankyou for your help in making this become a reality. May your rats bow before you!

Steven M. Smith; backer 32. Thanks, Steven, for returning to back my project again. I hope you find Volume II even more engaging.

Joe Tilbrook; backer 33. I really appreciate your continued support, Joe. Thanks.

Rob Crewe; backer 34. Thanks very much for coming back to pledge for the second campaign - it's appreciated.

Scott H Moore; backer35. Thankyou for helping the *Steam Highwayman* legend continue, Scott. It couldn't happen without you!

Redmick backer 36. Thanks for your support and interest, Mike. May your students never become unruly and may their writing always make sense.

Ayanna Mitchell; backer 37. Thankyou, dear Ayanna, for your friendship and your support for my project. I hope that as you dip into the books, you find all sorts of stories to stir your imagination.

Shane Dunkle; backer 38. Great to have your support and interest, Shane. It's much appreciated.

Michael Reilly; backer 39. Thanks for your friendship and support, Michael, and of course for **Gamebook News**, which has helped me reach countless new readers as well as keeping me informed about other projects. Keep up the excellent work!

Mervyn Koh; backer 40. Great to have your support once again, Mervyn. May your water tank never run dry!

Kamarul Azmi Kamaruzaman; backer 41. Thanks for returning to back SH2. May you discover all the secret locations!

Anthony Impenna; backer 42. I really appreciate your pledge and your support, Anthony, and I hope that you enjoy discovering all the secrets of the quiet woods.

L Bailey; backer 43. Thanks, Leon, for your interest in my project. Happy adventuring on the midnight road!

Simon Day; backer 44. Thanks for your support for the project, Simon. It's much appreciated.

Niki Lybæk; backer 45. Great to have your help in bringing this project to reality, Niki. Thanks!

Y.K. Lee; backer 46. Your support is much appreciated!

Stuart Lloyd; backer 47. Thanks for your pledge, your interest in the project and for hosting such excellent and thought-provoking articles on your **blog**.

Jeveutout; backer 48. May France fear the Steam Highwayman, now that the second volume will chart your adventures!

Daddy Eduardo Adamos; backer 49. Daddy, words cannot express my gratitude for the love and support I have found in your house. Thankyou.

Sibi Jacob; backer 50. Great to have your support, Sibi! It's been a privilege to teach Nathen and a joy to share literature with him.

Dean Soukup; backer 51. Thanks for your help in making SH2 a reality, Dean!

Scott Ballantyne; backer 52. Thanks for your help in backing the project, Scott. It's much appreciated.

Jeffrey Dean; backer 53. Thanks for your interest in my work, Jeffrey. .Best wishes for *Westward Dystopia* and your other books.

A. Thompson; backer 54. My dear friend! Thanks so much for backing the project and believing in me. God bless you for your faithful friendship.

Pennington and Porcas; backer 55. Thanks Sophie and Steve! I hope you enjoy the adventure!

Richard Harrison; backer 56. Great to have your help, Richard.

Sherloth; backer 57. Thanks for your support!

Chris Trapp; backer 58. Thanks so much for helping Steam Highwayman II turn into a reality.

林立人 **Lin Liren the Sunrise-Chasing Bard**; backer 59. Thanks for pledging again, Lin. I love to think of *Steam Highwayman: Smog and Ambuscade* sitting on a shelf or open on a coffee table in distant Taiwan, intriguing your visitors and bringing a little piece of England to the Far East.

Prof. Dr. Oliver M. Traxel; backer 60. Thanks for returning to back once again! I hope you find the stories of Steam Highwayman II just as engaging and thought-provoking.

Alessio Ruscelli; backer 61. Thanks for your support, Alessio.

Jimmy Murray; backer 62. Thanks for taking the time to pledge for th project, Jimmy. I massively appreciate it.

Mr Mann; backer 63. Thanks for your support, Mr Mann! Now you too can become the Steam Highwaymann.

Michael Sousa; backer 64. Thanks for your support, Michael!

Philippe Jaillet; backer 65 Thanks for your help - I really appreciate it, Philippe.

Grimace71; backer 66. I hope the arrival of these books brings a happy grimace to your face!

James the Steamer; backer 67 and WANTED CRIMINAL. May Nevada quake at the sound of your approach, dear sir! I wish you every success in your robberies.

K Taylor; backer 68. Enjoy the romance of the road and the smell of the steam.

James Dickinson; backer 69. Thanks for your support, James. Much appreciated!

Copper Miner Dallimore; backer 70. Thanks for your pledge. Best wishes with your **Copper Mine Miniatures**!

Backer 71.

Demian Katz; backer 72. Demian, thankyou for your pledge but also for your support for the gamebook community through your excellent online database. The day I saw *Steam Highwayman* appear there, my heart leapt!

Joshua Abramsky; backer 73. Welcome back, Joshua. Thanks for your input to the campaign.

A Nony Mouse; backer 74. Squeak squeak, A Nony!

Alistair Davidse; backer 75. Thanks for your pledge. May South Africa quake at the approach of the velosteamer!

Per Stalby; backer 76. Great to have your support again, Per! Thankyou and best wishes.

Ed Hughes; backer 77. Thanks for returning to back once again, Ed. Best wishes.

Fabrice Gatille; backer 78. Welcome back, Fabrice! Your support is massively appreciated.

Jim Hartland; backer 79. Thanks Jim. I hope you enjoy both volumes of the adventure!

Andrew Shannon; backer 80. Thanks for your support, Andrew! I hope you and your family enjoy the ride!

Nicola Birch; backer 81. Thanks, dear Birchy, for your continued support and friendship. I hope the prospect of midnight robbery helps you to let off steam when you need it!

Quentin Antrim; backer 82. Thanks for your support, Quentin! May you always roll sixes!

Allan "Goggles" Jenkins; backer 83. Enjoy the adventure and may your goggles never mist.

Javier Fernández-Sanguino; backer 84. Gracias, Javier! Enjoy the continuing tale of your exploits.

Charles Revello; backer 85. Have a great time astride the Ferguson, Charles! Keep your pressure up!

Michael Bailey; backer 86. Enjoy the stories and the adventure, Michael. Best wishes.

James Elbro; backer 87. I hope you have a great time in the book, James. May you find the beer that satisfies... And I hope your screw compressors retain all their oil too.

Vécsei Zoli; backer 88. Köszönöm! Enjoy the book.

Kim Sein; backer 89. Thanks, old friend, for continuing to believe in me and my work..

Mark Buckley; backer 90. Thanks for your help, Mark. Enjoy the book.

Antony Quarrell; backer 91. My friend at arms and on the road! May your tyres ever stay firm and the road rise to meet you. I'm so glad to be sending you a copy of this sec-ond adventure. Thanks for all your support.

Peppe Fazzolari; backer 92. Thanks for your support, Pep! You inspired a lot of this by your example.

Godwin-Matthew Teoh; backer 93. Thanks for returning to back book two, Godwin! I hope you enjoy it as much as the first.

Anders Svensson; backer 94. Enjoy the ride, Anders. May your water-tank never freeze.

Stuart Whitehouse; backer 95. Thanks for your support, Stuart!

Matthew Taras; backer 96. Thankyou, Matthew for your pledge.

David Gillson; backer 97. Thanks for your support for the projcet, David! I hope you've enjoyed SH1 and wish you every happiness in your own gamebook renaissance.

John D Jones; backer 98. Thanks for your help. John. Enjoy the fruit of your investment!

Michael Hartland; backer 99. So great to have your support again, Michael. Enjoy the ride!

Peter Auger; backer 100. Thankyou, dear Pete, for your faithful friendship and your continued support for my writing. I really appreciate it.

Jörn Bethune; backer 101. Vielen Dank, Jörn. Enjoy the adventure, for YOU are the Steam Highwayman!

Moritz Eggert; backer 102. Vielen Dank, Moritz. Your support means a great deal to me.

Rebecca Scott; backer 103. Thanks for supporting the project and pledging, Rebecca! The projcet couldn't happen without you.

Cato Vandrare; backer 104. Great to have your interest, Cato. Thanks for pledging - and here's hoping you'll enjoy the books enough to return for number three!

Malcolm Webb; backer 105. Thanks for your pledge, Malcolm. Great to have your support.

Hans Peter Bak; backer 106. Thanks for pledging and making sure that the Ferguson continues on its journey, Hans.

Luca Skorpio; backer 107. Grazie! Thanks for supporting me again in my Steampunk madness.

Joshua Galinato; backer 108. Josh, it is so encouraging to have your help again to get this out into the world. I really appreciate it.

Paul, Noah, Jona & Elya Brueckner ; backers 109. I hope the whole family comes to enjoy the adventures of the Steam Highwayman!

Adeodatus Ronie Twumasi; backer 110. Thanks for your investment in my work, Ronie, and your friendship over the last year.

Fabian König; backer 111. Vielen Dank and my sincere appreciation for your contribution, Fabian. I hope that the adventures astride the Ferguson bring you pleasure!

CONSTABLES BULLETIN: HAVE YOU SEEN

Alex "The Red Bear" Chapman; backer 112 and S.O.S.A.G.E. gangleader; May the vision come to pass - a steam-powered, two-wheeled horde of splendidly-attired, splendidly-behaved steampunks, terrorizing conventions with cups of tea and little light robbery. I hope the volumes of *Steam Highwayman* are a continuing inspiration to you and the S.O.S.A.G.Ers and your generous pledge is, of course, much appreciated. Keep up the good work on the Facebook Page.

BEWARE OF DANGEROUS GANGLEADER

Cristovão Neto; backer 113. Thanks for returning to pledge for my second project - I hope you enjoy the book as much as the first.

Muffy; backer 114. Marcy, thanks for your pledge and for reading my steampunk adventures. Great to have your support once more. Stay splendid!

N. Tanksley; backer 115. Thankyou for your generous pledge, Nicolette! I hope you enjoy the adventure.

Adrian Jankowiak; backer 116. Thanks for your support, Adrian! Enjoy the adventure.

James Catchpole; backer 117. Great to have your support, hootmeister!

John Hagan; backer 118. Thanks for your pledge and support, John. May the Mersey echo to the roar of the velosteam.

Lorraine and Mark Jackman; backer 119. Thankyou, dear Mark, for continuing to support me in my writing and remaining such a faithful friend. God bless you and your family.

Scarlett Letter; backer 120. Stay splendid, Scarlett, and enjoy the attentions of the Constables!

Eamonn McCusker; backer 121. Thanks for your support and encouragement, Eamonn. Enjoy the ride!

James Pearson; backer 123. Thanks for your pledge, James. I hope you feel a little of the old Fabled Lands magic in Steam Highwayman too.

Unai Gomez Onrubia; backer 124. Thanks for your encouragement and your pledge, Unai. Enjoy the book!

Jonathan Caines; backer 125. Thanks for your pledge, Jonathan. Enjoy the book!

Dave Bowen; backer 126. Cheers, Dave! May the adventures in the two books keep you entertained for many a comfortable armchair hour!

Joel Bridge; backer 127. Joel, thanks for your support and for all your engagement during the campaign. I hope you enjoy this extension to your adventures!

Leron Culbreath; backer 128. Thanks for your pledge, Leron. I'm so glad that you chose to support my project.

Andy Shrimpton; backer 129. Andy, thanks for your pledge. How good it was to meet you at Leiston and to enjoy your participation in the reading. I look forward to hearing of your adventures on the midnight road, sir!

Aaron W. Thorne; backer 130. Thanks very much, Aaron! Enjoy the book.

Riccardo "elfosardo" Pittau; backer 131. Have a great time with the adventure, Riccardo. Thanks very much.

Ian, Lord of Tickhill; backer 132. I hope your noble background has prepared you for an adventure and a half, Ian! Have a great time.

Dean Jones the Steampunk Magician; backer 133. My dear sir! Thankyou for your support and your friendship - also for your fabulous MC'ing whenever we seem to meet. Only one thing - beware your next tea duel! The Steam Highwayman has a long memory...

Francois Laisné; backer 135. Merci, Francois. I really appreciate your support and help in getting Steam Highwayman moving.

Mr Clottey; backer 136. Thank you, dear Eric, Sarah and girls for your pledge and your support for myself and Cheryl. God bless you!

Rod Hart; backer 137. Thanks for your pledge, Rod. I hope you enjoy reading the adventures as much as I have enjoyed writing them.

Neil Myler; backer 138 and WANTED CRIMINAL. My dear friend. I still don't know what I've done to deserve such faithful support and friendship from you. I hope that your terrifying reputation goes ahead of you and I wish you happy adventures on the road and in the library.

Pikey Berbil; backer 139. Thankyou for your pledge and for your support. May the road be smooth and unrutted beneath your wheels!

Mark Lee Voss; backer 140. Thanks, Mark, for your pledge and your support for the project.

CONSTABLES BULLETIN: HAVE YOU SEEN

Suze G; backer 141 and GANG LEADER. Thank you, Suze! I hope that you enjoy reading the books as much as I have enjoyed writing them. God bless you.

BEWARE OF DANGEROUS GANGLEADER

Scott Moles; backer 142 and WANTED CRIMINAL. Thankyou, dear Scott and family, for your friendship and your support. Scott, I'm sure you could never have guessed how your obedience in worship would have fruit like this - but your example of worship in creativity has gone far ahead of you. God bless you all.

Martin Randall; backer 143. Thanks, Martin, for your support and interest for my project over the last year and more. Don't let the Guilds get you down!

Martin Bailey; backer 144. Thanks for your support for the project, Martin. I really appreciate it.

Afia Yale; backer 145. Dear Afia! May the Lord bless you and your family - and thank you for all of your friendship and support for my work.

Simon Scott; backer 146. Enjoy the books, Simon! Have a great adventure.

Nicole (germie) Moyle; backer 147. Thanks for your support, Nicole! Enjoy the books

Hannah Quarrell; backer 148. Dear Hannah! Thank you so much for your continued support and friendship during my writing project. I really appreciate you and your dear husband and I'm so glad that Cheryl and I can be alongside you in life. I hope that you have some chance to enjoy the adventure in these books in the next year!

Jerry and Dorothy Mendoza; backer 149. My dear friends! Thanks so much for continuing to support the project in prayer and with your pledges.

Jojo; backer 151. Thankyou, Ading Jo, for your generous support for my writing. God bless you and continue to direct your path!

Ian Hayward; backer 152. Thanks for your support, Ian! May Basingstoke quiver at the approach of the dreadful Steam Highwayman!

Joseph Boeke; backer 153. Thanks so much for your support, Joseph. The book couldn't happen without you.

Draconis; backer 154. May your fire never go out! Thanks for getting on board.

Rabih Ghandour; backer 155. Thanks for your pledge, Rabih! Have a great time as the Steam Highwayman.

Bradley B; backer 156. Thanks for your help in supporting the project.

Jonathan Lightfoot; backer 158. Jonathan, thanks for your support! May your boiler ever stay at pressure.

The outlaw Rob MacArthur; backer 159. Thanks for your support, Rob.

Vijay Khutan; backer 160. God bless you, Vijay, for your friendship and your generosity towards my project. Continue in your faithful walk, my friend!

Tim Lawrence; backer 161. Thanks for your pledge and your support for the project, Tim.

Michael Blackwell; backer 162. Great to have your support, Michael. Thanks very much.

Jon Ingold; backer 163. I've said it before, but thank you again for your writing, your inspirational example and for your pledge as well. Best wishes for the (eventual) launch of **Heaven's Vault**.

Baron Von Swodeck; backer 164. Your secret is out, Baron! YOU are the Steam Highwayman!

CONSTABLES BULLETIN: HAVE YOU SEEN

Joshua Warner & Ryan Lynch; backers 166 and GANG LEADERS. Thankyou, Joshua and Ryan, for your generous pledge. I hope that your biking friends all remain in fear of your leadership - or democratically supportive of it, as you prefer.

BEWARE OF DANGEROUS GANGLEADER

Ninang Andrea and Ninong Leo Galinato; backers 167. Thankyou, Ninang and Ninong, for your friendship, prayer and support. God bless you richly!

Graham Wilson; backer 168. Great to have you joining the *Steam Highwayman* community, Graham. Thanks for backing my **Write Your Own Adventure** project too!

Alan Halpin; backer 169. Thanks for your pledge and also for all your interest in the project, Alan. May the people of northern Italy tremble at the approach of the Steam Highwayman!

Alex Papadakis; backer 170. Thanks, Alex, for continuing to pledge and support me in this work. I'm so appreciative.

Falco Czirsowsky; backer 171. Thanks for your support, Falco! Enjoy the adventure.

Otis Parker; backer 173 and WANTED CRIMINAL. Thank you, Uncle Otis, for your generous pledge and your support for my writing. I hope you, Otis Jr and the entire family enjoy the adventure and the ongoing series.

Amanda and Matthew Towler; backer 174. Enjoy the adventure, Towlers, for YOU are the Steam Highwayman... men... man and woman. You're them, anyway.

Ang NamLeng; backer 175. Thanks so much for your pledge! May the Singapore steampunk scene be shaken!

CONSTABLES BULLETIN: HAVE YOU SEEN

Emilie Butler; backer 176 and GANG LEADER. Thankyou, Emilie, for your generous pledge and your interest in *Steam Highwayman*. I hope that, wherever you go and wherever you share your copies, the members of your own gang are splendid and honourable. Steam on!

BEWARE OF DANGEROUS GANGLEADER

Clay Skaggs; backer 177. Thanks for your support, Clay. I hope you find the Steampunk world of *Steam Highwayman* inspires your modelmaking.

Leeton Hanson; backer 178. Thankyou, my dear friend, for all your support and friendship.

Mrs Verity Stephanie Sharpe; backer 179. Philgarians Unite! Thanks so much for supporting my writing. I hope the book intrigues you!

Martin Noutch Snr; backer 180. Daddy, thank you for everything. This pledge for this book, but much more. The shelves and shelves of things to read at home - the Sunday afternoon showings of *Scaramouche* and *Treasure Island* - the wargames on the shed table - and most of all, your love for each of us in the Lord. Enjoy the book, Dad.

Richie Aspie Stevens; backer 181. Thanks for backing again and for pledging so generously, Richard.

Elijah Dobner; backer 182. Thank you, Elijah, for your love, friendship and your support for my writing.

Sir James Terence Nelson Cleverley; backer 183. You've an adventure ahead of you now, James! Enjoy the books.

Anabelle Santiago; backer 184. Thankyou, Ate, for your friendship and your prayers, your support for myself and Cheryl in all that we do, not just in my writing.

Paul Kelly; backer 185. Paul, thanks so much for your pledge! I really hope you enjoy the adventure on the midnight road.

Magnus Johansson; backer 186. Thankyou, Magnus, for faithfully backing my second campaign. I am sincerely grateful.

Pablo Martinez; backer 187. Gracias, Pablo. I hope that the adventures inspire and excite you.

Larissa Sena; backer 188. Thanks for your pledge and I hope you enjoy the stories and the adventure. Steam on!

James Rocks; backer 189. Welcome aboard, James! May you find the wind always at your back.

Jon Mann; backer 190. Thanks for returning to back again, Jonathan. Best wishes.

Greg Merwin; backer 191. Greg, thanks for getting involved and for backing the project. I hope you enjoy the adventure and the mystery of a ride on the midnight road.

Adam J Purcell; backer 192. Thanks, Adam, for returning to pledge for the second volume. The look great on a shelf together - take it from me.

King; backer 193. Thanks very much for your pledge and your support. May the Ferguson roar across the Netherlands once more!

Matt Sheriff; backer 194. Thanks, Matt, for your contribution to the project. Enjoy the book!

To DANIEL, from Ms H Taylor; backer 195. Thanks for your pledge - I really appreciate your help in making SH2 a reality. Daniel, enjoy the adventure!

Jason O' Mahony; backer 196. Thanks for your support, Jason. Give those Yaks hell!

Damon Richardson; backer 197. Thanks for your support, Damon. I hope you find time to enjoy the adventure between all the game design and testing!

God-Keizer Kos Petoussis; backer 198. Thanks for all your comments and interest during the campaign, GK. Much appreciated.

Jared Foley; backer 199. Stay splendid, Jared! Thanks for your friendship and support. Let the TENTACLES flourish!

Ben "phantomwhale" Turner; backer 200. Enjoy the adventure, Ben! I hope you enjoy being transported to an England that never was.

Todd Weigel; backer 201. Thanks for your pledge, Todd. I hope you enjoy lacing the two adventures together.

Gray Board Gamer; backer 202. Daniel, I really appreciate your pledge and your interest in the project. Enjoy the adventure!

Chris Semler; backer 203. Thanks for getting involved and contributing to the project. I hope you enjoy every page.

Louise McCulloch; backer 204. Thanks for your contribution, Louise. It's appreciated.

Andreas Froening; backer 205. Vielen Dank, Andreas. I hope you find the world of *Steam Highwayman* engaging.

Danny Powell; backer 206. Great to have your support, Danny. Enjoy exploring, robbing and duelling.

Mark "Daelhoof" Johnson; backer 207. Welcome to the world of Steam Highwayman, Mark! Enjoy exploring the midnight road!

Peter Ljungman; backer 208. Peter, I really appreciate your support for my project. May the high roads of Sweden tremble before you!

Dr Vincent Robertson; backer 209. Thanks for your generosity and your faith in me, Fraser! I hope you enjoy the adventure.

Ken Finlayson; backer 210. Ken, your support is much appreciated. I hope you enjoy the adventure!

Yew Turk; backer 211. Great to have you aboard, Turk! Thanks for your support.

Michael Doberenz; backer 212. Thanks for your pledge, Michael. May all your robberies be profitable!

James "Desperado" Schannep; backer 213. Thanks, James, for your support and for your friendship. Every success with your **Click Your Poison** gamebook series!

Jack "Duke Box" Bicknell; backer 214. Dukey, thanks for your encouragement and support. I've been looking forward to getting this one into your hands.

Allan Richmond; backer 215. Thanks for your pledge, Allan! I hope you enjoy the adventure!

Jerica, Rico and Sebastian Castro; backers 216. Dear friends! Salamat for your friendship and your support for my books. May your boy grow into a ruthless - but principled - little highwayman.

Ondrej Zastera; backer 217. Ondrej, thanks for your support for the campaign. Great to have readers in the Czech Republic!

Mike Migalski; backer 218. Welcome to the *Steam Highwayman* tribe, Michael! Thanks for your pledge and your support.

Gaetano Abbondanza; backer 220. Thanks for your pledge, Gaetano - and for all your feedback after Volume I. I hope that you continue to enjoy the adventure.

Steve Lord; backer 221. Welcome back, Steven! I hope you enjoy this as much as Volume I.

Ian McFarlin; backer 222. Thanks for pledging to see the legend of *Steam Highwayman* extended, Ian. Enjoy the adventure!

M Phelps; backer 223. Great to have you back, Mark! May you outrun the Constables at every turn.

Joseph Snape; backer 224. Thanks for returning to pledge again, Joseph. Enjoy the open road and the open sky!

Bavo Thuwis; backer 226. Bavo, great to have your support and interest in the project.

Paul Gaston; backer 228. Thanks for pledging again, Paul. I hope that Steam Highwayman is beginning to look the part on your gamebook shelf. Happy adventures!

Jack Barrow; backer 229. Thanks for returning to support me again - and to keep the pressure up on the nobility. Long live the revolution! Wishing you every success with

#InSatNavWeTrust

Post-Kickstarter Supporters:

Luke Sheridan; backer 230. It's been great to have your interest and commitment to the project, Luke, even once the campaign has finished. Enjoy your special copies.

Mr K Vincent; backer 231. Thanks for your pledge in person at the Suffolk Steampunk Spectacular - and for your enthusiasm for my reading! I hope you have as much pleasure in your adventures as I do reading them.

Dan Usher; backer 232 Thanks for your contribution, your prayers and your interest, Dan!

Tita Edna Naongayan; backer 233. Salamat for your kind generosity and support for my writing, Tita! I hope that you will burst onto the Filipino Steampunk scene, inspired by what you read.

❧ NOTES ❧

BEER NOTES

	Name of beer	Location	Notes
1.			
2.			
3.			
4.			
5.			
6.			
7.			
8.			
9.			
10.			
11.			
12.			
13.			
14.			
15.			
16.			
17.			
18.			
19.			
20.			
21.			
22.			
23.			

CODEWORDS

- ☐ Baggage
- ☐ Balance
- ☐ Barbaric
- ☐ Barchester
- ☐ Bargain
- ☐ Bark
- ☐ Barnet
- ☐ Barrowboy
- ☐ Bearclaw
- ☐ Beaurigarde
- ☐ Before
- ☐ Befriend
- ☐ Believer
- ☐ Bellbottom
- ☐ Bellingham
- ☐ Bellyache
- ☐ Benediction
- ☐ Benign
- ☐ Bent
- ☐ Bergen

- ☐ Beringed
- ☐ Bermondsey
- ☐ Bernadette
- ☐ Bespoke
- ☐ Best
- ☐ Bested
- ☐ Bestial
- ☐ Betrayed
- ☐ Betterment
- ☐ Beyond
- ☐ Birthright
- ☐ Bitten
- ☐ Blabber
- ☐ Blameless
- ☐ Blarney
- ☐ Blasted
- ☐ Blended
- ☐ Bloodied
- ☐ Blotchy
- ☐ Blouse

- ☐ Blown
- ☐ Bodacious
- ☐ Bolster
- ☐ Bonehunter
- ☐ Bonnington
- ☐ Bonny
- ☐ Boorish
- ☐ Boosting
- ☐ Bootlicker
- ☐ Botanical
- ☐ Bother
- ☐ Bottle
- ☐ Bought
- ☐ Bragging
- ☐ Brand
- ☐ Brazen
- ☐ Breadbasket
- ☐ Breaker
- ☐ Bressingham
- ☐ Brigade

- ☐ Brilliant
- ☐ Brimming
- ☐ Broadly
- ☐ Brock
- ☐ Broken
- ☐ Brokenhearted
- ☐ Bronte
- ☐ Bubbling
- ☐ Bullring
- ☐ Bumpkin
- ☐ Burden
- ☐ Burdensome
- ☐ Burgundy
- ☐ Burnett
- ☐ Burnish
- ☐ Bursting
- ☐ Bushy
- ☐ Bust
- ☐ Busybody
- ☐ Butterchurn

Friend of…

Member of the Compact for Workers' Equality ☐
Bargee's badge ☐
Guildsman's Medallion ☐

Coulters Bank Account

Guineas

DEPOSITS AND WITHDRAWALS IN
MULTIPLES OF 10 GUINEAS ONLY

Wanted by

Constables ☐
Telegraph Guild ☐
Haulage Guild ☐
River Guild ☐
Atmospheric Union ☐
Coal Board ☐
Wallingford Town Guard ☐
Locobus Co-operative ☐
And…
_____
_____
_____
_____
_____
_____
_____

Satchel FOR BANKNOTES, NOTES, AFFIDAVITS, CERTIFICATES, TICKETS ETC

Titles, aliases and other names

AT 50 SOLIDARITY POINTS GAIN THE TITLE
PEOPLE'S CHAMPION

Jewellery Pouch FOR JEWELLERY, KEYS ETC

Extra Skills

Moored at: _____

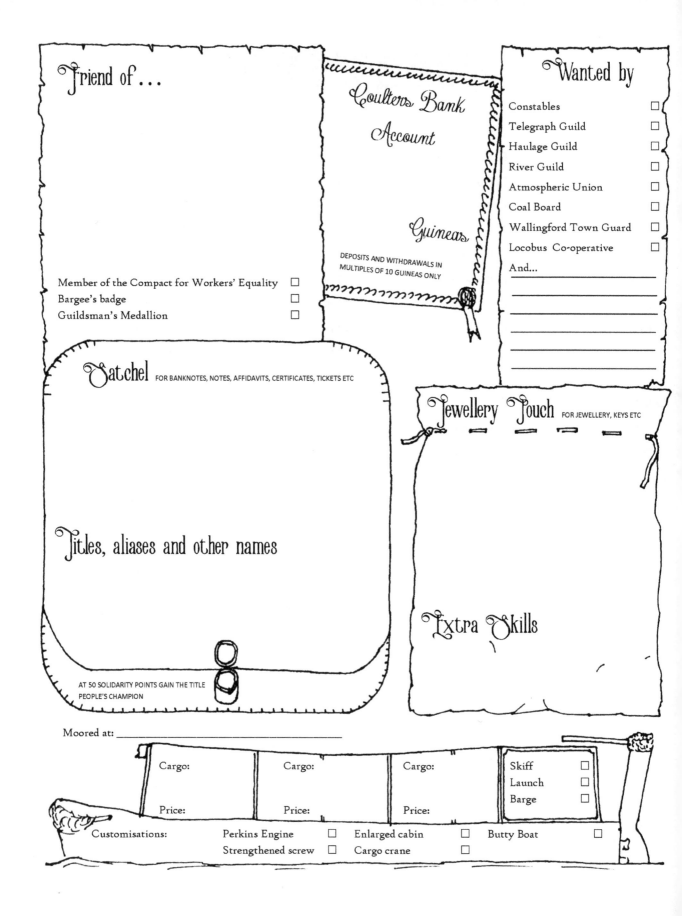

Cargo: Cargo: Cargo:

Skiff ☐
Launch ☐
Barge ☐

Price: Price: Price:

Customisations: Perkins Engine ☐   Enlarged cabin ☐   Butty Boat ☐
                Strengthened screw ☐   Cargo crane ☐

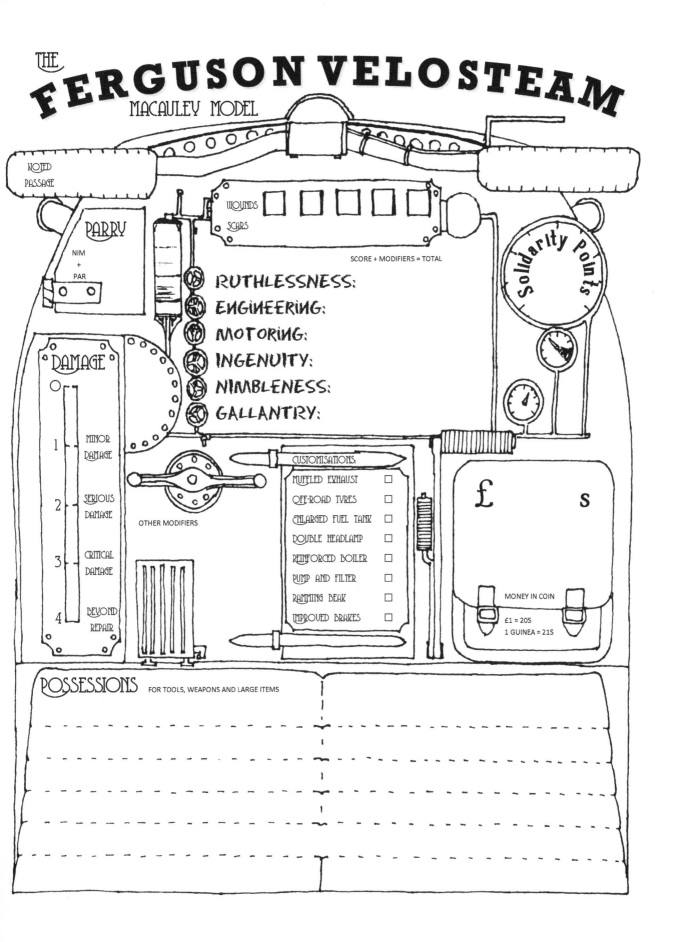

THE FERGUSON VELOSTEAM
MACAULEY MODEL

NOTED PASSAGE

PARRY

NIM
+
PAR

WOUNDS

SCARS

SCORE + MODIFIERS = TOTAL

Solidarity Points

RUTHLESSNESS:

ENGINEERING:

MOTORING:

INGENUITY:

NIMBLENESS:

GALLANTRY:

DAMAGE

1 MINOR DAMAGE

2 SERIOUS DAMAGE

3 CRITICAL DAMAGE

4 BEYOND REPAIR

OTHER MODIFIERS

CUSTOMISATIONS:

MUFFLED EXHAUST ☐

OFF-ROAD TYRES ☐

ENLARGED FUEL TANK ☐

DOUBLE HEADLAMP ☐

REINFORCED BOILER ☐

PUMP AND FILTER ☐

RAMMING BEAK ☐

IMPROVED BRAKES ☐

£   S

MONEY IN COIN

£1 = 20S
1 GUINEA = 21S

POSSESSIONS   FOR TOOLS, WEAPONS AND LARGE ITEMS

Lightning Source UK Ltd.
Milton Keynes UK
UKHW030952020119
334835UK00001B/3/P